No Good
to Cry

No Good
to Cry

A Rick Van Lam Mystery

Andrew Lanh

Poisoned Pen Press

Poisoned Pen Press
6962 E. First Ave., Ste. 103
Scottsdale, AZ 85251
www.poisonedpenpress.com
info@poisonedpenpress.com

Printed in the United States of America

To the memory of Lam The Do
1974-2009

Prologue

My cot is in the far corner of the barracks-like room. Twelve cots clustered together, no breathing room, and mine is by the crumbling wall where water seeps through the cracks. Chattering mice crawl in and out, scavenging for maggots or hard grains of rice. At night, restless, my stomach churns from the stench of stagnant sewage, rotting bamboo, and mice droppings. The worst cot in the room, given to me by the good nuns because I'm the worst of the boys—impure, a skinny twelve- or thirteen-year-old with forbidden American blue eyes and a rigid jaw. Sister Do Thi Bich, the old nun who runs the Most Blessed Mother Orphanage, refuses to say my name. Instead she sneers, "*Ma quy nuoc ngoai.*" Foreign devil. Satan's boy, beaten by the other orphans for sport.

But that changes.

One afternoon, returning from the market on Nguyen Tat Thanh with a heavy load of lemongrass—the reeds are wrapped in a cheap rag-paper flyer carrying Uncle Ho's benign face—I hear sobbing from the hallway outside La Vang Chapel. Then, a burst of high laughter, crazy, almost maniacal. I drop the lemongrass on the cook's counter and rush back toward the barracks.

The boy I come to know as Le Xinh Phong is surrounded by a gaggle of jeering boys, circling him, poking him, tugging at the cheap shirt he wears. Whore's son, they yell. *Nguyen rua.* Cursed boy. Leper.

My heart swells with a curious and welcome joy: another dust boy. *Bui doi.* Yes, the lazy, slanted eyes but the rich mahogany complexion of old coffee. A black boy.

Sister Mary Le Phan, who guards us, stands with her arms folded over her chest and watches as the others harass the boy, yet does nothing. A hint of a smile on her wrinkled face, which does not surprise me. She keeps a bamboo switch in her room. When she turns and catches me watching her, she fumes, wags a shaky finger at me, and croaks out my name. "Lam Van Viet." The boys stop poking the newcomer. One jeers, "The other one." A little boy looks up at the good sister and says, "*Nguoi pham toi.*" The sinner.

Barking orders, Sister Mary relocates my cot, forcing Phong to rest in my old spot—the sinner's corner. Quiet, shaking, he lies on his back that first night and stares at the ceiling. In the middle of the night, everyone sleeping, he sobs quietly.

The devil has come to the orphanage. *Qui Satan.*

Phong is bigger than the rest of us, a chubby boy with a wide face, a bulbous nose, so I am not surprised he becomes everyone's favorite leper. Especially mine, I'm ashamed to admit. For a few scant seconds of bleak eternity, I can catch my breath. Yes, I am punched and shoved, mocked—the whore's son, the American pig's boy, the familiar litany—but my cursed white blood oddly gives me a momentary pass. Not so Phong, whose G.I. daddy has left him that sable skin.

One afternoon I hear two nuns chatting about him. Sitting in the small garden, the scent of jasmine and burnt charcoal covering the yard, they talk of their Christian duty, one more cross to bear, yes, yes, yes. Sadly, yes. Wounds in the body of Jesus Christ. Some pesky government officials found the boy wandering in a village outside Ho Chi Minh City, stealing rice to survive, sleeping under a banyan tree, a boy covered with green bottle flies. When they located his family nearby, they learned his shunned mother had died—murdered, in fact—so an uncle pushed him out.

Phong is frightened of everyone.

Then I begin my own sinning. When the other boys taunt him, beat him so that there are always purple welts on his face and arms, I join in. I have someone to hate—to hit. My blows are furious and cruel, the worst of them. My fury is savage—so much so that the other boys somehow look at me with a grudging respect, if a little wariness. Never to be included in their games or talks or adventurous begging at the Soviet hotels on Nguyen Hue Street, nevertheless, I am the enforcer, my tight fist crashing into Phong's vulnerable ribcage.

He takes it. He even tries to be my friend because he has no one else. Lonely, yes, stuck in that corner, he tries to talk to me. I shun him. I call his mother a whore, his father a black bastard. I curse him. *"Ban se dot chay trong dja nguc."* You will burn in hell." The other boys applaud me.

One day there is a lot of scurrying in the hallways, the nuns frantic. We boys are lined up, headed back to the barracks after Sunday morning services, but the nuns hurry us, shush us.

"Quiet, quiet. Jesus is listening."

We are told our lunch is delayed, to stay in the room, to pray, but I sneak out to spy on Mother Superior, Sister Do Thi Bich. In her cramped office she is whispering to two men who've arrived in a noisy car. One man is obviously government, a small, officious man in pristine military uniform, his chest covered with garish braid and gleaming buttons. He speaks in a loud booming voice, like rocks smashing a wall, and Mother Superior keeps bowing and humming at him, squeaking out nonsense words. Next to him sits an American—or at least I assume him to be an American. A tall black guy with a scraggly beard. Bushy sideburns, a cigarette bobbing in his mouth. He wears a peasant's tunic, ill-fitting because the pants ride up a shin exposing old ripped socks.

When they stand up, I scurry back to my cot.

Within minutes, Mother Superior enters our barracks and points at Phong, who huddles under his thin blanket, frightened. "You," she thunders, and the black man shoots her a look. Phong stumbles toward them.

Late that afternoon I spot the man walking with Phong, too much space between them, but the uniformed man is nowhere around. When Phong returns to our room, he looks confused, but there is also fear in his eyes. Strangely, I catch him smiling at one point, but that stops quickly when he notices my eyes on him.

The boys buzz and titter about the visit. Someone says the black man is an American deserter who worked with the Viet Cong—an American traitor. He went into hiding when the Americans abandoned the country in 1975. Now working for Uncle Ho's Communist government, he is looking for his child, born in the last days of the war.

We call him the black American. *Le Den.*

The next day, at twilight, pruning the dead leaves from the mango tree near Mother Superior's office, I hear his voice from behind the closed door. He speaks Vietnamese with a thick lazy drawl, some words difficult to understand, stammered, broken. But what I do understand is that Mother Superior has reluctantly opened a huge ledger on her desk, which the man keeps referring to. His voice is stinging, harsh. Through a crack in the door, I watch as his fingers drum the sheets.

He doesn't look happy, and the good sister apologizes over and over. He stands up, he sits back down, he rocks in his chair. At one point his fist slams the ledger, and it shifts toward the edge, grabbed in time by the sister.

What I learn slams me: someone at the orphanage has recorded names, tidbits of information, birth certificates, family papers—all about the boys dropped off at the orphanage. But what the man discovers does not please him, and he fumes. Yes, the nun says, we have some information on the American fathers, if provided. An I.D. card maybe. In one case dog tags of a dead soldier.

Wide-eyed, I wonder—me? What about me? A dim memory of my mother when I am around five, a woman who holds me tightly in her lap, who tucks into my breast pocket the slender volume called *Sayings of Buddha* that I will carry to

America—and cherish all my life. Does the ledger have her name? I quake—the name of the American soldier? My father? My family? I stare at the ledger through the tiny opening in the door as though it is a holy talisman, a grail lit by fire and wonder.

The man never returns to the orphanage.

Phong sleeps with his face to the stinky wall.

Within the year I am sponsored to America, shuffled off with little notice, a paper bag with a change of clothing and that slender volume from my mother. Nervously, I huddle in the backseat of a Soviet car next to Sister Mary Le Phan. As the car pulls away from the orphanage, I spot a gang of boys chasing Phong into an alley. He trips over a basket of stale bread, an old woman cursing him, pummeling him. The boys land blows on him, and his helpless cries mix with their horrible laughter. Dazed, he lies there, his right arm bent under him.

Suddenly I am sobbing. Startled, the nun slaps me, though she glances at the man sitting in the passenger seat up front. She apologizes to him, a rasp in her throat.

Pinching me, she whispers, "Shut up, you bastard. No one cries in America." She snarls her words. "*Con de hoang.*" Bastard boy. "Do you want to go back to the orphanage?" She draws her face close to mine. The stink of chewed betel nut. "Do you, you ungrateful boy?"

Chapter One

The phone inside my apartment was ringing as I fumbled for my keys. It stopped, then started again. Then my cell phone jangled, a ring tone that blared a few swollen bars of Billy Joel's "Piano Man" I'd been meaning to change. I reached into my pants pocket, but realized I'd left the phone in a jacket hanging just inside the locked door. It stopped jangling. The land line rang again, and now I could hear an anxious voice, calm but laced with worry. Liz's voice. My ex-wife.

Disaster, I sensed.

"What?" I yelled into the phone. But Liz had hung up.

I toppled into a chair, caught my breath.

I'd been jogging on Main Street, across from the campus of Miss Porter's School, enjoying the late-afternoon April air, brisk and invigorating, the first hint of a glorious Connecticut spring. But I'd run too far, savoring my rhythm, a song in my head, the crisp air slapping my face.

I dialed Liz back. "Liz? Tell me."

She breathed in. "Jimmy."

One word. My mind went blank.

My partner in insurance fraud investigations, based out of Hartford. I was *his* partner in Gaddy Associates. Jimmy Gadowicz, the seventy-something blustery man who took me in as his partner years back and became a man I loved and respected. Steel-eyed Vietnam vet with the no-nonsense work ethic, he wouldn't let me get away with anything but ironically let me get away with everything. I know that sounds contradictory—if a little glib—but the man had a way of making sure your aim was true because, in fact, that's the way he demanded the world behave.

"Tell me," I whispered.

"He's been hurt. Alive—but hurt."

I slipped back in the chair and gripped the telephone. "Tell me."

I could hear Liz's heavy sigh. "It just flashed across the TV, his name, misspelled of course, and I called a friend at Hartford PD…"

I broke in. "Liz." My voice too loud. "Jimmy."

"He was walking on the sidewalk near your office. Down Farmington Avenue. With his friend, Ralph Gervase. Two muggers attacked them. One slugged Ralph, who fell, hit his head." A deep intake of breath. "He died, Rick."

"Oh, my God." I closed my eyes.

She waited a heartbeat. "Jimmy was hit by a car."

"What?"

"I don't have all the facts. When Ralph was clobbered, Jimmy stepped back into the street and a car hit him."

"He's alive."

"He's alive," she echoed. "He's at Hartford Hospital. I'm headed there now."

"I'll meet you there."

I hung up the phone and realized I'd been gripping the receiver so tightly my knuckles were white.

Standing up, I was momentarily dazed as I glanced around my apartment, staring at familiar objects—that old Tiffany-style lamp I bought at Goodwill and painstakingly rewired, the country-store work desk with my computer and green-glass desk lamp. Oddly, everything now struck me as alien, objects lit by a curious glow.

Shaking myself out of my trance, I rushed into the bedroom and stripped off my running clothes, dropping everything onto the floor, kicking my sneakers across the room. I slipped on old jeans and a flannel shirt, buttoned it so quickly I had to begin again because I'd buttoned it crookedly. I grabbed my spring jacket, checking to see whether my cell phone was in the pocket. Then I lingered by the front door, hesitant, taking in my comfortable rooms. An ivy plant on a sideboard needed to be repotted. Why hadn't I noticed that before? I was afraid to leave—afraid to drive the fifteen or so highway minutes into Hartford—afraid of what I'd find when I entered Jimmy's hospital room.

My apartment is on the second floor of a glorious Victorian painted lady, all gingerbread decoration, its clapboard sides painted a brilliant canary yellow, the favorite color of my landlady, Gracie, who lives on the first floor. Threadbare orientals cover the landing, but the boards creaked and moaned with each step I took.

A shaky voice drifted up from the first floor. "Rick." Tentative, shaky.

Rushing down the steps, I met Gracie, her wrinkled face trembling. "Rick," she repeated.

"Gracie, what?"

"The radio." A deep sigh. "Jimmy."

So she'd heard.

"Jimmy's all right," I assured her, though I wondered about my own words.

Gracie took a small step toward me. She was dressed for going out in her black opera cape. An old woman, probably early eighties, tall and slender with abundant white hair forming a bushel barrel of loose ends speckled with hairpins, she'd been an "entertainer"—her favorite word—since she was a young girl. A Radio City Rockette until an enterprising young businessman, hopelessly smitten with the beauty, had squired her off to Connecticut and this gigantic home. Now, standing close to me, her face flushed, she drew the cape tighter around her body and nodded toward the front entrance.

"No, Gracie, I'll call you."

She shook her head vigorously. "You can't tell an old lady what to do, Rick."

I smiled. "I've learned that."

"Then why are we standing here?" She pushed by me. "Move, then."

I shrugged and followed her out the door.

Gracie was smitten with Jimmy, as he with her, though both skittered around each other. It often reminded me of a scene from an old Annette Funicello-Frankie Avalon teen movie I'd watched one night on MeTV. For a boy who hadn't stepped onto American shores until he was thirteen or so, fresh from a Vietnamese orphanage, such black-and-white late-night reruns were a wonderful education, if skewed. I baited Jimmy and Gracie, we all did, our gang of friends, but we loved them to death.

"I'll bring the car around," I told her.

"Rick." A squeaked-out word.

"What?"

"They said Ralph Gervase is dead."

"Liz told me."

Her eyes got moist. "I never liked him, Rick. That Ralph. The few times we met. I *disliked* him." She shivered. "I always thought he was unpleasant. I didn't like him hanging around with Jimmy."

"I didn't like him either, Gracie."

She looked over my shoulder. "I feel bad saying that."

"It's all right. You can't like everyone."

She clicked her tongue. "For an educated man, you do like to use clichés."

I smiled back at her. "I learned a long time ago that in America they serve as wonderful transitions when you need to say something."

Without smiling, she glared at me. "How about this—Silence is golden."

I left her on the front porch, headed out back to get my car. Ralph Gervase, dead.

I stopped walking as I recalled that Jimmy had invited me for lunch with him and Ralph that afternoon. He'd asked me to meet them at our new office in a three-story building on

Farmington Avenue—we occupied the second floor, Jimmy huffing and puffing his way up one flight of stairs, a glowing Lucky Strike bobbing in the corner of his mouth—and the three of us would go for a bite at some local eatery. Now, thinking about that invitation, I bit my lip. I'd dug in my heels, refused because, like Gracie, I disliked Ralph Gervase.

"Christ, no, Jimmy, that man looks at me like he wants to kill me."

Jimmy had dismissed that. "You got an imagination, Rick boy."

"No, he's hateful."

Talking with Jimmy on the phone, I'd been ready to do battle over his newfound friendship with the old veteran, but backed off. "No," I'd told him, "I got things to do."

I'd lied. I had nothing to do. Jog around town, maybe go for a swim at the Farmington College pool, prepare a lesson for the one-night-a-week class I taught there in Criminology. Perhaps review a fraud case I'd been wrestling with. Dawdle the afternoon away. No, eating a sandwich while the mean-spirited Ralph glared at me across the table was not a good idea.

"C'mon, Rick." Jimmy had urged.

"No."

Ralph Gervase, dead now from a mugging. Ralph Gervase, recently moved to Hartford from a great-niece's home in White Plains, New York. Without options—I believed the man hadn't a friend in the world—he'd moved into a boardinghouse filled with old veterans, restless wanderers across America, casualties of a war that ended decades in the past. Ralph ended up in Hartford because he had a distant cousin in the same rooming house, another ailing veteran who died the day after Ralph moved in with his battered cardboard suitcase, a plastic ShopRite bag containing a six-pack, and the work dungarees he wore day in, day out. A small, wiry man, his bullet head with cloudy eyes always a little too red, he strutted around like a bantam rooster, his voice a mosquito whine, always standing too near so that you recoiled at his rancid tobacco odor.

Jimmy and Ralph had bumped into each other on the sidewalk outside our office. Jimmy was headed for cigarettes at a
Quik-Mart. Ralph, so Jimmy confided, had just shoplifted a
pack of Camels from the convenience store and nearly collided
with him. They'd known each other in Vietnam for a couple of
months near the end of the war, but had never gotten along. "A
weasel," Jimmy confessed to me. "No one trusted him. We all
thought he'd buy lunch with friendly fire one day."

"He sounds delightful," I'd said at the time.

Jimmy smirked. "Christ, how you talk."

He didn't like Ralph, a crusty drunk even less politically cor-
rect than Jimmy himself, though Jimmy's biases were couched
in an engaging humanity that somehow gave him a pass. But
he held a confused loyalty about old Nam veterans, especially
the ones he'd served with. Which was why he hung out—"Not
often but just enough"—with the old-timer.

After that first encounter Jimmy insisted Ralph meet me. A
big mistake, immediately evident. Ralph harbored ugly attitudes
carried from his younger days in the jungles of Nam. The stink
and horror of the underground tunnels of Cu Chi. So here,
unexpectedly, he found himself sitting across from the dreaded
yellow peril—yellowish peril, perhaps—a forty-year-old man
in a Brooks Brothers suit merrily chomping on a salty potato
chip and downing a salt-free margarita at Moe's Southwest Grill.
Jimmy hadn't told his old army buddy that his younger partner
in solving routine insurance fraud in the Insurance Capital of
the World was that curious product of the troubled war that
continued to define Ralph's dead-end life.

"Jimmy ain't told me you was a gook."

"Pleased to meet you, too." I'd offered my hand. He refused
to take it.

I'd stared into his rough, leathery face. He constantly tapped
a breast pocket where he kept a pack of cigarettes, as though any
situation that bothered him called for a necessary light. He'd
glanced out of the window and I expected him to hurry out,

slip a cigarette out of the pack, and snap on the Bic lighter he'd been playing with since he sat down at the table.

He avoided eye contact. "You're one of them boys, you know, who..." He glanced at Jimmy. "Like white blood or something."

"*Bui doi*," I'd helped him along. "One of the dust boys. My father was an American soldier..." My voice trailed off. "A story you've heard before."

Squinting at me, suddenly amused, he'd snickered, "I probably dropped a few squawking babies like you along the way. Half-breeds. Rest and relaxation from the Cong, as you'd say. There was one taxi girl, in fact, love-you-all-night whore who..."

Jimmy shot out his arm, grabbed Ralph's shoulder. His voice shook. "Ralph, I don't think Rick needs to hear about your days in Nam."

Ralph narrowed his eyes. "Yeah, we come back home, goddamn heroes we think, and no one gives a shit about the war—or us. A forgotten war, dammit. Like we was doing something mean and rotten to them godless people. America turned its back on us. Who the hell remembers?"

"Well, I guess that's why I'm here in America," I'd said quietly.

He'd snarled, "And just why is that?"

"To help you remember."

Chapter Two

Gracie and I met Liz as she was signing in at Hartford Hospital. Catching my eye, she nodded toward Gracie, and I understood her worry. She gave me a peck on my cheek and then embraced Gracie, who started to sob.

"It's all right, Gracie," she whispered. "Jimmy's fine. He'll make it."

Gracie glanced at me. "Old people die in hospitals."

Liz squeezed her hand. "The cranky ones like Jimmy live forever."

That made Gracie smile.

Liz had come directly from work. Dressed in a snug cranberry-colored suit, a simple white scarf draped around her neck, a white silk blouse, she looked the part: the serious criminal psychologist on staff at the Farmington Police Department. A gorgeous woman at forty with her gym-workout figure, she'd lost some of the alluring softness in her face, those large midnight black eyes too stark against her alabaster skin. Still, a damned beautiful woman. She caught me looking at her, something I often did whenever I started to sentimentalize the brief marriage we had, and the look she returned was a familiar if comical one: Behave yourself.

But now, watching me, she leaned in, touched the sleeve of my jacket.

"Are you doing all right, Rick? Yes?"

The identical words she'd used years ago when the two of us lived in a Riverside Avenue walk-up in Manhattan and I'd return from my job as a beat cop in Chelsea. Weary, I'd slink into the apartment where I'd find her tucked into a corner of the old sofa, a textbook cradled to her chest, books strewn across the floor. Yellow-pad notes for her master's thesis on Karen Horney scattered around her feet. "Are you doing all right? Yes?" Concern in her voice, a mixture of fear and wonder that she had a husband who carried a gun and sometimes shot at people. Worse, bad guys shot at the man she loved. I would lean in to kiss her.

My response was always the same. "Compared to what?"

Which always made her laugh. Made *us* laugh.

Now, her lips near my neck, she whispered, "Okay?"

"No."

"I didn't think so." She glanced at Gracie. "But it's going to be all right."

"Liz the optimist."

She smiled. "Rick the eternal pessimist."

Gracie was frowning at both of us. "You two talk at each other like you're an old married couple."

I gave Gracie a quick hug, staring at Liz over Gracie's shoulder. "We'll always be an old married couple."

Liz, in a matter-of-fact voice, said, "Rick forgets that I keep the divorce papers in plain sight."

Walking ahead, Gracie pressed the button of the elevator and ignored us.

The fifth-floor reception nurse indicated a room down on the right. "The cops are still in there." She peered down the hallway. "Like Times Square at New Year's in here today." A young woman, perhaps late twenties, her eyes drifted from me to Liz and finally rested on Gracie, whose flamboyant cloak looked out of place in the stark setting. "I don't think they're expecting a crowd."

Gracie smiled an unfriendly smile at her, clearing her throat, but I tucked my hand under her elbow and maneuvered her down the corridor. As we neared Room 515, the door suddenly opened and a uniformed cop stepped out, trailed by a man in a baggy suit who was berating him. "You ain't got the brains you were born with, Reilly." He got louder. "Your mama drop you on that pinhead of yours?" The young cop flushed as he faced us, which caused the man to glance our way. His eyes got wide and smoky.

"Shit. He's back. I knew it would happen."

Solemnly, I half-bowed at the rumpled man. "Detective Ardolino."

"In the flesh." He poked the young officer. "Don't just stand there. Get moving." The detective arched his back and turned back to me. "And, I suppose, a lot more of it than you remember, Rick Van Lam." He thumped his protruding belly, the faded blue dress shirt looking ready to burst some helpless buttons. A sliver of white flesh peeked through.

It had been more than a year since I'd see the homicide detective, the two of us reluctantly working together to solve the murder of Vietnamese twin sisters. A cop who had little patience with others stepping into his territory, he'd never returned my calls after the Hartford PD stamped *finis* on that file.

"I thought you were going to retire."

He glared. "So you remember that? Well, the wife nixed that idea. The idea of me being home all day long was just too much pleasure to bear." He chuckled to himself.

"A lucky woman."

He narrowed his eyes. "I'm glad one of us thinks so, Lam. I should be lying on a white beach in Porto Gordo at this moment. Instead I'm tucking a body into the back of a van headed to the morgue."

I stepped toward the closed door. "Anyway…"

"Anyway, I figured we'd meet again. Once I learned that Gadowicz"—he jerked his head back toward Jimmy's room—"is your partner in crime."

"Crime-*solving*."

"Every PI I've ever met is a criminal at heart."

"Bless you, Detective."

"Yeah, yeah."

True, Ardolino had packed on a few pounds since I'd last seen him, but the dumpy suit looked the same, if shabbier. A blot of reddish-purple covered an elbow, as though he'd dipped it into blood splatter. Poorly shaved with three resistant strands of hair now silvery gray combed across his blotchy scalp, Ardolino seemed a homeless derelict—and probably an incompetent one. I knew better. I'd learned the man's mettle. Appearance had nothing to do with his incisive, dogged mind. When the man chose to employ it, he had few rivals.

"Good to see you." I smiled again.

"Yeah, yeah." He looked at Liz, a lopsided grin animating his face. "And who are you?"

Liz had been watching him closely, amused. "Liz Sanburn. I'm a friend of Jimmy." She stuck out her hand. He held onto it too long.

"But who *are* you?"

She waited a second, and I knew what she'd say. "I'm Rick's ex-wife from his Manhattan days."

Ardolino raised his eyebrows as he shot me a glance. He squeezed her hand tightly, his eyes twinkling. "A fool, obviously." He shook his head mischievously. "Any man that puts an 'ex' before a gal that looks like this gotta be a damned fool."

"I've been telling Rick that for years." She pulled her hand away.

Gracie cleared her throat. "I'm here, too."

Ardolino's eyes swept down Gracie's opera cape, ready to hurl a barb her way. But then, a phony smile emerged. "Are you somebody's mother?"

Gracie drew in her lips. I expected her to let loose a stream of delicious fishwife invective. Instead, she turned away, dismissing him.

"This is Gracie Patroni," I told him. "A good friend."

"You three…" Ardolino paused. "Lam, where's your Batman-and-Robin sidekick? That youngster who tagged after you like you had the recipe for cheddar biscuits at Red Lobster."

I smiled. "Hank Nguyen."

"Yeah, that smart-aleck boy."

"Well, I wouldn't call him a boy, Detective. He's at the Connecticut State Police Academy, finishing up his studies. He'll be a state trooper within weeks, sworn in…"

My cell phone chirped. Startled by the buzz, Gracie jumped as I dug into my pocket.

I pointed it at Ardolino. "Speak of the devil. A text from him." I read: Local news mentions Jimmy. Stuck here. Call me. I looked at Liz. "Hank is worried."

"Call him after we see Jimmy."

Ardolino took a step away, but I held up my hand.

"Detective, how is Jimmy? What can you tell us? Is he awake?"

He put on his serious face as he took out a pad from his breast pocket. "Well, you heard it on the news, right?"

"Fill us in. We don't have any details."

Ardolino looked toward the closed door as it opened and a nurse walked out, stopping as she came up against the bunch of us clustered outside Jimmy's room. She skirted past us, though Ardolino called after her, "He's got visitors, sister."

She looked back over her shoulder. "He's sleeping." A wry grin. "And I'm no blood relative of yours."

Ardolino frowned at her back. "Well, he's been out of it all afternoon. How am I supposed to do my job, lady?" She kept walking. He leaned into me. "Actually he was awake for five minutes and told me some of the story." A low rumble. "All right, gang. Here's what we know." He glanced down at the pad in his hand. "Your buddy Gadowicz and this other guy named"—he looked down again—"Ralph Gervase left the Burger King on Farmington, home of fine dining, headed up the avenue, when two low-lifes come running up from behind. Both heads covered in hoodies, the disguise of choice these days. They rushed the old guys, and one shoved Ralph, who I gather was an ornery old drunk. Looks like Ralph was pissed—pardon my language— but maybe slugged one of the muggers. Surprised, said mugger punched Ralph on the side of the head, a blow that made him topple over, hitting his head on an iron fence post. When cops arrived, he was already dead."

"And Jimmy?"

Again he checked his notepad. "When all this was going down, Jimmy, I guess, got startled and stepped back off the curb, just as an old beat-up Honda cruised by, breakneck speed and all over the road, and clipped him. Driver is some under-age Rican, the smell of weed covering him like you stuck your head into a Christmas tree. Sent Jimmy flying over the fender. Kid hits the streetlight and then sits there with his eyes closed, a dreamy look on his face when we knocked on the window. I guess he needed a nap."

"Jimmy's injuries?" From Liz.

"Hey, lots of bruises. A concussion, it seems. A fractured ankle. Bruised lungs. A full menu of this and that, like he was tossed around like a rag doll. He ain't a spring chicken, you know. He'll be out of commission for…"

Gracie interrupted. "But he's all right?"

"He'll live. You didn't hear me say he was on life support, did you? But he won't be walking around for a while, the doctors said."

"What else did Jimmy tell you—when he was awake for that five minutes?" I asked.

Ardolino eyed me closely. "It may have been more than five minutes. I round off numbers for the lay public when they grill me."

My own words overlapped the last part of his sentence. "What did he say?"

"He can't remember much. Yeah, he's mostly groggy, out of it. Christ, I wish I had the drug they feed people at this hospital because it would make my nights at home with the missus bear-able. But he said there were two punks, skinny kids, hoodies. He only saw the back of one guy's head as he pummeled the late departed Ralph."

"Maybe he'll remember more tomorrow—or when he wakes up again."

"Yeah, that's when they usually make up stuff for the head-lines. How I acted the hero in the face of…You know the drill. Wanna see themselves on Channel 3."

"Jimmy isn't like that." Gracie was peeved.

Ardolino squinted at her. "Lady, everybody wants their fifteen minutes. Life ain't exciting for most folks. They gotta make up things. That makes my job tough."

With that, he nodded, performed a half-bow to Gracie and gave another squeeze to Liz's hand, tucked his notebook back into his breast pocket, and walked down the corridor.

"Can I catch up tomorrow?" I yelled after him.

Barely a pause in his stride. "Hey, I worked with you before, Rick Van Lam. I don't think I got no choice in the matter. You probably still got my home phone number."

"I do."

"I was afraid of that."

He disappeared around the corner.

Quietly, the three of us walked into Jimmy's room. He was asleep, a rough, wheezing hiss escaping his throat, his head twisted to the side.

I had trouble looking at the pile of man lying in that sterile bed, the big man lost under whiteness and IV tubes. I never thought of Jimmy as an old man, though of course I knew he was. After all, he'd been an infantryman during the Vietnam War years, the harrowing days of his young manhood, a war that somehow gave him a solitary life in small efficiency apartments. A life spent holed up in an office ferreting pedestrian fraud among the insurance high rollers. A man with few friends, no close family. Until he met me, that is. Somehow he'd kept a lingering affection for the muck and grime of war-ravaged Saigon, a loyalty to a boyhood spent in nighttime sweats and fear. Bizarrely, I was that link—the partner he said he'd never take on. A young man born on those bombed-out streets he'd patrolled. In the process we'd forged a friendship that was golden.

Not that we always got along. He was a big shock of a man in oversized Patriot jerseys and faded XL jeans that sagged at the bottom, a Red Sox baseball cap rarely absent from his head. A cigarette somewhere near his yellow-stained fingertips. We worked together, he with his scribbled notes, me with my laptop and Twitter account. He watched me with jaundiced eye, often mocking my life—"spoiled by living in New York among those people"—and finding fault with my polished loafers and J. Crew sweaters. Even my cozy apartment in Gracie's home with its old recycled furniture and walls of books and modern art. We rarely discussed politics or religion or—well, any topic that would result in explosive streams of curses hurled my way.

Although at times, frustrated, I was tempted to do so.

I never did.

Or rarely.

Now, lying in the hospital bed, he looked so weak and vulnerable, a man who'd always struck me as steel and spit, leveled now, hooked to apparatus that mimicked his labored breathing. I'd never considered that he could be—hurt.

Gracie began sobbing, clutching Liz's arm, her body sagging. And Liz, stepping close to the bed, reached out to touch his arm. She faced me, her eyes moist. "My God."

I couldn't move. The left side of his face was black-and-blue, a deep purple blotch on his temple. One arm, lying palm up, showed dark welts, pitch-black. His chin had red abrasions. A bandage covered his left ear. A foot in a cast. He looked—broken.

We stood there, silent, silent, nervous, not knowing what to do, until finally, stepping forward, I bent over him, my lips near his face. "Jimmy." A flicker of the eyelids. I looked at Liz. "He can hear me."

"Jimmy," she echoed. "It's Liz."

"And Gracie." My landlady's voice arched over Liz's, too loud for the room. Again, the flickering of the eyelids. Gracie bumped into the bedframe, tottered, and Liz grasped her elbow. She nearly toppled onto the bed, and a hand grazed Jimmy's side. I swear he winced.

"Jimmy, can you hear me? It's Rick."

Nothing.

"We need to go," Liz said finally.

But at that moment Jimmy flashed open his eyes, so rapid a movement that his eyes seemed to pop. His neck twitched. Gracie gasped. Suddenly his lips began to move slowly as he ran his tongue over them, like a thirsty man.

He said something.

"What?" From Gracie.

His lazy eyes slowly drifted from Liz to Gracie to me. A thin smile broke at the edges as he mumbled some words, groggy, slurred.

"I can't understand you," I said. "Tell me."

Then, each word spaced out, a man in a blissful narcotic stupor, Jimmy said clearly, "I must of died and gone to hell 'cause I'm looking up at three damn fools."

Chapter Three

The following afternoon, a Saturday, Hank knocked on my door. I'd been expecting him. Last night, leaving the hospital, I'd texted him back. We'd talked for a few minutes on the phone. Before bedtime, restless, as I stared at the TV screen and sipped lukewarm Chinese white lotus tea, I got a Facebook alert. Hank, ready for bed, wanted to know what I'd learned. His frenzied message was in block letters, an annoying affectation young folks use to suggest shouting. I don't like being shouted at. However, it was Hank, and, frankly, friends have license others lack.

YOU DO KNOW THAT WE HAVE TO DO SOME-THING. THIS NEEDS LOOKING INTO.

Well, I'd learned nothing new since our earlier talk, but we chatted back and forth, thankfully using lower case alphabet. We did discuss Detective Ardolino's role in the investigation, which intrigued him. Hank's final comment before signing off: "Does he still love you to death?"

I smiled at that.

Now, wearing a faded UCONN sweatshirt and baggy khakis, he strode into my apartment, an expectant look on his face. I hadn't seen him in some time, what with his intense training at the Connecticut State Police Academy, where he lived in the dorm during the weekdays. His boyhood dream of being a trooper was a month or so away, courses completed and the grueling physical training accomplished, the swearing-in ceremony at the State Armory something all of us looked forward to, though I knew his parents and grandma worried about a dangerous life spent in crime-infested neighborhoods.

Having been a cop myself, I tried to reassure his family, but I couldn't convince myself. After all, I'd been a cop in New York's Hell's Kitchen where I'd blown away a piece of filth who'd just beat up some poor slob for a few dollars and then put a cocked gun to my own head.

I still had nightmares about that night. That trauma propelled me to leave the force—and my marriage. A desire for calm led me to a life in placid Farmington, Connecticut, where my only real danger resulted from painful paper cuts as I painstakingly skimmed through personnel and audit records at Aetna Insurance.

"You've buffed up," I told Hank now.

He beamed. The physical rigors of training throughout the past year at the Academy had transformed the tall, slight Vietnamese boy who'd been a student of mine in a Criminology class at Farmington College. With his shaved head, his broad shoulders and wide chest, he was more competitive wrestler than the lithe young man I'd played tennis with. A handsome man with wide nut-brown eyes in narrow, slanted sockets, high cheekbones, and a rich mocha complexion, he was a charmer who bucked his family's expectation that he wed a chosen Vietnamese girl—preferably some FOB, Fresh Off the Boat—and fashion a career in an office building in downtown Hartford. Computers, they suggested. The IT department at, say, Cigna.

Our friendship had a rocky beginning because he'd harbored pureblood Vietnamese bias against mixed-blood mongrels as myself, but his warm heart and keen intelligence had defeated such provincialism. These days he was my buddy, though largely an absent one. Before his days at the Academy, he'd been my tag-along companion as I did my meager fraud investigations, which he found more interesting than I did.

He walked to my refrigerator and took out a quart carton of orange juice, jiggled it, frowned, and then chugalugged the contents.

"Hey," I said. "Manners?"

"You only had a little bit left." He tossed the empty carton into the trash. "Never mind. Tell me what you're gonna do about Jimmy? What *we're* gonna do."

Flummoxed, I watched his eager face. When I didn't answer immediately, he scratched his head and pointed a finger at me. "You are the PI here, you know."

I grinned. "I keep telling myself that."

"Well." Impatience in his voice, an edge. "I got time now—the Academy is done."

I hesitated. "I don't think Detective Ardolino wants my help." I waited a moment. "Hank, a street mugging—a random attack. Anonymous thugs. Just where would I begin…?"

He wasn't listening. "Ardolino didn't trust you last time either, and then you brought it all home."

"Lightning doesn't strike twice in the same place."

"God, you do love to speak in clichés." He dropped into a chair, threw his legs up onto the coffee table.

I squirmed. "You know, Gracie told me the same thing yesterday."

A sloppy grin. "Well, now you know how your friends view you. Sad, isn't it?"

I grabbed my jacket. "C'mon. I do plan to ask a few questions. Maybe I can't track the muggers, but I'd like to see the scene in my own mind. This is Jimmy we're talking about."

"Now we're talking." He jumped up.

"But let's avoid Ardolino."

"He casts a large shadow."

Now I grinned. "Bigger than you remember, I'm afraid."

Since the assault had taken place on the sidewalk near the new office of Gaddy Associates, I pulled into the rear parking lot. Hank and I trudged up the back stairs to the second floor. Although I did most of my insurance investigations out of my Farmington apartment with a modem and a phone, I checked in often at "fraud headquarters," as Jimmy termed our cramped catacomb on Farmington Avenue. Jimmy lived in a tiny studio apartment on a tree-lined West End side street two blocks away, a cubbyhole apartment that looked out on Dumpsters and broken asphalt pavement. Since our move into this space from the storied Colt Building, now gloriously gentrified, he spent a lot of time in the office. Despite the climb on narrow, creaky stairs, he liked the expanse of roll-up windows that front the avenue. "I can see the late-night crowd getting nasty 'cause KFC is out of crispy chicken."

Our building was a three-story 1920s office building with cracked cement foundation, crumbling brick, water stains on the flaky plaster ceiling. Yes, too many insensitive landlords had slathered hideous green deck paint on the walls or used a cheap varnish on the old oak floorboards, and, yes, when hurricane-force winds or blizzards rattled the windows, there arose the feeling that Doomsday had finally arrived—and not a minute too soon.

On the first floor was an ancient lawyer-owner named Riverbend—that, unfortunately, was his first name, his parents obviously dipsomaniacs—whose clients were old-guard Hartford WASP gentry who lived in ivy-covered mansions on Prospect. On the third floor was his dilettantish son, Herman, who ran some fly-by-night video production operation, grinding out indie films no one wanted to see, especially the juries at Sundance, but occasionally the scattershot cinematographer was thrown a few bucks by his father to tape lawyerly depositions in court cases.

Gaddy Associates occupied the second floor—above the awful stillness of the first-floor gentility yet below the raucous MTV soundtrack baseline that drummed overhead.

Walking into my office, Hank right behind me, I balked: Jimmy had obviously been spending time in the rooms because the noxious odor of cigars covered the room like a fog. His cigarettes I could tolerate—but his cheap Panama cigars did me in. In that instant I flashed to the man lost under crisp white sheets at Hartford Hospital. I turned to face Hank. "Smells like Jimmy."

"Only the cigars. What's missing is the familiar whiff of pepperoni in the air."

But his words were swallowed. Bothered by Jimmy's absence, he stepped close to Jimmy's small pine desk by the front window, and his hands rustled some of the papers on the desk. He breathed in and crumpled up his face as he picked up a note and handed it to me. Jimmy's barely legible scrawl: "Call Rick. That fool left the damn lights on again."

I smiled.

"Let's go," I told Hank.

Hank was grinning. "Don't forget to turn off the lights."

Late in the afternoon Farmington was jam-packed with cars maneuvering around illegally double-parked cars that clogged the avenue. At a bus stop three old black women dressed in winter cloth coats chatted and laughed, though one kept stepping into the street to check whether a bus was near. A young woman gingerly carried two cups of Starbucks coffee as she headed into a laundromat, talking in a high-pitched voice into the microphone she'd attached inches from her mouth. Two schoolgirls walked shoulder to shoulder, each one intently reading her phone. One girl raced her fingers over the keyboard, furious texting. That impressed me. I texted with one finger, the index finger of my right hand, at a pace that allowed empires to rise and fall.

Hank pointed to the crowds. "Had to be witnesses, no?"

A teenager pushed by him, banged into his side, mumbled a curse.

"Here." I stopped walking. "This is where it happened."

We stood next to a low, foot-high wrought-iron fence fronting the entrance to a small Italian coffee and pastry shop. A neon sign, flickering in daylight. Roma Bakery. The display window, set back ten or so feet from the sidewalk, featured replicas of ornate wedding cakes.

I pointed to a dried reddish-brown blot on the iron post. "This is where Ralph hit his head." On the sidewalk the familiar chalk outline of a body, a cop's rapid handiwork, smudged now but still jarring.

Hank bent down to examine the railing. "It strikes me that the muggers didn't intend to kill, just rob. I mean, if he fell a foot ahead"—he pointed to a clump of overgrown ornate yews lining the sidewalk—"he'd have toppled into the bushes."

"Ralph was a feisty guy. He fought back."

"And died because of it."

"There had to be witnesses." I checked out the neighborhood. "Crowds everywhere. Around four in the afternoon. The suburbanites fleeing Hartford. Farmington Avenue into West Hartford."

"A busy street," Hank agreed, but added, "but not so much right here."

He pointed to the red-brick three-story building next to the bakery, the entranceway cluttered with overgrown evergreens, an ancient metal rental sign on the wall, plywood covering the windows, another wooden sign nailed to the door. FOR SALE. A number to call. To the right of the bakery was a nightclub. Lola's Fantasy Club. A lit neon graphic of an upturned cocktail glass in the window, but an otherwise dark building.

"Nightlife," I said. "Closed now."

"So the muggers chose their spot carefully."

I shook my head. "But there's sidewalk traffic. A busy avenue. Cars, buses. Broad daylight."

"And their victims. Two old men, walking slowly."

"What about across the street?" I asked.

A line of apartment buildings, canopied, shadowy in the afternoon light.

"We'll see."

Hank sounded frustrated. "Somebody had to notice something, no?"

The woman behind the display counter of Roma Bakery greeted us as we walked in. A plump woman in her forties with a round, flat face and a pin-curl hairdo, she smiled warmly. "Hello," she sang out.

I introduced myself and Hank, told her I was an investigator and the partner of Jimmy Gadowicz, the man injured yesterday. I lowered my voice. "Ralph Gervase, the dead man, was his friend." Immediately her welcoming expression became mournful.

She stepped out from behind the counter. "Maria Lombardi." She grasped both our hands. "The owner. Please, have a seat."

We sat on white ice-cream parlor chairs around a small marble-topped table. Without asking, she poured us cups of coffee and placed them before us.

"A pastry?" she asked. "On the house." She glanced back toward the kitchen. "A warm almond cookie?"

Both Hank and I shook our heads, though I did welcome the aromatic, rich coffee. This was a place I'd return to. The tantalizing aroma of baked bread wafted from the unseen kitchen. My stomach growled. Yes, an almond cookie. She must have read my mind because she scurried to the counter and returned with a plate of them. I bit into one, and smiled. She was watching me closely, a smile on her face.

Dangerous—this bakery was down the street from our office. I figured Jimmy already lived here.

"I'm so sorry about your friend. Jimmy—him, I know." I nodded. "He buys…" She stopped. "So sorry the man died." She looked down into her lap. "I was the one who called the cops, you know. I was standing by the front door." She pointed. "Sometimes the smell of baking bread pulls them off the sidewalk."

"I can believe it," I said.

"Anyway, I sort of notice the two old men walking, pausing, and I thought they was arguing. I ain't really paying attention. The fat one—I couldn't see that it was Jimmy—raising his fist. Like making a point."

"Sounds like Jimmy." I looked at Hank.

"Then out of nowhere these kids come running, so fast I didn't understand what was happening. One of them is running real fast. He bangs into the old guy who starts to fight the kid. Then I seen him fall. I mean, the kid…slugged him in the head. I mean, an *old* guy hit like that. It was like TV and I don't believe it. Years here, and nothing like this happens. Then I hear tires screech and I seen the fat man flying forward, landing on the curb. The car up against the pole. I screamed and reached for the phone." For a second she closed her eyes, shivered.

"Can you describe the muggers?"

She shook her head back and forth. "Kids. Skinny-like. Maybe one tall, one short. But dressed in black sweatshirts. Sneakers. These black hoods up over their heads. All the kids look the same. They come in here for bus change, and I scoot them out. Even my teenage grandson dresses like that these days. The sullen face that goes with it. Moody, angry. Like a thug, I tell my daughter. Why let Mario dress like that?" She shrugged. "But then they're gone and the cops come."

"You didn't see their faces?"

Again the vigorous shaking of her head. "I seen their backs running away."

"Then it was over."

"Over," she echoed. "The ambulance, the police, the body laying there on the ground." She made the sign of the cross. "Mother of God, what a world!"

The door opened. A roaring voice filled the room. "Christ Almighty, man."

Detective Ardolino glared at Hank and me. "Clark Kent and boy wonder, Jimmy Olsen. I bet you ain't here to buy a damned cannoli."

Ardolino slid into an empty chair and faced me. But he spoke to Maria.

"*Maria, qual e il problema con te? Sei matto?* Such criminals you serve here. I should shut you down." His eyes danced. "Charge these hoodlums double for everything."

Maria waved at him, pleased. "Tony, you scare away the customers."

Again in Italian. "*Io son oil tuo miglior cliente.*" I'm your best customer.

She pointed at his potbelly. "Too much sfagliatella."

Hank looked dazed by the exchange, and I translated. "If my high school Italian serves me, the detective questions Maria's sanity serving us. You and I are criminals."

Hank beamed. "Detective Ardolino, you do know I'm gonna become a state trooper within weeks."

The cop threw his hands up in the air. "Yeah, big deal. You'll spend most of your time catching drunks leaving Enfield gin mills and trying to get back across the state line to Massachusetts which, as we all know, is a lawless state run by Communists."

Not amused, Hank bit his lip. "Or I could hang out in donut shops." His hand swept the room and landed on the display case of colorful pastries.

Chuckling, Maria went behind the counter to brew Ardolino an espresso, which he downed in one noisy gulp. Likewise the ricotta confection she placed before him, swallowed in three generous bites.

"That good?" I asked him.

A twinkle in his eye. "You know it." He nodded at Maria. "If she wasn't married to my best friend from Bulkeley High School, I'd marry her."

"But you're already happily married," Maria teased.

"Don't remind me." Ardolino scratched his belly. "You boys are wasting your time here."

"And why is that?" Hank asked.

"I'm wrapping up the case. I *know* who did it."

I sat up. "Tell me."

"My, my." He looked at Hank. "Here's a lesson in good police work for the soon-to-be trooper. Lessons from the master. None of that kung-fu Confucius philosophy Rick spouted at me last time."

I quoted a line. *"Con song con hoc."*

"Spare me."

"Live and learn." From Hank.

Ardolino sang out a line. "Yeah, right down to the ABCs of it. Teach me tonight. Teacher's pet."

"What?" From Hank.

Ardolino sat back, a contented look on his face. "Well, I figured these punks ain't exercising their right to annoy the public for the first time. Mugging can become habit-forming. Bigger and better thrills, you know. Write that down, young man. Not that you'll ever deal with common street muggers. As it turned out, the two punks ran around the corner, so we're told, headed across Sisson to the convenience store where everyone in town buys loosies for a quarter a pop, the grammar school kids handing over their lunch money. We got this tape of two guys skipping along. One of them bumped into the super of a building, and he called in. Only a flash of a look, too quick to really remember features, but he said one was like a white or Spanish kid and the other was"—Ardolino paused dramatically and put a finger into Hank's chest—"you."

"Me!" Hank half-rose from his seat.

"Well, not *you* as in *you*. But an Oriental like you. At least he thought the kid looked like that boy who delivers moo goo gai pan or General Tso's chicken to the drug dealers every Thursday night."

"Chinese?"

"Oriental. Like I said."

"And this led you to conclude what?" I prompted.

"A familiar M.O. That's what I mean. A white thug and an Oriental thug. Racial harmony in the insurance capital of the world."

"But," I protested, "they could be any two kids in hoodies, no? Just walking up Sisson."

Hank jumped in. "No one saw who hit Ralph."

Ardolino held up his hand. "I ain't stupid, guys. I can add two and two. Two guys running up Sisson? An Oriental? You see, awhile ago we had this string of muggings in the neighborhood. Two boys in hoodies would come from behind, running, whooping it up, knock folks over. Party time. Having a good old time, but some folks got hurt—smashed elbows, black eyes. Most not harmed, just frightened and somehow blaming me for not hanging them by the balls. Well, we sort of caught the two boys in the act, *flagrante* as I like to say, and they were underage creeps. One white, one Oriental. Looked like your younger brother." Again the staring at Hank.

Hank fumed. "My younger brother is a Dean's List student and…"

"Yeah, yeah. Gonna be President of the U-S-of-A someday."

"So you think they're the ones now?" I asked.

"Funny thing. Back then, they were caught after a shopkeeper calls in a shoplifting incident. There they are, on tape, the two boys. The little Oriental comes clean. I mean, he doesn't believe in lying, he tells me. Go figure. Gives me hope in a world going down the toilet. Kid blurts out that he and the other creep did the muggings—if you can call it that—six times. Christ, he gives me a number. Admits to shoplifting all over town. This and that. You couldn't shut him up. Like he's on *To Tell the Truth* or something. The other kid yells—shut the fuck up. So we nailed them—and the fact that they were carrying weed in their pockets." Ardolino rubbed his palms together.

"What happened to them?"

"Both boys sent for a four-month rest and recreation at Long Lane Juvenile in Meriden, a training ground for future murderers and rapists and politicians."

"So they're away at juvie."

"Hold on, Lam boy. A month back both got home, happily reunited with their loving families."

"And you think they're back to their old tricks."

"I'm positive." He fiddled with something in his breast pocket.

I looked at Hank. "I wonder."

"No wonder about it." Ardolino withdrew an envelope from his breast pocket, then debated whether to share the contents. Finally, shrugging, he handed small black-and-white photos to me.

"The white boy is Frankie Croix, a sixteen-year-old dropout from Bulkeley High School. The Oriental is Simon Tran, a.k.a Sy, or as the locals call him, the Saigon Kid. Also sixteen, also skinny, also a pain in the ass."

"Not much proof."

Ardolino frowned at me. "Then prove me wrong."

I stared down at the photos. Frankie looked like a wasted drug punk with deep-set blank eyes, a pimply face, and electrified hair.

Big ears made his face clownish, though the dullness in his eyes mitigated that comic look. Simon Tran looked Spanish, dark skin and black eyes in narrow sockets. Close-cropped hair. A bony face. But his eyes, staring back at the camera, were filled with anger, his lips drawn into a thin, razor line, menacing. A boy who resented the police photographer.

"Can I keep these shots?" I asked him.

That surprised him. "Go ahead." A befuddled smile. "Knock your socks off."

I pocketed the two photos.

I looked at Hank. "Do you know this Simon Tran?"

He shook his head. "I know the family, sort of. Dad's a mechanic. Hard workers, the kids over-achievers in school." He smiled. "So local legend has it. The Vietnamese venerate the scholars in the community." He offered a cynical grin. "One of Confucius' seven precepts, Detective. *Tri*."

Ardolino grimaced. "Tree?"

"*Tri*. Learning. The importance of it."

Ardolino scoffed at that. "Real nice. Kill a tree and make a book. Yeah, this Saigon Kid is a scholar, all right. This is someone who'll spend his life being *booked*—not *reading* books." His eyes got wide as he laughed out loud over his own joke. "Do you get it?"

Neither Hank nor I said anything.

"Well?" he goaded.

"Yeah," Hank finally answered. "Maybe we should book you at a comedy club."

Chapter Four

"Big Nose."

The first words out of Hank's mouth late that night when he called. I'd been lying on the sofa, the *Hartford Courant* spread over my chest, thinking about Jimmy—and the two hooded attackers. The front-page article chronicled the sad story—Ralph Gervase described as a "Vietnam veteran fallen on hard times." I thought the word choice questionable. Jimmy, however, was a "celebrated Private Investigator." Celebrated? That made me smile. I could imagine his horror at that description.

"What?" I said into the phone.

Hank repeated the words. "Big Nose. I like saying that."

A little impatient. "What, Hank?"

"Remember when everyone thought Willie Do pushed the cleaning lady off a bridge? Well, do you remember his grandson?"

"No." I sat up, and the newspaper slipped to the floor.

"Big Nose. That's what everyone calls Anh Ky Do. Roger in his legal American world. Big Nose to the rest of the world."

"And he doesn't mind?"

Hank laughed. "It's the name he answers to. He *likes* it."

"Okay, Hank, what's your point?"

"Well, he's sometimes a troublemaker, most times an all-right kid. Anyway, he's a buddy with Simon Tran, the Saigon Kid, or so my father told me."

"And? You going somewhere with this?"

"Simon Tran's father called my house last night because Willie, Big Nose's dad, gave him the number." He paused. "Mike Tran was trying to reach me—actually *you*."

I sat up. "The reason?"

Hank made a clicking sound. "Ardolino pulled in Simon and this Frankie kid, accused them of the brutal attack and causing Ralph Gervase's death. He threatened murder charges. I guess the scene at the precinct got real ugly because both kids got hot tempers. Mike Tran went with his son, and told Willie that Frankie slammed a fist into a wall, bloodied his knuckles, and pipsqueak Simon threatened to beat the daylights out of Ardolino."

"God, no. Did he arrest them?"

"That's it. No. He was in their faces. You know the drill—scare them."

"So Ardolino has nothing concrete on the boys—yet. That's clear."

"Bingo. But he's convinced…"

I broke in. "Maybe forensics will help nab the boys."

Hank sighed. "Simon's father is running scared and wants to talk to—you."

I rubbed my eyes. "What can I do, Hank?"

A long pause, quiet a moment. "Well, he wants you to move mountains. To prove his son innocent."

I hesitated. "And is this…Simon…innocent?"

Hank waited a second. "That's what you gotta find out."

"What does Simon say?"

Hank made a *tsk*ing sound. "The boy refuses to talk."

"Makes my job easy then."

"I promised Big Nose you'd look into it."

I smiled. "You were sure I'd say yes?"

Hank's voice rose. "I know you. They're Vietnamese. You imagine sins you're always atoning for."

"Atoning for?"

"And you got a heart."

"So I'm supposed to meet the family? When?"

Hank chuckled. "Well, tomorrow morning. Minh Loc Tran—everybody calls him Mike—has the day off. He's a grease monkey. Sunday morning. They'll give us *mi ga*."

"Us?"

"You don't expect me to miss homemade chicken soup, do you?" A pause as he rustled papers near the receiver. "They live in a small Cape Cod off Campfield on Milton Street in the South End."

"Tomorrow morning?"

"Didn't you hear what I said, Rick? *Mi ga*. Chicken soup for the Vietnamese soul."

◇◇◇

The driveway of the small Cape Cod home looked like a used-car parking lot: a rusted Dodge pickup up on cinder blocks, a decade-old Honda with a smashed-in right fender, mud smeared, and an ancient black Cadillac that might have seemed cool when Gerald Ford assumed the Presidency.

"God, Hank," I mumbled, "this looks like a salvage yard." I pointed to a vintage Jeep, primer paint slathered on the door, parked on the muddy lawn, its rear tires imbedded in dirt.

"They got a lot of cars." Hank did not sound happy.

"Are any of them running?"

Hank bristled. "They're poor people, Rick."

I shut up.

The house was painted a robin's-egg blue, eye-catching, a color so brilliant the house seemed a wonderful toy lifted from a children's fairy tale. The houses left and right—in fact, up and down the curvy street—were cookie-cutter homes, some building contractor's unfortunate hiccough back in the 1950s, the sameness relieved only by the different color siding.

Sitting in front, checking out the derelict cars, I sensed movement in an upper dormer window, a flash of a young face glancing out and then disappearing.

"They're expecting us," Hank said firmly. He jerked his head toward the house. "We just gonna sit here?"

"In a minute," I told him. "I want you to tell me what I'm walking into—and why you're being evasive."

On the way over Hank had been uncharacteristically quiet, answering mostly in monosyllables, his clipped responses unnerving me. "Did you ever meet Mike Tran?" I'd asked him.

"No."

"Anyone in the family?"

"No."

"Christ, Hank, help me out here."

"Grandma knew the wife a long time ago."

"And?"

"They tend to stay to themselves."

On and on, maddening, a scant biography that told me little. Hank's face was unusually frozen, his eyes avoiding mine.

No, he said, they rarely attended the Tet New Year's parties at the VFW hall in East Hartford. No, he'd never seen them in Little Saigon or shopping at A Dong, a supermarket a mile away in Elmwood.

"No, no. no."

"You're not telling me something," I'd insisted, and his feckless smile convinced me I was right.

"It's not important."

"I'll decide that."

So, frustrated, idling in front of the house, I put the car in gear and pulled away from the curb. "Let's just spin around the block, Hank. You gotta give me more. I want to know who this family is."

At the end of the block, I pulled up to a curb and sat back, waited. "I got all day."

A sheepish smile. "*Mi ga* waits for no man, Rick."

"I'll sacrifice the pleasure."

"Okay. I asked Grandpa, but he turned away. Nothing, not even his usual dismissal of folks he finds fault with. You know that he has Pop's biases—big time. So I asked Grandma, who was reluctant but—you know Grandma. She wants to like everyone. I kept at her. She told me that Buddha said, '*So nguoi o phai nauoi cho an.*'" You can't put blame on good and decent people.

I laughed out loud. "Which tells us nothing." I quoted Buddha back at Hank. "*Dau xuoi duoi lot.*" Good beginnings make excellent endings. I punched him on the shoulder. "So begin."

He scowled. "You and Grandma—a goddamned road show."

"I like that idea, but—start."

"Minh Loc Tran—Mike— is an embarrassment for the Vietnamese community, that is, for folks like Grandma who believe in decency and…and the rightness of things. I mean, the way *he* was treated. Not that *he* did anything embarrassing. You see, Mike Tran and his family are a whopping success story. He's an American dreamer who made his dreams come true."

I watched his face closely. "Okay, this sounds like good news—and bad."

He sucked in his breath. "Here's the story. A hard-working man, come up from nothing. You see, Mike Tran is half-black, Rick. *Bui doi,* but with an added cruel twist. Born in Saigon to a woman who went with a black guy, he was a leper twice over in the old country. There's taboo—and then, well, there's big-time taboo that chills the Vietnamese soul. Not only a mongrel but also a black mongrel." Hank had trouble looking into my face. "Not his fault, of course—not any baby's fault—but that's not the embarrassment to the Vietnamese I'm talking about. I mean, for the Vietnamese living here in America. In Hartford." He paused.

"Go on, Hank."

"You see, back when America was flying in all the half-American children in the 1980s—that Operation Amerasian Homecoming airlift that tried to right a wrong—a time when thousands of mixed-blood kids ended up here…" He stopped, nodded toward me.

"Yes," I half-bowed, "I know. I'm one of that gang."

"Anyway, in Vietnam, under the Commies, packs of half-American kids roamed the streets, begging for food, sleeping in alleys, beaten, forbidden to go to school because they were… the product of collaborators."

I bit my lip. "I remember, Hank. I don't need a history lesson."

"I know, I know. But the sad thing was that so many Vietnamese families, desperate to leave poverty and Communism, sort of *adopted* these orphan kids, bought them, forged papers, brought them into offices, and said, 'This is my dead sister's boy.' Not only the white-blood ones, but—others. Yes, he's black as the night, but he got our ancient blood coursing in his veins. And so many like Mike Tran, then Tran Loc Minh, scrounging for crumbs, suddenly found a new family and the whole crowd—mommy, daddy, lots of children—was welcomed into America. So Minh's family was delivered to Hartford and given an apartment on Huntington. The father was given a job on an assembly line at Pratt & Whitney in East Hartford, food allowances, furniture, money. The Tran family—a father, a mother, and three other children, all Pure Blood. Capitalized. The mother spoke some English and was hired to teach the immigrant kids at Bulkeley High School."

"I know where this is going, Hank."

"Yes, the embarrassment is that within one month they put the thirteen-year-old Mike Tran into the street. Dropping him off on the corner of Main and Garden. Alone on a cold winter day."

"It happened all over America."

He swallowed. "I know."

"And the good Vietnamese hide their heads in shame."

Hank squirmed. "Well, Mike Tran was a hardscrabble survivor, even found friends to live with, stayed in shelters, slept under bridges, did odd jobs, grappled with the raw deal he got, drove himself, and he became a success story. A man driven to be a good American. A GED from high school, courses at a trade school on Flatbush Avenue, a good job in a garage making okay money. Honest, good, he saved his money, and he bought a house and paid his bills."

"Good for him."

"Yeah. But lots of Vietnamese turn their heads away from him when he walks by. For one thing he looks too—black. Yes, those slanted eyes, that Vietnamese frame, but that mahogany skin. That hair."

"Just awful." I shook my head.

"But a smart man, really. And a good man. He married a Vietnamese girl who could care less about him being an outcast—an orphan herself, shuttled here and there, ignored. And they had four children, high academic achievers, mostly. According to Grandma, Mike enforced strict discipline, real severe, afraid of failure. A man with a hickory stick. School first. Always. He lives in Hartford, but each kid got a scholarship to a private prep school. The oldest is now at Trinity in Hartford, Hazel is a scholarship girl at Miss Porter's, her twin Wilson a scholarship boy at Kingswood-Oxford."

"And our little criminal? Simon?"

"The last of the brood, always battling his father's whip. A bright bugger, I'm told, but a handful. The sixteen-year-old who rebelled against books and teachers and—his family. Suspensions, shoplifting, absenteeism, smart-mouthing the world. A teacher called him 'Sy' one day and someone morphed that into 'Saigon Kid.' Which he liked a lot. Rumor has it—courtesy of Big Nose—that he got a tattoo of that on his bicep."

"At sixteen?" My voice crackled.

"God, how shockable you are, Rick. One of his buddies did it. There's a shot of it on his Facebook page. On Instagram. I checked him out."

"Does his father know? His mother?"

"Maybe we'll find that out now." Hank pointed up the street. "Let's go. They probably think we've changed our minds."

We pulled back in front of the small house and I switched off the motor. A curtain moved in that same upper dormer window and a small face glanced out, disappeared again.

"Don't mention the tattoo, Rick."

I smiled. "Makes him easy to identify in a police lineup, no?"

"We're here to save him from a murder charge." Hank's eyes got wide.

"Let's just start with a steaming bowl of chicken soup." I tapped him on the forearm. "Let's move. I think everyone in the house is watching us."

Chapter Five

The front door swung open before we rang the buzzer. A small man dressed in a faded blue denim work shirt and dungarees rolled up over his calves stared at us, his face tight. A muscular man, sinewy. Quietly, he sized us up and then thrust out his hand, pumping my hand and then Hank's. His palm was moist, but his grip was firm. Callused fingers, a bandage on his thumb.

"Mike Tran. Come in."

He had a gruff voice, scratchy, and his free hand held a burning cigarette, the ash ready to fall.

But he didn't step back, locked in that position, until a voice from behind him prompted, "Minh, you gonna stand there all day?" His eyes flickered as he turned to face the woman who approached from behind. She lovingly touched his elbow as he moved aside.

She introduced herself. "Soung Bach Pham. Call me Lucy. Everybody does." She winked at her husband and grinned. "Minh ain't used to company."

He clicked his tongue but looked relieved. They exchanged glances—companionable, warm, necessary.

Lucy was as small as her husband, but slender, wispy almost, with a delicate oval face and a cupid's-bow mouth that brightened her look. She blinked quickly, a nervous habit perhaps, but her eyes glistened. They looked—"happy" is the word that came to mind, but happy with wariness. We held eye contact for a second, but she broke the look.

"*Chao mung ban!*" She bowed. Welcome! "It's Sunday morning," she sang out. "We have *mi ga.*"

"*Cam on.*" I thanked her.

We were ushered into a small dining room that seemed even smaller with an oversized walnut table and chairs, a breakfront taking up one wall, and an illuminated cabinet filled with cardboard boxes—packages of rice noodles with brightly colored Chinese lettering, boxes of straws and napkins, a shelf of mismatched old dishes and glasses. The family storage bin. Chopsticks and bowls were already laid out on the table.

When I glanced through the doorway into the kitchen, I spotted a teenage boy bent over a textbook at the table. Was this Simon? If so, my stereotyped judgment was challenged because the boy looked classically studious—goggle glasses, scrawny shoulders, a picked-at complexion. For a moment he looked up, distracted, probably bothered by my gaze, but there was no expression on his face. His face dipped back to his book. A pencil gripped in his hand scribbled something on a notepad.

Lucy Pham saw me looking.

"Wilson, come say hello."

The boy didn't move until his father stood up. "Now." A loud command. "Now."

The skinny boy, pushing up the eyeglasses that kept slipping down his narrow nose, ambled into the doorway.

He grumbled, "Hi." A half-wave. A cellphone beeped in a baggy pocket of his khakis, and he turned away. "Sorry. I got homework." He pointed back to the kitchen. "I don't wanna be late with my paper." He looked back at his mother. "I told you—call me Will."

"Eat first." His father's voice was firm.

"Mom told me to eat before." He glanced at Hank and me as though the presence of strangers would inhibit basic digestion.

Lucy spoke up, apology in her tone. "Mike, he's had his bowl already. I figured you want to talk...alone..."

That didn't make Mike happy. "You could've told me."

Lucy beamed. "Wilson is at Kingswood-Oxford. A scholar, my boy. A letter from Obama last year."

Wilson had already returned to the kitchen table. He let out an unhappy grunt, a teenager recoiling from a parent's praise to strangers.

Within seconds a young girl stepped into the doorway, but the look on her face suggested she'd been ordered to make an appearance.

"This is Hung. We call her Hazel." Lucy draped her arm around her daughter's shoulder. "Wilson's twin sister."

The young girl was beautiful, slender like her mother, with her mother's delicate face. She didn't look like Wilson, to be sure, but then his face was masked by the oversized black-rimmed eyeglasses. She wore a slight trace of pink lipstick, a hint of eye shadow, a bulky white cashmere sweater pulled down to reveal a bit of her left shoulder.

Yes, I thought, a younger version of her mother with brilliant black hair, lazy eyes a little too close together so that she looked as though she were always in deep thought—and a creamy complexion that looked painted on. A far cry from her dark-skinned father. But she had her father's blunt chin and wide nose, though both seemed to enhance her Vietnamese features. A charming package.

I glanced at Hank who was blinking a little too wildly, his eyes riveted to the pretty girl. Awkwardly I kicked him under the table and startled, he yelled out.

"Ouch. Christ, Rick."

"Sorry."

But he knew what I was doing. A sly grin covered his face as he sent a half-wave at Hazel Tran.

Hazel mumbled something about not being hungry, study-ing to do, and fled upstairs. Lucy apologized for her. "The twins have just turned eighteen." As though their newfound majority explained their behavior.

For a while the business of this visit was avoided as we ritu-alistically enjoyed the *mi ga*. Lucy rushed back and forth into the kitchen, carrying out trays of bean sprouts, thin yellow noodles, chopped cilantro and lettuce, spices. Hot steaming broth, delicate slivers of glistening white chicken breast floating in a tantalizing broth. My brow got sweaty as I leaned into the succulent soup, using the chopsticks to stir the aromatic liquid. Delicious, one of the best, which I noted. Lucy beamed. Hank ate his soup so rapidly, slurping noisily, that Lucy snatched his bowl and refilled it. I sipped aromatic jasmine tea, strong, sweet. I sat back, happy.

"*An nao!*" Lucy said over and over. Enjoy yourself.

Mike Tran cleared his throat. "I will talk of money now."

I held up my hand. "Mr. Tran, not yet. Could we talk about your boy first?"

"Mike. Call me Mike."

I nodded. He nodded. Lucy paused as she began lifting bowls from the table. In a low voice I barely understood, she said, "Simon."

"Yes," I said.

In the kitchen Wilson coughed. I looked at him. He'd stopped reading, staring at us with an icy look, but then he returned to his textbook.

Mike Tran cleared his throat again, confused. He looked at his wife who dropped back into her seat, interlocking her fingers, resting them on the table.

Mike Tran glanced toward the kitchen. "Wilson, take your books up to your room."

The boy hesitated. "Pop."

"Now. We have family business." He pointed to the stairwell.

"I'm family."

"Now."

Reluctantly the boy cradled his textbook to his chest and climbed the stairs, but slowly, as though afraid he'd miss some conversation. No one spoke until he was out of sight. But from my chair at the end of the table, at angles to the hallway, I spotted the tips of his sneakers as he sat on the top stair, out of sight, listening.

Lucy, fluttering, pointed to a family photo on the sideboard. "We are a good family. Hard working."

Mike grumbled. "You don't need to say that, Lucy."

"I like saying it."

"Not now." His look froze her.

She was shaking her head as she reached for the picture. "I'm sorry. A good-looking family, no?" Her fingertips grazed each member. Mother and father in Sunday-best clothes. Mike in a stuffy ill-fitting suit. Lucy in a simple dress, a gold necklace around her neck. A goofy-looking Wilson with a bizarre cowlick, annoyed, his mouth open. Hazel in a model's pose, her head tilted at angles to the camera, lips parted. A third boy, older. "Michael," she noted. "Our oldest. At Trinity. A National Merit Fellow. Brilliant." Tall, striking, with a long, angular face, his head turned away from the camera.

Then her fingertip tapped the smallest boy tucked into the shoulder of his father. "Simon." Her voice trembled at the word. "Our youngest."

"Tell me about him."

Mike waited a moment, collected his words. He wasn't happy doing this. "The youngest lives in the shadows of the others. Never a student, didn't like books. But a bright boy, my Simon. Quick, sharp, funny. He…we could *laugh*." A trace of pride in his words, though he looked down into his lap. When he looked back up and into my face, he swallowed his words. "My shadow. Not like the others—me."

I knew what he meant. Staring at the family photograph, the family illuminated by a photographer's garish brush, the differences hit you. Young Simon, small and compact like his father, a bantam fighter, was dark-complected. Indeed, he could pass for a black kid. Or maybe Spanish. His father's rough, honest gaze. Not so the others with their mother's fairer skin, though they still carried their father's features. Simon, the last born—and his father's reflection.

Mike went on. "Always had trouble in school. Skipped classes. Fought back. Doesn't go now—a dropout."

My eyes drifted toward the living room. A wall of awards—plaques, school honors, embossed certificates, blue ribbons. A family's wall of fame in eight-by-ten frames from Target. I breathed in. "I thought he'd be here today. I'd like to meet him."

Mike looked at his wife, who turned away. "We *told* him you were coming—to help us, we told him—but he gets angry. And he runs off early this morning." A helpless shrug. "He's always been...a runner. You yell at him—he disappears. I lock him in his room, but he escapes." His voice broke. "I made him a prisoner but..." His voice trailed off.

"But I need to hear him out," I said.

A mumbled voice. "Some days we never see him."

Hank spoke up. "He's facing serious charges. A man died."

Mike winced; his wife gasped.

The tapping of a nervous foot. At the top of the stairs a boy's sneaker moved.

"I *told* him." Mike's hand balled up into a fist. "That detective came here, that Ardolino. Simon didn't make it better. They took him and his buddy Frankie in for questioning, real quiet-like, me trailing behind all confused, but Simon yells and runs like a nut. Frankie tried to slug one. They throw them into a room to calm down." His voice a shout. "My boy is doing his best to go to jail."

"Tell me about his earlier arrests. Shoplifting. Muggings. Drugs. Four months in juvie."

At first his voice was so soft I had trouble hearing him, but then, banging his fist on the table so that the plates shook, he roared, "A foolish, crazy boy. He always tells me he's not good enough—smart enough—for the family. Christ Almighty. Even when he was small, he got in trouble. To everything—no, no, no. Fights me." A glance at his wife. "I *demanded* my kids be good in school. I...I locked them in their rooms at night. No nonsense. Study. They were *not* gonna have *my* life." A thin smile at Lucy. "I mean, my life is good, but I wanted..." He stopped. He nodded at her.

Lucy finished. "The best in America."

"Simon fought me. He used to follow his older brother around, like hero worship, Michael this, Michael that. But then Michael goes to Trinity and says life in this house—the junk heap in the front yard—embarrasses him. Little Simon got no one to talk to. Bad grades, mouthing off to teachers."

"Where did he meet this Frankie Croix?"

Mike's face closed up. "A bad apple, that one. Sneaky, rotten. I know, I know—I excuse my boy and blame the other. I don't excuse my boy. But this Frankie hangs out on Park Street in the Spanish neighborhood, drifts over to Little Saigon, maybe to buy drugs, finds this gang of boys…"

Lucy broke in. "The VietBoyz, they call themselves."

"A gang?" I turned to Hank.

"Yeah, I heard of them. A local band of thugs—the underbelly of Little Saigon. Petty criminals, mostly. Not exactly BTK."

I squinted. "What?"

"Born to Kill, Rick. Remember that notorious Vietnamese gang that made headlines with a wild shooting at a funeral in Jersey? Based out of Canal Street in Chinatown. They challenged the local Chinese tong gangs. The FBI moved in—closed them down. Murder without remorse—that bunch."

"But years back, no?"

"Shadow gangs still pop up. Phantom gangs."

"And Little Saigon in Hartford?"

"Yeah."

Mike added, "Lost boys hanging together, stealing stuff from groceries, trafficking drugs, flipping off the cops, extorting money from old Chinese and Vietnamese store owners, payoffs from scared shopkeepers, that sort of thing. They just rob their own. Intimidate, frighten."

"How many gang members?" I asked.

"Dunno." Mike looked off as though thinking. "Mostly Vietnamese, some Chinese, some troubled white boys. Ex-cons. But my Simon found his way there. Lots of street boys do. You know, I followed him there one time. Some old industrial

building, closed up. The thugs want young kids—do their bid-
ding, follow orders."

"Soldiers," Hank went on. "Street soldiers."

Mike was animated now. "Not in school but hanging in the
front room of an abandoned store on Russell, off Park Street.
VietBoyz. With a z. One word. You see the graffiti on the wall."

"Simon's a member?"

Mike didn't like that. "No, no. He, well, stops in there. Him
and Frankie."

"Best buddies?"

He sighed. "I guess so. Simon and this Frankie got caught
up in street stuff, the two of them like brothers, running the
streets, dressing like punks. I forbid him to leave the house but
he...runs off. He wanders back. I can't control him no more. I
guess they mugged this one old Chinese guy, asked for his cash
but didn't take it, pushed him around. Then, drunk with it, did
more and more and more. Shoving, just pushing folks around,
knocking into people. But the drugs. Shoplifting. Worse and
worse. Stealing cigarettes from a gas station."

"Then the police caught them in the act." Lucy drew her lips
into a thin line. "Thank God." She whispered again, "Thank
God."

Mike let out an unfunny laugh. "Simon confesses. Blabs the
whole thing. Like he's proud. The judge sentenced them to four
months at Long Lane. Simon tells us he hated it there. Rough
boys, fights, cruelty, mocking by the authorities, everybody
telling you you're a piece of shit. Back home, he still runs the
streets—it's like it's in his blood—can't help himself."

"But he still goes to...VietBoyz?"

"Yeah, I guess so."

"No more crime?"

A fatalistic shrug. "I don't know." Then, "Probably."

"But he hated juvie."

"Maybe he thinks he won't get caught," Hank added.

Mike grunted. "Kids think they can get away with murder
these days."

Immediately he regretted his words. "I don't mean...no... he wouldn't..."

"Did he talk to you about the latest attack? The death of Ralph Gervase?"

Mike's eyes flashed. "You know, I asked him after we got back from the police station. Ardolino told me they were getting evidence against him and Frankie. Convinced, they said, he's back to no good."

"But Simon denied it?"

Again his fist slammed the table. "Yes." He locked eyes with mine. "You know, that first time, dragging Simon to juvenile court, dealing with lawyers, hanging out in courtrooms, talking to the judge, my little Simon dressed in a suit too big for him, all those times I got him to talk. We *never* talk. But then he did. Maybe he was scared. I don't know. He admitted *everything*. No reason, he said, the nonsense he did. Just for the hell of it. Something to impress the guys in VietBoyz, maybe. But after this last time we talked again. He—like sought me out. I'll tell you, Rick Van Lam, he *swore* to me this ain't his doing. 'But nobody'll believe me,' he says to me. 'I believe you,' I said back. And he starts to shake. My boy, shaking. He ain't never did that. A hard nut, that boy. This black sheep. 'I ain't done it.' And I told him again, 'I will call someone who will believe us.'" He pointed a finger at me. "You."

Lucy tittered nervously. "Do you believe us?"

I said nothing.

"Simon don't lie to me."

"I want to talk to Simon," I said.

That answer didn't satisfy. Mike swung his body around and leaned into Hank. His voice got dark. "You talk to him." The *him* was me.

"We'll see," I said without conviction.

Mike folded his arms over his chest and rocked in his chair. "When he was found guilty last year, I condemned him, I yelled. I...*hit* him. I locked him up. He disgraced us. I *wanted* him to go to Long Lane because I *wanted* him punished. Otherwise, what are we? *Ac gia ac bao.*" He looked to see if I understood. You pay a price for evil.

Hank muttered, "You reap what you sow."

Mike went on. "But this time I looked into his face and I knew to my soul that he was not lying to his father."

He stood up. We all stood up.

"We'll find him and talk," Hank volunteered.

I nodded.

◇◇◇

Outside, Hank and I sat in the car, neither talking for a while. Bothered, I was staring back at the house, though I sensed Hank watching my profile. Through the front window I could see Lucy clearing dishes from the dining room table. Mike Tran at one point stood by the front window, looking out at us, his face pressed against the glass, probably surprised we were still there.

"Well," said Hank, impatiently.

"I believe him," I stated finally. "I think Simon was telling him the truth."

Hank grinned. "So do I."

"But it's only my gut instinct."

Hank laughed. "Good enough for me."

"Ardolino may not agree with me."

"Did you expect him to?"

"But I think Simon is going to be the worst evidence against himself."

I put the car in gear, though I shot a look back at the house. In the upstairs window a face stared out from behind a curtain, half hidden but staring. "Look, Hank." I pointed.

"Hazel."

"I'd like to hear her take on her brother. Maybe even Wilson's."

"A beautiful girl."

Hank waved to her, a foolish gesture, I thought, but Hazel, suddenly aware of our stares, had quickly moved away. She had pulled the curtain across the window.

Chapter Six

Little Saigon on a Sunday afternoon in April.

Up and down Park Street cars moved, bumper-to-bumper, jockeying for parking spots. Shiny SUVS with license plates from Rhode Island and Massachusetts turned off the interstate, whole families crowded inside, a day's excursion to shop for the week at Saigon Food Market. Husbands drank beer and played a round of pool at Ky Dien Parlor while their wives filled carts with lemongrass, mangoes, barbecued pork. Jugs of soymilk. Loaves of crisp French baguettes for *ban mi* pork sandwiches. Teenaged boys stood on corners, their hair primped in duck's-ass cuts from a decade they hadn't heard of, cigarettes bobbing in their mouths, cell phones beeping from the pockets of their baggy pants. Girls in plastic jackets flirted with them. A ripple of high laugher, someone yelling out to a friend. An old woman embraced another old woman. *"Toi nho ban lam!"* How much I missed you!

"Oh, my God," Hank whispered. "I actually heard someone talking in English."

A young girl, her blond-streaked hair freshly permed, paused as she moved in front of some boys, waited for them to smile at her. To whistle, to spin around, do an exaggerated boogie-woogie two-step for her.

They did.

She rushed by them.

Hank and I spent hours wandering through the neighborhood, interviewing shopkeepers, stopping stragglers who sat on benches and watched the buses going by. Mug shots of Frankie and Simon in hand. Over and over—"Do you recognize these kids? The afternoon of April 12? Around four o'clock?"

According to Ardolino, Frankie and Simon claimed they'd been wandering Little Saigon, aimless, an hour in an arcade playing video games, stopping for sodas at Le Vinh Grocery, goofing off on a bench in front of the small park off Russell. But no one remembered them. The kid in the arcade told us he was new there, so he couldn't help. Others glanced at the photos, shrugged, and moved on.

A wasted afternoon, perhaps, but our last destination was the VietBoyz storefront down on Russell—where, if the boys were to be believed, they'd hung out for some time. Ardolino had scoffed at that notion and told me it was a crock. Our last stop—and the most troublesome.

Street gang members as witnesses? As alibis?

The leader had told the cops that Frankie and Simon were there.

No one believed him.

"Down there." I pointed.

Perpendicular to Park Street, Russell Street was a narrow dead-end. A couple businesses on the corner. Binh Thanh Fashions. Bo Kien, a small eatery. But mostly shabby triple-decker homes dotted the street. The sidewalks were broken, littered with beat-up plastic trash barrels. A bicycle frame was chained to a streetlight post, the wheels and handlebars disappeared. A block down, a yellow-brick two-story industrial building blocked the end of the street, the second floor boarded up, plywood sheets covering the window frames. A gutter on the roof sagged dangerously, pitched downward. To the left of the entrance was a huge sign: FOR SALE. The sign was faded, peeling.

"That's what Big Nose told me," Hank added. "Command central for the VietBoyz."

"This should be interesting." I poked him.

"There's probably an assault weapon aimed out the front door." He poked me back.

"That's why you're walking in first."

"You'll miss me."

"I suppose so."

I looked up and down the street, but there was nothing to see. Russell Street had little life. An old man tottered out of a triple-decker, eyed us suspiciously, and headed away. Quiet, quiet. The building looked abandoned. I tried the front-door knob, but it was locked up tight. I knocked, waited, knocked again.

"How does a gang keep quarters in Little Saigon?" I wondered.

"Intimidation?"

I rapped again. "Who pays the rent?"

Hank grinned. "That's what I like about you, Rick. A pragmatic man."

"Who pays the rent tells us a lot about the folks inside, no?"

I peered through a murky window into a dark room. A ratty sofa, an upturned chair, folding tables and chairs stacked up against a wall, and a long counter that suggested the room had been a store at one time. Etched into a tiled wall: "Tate's Groceries. We Deliver to Your Home."

Well, not anymore.

"Coffee?" I suggested to Hank.

He nodded.

Back at the restaurant on the corner of Russell and Park, we drank potent Vietnamese coffee and had triple-color dessert. Bo Kien was a tiny, family-style eatery. We tucked ourselves into the end of a long industrial table already occupied by a young family of four who sipped *pho* and never looked at one another: the wife tapping on a tablet, the frowning father checking his iPhone messages, and the young boy and girl absorbed in some noisy tick-tock video game on the gadgets gripped in little fists. Hank nodded at them and whispered to me, "There is no hope for the next generation."

"Hank, everyone said that about your generation."

"And they were right. Actually."

The dimly lit family restaurant had mismatched tables, chairs with torn plastic, white-washed plaster walls lined with cheap, romanticized scenes of old Vietnam that alternated with innumerable glossy calendars handed out by other restaurants, mostly Chinese take-outs. A young man with green spiked hair was happily tapping into an iPad, chuckling to himself. At one of the front tables a rollicking gaggle of small children tumbled over one another, sipping soda from plastic cups. Across from them their parents were all talking over one another, a stream of high-pitched Vietnamese that I couldn't grasp.

"What are they saying?" I asked Hank. "Too fast for me." My Vietnamese was rusty—serviceable but woefully incomplete.

"Money," he said. "Somebody owes somebody money but took off back to Vietnam. Everyone has an opinion." Then he added, "*Co tien mua tien cung duoc.*" Looking into my puzzled face, he translated glibly, "Money does all the talking."

A middle-aged man walked out of the kitchen and yelled something to the boy at the counter, who ignored him. The man wiped his hands on an apron, repeated what he'd said, and then swore.

Hank saw me looking. "Looks like Mike Tran."

"Black," I said.

"That's Johnny Binh. Nice guy. He's a character in Little Saigon. Dishwasher, handyman, you name it."

"I have a confession, Hank," I began slowly.

Hank was shaking his head, his voice dropping. "Oh God, Rick. I hate it when people start with those words."

"Why?"

"Because it always means I have to turn someone in to the police. Like—you."

"Pretty soon you'll be the police."

"And what a quandary that'll be for me." He waited. "Okay. Spill it."

"Whenever I see a Vietnamese with black blood"—I nodded toward Johnny Binh—"I flash to my childhood—and not a good memory."

"The orphanage?"

I nodded. "All these years later I'm ashamed of my own behavior. I cringe."

His eyes narrowed. "Okay. Just what did you do?"

I took a sip of tea and swallowed. I couldn't take my eyes off Johnny Binh.

I breathed in, drummed my fingers on the table. "I was looking for someone worse off than me. I was always getting beat up or having the nuns flog me or—or ignored, shoved in a corner. Then one day there was this *bui doi* who was black as can be. His name was Le Xinh Phong. Everyone hated him, even the nuns."

"And you could catch your breath?"

"Yeah. But worse. I think I hoped that I'd be *included*. Other boys would talk to me."

"So?"

"So I had a chance to beat someone up. To hurt someone the way I was hurt."

"Jesus Christ, Rick. Nice guy."

I closed my eyes for a second. "You know, I regret it to this day. My face gets flushed when I think of it. And this morning, sitting opposite Mike Tran, I kept flashing back to that sad boy who had no life. *Den Phong.* Black Phong. A boy with less of a life than mine."

"What happened to him?"

"When I left, he was still there." I paused. "My last image of him—beat up, sobbing."

"Christ."

I nodded toward Johnny Binh. "Whenever I see black *bui doi,* it reminds me that I gave in to the worst of my character."

"A long time ago, Rick."

"No, Hank. Sometimes, waking up, it seems like an hour ago." I reached for my wallet. "Let's get the hell out of here." As I stood up, I leaned into Hank. "I beat myself up as a cautionary tale, Hank. A warning to myself every day of my life that everybody matters."

◇◇◇

The front door was wide open, secured with a red brick. But the room was dark. Hank and I stepped inside, bumping into each other because he paused, twisted around, fumbling for a light switch.

"Nobody's here." Hank's voice echoed in the quiet room.

At that moment I heard rustling in a back room, heavy footsteps, the faint *beep beep beep* of a phone, someone grunting. A light switch suddenly snapped on, the room flooded with overhead fluorescent light.

"Help you?" A thick voice, unfriendly.

A young man stood in the back doorway, his arms folded over his chest. His head was tilted to the side, wary, but as I approached, his right hand slipped quickly behind his back, dug into the back pocket of his jeans.

"I'm Rick Van Lam and this is Hank Nguyen."

He said nothing. He watched us, his face blank.

"You are?" I asked.

"Ain't your business."

At my side Hank's body tensed.

"We're here about Simon Tran."

His eyebrows shot up as he glanced toward the back room.

"He ain't here." He stepped back.

Hank cleared his throat. "Are you Joey Dinh? JD? Big Nose mentioned your name."

"Big Nose has a big mouth."

"Are you JD?"

"You seem to know a lot already. I guess you don't need me." He took another step backward, but he had no intention of leaving the room.

"Look." I was exasperated. "We were at his home this morning. He was supposed to be there. His father asked for help. You have to know the cops think he killed that guy up on Farmington." I stopped because his body tensed up, the muscles in his neck pronounced, a vein in his temple jutting out.

"Yeah, I'm JD, and he ain't done it."

"Well, can we talk?"

He debated that, once again looking behind him at the back room.

He leaned back against a wall, once again crossing his arms. "I got all day."

I watched him. He was a young guy, probably early twenties, if even twenty. Mixed blood, definitely, a Spanish cast to his face. The slanted eyes of an Asian, dark brown with a slight gold cast to them. Lanky, wiry, but muscular, dressed in a shiny black muscle shirt despite the chill in the room. Cargo pants worn through the knee and tucked into unlaced brown work boots. Close-cropped hair, cut unevenly. A wealth of haphazard tattoos. A sloppy dagger across one side of his neck, a green-and-red fiery dragon on a bicep, a red-and-blue heart with an arrow through it, a girl's name I couldn't make out. Prison-style tattoos, dull ink.

"You're VietBoyz?" Hank asked.

JD scratched his neck with a broken fingernail and contemplated Hank who stood there in his neat khakis and breezy L.L. Bean windbreaker.

A mocking tone. "A social club."

"Yeah, right." Hank was smiling.

JD sucked in his cheeks, mimicked Hank's voice. "Yeah, right. You got that right."

I shot Hank a look as he twisted his head to the side. "No offense, man."

JD was nodding his head to a rhythm playing inside his head. A sickly smile, difficult to read. "Saigon ain't done nothing."

"That's why we want to talk to him."

JD paused, looked back over his shoulder again, and then nodded to the chairs. He pointed. We sat down but he didn't, which surprised me. He circled behind us, as though checking us out, but then, standing only feet in front of me, he said, "Saigon hates cops and you two smell like cops." A sliver of a smile. "Viet Cong style. Uncle Ho's soldiers. Or Thai pirates. *Hai tac.*"

"And yet we're on the same side."

His eyes flashed. "I don't think nobody's on Saigon's side."

"That's where you're wrong."

"He tells me he's being set up."

"That may be true."

A fake laugh that broke at the end. "And you gonna take care of that?"

I waved a hand in the air. "Well, I believe his father."

"His father is an asshole." His fist punched the air.

Hank flinched. "Come on."

JD rushed his words. "He flies in here, accusing us. We ain't kidnapped the boy, you know. It's America. A free country. Free choice. Saigon walking in that door." He pointed to the open door. "And he can walk back out."

"He's in trouble." I stared into his face.

"Every day is trouble."

"Some days worse than others, no?"

Suddenly he slid into a chair opposite me, glared into my face. A broad smile, menacing, grotesque. I saw a broken tooth, missing teeth. A gold tooth. *Talk about your Thai pirates*, I thought. His eyes burned as he looked from me to Hank. "This is my kingdom here."

I waited a bit. "What's your point?"

"We don't like strangers wandering into our camp."

Hank frowned. "Look, man, we gotta at least talk to Simon."

A smirk. "The Saigon Kid."

"So we've heard." I sat back in the chair, watched him carefully.

"Who ain't never heard of Vietnam and Saigon and the Cong and Uncle Ho Ho Ho." Again, the phony laugh.

"I'm not his teacher," I said.

A hard, steely voice sliced into my sentence. "Well, I am."

Hank spoke rashly. "Is that why he was sent to Long Lane for four months?"

JD waited a bit, shot Hank a contemptuous look, then turned back to me. "He's the cop, right?"

"State police," I said. "Soon to be."

"I heard you two might come snooping around."

I smiled widely. "Big Nose. Big mouth."

For the first time he gave us a genuine smile. "You got that right."

I leaned forward. "But look, JD, we're not here to harm him. Just the opposite. I don't have any proof, but I believe his father. Who believes his son. Who, I guess, believes you are his son's alibi. The man strikes me as an on-the-level guy."

"He's an asshole."

"You said that already."

"He thinks we're thugs here." His arm shot out, moved around the room.

"Are you?" Hank asked.

"VietBoyz. A social club."

Hank wasn't happy. "Rumor has it you extort money, traffic weed, terrorize local shopkeepers."

JD rolled his tongue into the corner of his mouth and regarded Hank slowly. "There ain't a gun here. You can search the damn place."

"I didn't say there was."

"Saigon ain't a VietBoyz member."

"Neglected to hand in the application?" asked Hank.

Again JD watched him closely. "I don't know if I like you."

"Hank," I prodded, "leave it alone."

"That's right," JD said to me. "Maybe you should educate your *boy* better."

Hank fumed. I laid a hand on his elbow. Calm down, I nodded at him.

Something crashed in the back room, yet JD barely moved his head.

"We got company?" I asked.

"Rats," JD snickered. "This old building attracts them."

"Anything I should know about Simon?" I asked him.

He considered my question seriously. "No!" Then, he confided, "I got enough trouble keeping my fuckin' soldiers loyal."

Immediately he seemed to regret his words, tightening his mouth, looking away.

"What?" From Hank.

But JD was shaking his head. "I told that loser Ardolino the boys was *here* at the time of the…assault. Here."

"And he didn't believe you?"

"What do you think? Another asshole."

"Am I supposed to believe you?"

"I don't care what you believe."

Enough of this cat-and-mouse game, which he seemed to enjoy. I stood suddenly and JD, startled, rolled back in his chair, a hand nervously touching a back pocket. "Just tell Simon I gotta talk to him. Otherwise he's gonna be hauled in for a crime he didn't commit."

"Will do." Laconic, clipped.

Then, surprising me, JD leaned forward and thrust out his hand. A quick, nervous fist-bump. I glimpsed jagged letters on his knuckles. He stood up. "Later, dude." He turned away, but I noticed a vein on the side of his neck—admittedly shielded by the colorful tattoo unwittingly stolen from a Kandinsky canvas—was throbbing. I'd made him nervous.

His eyes shot to the open front door. A burst of laughter, teenage boyish *ha ha ha*, high and goofy, came at us. As I turned, two young boys darted into the room, rolling against each other. But they sobered up immediately.

Saigon Tran and Frankie Croix.

"JD," Simon yelled.

"Christ," Frankie sputtered and looked back toward the street.

Simon's savvy look took in Hank and me. He stepped backward, colliding with Frankie who'd shuffled his feet, rattled.

"Simon," I said in as quiet a voice as I could muster. "Your dad…"

A mistake on my part. Anger flushed his face as he swiveled away, and Frankie, leaning into his side, swore under his breath.

"I want to help," I began. "My name is Rick Van Lam."

But Simon was staring over my shoulder, past JD who'd taken a step closer to the boys.

"What?" I asked.

Hank nudged me. "Turn around."

Behind JD stood three souls who'd left the back room and now positioned themselves, shoulder to shoulder, in a tight line. They'd materialized so quietly they could have been ghosts. *Di dem co ngay gap ma.* If you walk out in darkness, you can run into ghosts.

I flinched, startled by the trio. An older Vietnamese guy, perhaps mid-twenties, a ferocious scowl on his face. A barrel-chested white guy probably the same age with a red florid face and small marble eyes, an X tattooed on his forehead. And a slender Vietnamese girl who looked thirteen but was probably older. The white guy's look screamed ex-con, an icy glare made more menacing by the pale green dagger tattooed under his left eye. The Vietnamese guy was skinny, wiry, a head shorter than the white guy, with slicked-back hair that shined as though he'd shellacked it.

The two men glanced at each other, the beefy guy grunting. Both stared at me, and none too friendly.

At my side Hank was making a whistling noise, which I couldn't interpret. The young girl, a kewpie-doll face with kohl-rimmed eyes and a slash of bright crimson on her lips, was nervously looking at JD.

"Out of here," Simon roared. "What the fuck?"

Frankie had already turned toward the open door.

I started to say something, but it was JD who surprised me as he yelled out to the two boys. "Wait. Don't fuckin' move. You gotta…"

But he stopped as Frankie darted outside and Simon, close behind him, grabbed the door, kicked the brick away, pulled at the knob, and slammed it shut. With a crashing sound, as though he'd knocked it from the hinges.

"Shit," JD bellowed. "The dumb kid thinks everybody is a goddamn enemy."

I waited a heartbeat. "That's because he doesn't know who his friends are."

Chapter Seven

Jimmy wasn't happy. Or maybe he was the happiest he'd been in years.

Released from Hartford Hospital but convalescing, his right foot in a cast, his hip bandaged, his shoulder dislocated, his skin a patchwork of bandages and gauze, he couldn't return to his tiny studio apartment. Nor could he climb a flight of stairs. He also balked at rehab—"You walk in there and you might as well sign your death certificate"—so he was compelled to accept the compromise worked out in a conference Liz organized one night at Zeke's Old Tavern, our hangout down the street from my apartment. Liz, Gracie, Hank—and me.

The reluctant conclusion: Gracie offered to house the irascible malcontent in her first-floor apartment, tucking him into her spare back bedroom, where she could baby him, coddle him, flirt with him—my conclusion, not hers—until he was able to manage on his own. Living above Gracie, I'd be able to squire Jimmy to the doctor's appointments, to physical therapy, to the all-you-can-eat buffet at Tokyo Szechuan in Plainville.

Reluctantly he agreed.

So one afternoon Hank and I delivered a grouchy Jimmy—"Ouch. Dammit. What are you moving—a piano?"—to Gracie's, and though she fussed and complained about the extra burden that was Jimmy on a good day, she glowed. Life suddenly had a delicious tick to it.

She bubbled when she saw me in the hallway, headed out. "He's simply horrible, Rick."

I smiled. "I know."

"Worse than you can imagine."

"I know."

I sat with Jimmy in his bedroom the next morning. He looked out of place under a fluffy pink blanket. His injured foot dangled near the edge of the bed as though he were contemplating an escape route. A storeroom for Gracie's years in the entertainment world, its walls were covered with black-and-white photographs from her early adolescent days as a hoofer in gin mills in lower Broadway, her brief shining moment as part of a troop that toured Korea with Bob Hope, and her fabulous years as a Rockette at Radio City Music Hall. There were photographs of Gracie in the chorus of high-kickers, but also Gracie looking winsome yet vigorously athletic in a solo shot. Personally inscribed pictures from Jack Benny, Georgie Jessel, Red Skelton, Gracie Allen. A lavish inscription from Patti Page (*"Bumping into you at the Automat made my afternoon!! Patti"*), and a host of others whose names probably meant something decades ago but now were minor footnotes in Manhattan and Broadway histories.

But Gracie had also stuffed the room with frilly curtains and chair coverings and plaster-of-Paris tchotchkes that made the small space seem a prop room for some period costume drama. Gracie was a blunt-talking, no-nonsense woman who'd fought her battles with stage-door Johnnies. She was a woman who drank Budweiser from a bottle. "The way we did it on the road." So the Betty Boop décor, well…surprised, but delighted us.

In that cluttered room Jimmy looked like a chunk of coal tossed willy-nilly into a splashy rainbow.

"Look at this room," he grumbled.

"It looks like Gracie."

"Exactly." He squinted at a pink bow stuck onto a teddy bear on the bureau. "A piñata that exploded."

"You need a little color in your life, Jimmy."

"What I need is to get out of here."

"Gracie is a generous—"

"Yeah, yeah," he interrupted. "Mother-goddamn-Teresa herself."

Gracie and Liz, who'd been banging around in the kitchen, walked in with trays of food: fluffy scrambled eggs, bacon, and biscuits. I helped Jimmy sit up in bed—he groaned as though I were removing a vital organ—and he gobbled down his eggs before I had a chance to take a sip of coffee.

Like a moon-besotted moth near a flame, Gracie fluttered near the bed, adjusting the blanket, trying to reposition a pillow, smoothing out the rumpled blanket, while Jimmy frowned at her. But when she pulled away, shrugging her shoulders in a gesture that suggested she'd been dealing with a jackass, his eyes followed her movements. When she turned back, repeating the same aimless reshuffling of bed linens, he seemed pleased. His eyes twinkled.

"Oh, Lord." I directed my comment to Liz.

She was smiling back at me. "Young love."

Jimmy eyed her closely. "You two still here?"

"Somebody has to be a chaperone," I said.

"Maybe you should be out catching a murderer."

I grinned. "This is more interesting. *Days of Our Lives. As the World Turns.*"

"I love them shows," Gracie said.

I pulled my chair closer. "I do want to talk about what happened, Jimmy. Now that you're back to normal. Sort of. I know you were groggy after it happened, you didn't see much, but maybe if we talk about it…"

Jimmy looked impatient, nibbling on a flaky biscuit. "I told everything to that jackass Ardolino."

"I know, but now, days later, perhaps…"

"Well, what do you want to know?"

"Tell me what happened. As you remember it."

Jimmy pushed away his tray, which Gracie immediately retrieved and put on a table. Jimmy noisily squelched a pleased burp, then looked up at the ceiling as though running through the thoughts in his head. "Not much."

I leaned forward. "Tell me about Ralph."

"You didn't like him."

"True. He didn't care for me either."

"You was supposed to have lunch with us that day."

"No, I wasn't. You invited me but I said no."

"So rude, Rick. Where did you learn your manners? Anyway, Ralph had this mean hangover like he always did. He was in a bad mood. 'What the hell's your problem?' I said to him, which set him off. He was a pain in the ass."

"Jimmy…"

"Don't interrupt. I already said you was rude." He smiled at Liz as though expecting her to agree with him—to provide testimony that her former husband was, indeed, a lout. "I wanted Mexican but he says Burger King. Maybe he wanted one of those paper crowns they give you."

"Anything happen at the restaurant?" Liz asked.

"Other than indigestion?" Gracie added.

Jimmy ignored that. "Let me think. Yeah. He argued with the kid at the cash register. I don't know why. Maybe missing a pickle from his dollar-menu hamburger. I wasn't paying attention to a lot of his gabbing. I was thinking—I gotta get new friends."

I went on. "The witness, Maria Lombardo from the pastry shop, says she thought the two of you were arguing."

"That may be. I don't know. We argued about everything because…he didn't understand that I'm always right. All I know is that all of a sudden I heard this rushing from behind. Like Indians whooping it up."

"Do you think someone was aiming for Ralph? Targeted?"

"Naw, I see some kid shoving Ralph, coming alongside and pushing. But Ralph ain't one to stand for that nonsense. I mean, his street instincts kicked in right away, and he hit back. The other one just stood there—like he didn't believe old people could fight back. The punk slugs Ralph. He falls into the post.

I hear him groan." A deep intake of breath. "I guess he died then." He shivered. "Christ, Rick, all of this took just seconds."

"Lord," whispered Gracie.

"Did you get a look at them?" I asked.

He shook his head. "Naw. Hoods on their heads, their backs to me, the big one grappling with Ralph. I mean, it knocked me off-balance. I didn't know what the hell was happening. I panicked, stepped back, my foot tripped on the curb, and I went flying."

"When you were hit by that car."

"Next thing I know I'm a pile of blood and broken bones on the curb." He waved a hand in the air. "I must have passed out. The rest is a blur."

"A witness spotted two guys in black hoodies running up Sisson. Around the corner. One was an Asian kid. The other maybe white. That's a problem…"

Jimmy spoke over my words, "I know, I know. That fool Ardolino brought me these mug shots of those two boys fresh from Long Lane juvie. He got a bug about them boys. Same M.O., he says. What? Knocking people over? Nobody else does such crap in town? 'The knockout game.' That's what he called it. A game? Like Scrabble for thugs?"

"There's a lot in the news about kids hitting old people in the head—for sport."

"Yeah, so says Ardolino. 'Take a look, Gaddy. These the boys who did it?' I tell him I didn't see them, but he keeps at me. He points to the Asian kid, and I say I don't know. Christ, pictures of those two boys—they look like confirmation pictures, little junior-high boys surprised to be facing a police photographer's camera."

"Ardolino is convinced the boys are Frankie Croix and Simon Tran, given their track record and their recent return home from juvie."

"Maybe yes, maybe no. I can't say." He stared into my face. "You're involved, right? A Vietnamese kid?"

"Simon's dad believes his son wasn't involved."

Jimmy's voice was grim. "Well, it's murder. Maybe not planned, but Ralph died."

"He wants me on the case—to clear his boy."

Jimmy considered my words, his head nodding. "Well, maybe a conflict of interest, no?" He scratched his head. "Your partner"—he thumped his chest—"is the victim of a brutal attack and you run off to represent the alleged criminal? Real nice, Rick."

"I don't want an innocent boy brought up on serious charges, Jimmy."

He sucked in his breath. "Well, me either."

"Nothing may come of it. For one thing, I can't talk to the kid."

Liz was watching me closely. "Rick, you're gonna get emotionally drawn into this."

I spoke too quickly. "Spoken like a psychologist."

An edge to her voice. "Who happens to know how you react to things." She hesitated. "Now, I'm not saying that's a bad thing, Rick…it's part of your character."

I smiled. "True." I shrugged. "Sometimes."

Jimmy was listening to her. "Liz, do you hear yourself? Rick's a big boy. You ain't got him on your couch."

My phone jangled. "Hank." A pause. "Save me." Hank's voice loud and clear. "I'm outside on the sidewalk."

In seconds he bounded into the room.

"You look alive." Hank's first words to Jimmy. He extended his hand.

"You sound disappointed."

Hank punched him in the shoulder, and Jimmy winced, though he winked at Liz. "Somebody arrest this cop."

Impatient, I nudged Hank. "Okay, what did you find out?"

Hank saluted me. "Yes, sir. Task completed." His gaze took in Liz and Gracie and finally rested on Jimmy. "Sir Lancelot's aide-de-camp here, fresh from buying a happy-go-lucky boy named Big Nose two McDonald's breakfast specials."

Gracie was mouthing the words "Big Nose," with wonder in her expression.

I explained. "Big Nose is a sometime visitor to the gang headquarters of VietBoyz, sort of friend of Simon a.k.a. Saigon Tran, and the one who got this ball rolling. He's Anh or Roger, but the world knows him as Big Nose because of God's cruel experiment with his facial physiognomy. Big Nose is also a happy chatterer and sixteen-year-old gossip. I asked Hank to get the dope on some characters we met at gang headquarters. Not only their leader, JD—Joey Dinh—but three souls who appeared, as if by magic, standing in a sort of police lineup."

Hank was nodding happily, itching to talk. "Big Nose resisted but once he began talking, mouth stuffed with a sausage burger, home fries dropped unceremoniously into his lap, a pile of ketchup packets filling the table, he told me the story. Then I called his father, Willie, who filled in some of the blanks. But Big Nose also gave me the name of an ex-gang member, a guy who broke away, married, fled to Springfield. The guy knew exactly what these guys are all about. I could write a book."

"And?"

"The Russell Street storefront is not exactly the Chamber of Commerce."

Hank settled in, sitting on the edge of the bed. "First off, this JD is an interesting soul. He's been wandering the streets since he was a kid, petty crime, shoplifting, his own stint at Long Lane. Supposedly a white crack-addict mommy who headed west after he was born, leaving him with a boozy daddy, a guy named Henry Dinh, a notorious con artist. He lived in ramshackle tenements in the north end of Hartford, later at the Dutch Point Housing Project, and his daddy used to beat up little JD so fiercely that DCF stepped in and put the boy in foster care. It didn't take. Back with his father, he was kicked out after a bloody brawl. A year later a frozen body was found under the underpass of I-91 near the garbage heaps. Henry Dinh, dead for days. JD became a wanderer. A charismatic personality. People like him, it seems, or the rebel kids do, and he put together this band of disaffected loners. VietBoyz. Though not all are Vietnamese. Some Viet Ching—you know, Vietnamese-born

Chinese. White ex-cons. The police are always pulling him in, but he's got the touch, ends up back on Russell Street."

"The others?" I prodded.

Hank deliberated. "I described the three people we met to Big Nose and then to Huong, the guy living in Springfield, though I was so traumatized it's a wonder I remember anything."

"So says a state cop," Jimmy broke in.

Hank grinned. "Be nice, Jimmy. Someday I'll arrest you for speeding."

"Hank," I prodded.

"Okay. The Vietnamese guy is Ming Tinh. They call him Mickey. A meth addict, says Big Nose, ready to fight, sometimes found filling his pockets with candy from the CVS on Prospect, tough guy, mean, the shopkeepers give him lots of space. He comes out of New York. Viet Ching. Tattoo of BTK on his rib cage. His father was Vuong Ky Tinh. Vick, so-called. An enforcer with Born to Kill. Machine-gun happy, supposedly one of the guys who sprayed that funeral in Jersey with an assault rifle. Shot to death in a shootout with the Feds."

Liz shivered. "Good God."

Jimmy added, "The Feds got a squad dedicated to them—VCA. Vietnamese Criminal Activity. To shut them down. BTK. Oriental Boyz. D.O.A. Lonely Boys Only. Stop one gang, another pops up."

"Like the VietBoyz," I said.

Hank spoke softly. "*Dat khach que nguoi.* The lost and lonely souls far from home."

"So Mickey Tinh ends up in Hartford?"

"He had to get out of New York. Played enforcer in Bridgeport, picked up on a home invasion. Lots of jail time. That's where he met the beefy white guy. Travis T-Boy Taylor. Cellmates. A piece of work. Attempted murder charge. Released for good behavior—that's hard to imagine—he drifted to Park Street, hung out in a bar opposite Pho New York, and reunited with Mickey Tinh. JD may be the leader of VietBoyz, but these two guys don't give a damn. For them, it's a place to hide out—to plan crimes. JD has no control over them, according to Big Nose, who is scared of them."

"And that girl we saw?"

"JD's girlfriend. Linh Dao. Calls herself Lana. Pretty as all get out, but no brains. Sits there and moons over JD like he's the last piece of cheesecake in a midnight deli. JD likes her to dress up like she's one of the taxi girls he's heard about in Old Saigon."

I nodded. "Good job, Hank. But I can't see Simon and Frankie hanging out with such punks."

"They don't, Big Nose told me. They just like JD. He gives them a place to run to. Maybe feeds them bucks, has them run some drugs."

Jimmy had been listening closely to Hank's long narration, but now I could see him start to drift off, slumping in the bed, his head lolling to the side.

Gracie shooed us into the living room and immediately began to brew tea. She placed cookies on a platter. "These characters sound dangerous, Rick," she commented, but she was looking protectively at Hank.

"I'm gonna be a state trooper in a few weeks," he told her.

"More reason to worry." She tapped him on the cheek.

She turned to Liz. "Can't you talk some sense into Rick?"

Liz laughed out loud. "Gracie, I never could when we were married."

"Well, my husband always listened to whatever I said."

Hank smirked. "Is that why he died?" He squeezed her hand affectionately.

"Fresh mouth." Gracie made believe she was slapping his cheek. He beamed at her.

Liz ran a spoon around the edge of her teacup. "I met Simon Tran, I think. Assuming there's only one Simon Tran in town."

I sat up. "What?"

"Remember last year how I mentored the three scholarship girls at Miss Porter's? That program I volunteered for? One girl was Hazel Tran. Hung Tran. A beautiful girl, very bright, a little insecure being at the rich girls' school, but popular in her own way. For a short time we became friendly. She'd call me at home for advice. One time, walking through Target, I met the whole family. Father, mother, Hazel's twin, and a boy who looked like he didn't want to be there. Hazel introduced him. Simon." She chuckled. "I remember that he overlapped his father's introduction with a nervous 'Saigon.'"

"Lord, Liz. I can't find him—he spots me and runs away—and you've already met him."

"In passing, Rick."

"Are you still friends with Hazel?"

She shook her head. "No, the mentorship program was short-lived." She hesitated. "I had some problems with her boyfriend at the time. He's…sort of a junior-grade womanizer who stood too close to me. But I know she's still at Miss Porter's. I get updates."

"Call her."

"Why?"

"I'd like to talk with her. Away from her family."

"Surely she's not a mugger." Liz blinked her eyes merrily.

"No, but I want to understand little Simon. I want to understand why, in a family of high-achievers—prep school wonders—why the youngest drifted into the dangerous world of the streets."

Hank spoke up. "Maybe because he felt like the outsider in that family, Rick. He *looks* different."

"Maybe his sister has something to tell me. I have this image of her in an upstairs window, half-shielded by a curtain, watching us drive away."

Gracie wore a perplexed look on her face. "A stretch, Rick?"

Jimmy added, "You think the secret of that boy lies in the family?"

"It always does." I sipped my tea. It was lukewarm now. "It always does."

Chapter Eight

Hazel Tran was a stunning girl. She knew that about herself. You could tell that by the way she withdrew a compact every so often from the Vera Bradley bag she'd tossed casually onto the seat next to her. She sat back, a broken smile on her lips as she ran her fingertips across the rim of the water glass.

She looked at Liz. "I was so surprised to hear from you. It's been…like a year, no?"

Liz nodded. "Yes, a year. How have you been?"

Hazel shrugged. "My last year at school."

"And next year?"

"Vassar." She smiled as she said the name.

"Not bad," I said to her.

She twisted her body and looked at me, baffled. "I don't understand why we're here." She waved her hand around the small sandwich shop just down the hill from her dorm at Miss Porter's, steps away from the Farmington Country Club. Liz had phoned her, and Hazel agreed to meet both of us for lunch between her classes.

Liz assured her. "I told you…"

I cut in. "You do know that I'm trying to clear your brother, right?" I was a little impatient because I watched her eyes glaze over as I spoke. "We did meet at your home the other day."

She smacked her lips, annoyed. "My parents insist I go home on weekends. Sometimes."

"You don't like that?" I asked.

"What do you think?" An edge to her voice.

We'd ordered sandwiches—a bacon cheeseburger for me, a turkey club for Liz, and a tuna melt for Hazel, which she ignored. A diet Coke also untouched. Repeatedly one fingertip traced the rim of the water glass, either a nervous gesture or idle boredom.

She dabbed the corner of her mouth with a napkin, though she'd not touched her food. A girl conscious of curious eyes on her. She was wearing a peach-colored cotton blouse, snug, the collar turned up, a simple gold chain with a drop pearl around her neck. A teenaged boy, passing by, hesitated, as if he knew her, but it might have simply been that she looked up at him, smiled, but then turned her head away.

Liz caught my eye. "Hazel, you still can get any boy's attention."

"Thank you."

Liz wasn't happy.

"I'm trying to get to know the family," I continued. "I figure perhaps you can help me understand what makes Simon tick—why he's taken a road so different from you and your other brothers."

She was in a hurry to speak. "I have no answers."

"Of course you do," I said a little hotly, which surprised her.

Liz glanced at me. "What he means is that you can tell us about Simon, anything, something, bits and pieces of growing up with him. If Rick is to help him. The why…"

Hazel tossed out a line. "He's always been the baby of the family. Two years younger." She sat back. "That's it."

"And you're the only girl."

She clicked her tongue. "Yeah, you'd think *I'd* be the baby, but not in a Vietnamese family." She glared at me. "You *know* that. Boys rule the roost. Men call the shots."

"Yet your parents are proud of you. Miss Porter's on a full scholarship. Vassar next year."

Her voice crackled. "My father is a slave driver. You've *met* him. All A's in school. No B's. Study, study, study. He wouldn't let us have—fun. That's why he bought that horrible little house in the South End."

"Why?" From Liz.

"He wanted the family away from the bad neighborhoods. The South End has, you know, Italians, Polish. We started out on a bad street—drugs, hookers—but we moved. When I was small, we lived in that house with almost no furniture. Money for the mortgage, that was all. Lord, I slept on the floor." She frowned. "Imagine. A house with no furniture. I was embarrassed to invite friends over." She bit her lip. "I never did, in fact."

"They sacrificed for you kids."

"I suppose so." She looked into my face. "A world of…not love but…*hoc*."

Liz looked confused.

"Studying," I translated.

Hazel picked up her tuna melt but then put it back on the plate. "But Pop hounded us. Afraid of failure. Drummed it into us. We gotta make it in America. What will the neighbors think? No slackers. Work, work. Lord, he *locked* our bedroom doors at night. That's what got to Simon, I think."

"The pressure?" I asked.

She nodded. "We're all bright kids, always were. Michael at Trinity now. Wilson at Kingswood-Oxford. Me here." She pointed out the restaurant in the general direction of her campus. Even little Simon was bright. Really. Always trying to please Pop. Quick, sassy, sharp as a button. Teachers loved him."

"But something happened?" From Liz.

"I think Pop was on his case about grades. 'Oh no! A B-plus in Spanish? Oh dear! Say it isn't so!' It just got to him. The *weight* of the family. The rest of us, you know, already shining lights… That and…" She hesitated.

"What?" I waited. Silence. "What?"

"Look at him."

"He looks like your father."

"My point exactly. Pop's half black. No big deal. But the rest of us look more like Mom—I mean our complexions." Nervously her hand tapped the compact, which she'd rested on the edge of the table. "Simon is, well, darker than the rest of us."

"And that's a problem?"

"Not to me—or most people. These days, especially. I think it's sort of cool that I'm…like a quarter black." She arched her neck, smiled. "Gives me a sort of cachet with some of the rich girls at school." She twisted her mouth into a cynical grin. "They come from different worlds—like Darien and Beverly Hills—and think street life is cool. Or something. Street cred. Like I would know *anything* about street life. Dr. Dre and me. Kanye West humming in my ear. Pitbull sending me tweets. Yeah, sure." A false laugh that broke at the end. "I celebrate it."

"But Simon doesn't?"

"I don't know. All I know is that he's had kids in school taunt him, that kind of thing. Half Asian, half black, whatever. He'd come home to tell Pop and Mom—'They call me dog-eater. A freak.'"

I debated what to say. "And you think that led to him to run the streets, hanging out with a gang? With Frankie Croix?"

She drew her lips into a thin line. "Frankie Croix. That loser."

"You know him?"

"A troublemaker. He got into it with my boyfriend."

"They know each other?"

"No, not really."

"What are you talking about, Hazel?"

She spoke over my words. "I really don't know what I'm talking about."

Liz was watching her closely. Hazel seemed pleased with her response, sitting back, tilting her head. For some reason she smiled and blinked rapidly. She excused herself, whispering to Liz, "Powder room."

We watched Hazel weave her way through the tables, pausing to say hello to a small group of girls sitting in a back booth. She leaned into the table, said something that made the girls laugh loudly, and Hazel glanced back at Liz and me, both of us unfortunately staring at her with a little too much interest. A half-wave, a shrug that communicated an exaggerated *whatever*, and she disappeared into the bathroom.

"What a difference a year makes," Liz said slowly.

"Meaning?"

"A scholarship girl, she was shy, charming really. Of all the poor girls I mentored—she'd already been there a year—leading them through textbook assignments and even manners and dinner etiquette, she was the most deferential, thankful. A quick, lively mind. A year later she carries herself with an unpleasant confidence."

"Well, she's found all sorts of approval at the exclusive school."

"She seems to take little interest in Simon's problems." Liz's eyes got cloudy. "That ticks me off."

"Yeah, I noticed. But she's also straining at the family leash."

"Her father's a man who wanted to save her and her brothers." Liz reflected, "He may have gone about it the wrong way, though."

"What a cruel, cruel man, no?" I wasn't happy.

"Last year she was so sweet. To me, at least. The *only* time I saw her bristle, become a little mean-spirited, was when her boyfriend, this lumbering football jock who oozed testosterone, acted smitten with me. Flirted stupidly, hung on my every word."

I grinned. "I can understand that."

"Hazel wasn't happy." Liz rolled her eyes. "Nothing like having a teenaged boy practice his feeble pickup lines on you."

"Good-looking?"

"Very."

"Smart?"

"Very."

"Winning ways?"

"None."

Hazel slipped back into her seat. "I *do* love my family," she insisted. "I hope I didn't come across as…" Her voice trailed off.

"Then you must be worried about Simon," Liz said in a curt voice.

Hazel drew her lips into a disapproving line. "He was always Pop's favorite, you know."

"You saw that?" I asked.

She tossed her head back, touched the edges of her hair. "It was obvious. Simon, as I say, looks like Pop, but Simon was... weak, he'd fall apart, he'd cry. He...he was real bright in school, but it was like he couldn't keep playing a part."

"So he turned to street crime?"

"I think he just got tired of it all...the expectations. He needed to break out, I guess. I did, too. In my own way."

An edge to my voice. "Teenagers rebel, Hazel, but they don't attack strangers on the street. Over and over. Shoplifting. Weed. God knows what else."

"He met that Frankie Croix, that's why. I *told* you."

"A bad influence?"

She puckered her mouth. "A piece of white trash. They met each other, became bros. Frankie's a lowlife, lives in a slum in Hartford. Simon is—like a follower. Frankie was...excitement maybe. A dropout. Made Simon drop out, too. Talks in this hip hop slang, you know. Swaggers, spits, gives the finger to the world. Simon saw that as...well, good. Low expectations, I guess." She shrugged and suddenly looked tired of the conversation.

"What did you think when Simon and Frankie were arrested and sent away?"

"I wasn't happy."

"I know, I know, but you must have..."

"Lord, who wants to live with a criminal in the family?"

"And now—maybe again. This time a man died, Hazel."

"Simon says he wasn't there."

"The cops don't buy it."

She lowered her voice. "Lord, his alibi this time—listen to this—is a gang leader."

"But did you feel sorry for him?" Liz asked.

"Frankie whispered in his ear that the devil has more fun than the angels."

"But what about his two brothers? Do they try to help him? He sounds like a boy who needs someone he can trust." Liz's voice rose.

"I don't know. I'm not there. Only weekends. Not always. I have a life…here. A boyfriend. Pop told me Simon runs to some hole in the wall off Park Street. Pop trailed him there once. This leader guy, covered with tattoos, told Pop Simon wasn't there, even though Pop saw him and Frankie wandering in."

"JD," I said to Liz.

Liz persisted. "I don't care. Two older brothers…"

Hazel's eyes sparkled. "You do know that Wilson is my twin. Fraternal, of course. What can *he* do? Simon thinks he's a nerd. Lost in his books, hunched over, those glasses slipping down his nose. Half the time he doesn't even know where he is."

"It sounds like you don't like him," I said.

"Wilson thinks that if he hugs a book to his chest, Pop will love him. That's not how it works. I don't think about him. We're twins, at one time always together in school. Too many comparisons by teachers. He doesn't like to look up from a book." Her eyes got wide. "How can you learn about the world unless you look around you?"

"What does he think of Simon's problems?" Liz asked.

"I don't know."

"What about Michael?" I asked.

She bit her lip. "He hides out at Trinity. I heard Pop on the phone asking him to talk to Simon. Simon used to follow him around, hero worship crap. Long ago. But Michael blew Pop off. Well, it doesn't take much to make them yell at each other. Michael has decided to become a white man."

I looked into her face. "But that's impossible."

A superior tone in her voice. "Oh, you can do it if you try hard enough."

"And Michael can do that?"

"He already has." She looked at her watch. "I'm being picked up."

We stood up. I dropped cash on the table as Hazel scooted out the door, quickly disappearing. Liz shot me a look and shrugged her shoulders.

Once outside Liz tensed up. Her hand reached out to grasp my elbow. "Rick." Under her breath she whispered, "Oh, Christ."

A tall young man stood beside a red Audi, the top down despite the spring chill. He leaned against the driver's door, an insolent posture, casual but possessive, and pointed at us, extending the index fingers of both hands. Double-barreled shotgun. A kind of worldly gesture you could imagine Tom Buchanan using in *The Great Gatsby* as he bumped into an old crony from New Haven.

"Judd, you remember Liz from last year." Hazel didn't sound happy.

A roustabout playboy, I thought, dressed more for an outing at an Episcopalian dinner dance at the Farmington Country Club. A blue dress shirt, gray necktie, prep school trousers.

Judd walked toward us and reached out his hand to Liz. He gripped her fingers too tightly, held on too long, and Liz twisted her body away.

Judd preened. "I thought I'd never see you again."

Liz sucked in her cheeks. "You almost got your wish."

Hazel opened the car door and motioned to Judd. She caught my eye. Her voice became low and sad. "Judd used to think Liz was the most fascinating woman in the world." Color rose in her neck.

"She is."

Judd laughed. "Hey, man, we agree on something." He made a clicking sound and wagged a finger at me.

Hazel slammed the door. "Sometimes Liz could be too charming." Now she eyed Liz, speaking through clenched teeth, "She has a way of making foolish schoolboys forget who their real girlfriends are." Her words sliced the air, but she looked as if she could cry at any moment.

"Hazel is my girlfriend." A flat-out statement, said loud enough for Hazel to hear. "For two years now." Unhappy words, thrown out at us. The look he gave her was angry, fiery. "What did I tell you about talking such shit, Hazel?" His words were snarled as he nodded toward her. "It's nice to have a pretty girlfriend, right?" She looked away.

"You're a lucky guy," I told him.

Judd was staring at me, his look none too friendly. "No, mister, you are." He winked at Liz.

Hazel, furious, leaned on the horn.

Chapter Nine

When Hank and I pulled up in front of Mike Tran's house, I got a queasy feeling in the pit of my stomach. Not only were all the lights on in the downstairs rooms, but in the upstairs rooms as well. The front porch light. A spotlight on a garage illuminated the small fenced yard with the battered cars. Eerie and unnerving. I turned to Hank, "What do you think?"

Hank said nothing at first, then slowly pressed his face against the car window. "Mike Tran is telling us this is a safe haven."

"He's telling us that his house needs protection from the bogeyman."

Hank shivered. "Simon Tran will not be home."

"Even though he promised his father he'd be there. The Saigon Kid has fled once again."

"You think so?"

"I know so."

Hank banged the dashboard. "Christ, Rick, what's wrong with that boy?"

"I suppose we have to find that out."

I was right. Inside, we faced a nervous Mike Tran who kept shifting his body from one foot to the other. "I'm sorry," he began, not looking at us. "I know I told you that you could, you know, finally *talk* to my son." He shrugged helplessly. "But when I told him you were coming, he bolted." He glanced toward the front window. "He runs the streets. He's like a pet that breaks free and runs." At that moment his wife approached from behind and rested a hand on his elbow.

Lucy looked as if she'd been crying, her face puffy and pale, her eyes red-rimmed. She attempted a smile, but stopped.

Quietly she looked into my face. "We are going to lose our son."

Mike faced her. "No."

"No," I said to her. "There has to be a solution."

Lucy's eyes were wet. A soft "thank you."

Lucy had none of Mike's thick, blunt toughness. She looked fragile, a slender woman given to some girlish plumpness in her arms and face. Wearing a housedress covered with purple irises, she looked uncomfortable, as though she'd dressed for our visit in her Sunday best. She ran her hands down the dress, smoothing wrinkles that weren't there. A woman who fretted her day away. I knew that she worked as a cafeteria helper at the local middle school, but I imagined her long days were the stuff of worry and pain.

Mike nodded, uncomfortable. "Sit, sit." He motioned to the living room. A tiny room dominated by a huge flat-screen TV, turned on, the sound muted. A plaid sofa, covered in plastic. A coffee table with a huge arrangement of paper flowers. A photograph on an end table: a wedding shot of Mike and Lucy, young, smiling, almost giddy in the way she threw her head back, Mike glancing at her profile with an expression that was both delighted and surprised. It made my heart leap, that photo, the heartfelt affection there, deep, real.

It gave me pause as I remembered Liz and me, newly married, having our photo snapped by my best friend at Columbia. He caught me looking to the side, Liz watching my face as if she couldn't understand the strange man she'd somehow said yes to. She always found that photo amusing—in fact, she'd framed it, kept it on her desk. "You are looking for a way to escape," she used to say, a ripple of laughter coming from her. Then, unfortunately, it became true.

That photo—I wondered if Liz still had it. I didn't.

Mike sighed. "Simon tells me you went to Russell Street. The VietBoyz. That JD and those...those..." Helpless, his hand floated in the air, then dropped back into his lap.

I smiled. "He wasn't happy about that. He ran away."

Mike glanced at his wife. "All his life he runs away."

The moment froze. No one said anything. Mike stared over our shoulders, his focus on the plate-glass window that looked out onto the street. I waited. Hank fidgeted.

Finally, clearing her throat, Lucy announced supper. She walked to the foot of the staircase and yelled upstairs. "Wilson, honey, now."

The young boy scampered down the stairs, two at a time, jumping the last three, and stood staring at Hank and me as though surprised there were visitors.

"Did you wash up?" his mother asked, and he nodded.

At the dining table he looked out of place among the adults, a skinny boy slouching in the chair, picking at his food, watching us.

I found myself comparing him to his sister. It was difficult believing they were the same age, let alone twins, because Wilson looked the little boy with his tiny bone structure, his thin shoulders, his broken fingernails, that shock of deep black hair in need of a trim. And those huge Coke-bottle eyeglasses with the wide black frames. It was, I supposed, the contrast with the slick young woman who could casually toss a designer handbag onto a luncheonette seat with the insouciance of a runway model.

And Simon. Saigon. Street runner. Wise guy.

Lucy served us a white asparagus-and-crab soup, a delicacy for special occasions. *Sup mang tay cuc.* Wilson kept sipping the soup, mumbling "Hot, hot, hot." Then Lucy served steamed white rice with thin slices of pork pounded into an inch of their lives, marinated with a caramel lemongrass sauce. Wilson took a second helping while his mother sat back and watched the men around her, checking every so often with Mike, who beamed at her, proud, satisfied. Lucy barely picked at her own food, though she fiddled with chopsticks, picking them up, grasping a piece of meat, then dropping it back onto her plate.

Mike kept checking out Hank and me, running his tongue over his lips. Every so often he looked to the front door. He'd promised us Simon, and that bothered him. But then, with a sidelong glance at Lucy, he'd nodded toward his son. It was clear what he wanted to discuss, but he chose to wait. Wilson nibbled on a piece of pork, oblivious. Instead, we discussed the brisk spring weather, Mike's job at the garage. Did we notice one of the cars on the front lawn? He was rebuilding a Ford Mustang from 1966, vintage, he said, tan with a cloth roof, a classic—and Lucy said that the tulips she'd planted last fall in the front yard were starting to peek through the old leaves and spring mud. Pleasant, surely, all of this, but killing time.

Hank got Wilson's attention. "How's school?"

The boy beamed. "Good." Then he looked back down.

Lucy smiled at her son. "Wilson studies all the time."

Wilson twisted his head. "If I don't, Pop'll get mad." He avoided looking at his father.

The remark bothered Mike, who struggled with a stiff smile. "I do let you out of the house to play basketball in the yard. And those goddamned video games you love."

Now Wilson seemed repentant. "I only mean…"

"It's all right." His mother tapped the back of his wrist.

"What's your favorite subject?" Hank asked.

Wilson brightened. "English. I'm gonna be a writer." A pause. "Yeah, a writer, I think."

"Cool." From Hank.

"A science fiction writer," the boy went on. He looked eagerly at Hank. "You ever read the Robotech series?"

Hank nodded. "Yeah, what kid doesn't?"

Wilson's face lit up. "I got all the books lined up on a shelf."

Mike interrupted. "If you're finished, Wilson, you can go upstairs."

But Wilson had found a sympathetic audience in Hank. "Sci-fi movies. Books." His eyes popped.

I spoke up. "Good for you, Wilson."

"Call me Will."

"Will."

"When I'm twenty-five, maybe I'll be famous. Maybe even rich." He blinked wildly.

Mike was frowning. "For God's sake, Wilson."

The boy spoke loudly, energetic. "No, no, I mean it. I'm the smartest kid in my class. The teachers tell me so."

Mike wasn't happy. "Wilson is in love with himself."

That stopped the boy. He got quiet, but he looked annoyed.

Lucy, fretting, said in a squeaky voice, "Hank is gonna be a state trooper, Wilson."

"I know. I heard." He narrowed his eyes at Hank. "But why? Isn't that dangerous? I mean—like *guns?*" Suddenly he looked uncomfortable, his head dipping into his chest.

Hank didn't answer him.

"What are you reading in school, Will?" He looked back up, relieved. I looked over at Hank. "What do kids read in school these days? I'm so out of touch."

Hank grimaced. "They read graphic novels about ghouls and vampires and…"

Wilson broke in. "Sci-fi at home. Even—like the Transformer series. I do. In school we're reading *Moby Dick*. You ever read it? I love it. We read *The Scarlet Letter*, which I didn't love. Hey, single mom with a baby. Deadbeat dad. Big deal. That's like turning on, you know, *Dr. Phil.*" He grinned. "And I thought *Moby Dick* would be, you know, boring. A whale. I mean, a *whale*. But it's not. It's my favorite book." He pointed to the upstairs. "It's a great book. No one in my class likes it, but me." He stopped, out of breath.

Mike made a grunting sound. "Okay, Wilson, you can go to your room, okay?"

Flummoxed, Wilson left the room, though he grinned at Hank.

Mike whispered, "We gotta talk now."

We sat in the living room, silent at first, facing one another, while Lucy poured tea into small cups. Her hand shook as she placed the cups on the table.

Finally Lucy broke the silence. "Hazel phoned today. She said you—even Liz, her old mentor—met with her in Farmington." Question in her tone, a glance at her husband.

I exchanged a glance with Hank. "Liz hadn't seen Hazel for a year," I explained as a puzzled look came into her eyes. "Liz is my ex-wife, Lucy. I thought it a good idea—to get her perspective on Simon's problem. How a sister sees his problem. You know…" I faltered.

"It made her nervous." She bit a nail. "She told me that."

"It wasn't meant to," I told her.

"Did she help you?"

Before I could answer, Mike interrupted. "She's got so high and mighty. Hazel has an attitude nowadays—holier-than-thou crap. A rich girl's school."

Lucy looked perplexed. "I still don't get…"

Mike's look told her to be quiet. "Ardolino called here again."

"What did he say?" I asked.

"I think he just wants me to know that this ain't going away. That's the message. Like—I know your boy is dirty, mister. A matter of time before I haul his ass in."

Lucy was watching me closely. "I still don't see how meeting Hazel at school can help."

Mike was impatient with her. "Christ, Lucy, he must know what he's doing."

"I don't understand. I guess…well, afterwards, she had a fight with her boyfriend. That—that Judd Snow."

Mike let out a nasty growl, then slumped back, looked sheepish.

"You don't like him?" From Hank.

Husband looked at wife, a glance that ran through chapter and verse of an unpleasant book.

Mike hissed, "Too goddamned possessive, that boy. Hazel is a girl who tells you what's what, but she always *obeys* that boy. Jumps when he snaps his fingers. He got too much control. He makes her—afraid somehow. She…you know…I can see it in her eyes."

"Charming," Lucy added, but it wasn't a compliment. "He's charming. Smart as a whip, they tell me, but"—she shook her head back and forth—"not good for our Hazel."

Mike's voice was biting. "He can get her to follow him into fire."

"What does that mean?" Hank asked.

Lucy shook her head sadly. "Sometimes she's up in her room crying."

Mike sneered. "Judd Snow. Dumb-ass name, no? Rich boy—buys her shit, then takes it back. He comes from over the mountain in Avon. He scoots around in a fancy car, blows the horn in the driveway instead of ringing the doorbell like a boy should. This boy don't like to be crossed. He sits in front, leaning on the horn, louder and louder. When I tell him to stop, his face gets blood red. Scary. Mouth got all tight. Nobody never says no to the boy. Respect for the family, I say. What boy does that?"

Lucy leaned in. "Hazel whispered to me that he flirts with other girls, wants their attention. Right in front of her—to make her mad. A cruel boy." She stopped, bothered. Then, looking at Mike, "We're worried about her."

I debated my words, but said, "I met him when he picked up Hazel. Johnny Cool. Last year he was taken with Liz, hovered around her, a pest. Liz is a gorgeous woman."

Lucy smiled thinly. "I know about that. It really boiled Hazel. For a while all Judd talked about was…"

"Liz," I finished.

"Her looks, her humor, her sophistication, even the perfume she used."

"Well, that ended."

Mike had been listening to Lucy and me. Suddenly he thundered, "Did it?"

I clicked my tongue. "Yesterday he was a little obnoxious, I thought."

"He's always obnoxious," Mike stormed. "I don't *like* him."
Again the helpless shrug. "But Hazel—another child of mine
who doesn't listen. She nods, obeys, afraid to *lose* the asshole."

Lucy admonished, "Mike, please. Your tongue."

"I don't care. My Hazel…"

"Then there was another girl," Lucy interrupted. "A young
librarian at Kingswood-Oxford."

"He goes there?"

Mike's eyes darkened. "Yeah, that's how he met Hazel. Dumb
luck. He's head of the chess club, a whiz kid. A jerk. In the
same class as Wilson. So he teaches our Wilson to play chess,
and Wilson *beats* him. That made him crazy. Wilson was in a
chess tournament, so we all went, and this Judd was the star of
the event. While we're watching Wilson win, Judd's eyes found
Hazel as she sat with us."

Lucy spoke quickly. "I think her eyes found him, too."

Mike lowered his voice, peering toward the staircase. "He
hounded Wilson about Hazel, but Wilson kept his distance. 'He
makes me nervous,' he told us. 'He's bossy, orders me—everyone—around. Even the teachers.' That's what Wilson told us.
Judd drove Wilson crazy. 'Where does she hang out? Who are
her friends? Tell me, tell me.' Wilson made an enemy by telling
him to leave Hazel alone. But that seemed to make Judd even
more determined."

"And here we are today, a couple years later." Lucy sat back,
folded her hands into her lap. "He's the big man on campus,
headed to Princeton."

"What bothers me," Mike spoke over her, "is this boy's father.
I mean, Judd treats *us* like—like old suitcases Hazel has to drag
around. He walks right by Wilson in classes, but his father calls
here. His *father*. 'Judd isn't answering his cell phone. I texted
him all day. Is he there?' When I say no, he says, 'Are you sure?'
Like we're hiding the boy in the attic. One time the flashy red car
is in the driveway, horn honking, Hazel getting ready to leave,
and I look out and it's not Judd, but the father. 'Hazel, it's his

father.' 'Oh Christ,' she says, but she runs out anyway. Watching from the window, I see him leaning in, laughing. Creepy."

Hank and I sat quietly.

"What's going on?" Lucy whispered to Mike as though Hank and I weren't in the room. An awkward moment, a husband-and-wife late-night talk about the children. Intrusive, my sitting there. A violation. I stared at my hands.

"We lost control of our kids." Mike's rough voice was a whisper.

Lucy shook herself out of it, addressing me. "Simon told us there was a real bad incident at the mall."

"With Judd?" I asked.

She nodded. "I guess Simon was walking with that…that rotten kid, Frankie…they're like mall rats, them two, in the arcade, loitering, and Hazel walks by with Judd. West Farms Mall. I guess Frankie opened his mouth, said something real fresh to Hazel, so Judd flipped out. He accused Frankie of flirting with his girl, and Frankie mouthed off something. It got bad real quick, and Judd *slugged* Frankie. Frankie dove into his chest, the two boys at each other. Security pulled them apart, but they tried to keep going—shoved the guard into a window. They arrested them both—took them to the station. Judd had to call his father—it wasn't pretty, Hazel told me. He was humiliated. But Hazel defended him. 'Frankie started it.' Simon said Judd yelled, 'I'll get you. Watch your back.' Something like that."

"Simon told you this?" I asked.

Lucy looked surprised. "Yeah, why not? Simon always talks to me." She paused. "Or *talked* to me. He liked to talk to me. Used to. We'd sit in the kitchen"—she pointed—"and he'd go on and on." A slight sob escaped her throat. Mike frowned at her.

"Simon." Mike's one word filled the room.

"They're gonna put him in jail for life." Lucy's voice shook. "Frankie ruined him. He was a sweet boy, lovely, my Simon, but he's turned…bitter. We never see him. Juvie. Jail." She shuddered. "We can't call anyone. Who do we talk to? Who understands? We don't want…"

"No."

We all jumped.

Wilson had walked down the stairs, unseen, and slipped into the living room. He stood there, a book—*Moby Dick*? I stupidly wondered—cradled against his chest. He was shaking. His eyeglasses were crooked on his nose.

"No!" Louder this time.

"What?" From his father.

He started to say something, but the words were a mishmash. He breathed in and started again. "You all talk like he's this... this evil kid. He's...Simon." His voice broke. "Aren't you supposed to love him to death?"

With that he spun around, bumped into a wall and stumbled back up the stairs.

Mike dropped his voice again. "Wilson. Christ Almighty." He looked at me. "You have kids, easy, but you spend a lifetime not understanding what the hell they're talking about."

Chapter Ten

We sat in the kitchen watching Hank's mother chop cilantro on a cutting board, her head bent in concentration. Occasionally, listening as Hank and I chatted about Jimmy and the death of Ralph, she'd flick her head toward us, but avoiding eye contact. Finally, placing the sharp knife on the board carefully and wiping her hands on her apron, she faced us, her face flushed.

"You two bring death into this house."

"Mom," Hank began, but she held up a hand.

A forced smile directed at me, the visitor. "It's like the bad luck people bring into the house after a funeral. Sometimes the dark spirits come off the clothing."

Hank was exasperated. "For God's sake. Mom, this is America."

His mother frowned. "And there aren't dark spirits in America? Seems to me they follow *you* around."

Hank laughed. "Some folks get lint on their clothes. I get the dust of death."

His mother started to admonish him, but looking down into her son's face, she found herself smiling. "You have all the answers."

Hank beamed as he reached over to touch her forearm. "I'm glad the world is starting to pick up on that."

She faced me. "I'll never win any battles with my son, Rick."

I was sitting in the warm kitchen of the Nguyen household in East Hartford. Once an alien space for me because my mixed blood made me unwelcome, I now was comfortable there—in a fashion. Hank's obsession with making me part of his family hadn't been easy, although his mother and grandmother—the old woman I called Grandma—drifted into companionable and sweet attention. His father and irascible grandfather—Hank's father's father, not Grandma's husband—were bitter holdouts, although Hank's father now talked to me. Battles are won, I soon learned, in tentative baby steps. But the craggy grandfather was the cement wall I constantly crashed into, ego bruised, feelings hurt.

"Everybody's gonna love you, Rick." Hank's mantra.

I'd shaken my head vigorously. "If everybody loves me, I'm doing something wrong."

"Did Buddha tell you to say that?"

"Not specifically, but he'd agree." I grinned. "Ask Grandma."

I loved the feel of the small kitchen with the wrinkled wall calendars from Chinese and Vietnamese restaurants, the small altar suspended near the ceiling with its allegiances to two cultures—a gilded Buddha with the bright-red oranges, joss sticks, and incense—and the Virgin Mary, equally glossy, a crystal cross speckled with gold chips, and dried palms. A happy marriage, that union, though sometimes there were field skirmishes.

Hank, the infidel, viewed it all as anachronistic, though he honored it all. On the other hand I welcomed its power over me because it filled me with dreams I carried from my own childhood.

Hank looked toward the doorway. "Where is Grandma, Mom?"

"I'm right here." A voice in a shaky Vietnamese, but laced with laughter came from the hallway. She stepped into the room. "It is nice to know I'm missed."

She headed toward me as I stood up, bowed down to kiss the tiny woman on the cheek. Probably in her eighties, she got smaller each time I met her. Her white hair, so skimpy her scalp showed through, was covered with a small white bonnet.

Her eyes were lively in a wrinkled face. She grasped my arm affectionately.

"Sit down, sit down." She pointed to my chair.

While Hank's mother poured jasmine tea, Grandma leaned against the counter, picked up a knife, and began working on the evening meal. Hank sat back, stretched out his long legs. No one wore shoes in the home, of course, and Hank's white socks caught his mother's eye. "A disgrace, Hank." She pointed. "You walk through mud?"

He smiled. "Rick's apartment, Mom. It's been condemned."

We were having *pho*, the Vietnamese comfort soup, strings of raw beef, some clinging to the bone, cooked in a hot broth that simmered for hours on the stove. An aromatic feast: charred onion, potent ginger, fresh ground cinnamon, star anise, thin white rice noodles. A dash of hoisin sauce, speckled Thai basil, a handful of basil sprouts and cilantro.

"Let me help," I suggested, but the women paused, both with knives held out, frozen in place, a moment that looked like a scene from a comedy skit.

Hank groaned. "You know they won't let you." He teased his mother. "You know, I offered to do all the cooking in the household."

Grandma eyed him, a twinkle in her eye. "Then I would have to say prayers for the dead."

Hank's Mom groaned. "I was just telling them"—her knife motion included me and Hank—"that they talk of nothing but death."

Grandma shrugged. "Is there any other topic? Death defines us. Listen to Buddha." A pause as she furrowed her brow. Then her voice got soft, "*Sang hen cung ba tac dat la xong.*"

My Vietnamese failed me, as she noticed. So she whispered, "In the end even the great become a pile of ashes."

Hank's Mom rolled her eyes to heaven.

"Grandma saw you, Mom," Hank teased, delighted with the exchange.

Grandma ignored that. "Did you see the photo of Hank in his uniform?"

I smiled at her. "No. I didn't know he allowed such pictures to be taken."

Hank grumbled. "I had no choice. State troopers gotta follow orders."

Grandma swelled with pride. "The handsomest boy on the earth."

Hank blurted out, "Grandma, no. Well, maybe…in Connecticut."

Again his mother rolled her eyes.

"Let me see."

Grandma reached up into a basket on top of the refrigerator and took down a manila folder.

"Here." She handed it to me.

I slipped the large color photograph out of the sleeve and stared into a resplendent Hank in dress uniform. When I glanced at him, he was watching me closely, a little embarrassed though a little bit tickled. In the photo he looked boyish, and I was reminded of the skinny young man who'd sat, years back, in my criminal justice course at Farmington College. Dressed in his uniform, he seemed even younger, a fresh-scrubbed boy, that severe face unsmiling, determined to look authoritative, but like he was suited up for a parade.

At that moment, gripping the photograph, panic swept through me. I was young, fresh from Columbia College, newly sworn in as a policeman in Manhattan. Liz, my new bride who frowned on my decision to become a cop, stood next to the photographer as I was photographed in my dress uniform, a cynical smile on her face. "A little boy." That what's she'd said then.

There I was, filled with hope, idealism, drunk with the same unbridled passion Hank possessed. That uniform suggested I could change the world—make things right. Yet the photo of Hank brought me back to that awful night when I struggled with a crazed druggie. I fired. Over and over, insane, out of control. The moment took away my hope and led, ultimately, to my leaving the force.

I sputtered. "You look very handsome."

Hank was glowing. "Yes, I know. Women will follow me in the street."

"Most of them will end up in the backseat of your cruiser, handcuffed."

A sly grin. "Don't get me excited."

"Stop this," his mother chided. "You two are..."

Grandma broke in, delighted. "Boys."

Within minutes, Hank's father joined us, slipping into the room quietly and sitting down at the end of the table. His hands fiddled with a pair of chopsticks. He nodded at me, a slight movement of his head that communicated volumes. Nguyen Tuan Tan was a sinewy man, a warrior's body with wide shoulders and a barrel chest, a Saigon native who'd battled the Cong, endured a year in a Reeducation Camp, and whose long journey into America was hated exile. America, to him, was a failed enterprise—too much softness, too many souls who didn't understand that life was an endless test.

Now, listening as Grandma talked of Hank as trooper—"The rhythm of life, the wheel of justice rolling on"— all spoken in high-pitched Vietnamese—he drew his lips into a thin line, buried his head in the pages of a newspaper rolled up on the table. *Tien Phong*, a Vietnamese language tabloid from California that he bought weekly at A Dong.

He tapped the paper. "In some parts of America they are waiting for rain."

His words shut Grandma up, though I detected a whisper of a smile as she walked back to the counter.

"Where's Grandpa?" Hank asked.

His mother nodded toward the back of the house. "Napping. He'll eat later on." She shot a glance at me. "He says he's under the weather."

"A family eats together." Then Grandma added, "If you are sick, food is medicine."

I squirmed in my seat. When I'd arrived an hour or so ago, I'd heard Grandpa's irritated growl coming from a back bedroom. "He's here."

The ghost in the house.

Dust under foot.

Hank's younger brother and sister trooped in from their rooms, jostling each other, and settled at the table.

We ate in silence, our chopsticks dipping into the broth, the long strands of vermicelli noodles twisting on the ends, delivered dripping into our mouths. Slivers of beef, gleaming red when placed in the hot broth, immediately darkened. Finished, we sat back, sated, Hank groaning his pleasure with a belch that met Grandma's approval, me with a lazy drawl of thanks.

"Tell Rick about Lucy," Hank began.

Finally. The reason for the invitation to supper: Hank's insistence that his grandmother flesh out the biography of the Tran family.

"That sad family," his mother hummed. "Simon. That poor little boy. In the market on Saturday everyone talks of him."

His father sneered, "A delinquent. A disgrace. Sent away to a prison, that boy."

"To juvie," Hank said quietly.

"Same thing." He thrust out a hand, an abrupt gesture, and pushed back his chair. He fumbled for his pack of cigarettes and headed out the back door. I could see him standing on the back landing, lighting a Camel and staring out into space. A cloud of smoke covered his head.

Hank's Mom shooed the younger kids out of the room, "Homework? Yes?" They nodded at everyone and left the room.

"Well," Grandma began, savoring the moment. "I have a story to tell, and it does not say good things about myself." She stretched out the Vietnamese words, lots of space between them.

Her words surprised me. "I don't understand."

She began again as she sat back, folding her hands into her lap. "Before she was the wife of Mike Tran, she was Lucy, a little girl I knew briefly in Saigon. I knew her family, especially her parents. They were not good people, lazy, conniving. The mother, I am sad to say, ran the streets. Their children were in the way. They bit into bitter lemon and demanded that it be gold."

"What does that mean, Grandma?" Hank looked puzzled.

"They were lost in a world of scrounging for money. Pennies here, there. They didn't like working." She paused. "*Tay lam ham nhai.*"

I translated the old saying in my head. If you don't work, then why should you enjoy food?

"Sometimes they remembered to feed their children—two boys, the little girl Lucy. Sometimes the children stole mangoes from the market stall to fill their stomachs. A handful of old rice, thrown away."

Hank's Mom *tsk*ed. "Children in the way."

"But they came to America, all of them, right?" Hank went on. "They settled in Hartford."

"I heard they stole gold coins and bought their way to America."

"The whole family?"

"All of them. Two streets over. In a housing project. The worst. Dutch Point. Crime everywhere. Bars in the windows, rats in the hallways, gunfire at night, needles on the doorsteps."

"Where is this going, Grandma?" Hank was impatient.

Grandma smiled. "Impatient, impatience. In America children rush the conversations of their elders."

Hank laughed. "Grandma!"

Grandma put her fingertips on her lips. "Shush, boy. Then they died, the two parents. Within months of each other. The father drinking. The mother weeps. She got afraid of everything. Of everyone. Well, she stopped caring about living, hiding away. It was hard for us to believe she really loved that cruel man, but she did. She faded away. A late summer flower afraid of winter."

"People die *for* love, Grandma, not *from* love."

She eyed him closely. "They're the same thing, my boy. Remember that love doesn't start or end—it's just there."

I smiled. "Don't look for love in the sky. You find it in your heart."

Hank groaned. "You two should write romance movies for the Hallmark network."

Grandma nodded at me. "My Buddhist son." Then a look at her real grandson, sitting with his arms folded across his chest, his long legs stretched out in front of him. "And the American shiny coin. A boy with too much love." *Thuong nhieu qua.*

Hank saluted her.

"You were friendly?" I prompted.

"Lucy and her brothers lived with cousins who didn't want them around. Lucy was shuttled around, unwanted, until the state gave her to a couple for safekeeping. When she was a young woman, maybe eighteen or so, I met her in the market. We talked. I liked her. Another daughter for me. Then her brothers disappeared. One sent a postcard from Texas. She showed it to me. 'People here like me.' That's what it said. The other went to California to look for happiness. Then silence. Lucy lived a street away. We'd walk to the supermarket and then have tea at Pho Linh on Park. We *liked* each other. She called me her mother." She stopped, her voice trembling.

Into the silence Hank's mother spoke. "She was a friendly girl. I remember her." She shrugged. "But...so lost."

"What does that mean?" said Hank.

"Always looking over her shoulder or staring into space. Like she was hoping something good was waiting for her."

Grandma spoke over her daughter's words, "Yes, lonely."

"But what happened to your friendship?" I asked.

Grandma was nodding her head vigorously. "What happened is a failure of my spirit."

Hank, exasperated, "What?"

"I betrayed her."

Grandma's words hung in the warm kitchen, and we waited.

Her small gnarled fingers trembled. "We were close, the two of us. She had no one else. We chatted, gossiped, even prayed together. She had settled her life into mine, and welcome."

"I don't understand."

"One day, excited, she told me she'd met a man, but she kept him away from me. I asked her over and over about him, this mysterious man. She was happy, always laughing, never so happy. She talked about the man who had no name. But one day in Walgreen's, I spotted them." A deep intake of breath. "She was arm in arm with Mike Tran."

Hank's Mom muttered, "*Tran den.*"

The black man.

A long silence, painful. The words exploded in the room, whole paragraphs filling in the blanks surrounding his mother's terse phrase.

"Yes." Grandma stared into my face. "A different world back then, Rick. So close to the old country—the war, the American GIs in the street. The Cong soldiers. Mike Tran was left out of the Vietnamese community. You know that. He had been brought to America with deceit, then tossed onto the street. But a man who was not only forbidden—a dust boy"—her voice lingered on the words *bui doi*—"but the impure blood was…African."

The black man.

Suddenly I flashed back to the orphanage in Saigon and Le Xinh Phong, the black kid shunned by all—and gleefully attacked by me. Sitting in Grandma's kitchen now, I found myself alternating pictures in my head of Mike Tran and that never-forgotten kid in Vietnam. The memory of my cruel hand across the side of his trembling face.

Wildly I thought—karma. *Dao phat*. It waits decades to find you, and then you lie awake at night.

Grandma sighed. "Lucy fell in love with him. A good man, hard-working, who saved his pennies, sweated away at every job he could find, and managed to create a life."

Hank finished. "Still not enough to satisfy some people."

Grandma nodded. "Yes. So many years ago. Decades. I was a foolish woman. Like the others, I shunned her. I let the friendship drift away, slowly, so that one day I realized I hadn't talked to Lucy in years. In the markets the women turned their backs on them. It is easy to forget about the devil in America. I forgot that he was inside of me already—a part of me. You'd see them shopping on Park Street, see them on Sunday morning in Saigon Kitchen, ignored by most but not all. After a while Mike Tran earned—they earned—the respect of the community. But I never talked to her again." Grandma trembled. "My failing, I tell you now. I listened to the wrong heartbeat."

"Grandma," Hank began, "that was then." He looked at me. "We all had these views." He addressed me. "Rick and I…" His words trailed off.

I cleared my throat. "You never talked to her again?"

"My shame." Grandma closed her eyes. "My own disgrace. Now, years later, I see myself as a foolish woman who listened to the wrong birds circling in the sky."

Her daughter was watching her closely. "But now her son Simon is in trouble. A man died."

Grandma seemed not to be listening. "So long ago." Her words fluttered in the air, silenced us. "Too long ago."

Hank's Mom looked into my face. "Tell me, Rick, do you believe young Simon is innocent?"

"Actually I do. I have no proof but his father's strong belief."

Hank's mother went on, "Lucy and Mike Tran built a life that everyone now knows is…"

She stopped, gasped. We heard banging on the floorboards and jumped. Hank's grandfather stood in the doorway, his body swaying, his face an awful scarlet, his lips quivering.

"Grandpa." Hank half-stood, nervous. "What?"

The small, wizened man was staring at me, so intense a look that I turned away, unnerved. Hank, protective, stammered— "I…we…"—but then fell silent.

The old man shuffled in, grasped the top rung of a chair, and steadied himself. Spittle formed at the corners of his mouth as he spat out the words, "The black man." He shook his fist in the air. "A man whose name should not be mentioned in this house."

Hank protested. "Grandpa, no. Mike Tran is…" But a look from his mother shut him up.

Respect, I thought: the careful protocol of patriarchal Vietnamese families, violated now as the American Hank sputtered and squirmed. His grandfather eyed him closely, and Hank turned away, eyes dropping into his lap.

The old man spoke through clenched teeth, a slow methodical spacing of words. My fractured Vietnamese was faulty, to be sure, but there was no mistaking the man's venom.

"You talk of a son who runs foul of the law. This…this Simon. A youngster hell-bent on evil. Well, that evil springs from the soul of that man."

Grandma spoke in a hesitating voice, though she never looked at the old man. "A boy who has to find his way back, who…"

He never let her finish. "Who knows what evil possesses his children? All of them. Mongrels. America rewards them for reading a book? Black hearts."

"But…" Hank sputtered.

He got no further.

"It doesn't matter," the old man said, his voice creaky. "It only takes one evil child to blacken the soul of an entire family."

He shook his head and left the room.

Chapter Eleven

Big Nose brokered a meeting with Simon and Frankie. The gadfly boy was proving to be a valuable intercessor. A sometime friend of Simon Tran and someone who liked to singe his fingertips on the edge of trouble—Hank told me he'd flirted with petty lawlessness a few times, picked up for shoplifting Transformer action figures at Walmart—Big Nose also liked to be in the mix of things.

Hank summed up, "Ever since his father had me ask you to help little Simon, Big Nose has been calling me, sending me tweets, begging for information," Hank told me. "He's afraid some juicy tidbit might pass him by. So I asked him to talk to Simon. Guarantee a meeting. Promise that Simon won't head for the hills again."

"Simple as that?"

Hank grinned. "Who would have thought it? The boys run from everyone. Big Nose sends one text, probably ungrammatical and filled with hieroglyphics like LOL, LMAO, and other emoticons, and the delinquent boys jump at the chance to catch lunch."

"How civilized," I said, grinning.

Hank and I drove in my car to a greasy eatery on New Britain Avenue. "I had to promise them lunch. Whatever they wanted."

"A small price," I told him.

"At the Coffee Pot?" Hank frowned. "The price is acid reflux and possible emergency flight to the ER."

I got serious. "I wonder about this change of heart."

The Coffee Pot was a converted gas station now masquerading as a working-class diner. A Mexican take-out one lot over. An all-night laundromat on the other side. At the end of the block a "Welcome to Hartford" sign covered with Keith Haring graffiti. A painted sign with a spotlight on it. "Eats." No neon. White stucco façade, windows with rusted bars, a faded Exxon sign poorly painted over, and on the side an ancient Ford station wagon tucked between two Dumpsters.

Hank pointed to it. "Looks like something you probably drove when you were begging girls for dates back in New Jersey."

"Yeah. A tin lizzie."

His eyes got wide with glee. "Was that your nickname for Liz?"

"Yeah. Why don't you ask her that when you see her?"

"She'll be mad at you."

"Liz has a sense of humor."

He opened the car door and stepped out, leaned back inside. "She must have. She married you, right?"

I groaned. "Junior-high humor, Hank?"

"Nowadays we call it middle-school humor."

"Hey." A voice startled me, approaching from the left. "Hey, youse." Big Nose stood next to my car, staring at me. Stepping out of the car, I extended my hand, foolishly expecting a handshake, but Big Nose stared at my hand as though it were covered in toxic waste. Instead he rolled a few fingers against my palm, so quick a gesture I might have imagined it. A small, round boy, around sixteen now, with a round head and a shabby haircut underneath a backwards Red Sox cap, he grinned at me, in the process his small eyes disappearing into the folds of his plump cheeks.

"Hey," I said back.

"Hank, what up?" He waved at Hank.

Hank, one toe gingerly in the real world of adolescent boys, performed the handshake ritual with aplomb.

"Everybody's late." Big Nose pointed back to the street.

"We're on time." My wave included him and Hank.

"Yeah, I suppose so. Whatever." He jerked his head toward the doorway. "Follow me." He looked over his shoulder. "I hope you guys like mean-ass chili dogs."

Inside we discovered that Simon Tran and Frankie Croix were already tucked into a back booth by the bathrooms, partially shielded by a pile of cardboard boxes labeled Dixie Cups. The corner smelled of some disinfectant, and my nose twitched.

Big Nose, spotting the two, looked unhappy. "You was supposed to meet me outside," he yelled across the room. A few diners looked up from their burgers and fries, squinted at the angry, roly-poly boy.

Frankie got up as we approached and slid in next to Simon, so that Hank and I faced them both. Big Nose, looking at the narrow space, pulled up a chair from a nearby table and sat on the end.

"Now what?" he said into the silence.

Both boys watched me closely. Dressed in the uniform of the day, they wore baggy dungarees bunched up, accordion-style, over untied work boots, oversized football jerseys—the New England Patriots, displaying a certain loyalty to the region—and Boston Red Sox baseball caps, turned backward. They struck me as partners in primary colors: Simon in a red windbreaker, Frankie in blue.

"We ain't done nothing." Frankie spoke first, his face scrunched up.

A lanky boy, stringy, light brown hair falling over his forehead, dull hazel eyes that looked a little glazed over, a jutting chin, exaggerated now, defiant. He kept flicking his head toward the window, checking the parking lot.

Hank was impatient. "Well, you *did* do something."

Frankie's voice rose. "That ain't what I mean, and you know it. This time. Yeah, we did some stupid shit, Saigon and me." He glanced at Simon who had slumped down in the seat, uncomfortable, his head dipped into his chest. Frankie had a deep, rumbling voice, syrupy, so many words swallowed.

"All right, all right." I nodded toward Hank—slow down.

"Why do you keep running away?" I asked Simon.

Frankie answered for him. "Everybody's out to get us." He jerked his hand toward Simon's sleeve. "We were stupid, me and Saigon."

"But I've been asked to help you boys, no? I'm an investigator." I paused because Frankie twisted his head to the side and made an exaggerated comic face. "In-ves-ti-ga-tor." Frankie spaced out the word, stressing the syllables.

"I do insurance fraud, Frankie. Not…well, street muggings and assaults and a possible manslaughter charge."

Frankie yelled at me. "We ain't done that."

For the first time Simon looked up, blinked wildly. "No." One word, stretched out.

"Then help me, boys. Help us." I indicated Hank.

Frankie sneered, "How? It ain't possible. What we gonna do? Find the real criminals and haul their asses to you? It's bad enough that asshole Ardolino is on our case. The fat fuck got his mind on crucifying us, and nothing ain't gonna change it."

I sat back. "Then we're gonna have to find an answer. Help me."

A waitress approached the table, delivering plates filled with oversized cheeseburgers, fries, and huge glasses of Coke.

Frankie smirked, "We figured we would order, seeing how you was gonna pay anyway."

I smiled. "Be my guest."

"We got ice cream coming, too."

"Why not?" I nodded at the waitress.

Big Nose was fussing, tapping a menu as though he'd missed his one chance to be a glutton. Eying the food on the table, he pointed. "I want *that*. And a chili dog. Two of them."

I nodded at the waitress. Hank and I got cheeseburgers and Cokes. Frankie nodded his approval.

Simon spoke up. "Pop is on my case."

"He knows you're innocent," Hank broke in.

"That's what he *says*." Restless, the boy bumped against Frankie's side.

"C'mon, Simon."

"Saigon."

"All right. Saigon. You don't believe that he thinks you're innocent?"

"All he thinks is that I screwed up the family."

"Well, he's on your side." Hank softened his voice. "He told us you never lie to him."

Wide-eyed. "I don't."

"And I'm not lying to you now," I went on.

A thin smile. "You ain't Pop."

"That's not the point."

"Pop thinks I'm a fuck-up. Cuz I dropped out of school."

I waited a bit. "Why did you?"

He stared out the window. "I couldn't do all the shit he wanted."

"Which was?"

"Like the pressure. When I got good grades, he yells, ninety-five, why not one hundred? What's the matter with you? Your brother Michael…he…"

Frankie spoke up. "Bullshit. His Pop says, 'Go to Yale or something.'"

"What about you?" Hank asked.

Frankie laughed sarcastically. "When he was around, my own dad ain't heard of Yale. If you ever find the bum, ask him. And Ma…the only thing she asks me is to go to the corner bodega and pick up a pack of Marlboros. Red box, filters. Keep the change. All fifty fucking cents, just for me."

Hank's voice was biting. "Your dad loves you, Saigon. Christ, you *look* like him."

The boys swiveled to look into each other's faces. Simon grumbled, "Yeah, like that's supposed to make me feel good? The black boy in the family. Hazel is prom queen with a fucking tiara on her head, and Michael plays lacrosse at prep school. In school the teachers say—'You don't look like your brothers. Your dad remarry?' What kind of fuckin' question is that?"

"So what?" From Hank. "Families…" His voice broke.

"Families don't count for much." Frankie arched his head, stuck out his bony chin. "You know what I'm saying?"

"Look it…" Simon began, but Frankie nudged him, and the boy shut up. Both stared stonily at me, Simon slipping down in the booth while Frankie sat straight up, ramrod. A fiery look in his eyes.

Hank nodded at me, a look that communicated: Frankie is kingpin here, Simon the follower. In fact, Simon looked at Frankie repeatedly, as if they'd orchestrated a strategy beforehand and now, in the eatery, he'd forgotten his rehearsed lines.

"Tell me about the arrest—the one that got you four months in juvie?"

I waited. Again Frankie seemed to be debating what to say.

"Hijinks." Frankie savored the word. "Yeah, hijinks."

Hank squinted. "Meaning?"

"Goofing around."

"Well," I began, "assaults on people, knocking them…"

Frankie's voice was triumphant. "We just did it for fun. I mean, we just pushed through people walking by. Fun."

"What do you mean—do it for fun?"

Frankie munched on a French fry, smeared ketchup on his fingers, licked them. "I dunno. You know, there was that stuff online, like YouTube, about these kids doing a knockout game, you know, coming at old guys and punching them in the head, knocking them over."

"Yeah?" I prompted when he paused.

He shot a look at Simon. "I…well, we thought it was cool. But not to *hurt* anyone."

Hank was having none of it. "But people *did* get hurt. Broken limbs, in one case. An ambulance took a man to the hospital. How many times did you do that?"

Frankie ignored him, but stared into my face. "Like until we got caught. That last time. Real dumb. Then we got caught shoplifting. Just candy and stuff. But they seen the video and then it, you know, came together."

"And drugs." From Hank.

"Just a little."

"It was nothing," Simon whispered.

"No," I insisted. "You can't say that."

Frankie pounded the table. "We just knocked people over." He stifled a giggle. "Fun."

I glanced at Hank. "Are you telling me you never robbed folks, Frankie?"

"Naw." Frankie bit into his cheeseburger. "Well, one time we banged this guy and his wallet flew out of his pocket."

"But we didn't take it," Simon finished.

"Really?"

Frankie snapped, "Goddamn it, man, whose side you on?" His face flushed, a vein popping in his neck. He shuffled in his seat, and I sensed he was ready to flee.

Nervous now, with a sidelong glance at his buddy, Simon looked like a skittish kid dragged into the principal's office.

I shifted the conversation. "JD says you two were at the storefront—when Ralph Gervase died. He's your alibi."

"Lotta good it does. Like the cops believe him."

"Well, tell me. You gotta tell me everything. Every place you went to that day. A timetable. When you arrived at JD's. What you did before. I'll trace folks down who met you. But you got to give me something to work with."

Frankie shrugged. "Here and there. All over Little Saigon. Mostly at JD's place."

"That won't help." From Hank.

"Some more," I prodded.

But the boys were closing up, shrinking in their seats.

Hank sensed the tension, and he said in a cheerful voice, "You into music? I see you got your music with you." He pointed to the ear buds hanging around their necks.

Simon beamed. "We're gonna be rap stars." He grinned widely, but Frankie, pursing his lips, punched him in the elbow, as though Simon had revealed secrets.

"Cool." From Hank.

"Yeah, ain't it?" Frankie's words were snide.

"Music," Hank went on. "Like what?"

Frankie put down his sandwich. "Enough of this shit."

"I'm only…"

Frankie cut Hank off. "Phony."

Hank smiled and shook his head.

I changed direction. "Saigon, we talked with your sister, Hazel, the other day."

"I know," he said slowly. "She phoned Mom. You and your girlfriend."

"Liz is my ex-wife."

Simon grunted. "Same thing. Like if you're still hanging around with her, you're…like married."

That gave me pause, and I found myself laughing. "You may have a point, Saigon."

My remark puzzled him. "Hazel ain't happy."

"Why?"

"*You* know." He waited. Then he stressed, "*You* know."

I must have looked helpless because Frankie jumped in. "Her asshole boyfriend. Judd Snow, white supremacist in charge of bullshit."

"I hate him. Everybody hates him but stupid Hazel. I mean, like he orders Hazel around like she's his slave." Simon's words were whispered. "She afraid to say no to him. Scared."

I looked at Frankie. "You had a fight with him, right? At the mall?"

Frankie smirked. "Yeah, I got hauled into the police station, but so did that loser. For me it's no big deal—I know the game. But not for hot-shot Judd. Romeo creep. This rich white dude from Avon finds himself calling his daddy. 'Oh help me, help me, Daddy. The mean old cop's gonna rape me.' Christ Almighty man!" He munched on a French fry, but started choking. "They shoulda hung him by the balls."

"What happened?"

Eager to talk of it, Frankie sat up straight. "He's a freak, that guy. Says I was moving in on his girl, like I would tap Saigon's sister, come on. I ain't stupid. So he pushes me. I shove him, he lands a blow, we wrestle. I knock the air outa him, and he's bigger. When I ain't looking, he takes my backpack and empties the shit out on the floor, kicks it around like it isn't nothing. Pulls out a little weed and waves it in the air for the world to see. Stuffs a new video game I just got in his pants. Brand new. I knocked him over. The security guard comes rushing in. Asshole. They take us both in."

"No charges?"

"His daddy comes running in with a million lawyers, boo hoo, boo hoo, wink wink, let my boy go. Daddy is a flashy guy who likes to wave dollar bills in the air. He's all slicked over, like he's going to the prom or something. They send us home. But Judd boy is like shaking, *crying*, the big baby, and says he's gonna kill me next time he sees me." Angry, Frankie pushed his plate away. Some fries slipped to the floor. "I can't wait for that clown. He hid my fucking weed in his pocket or sock and I never got it back."

Simon looked up, his lips quivering. "Tell them about the car, Frankie."

"Nothing. Just that I swear I seen him following me. I come out of my house in Frog Hollow and this convertible cruises by, top down. Nighttime. Chilly. I swear he was driving. What's he doing in Hartford?" He stopped, folded his arms over his chest. "It ain't nothing. I take care of my own troubles."

"Tell us about the VietBoyz gang," Hank asked.

"Yeah, we seen you two there that day." He locked eyes with mine.

"You part of that gang?"

"Naw. JD lets us hang out there. We run favors for him, like around town." He mimicked smoking a joint, his index and thumb holding an imagery joint. "Sometimes we got nowhere to go so we hang out there."

"JD is cool," Simon added. He nudged Frankie.

"But?" I smiled. "I sense there's a 'but' coming."

Simon shivered. "I mean, those other dudes scare us. They're like real…*criminals*. Ex-cons. Christ, one of them is like the son of a Born to Kill thug from Chinatown. When we go there and see them, we beat it outa there. JD tells us to get out. Other times we just *hang*."

"That's where I can find you?" I asked Simon.

Frankie muttered something.

"Shut up." From Simon.

"What?" Hank asked.

"Saigon hides at Michael's," Frankie said, smirking. "His brother."

"Shut up, Frankie." The small boy's face crumbled.

Hank leaned in. "Maybe you should stop hanging out on Park Street."

Frankie flared up. "They're gonna arrest us for killing that guy anyway."

Simon was moving out of his seat, but dropped back in. "What's gonna happen?"

"Well, for starters, I'm gonna believe you, Frankie. You too, Saigon."

Simon blinked his eyes rapidly, half-rose from his seat. "Yeah?"

"Yeah."

A wise-guy voice. "I don't believe you."

A horn blared, someone leaning on it. A low-slung Toyota with black-tinted windows and under-inflated tires idled just outside the window. The driver's door swung open and a guy stepped out. He was peering at the eatery, an angry look on his face, and he said something to a passenger. An Asian man, short, maybe early twenties, lean but muscular in a loose black linen suit with polished black shoes. A collarless black shirt buttoned to the neck. A spiked, shaved-on-the-side haircut that exaggerated his long head. He was wearing black wraparound sunglasses but he'd slipped them onto the top of his head. He lit a cigarette with a lighter, blew a smoke ring, leaned into the car, said something to the unseen passenger who stepped out and lit a cigarette. Another

Asian, Vietnamese probably, shorter than the first, skinny, with a pinched wild-dog face. A similar black suit, oversized, button-up shirt, the prominent wraparound sunglasses. Street thugs, I thought, watching the cheap macho swagger and calculated blank faces. VietBoyz, maybe, gang soldiers.

But at that moment Frankie punched Simon in the side and muttered, "They're here. Shit. Get up." He had a scared look on his face.

Frankie nudged Big Nose, who'd kept his mouth shut the whole time. "C'mon, Big Nose."

"No," he said to Frankie.

"Why not?"

"You think I'm fucking crazy?" Big Nose looked away.

But Simon, energized, rolled out of the booth, nodded at me as if to say—That's it. Okay? He bolted away from the table, pushed along by an antsy Frankie. Outside the boys jumped into the backseat of the car, the two slick thugs tossing their cigarettes away, sliding back inside. The car squealed out of the parking lot, a deliberate run of rubber that made everyone in the restaurant turn their heads. From where I sat I could see the car pause at a red light and then gun it, flying through.

Chapter Twelve

Liz wanted to know what I thought of Simon and Frankie. "They look so cute in their mug shots."

"Yeah. Adorable." I stared into her grinning face. "Bad boys with dimples."

We were having an early dinner at the First and Last Tavern in the South End of Hartford, sharing a plate of lasagna, a Caesar salad, and a bottle of pinot noir. I'd dressed in oxblood loafers and a blue blazer, tan slacks. My outfit for first dates. Actually any date.

She was coming from a meeting at Hartford PD and looked tired. "It's dangerous having a criminal psychologist in the room when department higher-ups are trying to define police policy and their body language says they'd rather be at Duffy's Bar across town."

Dressed in a tailored light blue suit with a white silk blouse that accentuated her creamy complexion, she looked all business. An attractive FBI profiler on TV, maybe. Until, that is, she twisted her head to the side and smiled. Then she looked dangerously mischievous. Alluring. I found myself smiling at her.

"Stop it," she said.

"What?"

"You boys are all the same. You looked at me that way when we first met in the stacks of Butler Library a hundred years ago."

I grinned. "Little Simon said you're my girlfriend."

"What?"

"Hazel told Simon about our lunch in Farmington. I told him you were my ex. That the two of us stayed good friends—friendly." I debated which word to use, which Liz noted, her eyebrows rising. "He suggested we'd always be married."

The tip of her tongue brushed her lips. I noticed a trace of lipstick on a front tooth. "Smart boy, that Simon. For a young kid he seems to understand something about the weird rituals of formerly married friends."

"Well, I did think it was cute."

Liz frowned. "Wrong word, Rick."

"Sorry."

Now she laughed. "When we were married, every time you felt you won an argument, you'd say 'sorry' and hoped I wouldn't notice."

"Sorry."

"I rest my case." She waved her fork in the air. "Tell me about the boys."

"Well," I said slowly, "they come off as bratty boys, filled with spit and anger and tough-guy attitude, especially Frankie, who strikes me as a boy hardened by whatever life he's led. But there is something childlike—even childish—about Simon, also known as Saigon."

"They knocked folks over." Liz looked into my face. "Enough times that they were sent to juvie. They *hurt* folks."

I scratched my head. "I know, I know. But that's the thing. It was malicious and wrong and stupid, but I believe they thought they were only fooling around, sort of like—well, I dare you to be bad."

Liz's eyes widened. "But they *did* cause harm. Don't excuse them, Rick."

I rushed my words. "I'm not. Really. But that's the real problem. It's a game for them. Or at least it *was*. Like playing one of those mindless, violent video games the kids are obsessed with. Fantasy slips over into ugly reality. A blurring of lines."

Liz held my gaze. "But it seems to me that, if what you say is true, they're gonna stumble into some serious crime. Assuming, as you obviously do, that they did *not* attack Jimmy and cause the death of Ralph."

"I can't see it. Even Frankie, as tough as he comes off, seems wrong for such a brutal attack."

"And Simon?"

"The follower. Always."

Liz's eyes got a faraway look. "You know that he's like Hazel, Rick. A bright girl, clever, beautiful, a lot going for her, but she nods at her caveman boyfriend, follows his lead. I watched *that* unfold last year."

"Did you talk to her about it then?"

"Of course. But she's smitten, though ambivalent. Some fear in her eyes when he approached. And then she got mean because of his attraction to me."

"You home wrecker."

"It's not funny, Rick."

I nodded, penitent. "I know that."

"Hazel, like little Simon, has her own way of rebelling against the family."

"Liz, the truth of the matter is that Mike Tran comes off as a demanding father. He's scared of them failing, of America crushing them, so he drives them, almost relentlessly. Study, study, books, school. He doesn't want them to have a tough life."

"So in the process he makes them sheep," she concluded. "These kids are programmed to follow anyone's authority but their father's."

"It's especially dangerous for Simon a.k.a. Saigon, no? The lethal combination of follower coupled with a rebellious streak. That leads to…"

"The wrong crowd," she finished.

"Yes. VietBoyz. But Simon and Frankie didn't cause Ralph's death."

"You don't have to convince me." Her eyes sparkled. "I've always trusted your instincts."

"Always?"

Hesitant. "I should never speak in absolutes." A pause. "I leave that to you."

"The problem is—how to trace those boys' footsteps the day Ralph was killed. A timeline. Places they went to before Russell Street. Or, maybe, someone who saw them in the vicinity of JD's evil little empire."

"You know kids think they're indestructible."

I sat back, interlocked my fingers. "Maybe I have to locate two anonymous street thugs in dark hoodies in a city where that's already the obligatory tough-guy spring-fashion look. Abercrombie and Son-of-a-Bitch. While I wrap up two fraud investigations for the Travelers and Aetna, teach Criminology one night a week, as well as handle Jimmy's cases while he's tucked away under Gracie's doting care."

Liz smiled a long time. She took a sip of wine and watched me over the rim. "Gracie has never been happier."

Sourly I added, "This cannot have a happy ending."

"You cynic. Even Gracie knows that. Hey, we've all met Jimmy." She fiddled with a bread stick, broke in, nibbled on an end, her eyes catching mine.

"What?" I said. "You're not telling me something."

"True."

"Which you'll tell me eventually."

"True." She sighed deeply. "I don't know how to read this. Hazel's boyfriend."

"Judd Snow?"

"I had a phone call from him."

I sat up. "Why? For God's sake, Liz."

She shrugged. "It may mean nothing." She twisted her head to the side. "But I don't believe that."

"Tell me about it."

"It's only that you have enough on your plate now, and I don't want you stepping into my problems—if problem it is."

"Tell me." My voice rose.

"That crush on me last year? A puppyish crush, unnerving, but I thought—harmless."

"I never thought so, and it's a mystery to me why he's Hazel's boyfriend."

She fiddled with her napkin. "Another example of one of the Tran kids following someone else around. Humble servants." Her hands made a what-can-I-do gesture. "Last week when we met him outside the Farm Shop, well, I…well, he looked at me a little too long."

"Yeah, an obnoxious kid. I didn't like him."

She snapped, "Not a kid, Rick. He was always a little scary. All that swagger. The way he assumed I'd be flattered by the attention of a young boy."

I counted a heartbeat. "What did he say on the phone?"

"A brief conversation, which I ended. I was surprised he had my number, but of course Hazel had it last year. The caller I.D. said 'Unknown,' but I picked up anyway. For a minute it was harmless. 'Good seeing you again. A surprise. You still look the same. You don't change.' I interrupted. 'What do you want, Judd?' That bothered him, I could tell. He said he just called to say hello—to thank me for helping out the Tran family in what he called 'their hour of need.'"

"That's it?"

"That's enough. It's not so much what he said, Rick, but the fact that he *called*."

I waited. "There's more, right?"

She made a face. "Smart boy. There's always more. I told him not to call me anymore and he said all right, but I picked up anger, the way he slurred his goodbye, the abrupt click of the phone. Since then I've had a few calls, all I.D.'d as 'Blocked' and 'Unknown.' I think it's him."

I burned. "Not good."

"Just when I was leaving my apartment, an ostentatious red Audi turned a corner. Yes, I know there's more than one in the world, but the coincidence made me think…"

I sat back, drummed the table, thinking. "Frankie had a lot to say about the fistfight he had with Judd. Lots of anger. I'd like to hear Judd's side of what happened—to get a handle on

Frankie. What's he capable of? Frankie also claims Judd was following him one day. The wonderful red Audi."

"Frankly, I'd avoid Judd."

"But I'd like to get his take on the Tran family. Hazel—and even Simon. Maybe he picked up something that can help me."

Liz wasn't happy. "You're gonna have to go through Hazel."

"She'll know how to find him."

"If he wants you to find him." A pause as she stared into my face. "Don't say anything to him about the phone call, Rick. I can see what you're thinking. I can handle that."

"I can't promise that."

She made a face. "Ah, the old knight in shining armor defending the damsel in the bell tower."

"That's not what I mean. Liz."

"I'm a big girl. I fight my own battles."

"I know that—I respect that. But, you know…" I faltered.

She smiled. "You worry about me." She touched my wrist. "Like I worry about you."

"But keep in mind what Simon said. 'You'll always be my girlfriend.'"

"Yes, Rick, but it's not 1950. And you're not Wally Cleaver on *Leave It to Beaver*. Menaced virtue, my hero plunging into battle, sword at the ready."

Now I laughed. "When knighthood was in flower."

"Well, knighthood has gone to seed these days. Thank God." She locked eyes with mine. "*Try* not to say anything."

"That's better."

◇◇◇

I dialed Hazel's number at Miss Porter's. Surprising me, she answered on the first ring, hissing, "About time," then was irritated when she heard my voice.

"I'm disturbing you."

"I…I was expecting a call. Oh no, really. I don't mean to be…so abrupt but…"

I stopped her. "It's all right."

But almost immediately she snapped, "Well?"

"I'd like to talk to Judd, Hazel."

A long silence, then in a whispered voice, "Why?"

"I want to talk to him about that fight he had with Frankie. I'm curious about Frankie's public behavior. I'm trying to prove..." I stopped because I could hear her clearing her throat, ready to jump into my words.

"That was ugly, that fight. Judd is—like too possessive. Frankie talked to me and...God, it was nothing, but Judd—like he's afraid I'll look at another guy."

"Could you give me his phone number?"

She hesitated, her voice suddenly buttery. "I'll call him. He's at the Avon Country Club on Simsbury Road. At the indoor tennis courts. He's playing till four."

"I can meet him there."

Again the hesitation. "I guess so, but let me reach him. I'll tell him you're coming." She spoke into the phone, her voice loud now. "Should I be there?"

"You don't have to be, Hazel. I just want to hear what he has to say about Frankie."

"I can tell you that right now. He doesn't like him."

"Let him tell me that."

I started to thank her, but her voice got gravelly. "You're not gonna bring Liz with you, are you?"

"No. Why?"

Anger in her voice. "I don't want a repeat of what happened last week."

"Meaning?"

"Didn't you *see*? My God. Judd all in Liz's face, flirting, talking about nothing. Lord, you'd think she was...like Michelle Obama or something. It embarrassed me. Like Liz is a great person and all, but she could be his *mother*."

"Liz has no interest in your boyfriend, Hazel."

"Sure, I know that, but she was supposed to *stop* it."

"She didn't encourage him, Hazel."

A high, false laugh. "Well, it doesn't take much to encourage Judd. All she had to do is show up in that parking lot."

"Four o'clock." I wanted the conversation over. "I'll be there. Tell him."

"Maybe you can tell him to stop talking about her. Lately he brings her up in every conversation."

"Four o'clock," I repeated, shutting off the phone.

◇◇◇

The lounge of the country club, a spacious room off the main entrance of the rambling Colonial-style building, mimicked aristocratic British décor: burgundy-tinted walls, understated lithographs depicting foxhunts that had never taken place anywhere near Avon. A wall of uncut leather-bound volumes secreted behind locked leaded glass panel doors, volumes so uniform I imagined they were some interior decorator's faux-laminate addition. Pristine oriental carpeting so deep you felt as if you were walking in your slippers. A brick fireplace with gargoyle andirons. And deep, bulky leather chairs in forest green, three of which now contained men engaged in a spirited conversation about some item in the *Hartford Courant*. I watched them as I sat across the room, waiting for Judd.

Every so often the men would glance at me, deliberately, in a body, but then turn back to their current-events squabble. A little insecure, I tugged at the lapels of my corduroy sports jacket, pressed my hands across the seam of my ironed khakis, and noticed that my loafers were suitably worn at the heels. A burgundy knit tie and a pale blue shirt. Slightly shabby, but very Ivy League, I looked as if I belonged there.

Judd Snow smiled as he rushed across the room, hand extended. Dressed in a white polo shirt, white linen pants over white deck shoes, a white cardigan sweater across his back and the sleeves tied in front, he looked like a Hollywood wannabe from Leonardo DeCaprio's vision of *The Great Gatsby*—or an upscale Good Humor man who couldn't find his truck.

"Hey, Rick," he began, affecting a casual familiarity.

"Judd."

"We have to make this fast, I'm afraid. My father's probably pulling the car up as we speak."

He toppled into one of the deep chairs, sat back, an angelic smile on his lips. He waited.

"Frankie Croix," I said, and watched his face close up.

"Yeah, I know that. Hazel told me you were working to save that scumbag from the electric chair."

"Well, that's a real extreme fate for him, no?"

The smile disappeared. "It should be."

A good-looking young man, I thought, strapping, his long legs stretched out in front of him, one knee rocking back and forth to a rhythm only he heard. An athlete's grace, cool, confident, a body toned perhaps by that tennis court he just left. A square jaw, like a roaring twenties Leyendecker model, high cheekbones, deep blue eyes set far apart so that he seemed a little dim, though the wariness in his eyes suggested otherwise. A lock of bushy straw-blond hair was allowed to drift haphazardly over his forehead, but the haircut looked expensive and designed for a millennial stockbroker or a baby boomer millionaire. He was a young man who never questioned his own place in the scheme of things.

"You look like you were born to be a member of this club."

His eyes flashed, surprised. "That goes without saying."

"That's exactly the remark I expected you to make."

He didn't know how to answer me, a quizzical smile on his lips.

I switched gears quickly. "What do you think about Simon Tran and Frankie Croix attacking Ralph Gervase?"

He watched me closely. "Well, I wasn't surprised, if that's what you mean, but I don't really think about it. I don't *care*."

"Simon is the brother of your girlfriend."

"Yeah, and a kid I don't know. One I barely saw."

"But you don't want a member of your girlfriend's family up on charges, right?"

He was getting irritated. "I told you—I don't *care*. Hazel tells me he's a goofy kid, and I don't know that creep Frankie"—a big smile—"other than as someone whose face met my fist. A criminal who ruined a good part of my day."

"That's what I want to find out about."

"But why?" He squinted his eyes, looked over to the three men who were quiet now. "I mean, that stupid scene had nothing to do with—*killing* someone."

"Yes, I know that. But if I'm to prove Simon innocent, I've got to understand his buddy, Frankie. The fact that he tangled with you suggests, well, a short fuse, a propensity for violence…"

"Listen to you," he broke in, amused. "'A propensity for violence.' *CSI: Farmington. Special Idiots Unit.* An HBO After School Special." He laughed at his own humor. "Look, Rick. I caught the creep making goo-goo eyes at my girl, and that's taboo big-time. A few words and the dirt bag rushed me, surprised me. So, yes, he's given to hair-trigger anger. I'm not, although I had to defend myself. It happened so fast—bang bang. He hits, I hit. The mall cop frowned on it. The fucking nightmare ended with both of us arrested. Arrested, Rick. Me—minding my own business. Thank God my father got it hushed up, although that also meant that creep got off with a slap on his wrist."

"That's it?"

His voice rose. "Do I think he killed that man? It wouldn't surprise me. But, as I said, I don't care." He pointed a finger at me. "Christ, I had to hear Hazel babbling on when her brother was first arrested—sent away. Knocking people over on the street? The *Courant* had a field day with that. Lucky no names—underage and all that. But Hazel's dad went ape-shit."

"You followed the case?"

"Hazel felt the need to bore me."

"A hearing in juvenile court?"

"Whatever."

"When you had that fight, he says you stole a video game and some weed."

A wide grin. "To the victor goes the spoils."

"Still and all…"

"If you're here for a character reference for Frankie, you've come to the wrong place." Suddenly his face turned dark, his eyes narrowed. "He's a piece of white trash from a Hartford project."

"So your parents were bothered?" I asked.

That gave him pause. Absently he ran his hand down the front of his polo short. "For your information, my mother left my father—and me—a decade ago, moved to one of the plains states where no one with any sense goes, and that's the end of it." For a second his face tightened. "My mother ran off with a scumbag car salesman, and she never looked back. I'm there waiting for someone to make my lunch. I'm still fuckin' waiting." A confused grin. "My father sits on bags of money and thinks he's younger than me. An embarrassing second childhood. Maybe I mean—second adolescence. I've had a hundred almost-stepmoms, each one with the conversation skills of a vacuum cleaner filled with dust. So…that's my biography. Happy? My father wasn't happy heading to a police station with a two-hundred-dollar-an-hour ambulance chaser at his side. One cop even knew my dad. But he couldn't let the heir apparent languish behind bars."

"Have you seen Frankie since?"

That perplexed him. "Why should I?" Then, his face even darker, a vein in his neck throbbing. "But I'll tell you one thing, Rick, my friend. He crosses paths with me and looks at me the wrong way, well, there's gonna be fireworks. I'll go George Zimmerman on his sorry-ass head."

I leaned forward, watched his mobile face shift, the anger growing. "Sounds to me like you also have anger issues."

His jaw went slack as he contemplated me quietly. "Anger issues? Christ, does everyone your age talk like they're auditioning for Dr. Phil's afternoon housewifey TV interrogation?"

"You're a smart-aleck."

He grinned. "It took you this long to pick up on that?"

He stood up, smoothed the front of his polo shirt again as though he'd managed to wrinkle the fabric by standing, and nodded at me. "My father is out front. Unlike me, he doesn't put up with the kind of bullshit you seem to be paid to do." With that, he strode out of the room, though he glanced back. "I don't think you can sit there all day if you're not a member." A sly grin. "Even Walmart-loving nouveau-riche Avon has its standards."

I followed him outside, headed to my car that, it turned out, was parked near that red Audi, the top down. Judd sauntered toward it, a cavalier stroll that made the man behind the wheel frown. As I passed by, I looked into the driver's seat, and the man fingered the sunglasses that covered his eyes.

Judd, beaming, paused by the passenger door, and announced in a loud voice, "My father, Rick. I know he looks like the playboy of the Western world in those Italian sunglasses, but he's just the simple man who gave me life on this planet."

The man removed the sunglasses and leaned across the seat. "Judd told me you were meeting him. Rick Van Lam?"

I nodded. "Yes."

"Foster Snow."

We shook hands. He sat back, one arm thrown casually over the back of his seat, his head turned upward. Yes, a playboy, I considered, according to his son, with his longish slicked-back hair glistening from some gel best used on a car engine. The loud Ed Hardy summer shirt picked up the shrill red of the convertible. Here was a man trying to look younger than his son. Oddly Judd, with his oh-you-kid country-club mien, seemed the elder of the two. Foster wore a bemused expression, as though I'd uttered some *bon mot* he found delightful. I didn't like him. First impression, an instinct. From the look on his son's face, I surmised that his handsome progeny didn't either. I bet they spent their leisure hours at war. There was only room for one Romeo in a flaming red Audi convertible.

Judd jumped into the passenger seat, not opening the door but leaping over it like an action hero on TV, an acrobatic feat that was accompanied by a huge clownish grin.

Foster started the motor, revved the engine. A hot rodder. For some reason he laughed out loud.

Judd's eyes glowed. "Oh, by the way, tell Liz I said hello."

That caught me by surprise. "What?"

"Remember me to the woman who dumped you."

"Judd, no." His father pointed a finger at him, but was clearly pleased.

"Don't bother Liz anymore." My voice was scratchy. Echoes of Liz insisting she'd handle her own life. I didn't care. I could—well, defend the woman who dumped me.

Judd's head jerked back as his father shifted into gear and the car began to slide away.

"No one tells me what to do."

Chapter Thirteen

Hank left me a voicemail. "Michael." A pause. "Did you find it strange that Frankie mentioned Simon going to his brother's apartment at Trinity?" Another pause. "What do you think? You're the investigator here. Maybe you should…investigate. It's a clue, Sherlock. Call me."

I'd already wondered about that offhand remark, one that bothered Simon. Why the secret? From Hazel's remarks I'd concluded that Michael, the oldest child, had little to do with the young boy—or his family. Perhaps that was wrong.

He answered the phone on the second ring, not a pleasant "Hello" but "What?" with a comical inflection, as if he'd been expecting a call from a close friend and this was his way of being funny.

I chuckled. "What indeed?"

A hesitant bit of *tsk*ing. "Sorry. Yes?"

Still no hello, replaced now with impatience.

I identified myself, and he startled me by breaking in. "I was expecting your call."

"You were?" I was tempted to offer a variation of his "What?" But I didn't.

"My mother phoned to say you were helping the family out. The Simon nonsense and all."

"Nonsense?"

A strained laugh. "Have you met that little boy? He's a goofy kid. There's no way he'd assault—God forbid—kill someone. Impossible."

"He did accost folks, Michael. It got him four months in juvie."

"Oh, *that*. Foolish—but not murder."

"It happens in the best of families."

I meant that as a joke but he took me seriously. "If you're looking for the best of families, you had better pass by the royal house of Tran."

"I'm calling because I learned that Simon stops in to see you."

He didn't wait until I finished, his voice sharp. "Yes, that's true."

"Can I talk to you about Simon? I want to…"

He finished for me, making my remarks into a question. "Clear his name by interrogating the members of the family? I imagine princess Hazel had a lot to say about me."

"Can we…"

He made a resigned clicking noise and then seemed to cover the mouthpiece of the phone. I could hear a mumbled remark to someone in the room with him. Just as he came back on the line, I heard a girl's giggle.

His tone was serious. "I'm on spring break this week. Can you find your way through derelict Hartford?"

"My GPS knows the way to carry the sleigh."

"Then you better come now. Maybe an hour. I have things to do."

Click. The call ended.

His apartment was on the second floor of a beige-brick apartment complex of four floors, probably six apartments on each floor. A worn, dusty building on a small plot of land. Loud salsa music blared from a first-floor apartment, and a ragtag bunch of boys, maybe ten or eleven years old, bounced through the lobby, stopping to stare at me before they scurried out the front door. I pressed the intercom button next to the embossed name behind a glass panel: TRAN MICHAEL 3A. When the elevator door opened, two college students with backpacks stumbled out, a young man and a young woman, arms wrapped around each other.

A threadbare carpet in the hallway, peeling flowered wallpaper, but when Michael opened the door and bowed me in, I was surprised by the rooms: glistening glass-and-chrome coffee table covered with neatly stacked art books. A thick tome on top. I read the title. *Helen Frankenthaler: The Late Paintings.* A hard-polished walnut bookcase stretching across one wall, the lines of books arranged neatly, their bindings evened out. Gleaming black marble end tables, a black leather sofa so stark it seemed something appropriated from a New Age funeral parlor. A neat freak's domain, I told myself. Everything in its place. The magazines and newspapers on the coffee table were spread out with perhaps three inches of space between each issue, and, sitting down at his invitation, I noticed that they were ordered in the right sequence: December, then January, then February, then March. The precise, calculated life of Michael Tran.

From speakers high on bookshelves the sound of soft music, almost not there. I strained to listen. Maroon 5.

He saw me looking at the anal-compulsive spread of the *New Yorker.*

He smiled. "Don't touch anything. I'll get upset."

"I wasn't planning on it."

"I like an ordered life, but I can see by your look that you consider me…well, compulsive."

"That's exactly what I was thinking."

"Would you like something to drink?"

I shook my head. No. He was sipping pink lemonade from a tall glass.

"Are you sure?"

I nodded again.

There was a sudden movement behind me as a kitchen door swung open. A young woman walked softly into the room, her feet bare, a slender, red-headed woman in white painter's pants that never worried a can of paint. A rose-colored peasant blouse. A pretty girl with pale skin, hazel eyes, and faint rose polish on her long nails. I noticed because she quietly waved a hand in greeting, a fluttery gesture that seemed to exhaust her. She toppled into a red leather side chair, curled her legs beneath her, and then wrapped her hands around her knees. She was smiling at me.

Michael and I watched her languorous trek to the side chair, he with a look that suggested possession and delight. Me, however, baffled. Off-Broadway performance art in an off-campus apartment on a ramshackle side street that edged Trinity College campus.

"Cheryl." Michael pointed at her and she nodded at me.

"Rick Van Lam."

"I know."

Michael sat down opposite me. "What can I do you for?"

"Simon. Your little brother. Suspected of assault resulting in the death of an old man. And, I now understand, a boy who likes to visit his older brother."

Michael frowned. "I don't know whether he *likes* to come here. Frankly, I was surprised when he first showed up. He took the city bus and somehow found me."

That puzzled me. "When did the visits start?"

He rolled his tongue into his cheek. "The day after that detective Ardolino dragged him in for questioning. So, yes, recently. After he got back from Long Lane. He never came here before. It scared him, I guess. Ardolino can be a bulldog."

"So he came here?"

He glanced at Cheryl. "You seem surprised. He's not scaling Everest to get here."

"But the emotional climb to these rooms is probably…"

He thrust his hand out, blocking my face. "Oh, Christ. Introduction to Freshman Psychology."

I grinned. "Fair enough." I glanced at his girlfriend who was watching me closely. "On the phone you said you didn't believe he had anything to do with the new assault. Why?"

"Simple. Because he *told* me he had nothing to do with it. Yes, he did that nonsense that got him sent to Long Lane."

"You're excusing that?"

He rushed his words. "I didn't say that, did I? Let me talk." Flash fire annoyance, a tinge of red in his cheeks. "Of course not, but it was a boy's stupidity. Yes, people did get hurt. A broken limb, I believe. But this last incident was a whole different ball game, no? And he told me he got scared at Long Lane—never wants to go back. Certainly not a life of crime that leads to Somers and a cell shared with a prison-muscle freak named Jim Bob."

Again the glance at his girlfriend, who now sat with her eyes half-shut, a narcotic smile on her lips. His eyes finally stayed on her face, a twist of his head suggesting some communication between them. When he looked back at me, I detected irritation. What had they said to each other in their coded body language?

He reminded me of little Simon, I suddenly realized. Yes, little Simon was a short slip of a boy, while Michael was taller, also bone thin but lanky, his arms long and bony. And Simon, like his father, had a dark complexion, a chocolate smoothness, his black hair wiry, ragged. Michael was fair with the delicate mocha of so many Vietnamese, but similar facial structure, pronounced cheekbones, small dark eyes, rigid chin, ears a little too big. What they called Buddha ears—bigger than they should be, with elongated lobes—prized as symbols of longevity. But a wide, broad nose. Good-looking, I realized—no, more striking than good-looking. He thinks he's white, Hazel had said of her brother, dismissing him.

"I still don't understand why Simon started visiting you."

He rubbed his palms together. "Look, Rick. When I lived at home, when I was at Kingswood-Oxford prep, little Simon followed me around. So small, cute as a button. He would walk so close to me that if I stopped suddenly he sometimes bumped into my back. It was a joke—we laughed. Then I went away."

"National Merit Fellow at Trinity. Full scholarship."

His eyes widened. "You do your homework."

"I'm an investigator who knows how to Google."

He laughed. "I don't go home anymore."

"Hazel told me you think you're white."

He bit his lip. "Do I look white?" His question was addressed to the white girl sitting across the room. He made a *har har har* sound, exaggerated, and then closed up.

"You're Vietnamese."

"I'm an American college student."

"Why don't you go home?"

Again the quick glance at Cheryl, as if checking her response to a conversation she seemed to be ignoring. "I have a new life here. A couple more years at Trinity. A political science major. An internship planned for a state legislative office in Boston. Grad work at Harvard. A life *there*."

"You could still stop in at your folks'."

He waved a dismissive hand in the air. "You asked me why Simon found me. I never told him where I lived. I don't want anybody from my family visiting me. Yes, I talk to my mother because she worries and doesn't understand any of her children because she's not allowed to. I feel sorry for her. So I call her every so often. Community outreach, I call it. Charity. It's less painful than canvassing for a cure for cancer."

"Christ, you're cynical."

"That's not cynicism, Rick Van Lam. That's the first lesson in survival I learned."

"So Simon found you because…"

"Because this last arrest threat is serious business, and maybe he remembered bumping into my back. He's a boy hungry for… well, a safety net."

"And do you help him?"

"I let him sleep on my sofa. A few nights."

"Why?"

"He's my brother."

"His buddy Frankie?"

He shivered. "Christ, no. That two-bit street punk. Foul-mouth trash bucket. Simon brought him here once and I said—no, no, no. God no. Do I look like a halfway house for white trash? The next time Simon came alone. I'm an escape route. Underground Railroad. Three, maybe four times. As I say, it surprised me."

"I sense you want to tell me something scandalous about your home life."

He laughed. "Quick, you are."

But I noticed a bead of sweat on his forehead. The tilt of his head told me he was nervous.

"Your father." I let the two words linger in the air, explosive, accusatory.

"Quick, you are. Pop. I have a grudging respect for the man. But the pressure—the constant drive. The—pain of expectation."

"Your father made a decent life for you kids."

A smirk. "He did that. I told you I have a grudging respect. But we paid a price for *his* American dream."

"His noble dream, no? A boy dumped onto the Hartford streets, a boy taken in just to get some greedy folks to America. A boy living hand to mouth. A boy…" I stopped, deliberately. "*Tran den*. The black American."

He winced, pulled back in his chair. "I hate that."

"I know you do."

A low, clipped voice. "You don't think we heard it all growing up? 'Do good in school. Be polite. Make America love you. Get all A's. Go to prep school. Go, go, go. Christ, the family religion."

"He only wanted…"

"Stop saying that. Give me a fucking break. You must have seen that wall of awards. First prize, second prize. Spelling bees, Math competitions. Science fairs. Nutmeg Boys State. D.A.R Civic Award. Elks Club medals. A wall of fame—and, ultimately, shame. Each new addition a testimony to the wonder of the children he produced."

"Okay, so he went overboard. Lots of Asian parents put pressure on their kids."

"Pressure!" he bellowed. "You just don't get it, do you? Christ, we were held to the ground by the Plymouth Rock. Study, study, study. By the time I was in high school, I suffered from severe migraines, sobbing in my room when I got an A-minus on a fucking quiz. He's at my high school graduation, rushing in from the goddamn garage, a grease monkey, covered in oil and tar and…and…and he tries to hug me."

I sat up, gob smacked. "You're ashamed of your father."

He waited a long time. He seethed. "I told you I have a grudging…"

"Cut the crap, Michael. You're embarrassed."

He looked away, but then watched me with an unfunny grin on his face. "On my college application I stupidly wrote he was a master mechanic. It just popped into my head. It sounded good. But he saw it—I left it out by mistake. Christ, it bothered him. But I couldn't bring myself to say…what? He changes the oil in your brand new Infiniti…I'm sorry. He kept saying he was proud of me. Proud."

"You're blaming him for being proud?"

His two hands cradled the glass of lemonade. I thought he'd shatter it. "Let me finish, dammit. I feel sorry for little Simon because he's not gonna make it. Him and Hazel who will use her looks to wrangle a life with that scumbag from Avon Mountain, Judd the Dud. Or meek little Wilson with his eyeglasses falling off his nose, whimpering when he has to show Daddy a less-than-A grade in biology. He's not strong. You tell him to jump and he does. He's so fucked up he doesn't know that he can say no to the world. You wanna know why I let Simon sack out on my sofa? He needs a place to hide from the family. All good, good people who are doing their best to ruin his life because they don't know any better. Running the streets and flirting with some Viet Cong gangsters because they tell him he is worth something. Little Simon, the one my father coddled—his own image. But the one he demanded the most from. To become *him*."

"But your mother. You call her."

"Because she's helpless. And because she feels guilty because she didn't protect her kids from"—his eyes danced wickedly—"school."

"But you're here"—I waved my hand around the room—
"here at Trinity getting ready for a comfortable professional life.
Because of your father and mother."

"How trite you are, Rick Van Lam. Real Fresh-Off-the-Boat
thinking on your part. Do you think that I'm *that* superficial? I
don't want to be around my father but not because he's a grease
monkey who wants the best for his kids."

"But that's what it sounds like."

He sat back, smug, his head tilted up. "I haven't told you the
missing part of the Tran puzzle. Yes, he pushed us—continues to
push Hazel and Wilson. And even Simon. And he's made them
so helpless they follow the orders of any Nazi they meet. Frankie
Trailer Park or—or Judd the Crud. But I realized that Pop had
changed when he actually got what he wanted. When that wall
was filled with trophies and merit badges and imprimatur from
the Governor of Connecticut—when the world bestowed gold
dust on his progeny, well, he…changed."

"Meaning?"

A long, deliberate pause, deadly. "Simple. Real simple. He got
jealous of us. His own kids. I realized that one day by the look
on his face when I was feted in the *Hartford Courant*. My face
next to a fat Rotarian handing me a scholarship. The world loved
his high-achieving kids, and it left him behind. He got"—for
the first time Michael's voice quivered and his hands shook—
"jealous. We had something he could never have. That was the
day I realized a whole part of him resented us. That was the day
I ran away from home. Do you see why I let Simon crawl into
a fetal position on my sofa?" He actually pointed to the sofa I
sat on. "He needs me. And that's so—unfortunate."

Chapter Fourteen

The door to Gracie's apartment was open, the TV blaring. Inside, sitting on the sofa, his injured leg up on the coffee table, one arm cradling the remote control, Jimmy kept his eyes glued to the set. Behind him stood Hank, his phone gripped in his right hand, a look of utter wonder on his face. As I sat down next to Jimmy who was grunting at me without looking over, I started to say, "Jimmy, I need…" His free hand flew into my face.

"Quiet, dammit." He pointed at the TV and mumbled, "That damned fool, Jesse."

He was watching *Days of Our Lives*.

Last week when I'd stopped in, he'd been positioned in that same spot, his leg suspended, and the minute Gracie left the room he'd whispered to me, "Can you believe this shit?"

"What?"

"Look. All these pretty people yelling at each other and then locking eyes as if someone told them the world was coming to an end. Baloney, all of it."

Gracie had heard him because his stage whisper was loud enough to drown out the TV. "Jimmy," she'd explained, "these are people in the thralls of an emotional…"

"Yeah, yeah, crisis. We had this talk, you and me."

"When I was a Rockette in Manhattan"—Jimmy's eyebrows had shot up and his eyes popped—"I was offered a walk-on part in *All My Children*, but my dance life was more important." She'd pointed to the TV. "I could have been a soap opera star." She'd dramatically thrown back her head and her bonnet of white curls shifted. Her hand patted them in a deliberate stage move, as though she were being watched from the balcony.

At the time Jimmy had caught my eye, a look suggesting there was no guiding light strong enough to lead Gracie anywhere. Or—enough days in anyone's life.

They'd bickered back and forth. The War to End All Wars— Liz's description of Gracie and Jimmy's wonderful tit-for-tat exchanges, an old married couple's sniping that skirted the edge of meanness—or kindness, in fact—but ended with Gracie rushing into the kitchen to take the pan of walnut brownies out of the oven because she knew Jimmy didn't like them too chewy.

Now, a week later, he'd gone over to the dark side—to Hank's horror, if I could judge by the look on his face. If Gracie allowed afternoon time dedicated to her "shows," as she termed them, hell or high water, Jimmy, the reluctant captive who'd graduated from his bed to the living room, suddenly was entranced by the lives of the folks at Salem University Hospital. "Look, look, check out that creep. People don't got sense these days, Rick."

"You're telling me," I answered.

He pointed a finger at me. "What are you trying to say?" He never took his eyes off the TV. "You know better."

Then we smiled at each other. Jimmy was on the mend.

Hank scurried into the kitchen to help Gracie carry out a tray of coffee and cookies.

"Gracie," he said, grinning, "you've turned into a real girl scout with all these cookies."

From the sofa Jimmy made a grunting sound.

"You know, I haven't baked anything in years." Gracie fluttered about, nearly toppling the plate of cookies. "My first batch were like hockey pucks."

Jimmy looked over. "That was obvious to me right away."

"Yet you ate every one I gave you." Gracie tilted her head impishly. "You *gnawed* on those cookies."

"I'm a polite guest." His eyes on the TV. "What am I supposed to do—starve?"

Jimmy pulled himself up in the seat, tugging at the sweatshirt that rode up his tremendous belly, adjusting his foot as he let out a disturbing "Oww." A task punctuated by heaving and sighing and a scattershot of "goddamn" and "Christ Almighty man."

"Hurts?" I asked him, smiling.

He frowned at me. "This is a prison here"—he shot a glance at Gracie but there was merriment in his eyes—"and even the visitors are hell."

"I can't do this alone," she'd whispered to me. "It's like pushing a water buffalo upstream."

"You got an attractive warden." Hank pointed at Gracie, who beamed.

Jimmy eyed him. "And just why are you here today, Hank?"

"Well, Rick and I are headed into Hartford."

"When?" From Jimmy.

Hank checked his phone. "In an hour or so."

"I ask the time and he looks at his phone. What kind of world is this?"

"What's up, Jimmy?" I asked. "You demanded I stop in."

Jimmy turned to me. "Rick, two things. I wanted to talk to you about one of my cases. The Aetna one."

I nodded. "I got your notes, Jimmy."

"Great, but can you read my writing?"

"No one can," Hank said smartly.

Jimmy beamed. "That's because your generation never learned cursive. All you know is big block letters. You're only qualified to write ransom notes."

Hank threw back his head and laughed.

Jimmy straightened himself in the chair. "All right, Rick. But something else. The Ralph case. Some shit finally came back to me. You gotta tell Ardolino, I guess. Not that he cares to phone here." His fiery look at Gracie suggested she'd cut the telephone wires. "I woke up his morning and I remembered something. I think it's important."

I was reaching for a cookie when he bellowed, "Are you listening to me?"

With a mouth full of cookie, I managed, "Always."

"Anyway, when I woke up, I could smell bacon and suddenly I was back in that Burger King on Farmington Avenue."

"You saw something?"

He shook his head. "Naw. I *heard* something." He turned to face me, his face tight.

"Tell me."

I glanced at Gracie who was watching Jimmy closely.

"I mean, I was listening to Ralph yammer on and on about some nonsense. Christ, he was a bore, that man—God rest his pathetic soul. Anyway, he'd been drinking, I think—no, I know—after all, it was daylight, so his talk was a little too loud and stupid. He rambled on that I was an ass because I took Rick into the firm." Jimmy cast a disingenuous look at me, a sliver of a smile on his face. "He wasn't as free-thinking and tolerant as I am."

"Editorializing," Hank mumbled, and Jimmy's look shut him up.

Jimmy reached for a cookie, nibbled on the edge, then sucked down the whole thing. Crumbs dotted his chest.

"Anyway, Ralph was making a spectacle of himself as he munched on a cheeseburger. And then he mentioned some jackasses sitting at a table behind me. I didn't pay it much attention because—well, it was Ralph talking. But I guess some kids were talking *about* him, or making fun of him, or something like that. 'Creeps,' he called them. 'What?' I asked and he said, 'Punk kids. Someone should blow them away.' Nice guy, right? I didn't care. There are always kids in that Burger King, especially after school. They meet there, laugh it up, and bother people, you know."

"But this was different?" I asked.

He shook his head vigorously. "I guess so. Ralph mumbled that one of the kids gave him the finger—or Ralph thought it was the finger. I mean, he was boozy-eyed, so the kid could just as well been counting to one or something."

"But Ralph took offense."

"He muttered that they were doing some nonsense on their phones or players or some gadget they got nowadays. He gave them the finger. I should have turned around, but I didn't want to make the dumb scene into a—you know, big scene. Fighting with teenage punks in a Burger King? Come on. Now I wish I had. He imitated the sounds from their gadgets: *beep beep bam bam pow pow.* Something like that. I ignored it. Who cares what young people do nowadays?" He tilted his head toward Hank. "They ain't the greatest generation."

Hank commented, "That was World War Two, no? You were Korean War, right?" A dumb smile on his face.

"You know damn well I was shot at in Vietnam, Hank." He drew his lips into a thin line. "Probably by Rick's opium-smoking uncle."

I smiled. "Becoming Jimmy's partner was my family's revenge."

Jimmy smirked. "It worked."

I bowed.

Gracie spoke up. "They must have followed you and Ralph out, Jimmy. Ralph made them mad."

"If this is true," I went on, "the two targeted Ralph. Not so much you, but Ralph. This wasn't a random street attack."

"Maybe." Jimmy's brow tightened.

Gracie was getting excited. "Rick, you gotta talk to the folks at Burger King. Maybe somebody remembers the boys."

Hank jumped in. "Ardolino probably did that."

"Probably," I said. "He can be a pain, but he's a bulldog. It's logical that he'd retrace Ralph's steps."

"Anything else, Jimmy?" Hank asked.

Jimmy waited a bit, drumming his index finger on his chest. "Yeah, as a matter of fact. They were talking in a singsong voice, at least someone behind me was. Not that I could recognize a voice, mind you, but you know how you hear bits and pieces of folks' talk nearby. There was this, like...rhythm, *dud dud duh DUH.* Then again. *Duh duh duh DUH.* Like a goddamn rap song. Christ, you even hear that shit in elevators these days. *Duh duh duh DUH.*"

Hank was laughing. "So they were rapping."

"Maybe."

"Could it have been on their phones?" I asked.

"Who knows?" He paused. "No, Ii was a real voice because it was uneven, in and out, mixed with talking, I guess. Yeah, rap." His eyes got wide. "How come nobody these days remembers Sinatra? Or, you know, Bing Crosby?"

Hank started to defend hip-hop culture—he mouthed the words "Kanye West"—but I signaled to him. Be quiet.

"So what do you think?" I asked Jimmy.

He smiled at Gracie. "I agree with Gracie. Ralph pissed off these street thugs, and they followed us out and jumped him."

"But they probably never intended to have him die," Hank said.

"Ardolino will get them," I said.

"Tough luck for them when they get them." Jimmy's voice got mournful. "Ralph ain't much in the scheme of things, but nobody should take away his last breath."

Jimmy's words hung in the air, a curious valedictory. We sat there, quiet.

Then, with the implausibility of coincidence from, say, *Days of Our Lives*, my phone beeped and I saw Detective Ardolino's name on the I.D. "Speak of the devil."

"What?" asked Hank.

"Ardolino."

Chapter Fifteen

When Hank and I were led into his office, Detective Ardolino had both of his legs up on his desk, a paper napkin tucked under his chin, a mustard-smeared finger headed toward his mouth. "They got hot dogs in the vending machines now," he announced as a greeting. "Pretty soon you can buy a whole goddamn turkey."

Hank reached over to shake his hand. "Detective Ardolino."

"Yeah, yeah." The man sat up and wiped his mouth. He rubbed his palms with the napkin, then tossed it into a waste bin. He shook hands. "Wherever the Lone Ranger goes"—he looked at me as if I'd dragged along an errant child—"Tonto is sure to follow. Kemo sabe. Hi ho, Silver."

"Who knows?" From Hank, a little cocky.

"What are you talking about?"

"Kemo sabe. Sort of Spanish for—Who knows? *Quien sabe?* High-school Spanish. As in—who was that masked man?"

"No child left behind," Ardolino grumbled. "Some should be." He shuffled in his seat. "Out of the kindness of my heart I invited you to see a surveillance video some storekeeper on Farmington Avenue decided to tell us he had."

"Of Jimmy and Ralph?"

"No, of my wedding at the dawning of the Ice Age."

"Sorry," I said sheepishly.

"It's pretty lousy quality and all. And it's from a hundred yards away, more or less, but you can see a little of what happened.

Since Jimmy is your partner and you were close friends"—he grinned—"with that drunk Ralph, I figured you might spot something my trained eyes missed. Probably not, but, as I say, I'm a generous guy. I share evidence."

Hank piped in, "You know, with all our modern technology, I still can't understand why we can't get clear, vivid shots from those surveillance tapes in banks and gas stations."

Ardolino clicked his tongue. "Christ, Hank, we get eye witnesses who were standing four feet away who can't tell you if the killer was a man or a woman."

He led us into a nearby room where a sergeant was sitting before a bank of monitors. I told Ardolino what Jimmy had said about the scene in the Burger King—Ralph and the rapping boys, Ralph giving them the finger. "I'm assuming you interviewed folks there. The last place Jimmy and Ralph were."

He resented my remark. "I know how to do my job, Lam."

"All I meant…"

"I know what you meant." He clicked his tongue again. "Thanks for sharing the story." But his tone suggested I'd withheld crucial evidence. "And yes, of course. Some kid remembered Jimmy and Ralph, called Ralph a regular there, a drunk who complained about the pickles in the fucking burger, so people hated him, probably spit in his burger, which he deserved, maybe. Anyway, nobody remembered any kids following them out because no one paid attention to the old fools. Who the hell does? Christ, I pump gas and the blue-haired, tattoo-of-Satan girl behind the counter never even looks into my face. Hopped up on Molly, I wouldn't be surprised. Sad, but that's me—I live for courtesy and manners." An ah-shucks look covered his face. "That's the way my motor runs."

"Nothing then?"

He signaled to the sergeant—"You gonna sit there all day?" Then, to me, "The place was filled with kids in hoodies and baggy pants and backward baseball caps and phones ringing, everybody looking into their phones expecting tweets from the person they're sitting opposite in the restaurant. Nobody sees nothing nowadays."

"So that's a dead-end."

"Like I said."

The sergeant queued up the video, the edited section running perhaps ten minutes. An impossible tape, I realized, grainy, dim, shadowy, with stick figures sauntering by, a blur of speeding cars on the street. But at one point two murky figures come into view—Jimmy and Ralph—although so far from the lens they could be any two old guys ambling down the sidewalk. But in a flash two figures rush up the sidewalk, one disappearing from the frames for a second, but then reappearing on the edge of the sidewalk. Then out of the frame. As we watched, the taller kid lurched forward, a hand raised, a blow to the head, Ralph twisting around, pushing back, the two grappling, Ralph stumbling, crashing into the iron pole.

"You really can't tell anything," Hank commented.

"As I said," Ardolino went on. "Just the assault."

"But it's impossible to identify the kids."

"As I said," he repeated.

"But," I noted, "you *can* tell a couple things. First of all, the aggressor is a tall boy, a head or so taller that the other, wouldn't you say? And look at the shorter kid. He's standing back to the side, then disappears. When he reappears, he's not moving at first, then he runs."

Ardolino watched me closely. "So you're saying what?"

"I'm saying that the shorter kid didn't participate. At the end he runs away down the sidewalk, wobbling from side to side."

"So does the attacker."

"Maybe the other kid," Hank jumped in, "was surprised at the attack. Maybe unplanned. Maybe he didn't know that the taller boy would do such a thing."

Ardolino wore a slick grin. I noticed a bit of brown mustard had dried on his left cheek. Unconsciously he scratched at it, and the dried condiment flecked away. Ardolino examined his fingernail, and frowned. "Shit, the stuff that stays on me."

Hank looked ready to comment—the corners of his mouth twisted up humorously—but I shot him a look.

Ardolino caught the look, clever detective that he was. "Flies on shit? Is that where you're going?" He wagged a finger at Hank. "Anyway, I hear you, Rick. But what I also hear is that you and your state-police-boy-scout are saying that little Simon Tran was somehow the innocent here, a bystander—that the big bad wolf is Frankie Croix."

"I didn't say that."

Ardolino stood up. "Of course you didn't. I can read minds. You didn't know that about me, did you? I'm a fucking Houdini."

◇◇◇

Hank and I sat upstairs in the office of Gaddy Associates. I'd been stopping in nearly every day for a while now, sometimes only for an hour or so, catching up on my own fraud cases as well as moving through Jimmy's Byzantine note-taking, covering his cases for him. For all his hieroglyphics and scribbling and dog-eared printouts, Jimmy had mastered an intricate system of work: a diamond-cut logic belied the seeming chaos of his desk. In some ways working his cases was easier than my own because my pile of search-engine data towered dangerously on my desk and in the interconnected files on my laptop, while Jimmy's investigative world was laid out with the awesome clarity of a child's ABC primer.

While I worked at my desk, Hank sat by the front window, his tablet in his lap as he filled out some forms demanded by the state police. But his movements were desultory, lazy, as he leaned back on the wooden chair, two legs wobbling in the air, and quietly gazed down from the second-floor onto a busy Farmington Avenue. Handing him a cup of coffee, I noticed he'd abandoned his form and was tapping away on "Words with Friends."

"Words with Nerds," I joked.

"There's a disheveled and lonely gamer hidden in the basement of his parents' flat in London who resents your character attack."

But when I stopped to pour myself a second cup, he looked up, pushed his tablet away. "Ardolino is dead set on nailing Simon and Frankie for Ralph's death."

"Sounds like it." Then I smiled. "That's why I'm chasing after anyone connected with the Tran family. Somebody has to tell me something I can build on."

"What about Frankie's family?"

"I called his home, but his mother was evasive. She doesn't trust strangers."

"Even those helping her son's case?"

"She may not see me as her son's advocate. Just Simon's."

"But to clear one is to clear the other."

I rustled some papers on my desk, made an entry into the computer. I pressed SAVE. "But she said I could stop in to talk to her."

He went back to his tablet—"Christ, the state of Connecticut loves forms"—pecking away with three fingers, deleting—with a curse—then backtracking, muttering to himself. "I'd rather arrest a murderer than type a form."

I laughed. "Hank, one day when you arrest a murderer, you'll have hundreds of forms to fill out."

Suddenly the quiet of the office was punctuated with a thunderous rumble of motorcycles in the street. Hank leaned over the sill, frowning. "Bikers." He looked back at me. "Three of them disturbing the peace with their modified Harleys." The clang and sputter finally died. "One of them is yelling at a driver who pulled into a spot next to him. He's not happy."

I walked to the window and looked down. Leather-clad bikers in helmets straddled their bikes, two of them with arms crossed, the third pumping his fist at the driver, a twenty-something who'd stepped out of his car. The biker slipped off his helmet, cradled it to his chest, and swung his head around.

Hank blurted out, "Christ, is that—Frankie Croix?"

From the second-floor angle it was difficult to get a good look, but I understood what Hank was saying. The young man, swiveling his head back and forth angrily, happened to tilt his head upwards, and he did, indeed, resemble Frankie Croix. The long bony face, the long neck with the prominent Adam's apple.

"An older brother, I guess." I peered down into the street. "He's—what? Twenty or so?"

"Looks just like Frankie."

"Yes, and they burn with the same fire."

Hank looked puzzled. "Frankie has an older bother?"

"More than one, Hank."

"How do you know that?"

I pointed to my laptop. "I do my homework."

"You got files on everyone?"

I nodded. "It helps." I went to my computer, tapped some keys, and brought up my file on the Croix family. "Okay. He's probably Jonny Croix, aged twenty-two, a rap sheet for a thousand petty crimes, one year in Somers, paroled. The next brother is still in jail. The oldest is married and living in Waterbury." I waited a second. "He's a prison guard."

"All in the family."

"So this is Jonny." I zeroed in on an online photo from the *Courant* during his arraignment. "He does look like his brother Frankie, with the addition of a lightning-bolt tattoo on his forehead, a zigzag scar under his puffy left eye, and the emaciated skeletal face of a chronic Meth user."

"His buddies are yelling something to the driver now."

I went back to the window. Both buddies remained on the Harleys, arms still crossed belligerently, both with helmets cradled to their chests."

"I wonder who they are," I said out loud.

"Why?"

"I dunno. Check out the one on the left. An Asian guy. Watch when he swings his head around. Chinese? Vietnamese? Maybe gang members. Maybe he occupies a parallel universe from his little brother Frankie. Maybe..."

Hank, antsy, jumped up. "I'll check."

He bounded out of the office, and I could hear his footfall on the old wooden staircase. But as I watched the street below, the bikers revved their engines, Jonny leaped back onto his Harley, strapped on his helmet, and the three sailed back into traffic, heedless of the flow. Jonny did a U-turn, skirted close to the driver of the car who was standing on the curb, watching. Jonny gave him the finger and yelled something, and then flew off behind his buddies.

On the sidewalk Hank looked up at me and shrugged his shoulders. I waved back.

Hank turned to the driver who was already headed into the law offices that occupied our ground floor. Hank said something and the man paused. From what I could see he pointed at the annoying bikers and his mouth formed one word, evident to me from two floors away.

Assholes.

Hank gave me the thumbs-up.

Chapter Sixteen

Frog Hollow was an old neighborhood in the shadow of downtown Hartford. A few blocks to the west, it had a used-up feel, rows of stolid three-decker brick buildings faded from too much sunlight and too little attention. Here and there a window was boarded up with plywood. A door had posted a sign: *Do Not Enter. Condemned.* Faded green asphalt-tiled porches sagged under patchwork tarpaper roofs.

I pulled up my old Beamer in front of Frankie's home, squeezing it between a Toyota with a flat tire and a Honda Civic with no license plate. While I locked my car—I don't know why because it was twelve years old now, hardly a car to steal—a sloe-eyed drunk tottered against a lamp post, careened into the front fender of my car, and waited for me to say something.

As I reached the second floor, jarred by a swell of rap music coming from an apartment down the hall, the door of 2A opened slowly, and Doris Croix stood in the frame, arms folded across her chest.

"I don't know why you gotta talk to me."

"You're Frankie's mom."

She turned and walked back into the room. She flicked back her head. "He told the police it ain't him that done it."

"Still and all." I followed after her. "There's a good chance he'll be charged."

She turned quietly, her face near mine. Her breath reeked of stale cigarette smoke.

"I know the Orientals hired you to clear that Saigon kid." A hesitant smile. "I guess it's a two-for-one deal. Clear one boy, the other walks. My Frankie."

I smiled. "That's sort of the way it works."

"But what do you want from me?"

She pointed to a sofa, and I sank deep into the lumpy cushions. I caught her smiling. "You got you five boys in the house, and every spring gives sooner or later."

"Five boys?"

She held up her hand as if she planned to count her fingers. Instead she waved the hand, a throwaway gesture: what the hell. "Jail for one. Another got a job. Then there's Jonny and Frankie and little Pete, who's twelve. I had one baby that died. Hard to remember him. He was the first of them all."

"I'm sorry."

"He was the lucky one. He missed out on the hell that always follows us around."

Quietly I surveyed the large room. No curtains on the windows, a clay pot of failing geraniums on a sill, too much furniture. The fabric on the sofa was patched with bands of black duct tape. On a side chair a giant overfed black cat stretched its paws, yawning. A coffee table of pressed board, the surface discolored from water stains from wet glasses and cups, concentric rings that overlapped, spread out across the table. An old-fashioned TV on a wire stand, switched on but the sound muted. Snowy figures fluttered across the screen. Doris Croix rushed to turn off the set.

"I sometimes forget it's on," she apologized. "It's like— company."

"Frankie's not home?"

She looked toward the door but said nothing.

She caught me looking around. "Can't do much on Section Eight housing." Then she laughed. "Can you imagine what Sections One through seven look like?"

"Is Frankie here?" I asked again.

"They went to the bodega for cigarettes."

"They?"

"Him and his brother, Jonny."

"I'd like to talk to you—but also him."

Her body sagged. "I told him you were coming. He's not happy."

"I know. He's like Simon. He doesn't care."

She shrugged. "You're a stranger." She reached for a cigarette from a pack at her elbow. A Virginia Slim, which she lit by striking a match. She sat back and blew smoke into the air. "And maybe because they're just dumb kids who ain't got a clue how life works."

"He's coming back?"

Again the shrug. "I hope so. But I'll tell you something. None of them listens to me. My husband, Jack—he beat it when my youngest was born. I mean, it's a winter night and he says to me that he gotta get cigarettes. He throws on his coat, walks out that door, and that's the last I seen him. Ever. The cops didn't give a damn. The point is I'm stuck with five rat-assed boys, and one after the other pushes his way around me."

"They hit you?"

"One night I tell Jonny to do something—I mean, he's like fourteen then—and he smashes up the place. He breaks every dish in the kitchen, yelling and swearing at me. When it's all over and the place looks like a bomb went off, he stands up against my face, and says, 'If you ever give me another goddamn order, I'll do this all over again.' The other boys see that, and, well, you know how the story ends."

She offered me a soda—"I only got diet Coke"—which I refused. She looked disappointed as she left the room. I heard her opening the refrigerator, the sound of bottles clinking, and she returned, a bottle of Coke in her hand. "I drink so much diet Coke they should put me on TV." She held out the bottle, as if displaying it before a camera, and said in a deep rumbling voice, "Eats your insides out, folks. Pick some up today."

"Tough sell," I laughed.

"Don't matter." She laughed as she gulped some soda and then put the bottle down on the table, immediately picking up the cigarette she'd left burning in an ashtray.

"Maybe you can help me?" I said to her. "Tell me what Frankie said to you about that day. Anything? I know he said he was at the arcade on Park with Simon, that he stopped in at the...you know, the VietBoyz storefront."

She held up her hand. "Those are rotten hoods. Frankie talks to his brother about them. To Jonny. Like with admiration, I guess. But Jonny knows them. Christ, *he* goes there. He likes them thugs—the Oriental guy who comes from Chinatown. Killer, he says. Another guy just out of prison. Jonny knows him from a tavern on Capital. Piggy's, they call it. Jonny *likes* the fact that Frankie hangs out there."

"But that afternoon..."

"Frankie says he didn't know about the guy dying until later—when that detective knocks on the door. 'What are you talking about?' he says to him."

"But then he remembered that he'd been at the storefront, no?"

"I guess so. I don't know." Suddenly she looked exhausted.

"Was Jonny there that afternoon, too? I mean, the afternoon when Ralph Gervase died? Maybe he was there when the boys stopped in. Maybe he can tell me something."

She gazed off into space. "I dunno. Don't hold your breath. I only know what I overheard, and that ain't much." She hesitated. "But I can tell you that I hear Frankie and Jonny talking about it after the detective disappeared—and Frankie tells his brother it ain't him done it."

"Maybe he lied to Jonny."

She shook her head back and forth. "That would surprise me. You can't lie to Jonny, let me tell you. I seen Frankie try that, and Jonny smacks him across the mouth. Bloody nose. 'You lie to me, you little fucker, you pays a price.' His words."

"But now we're talking about a man dying."

"Don't matter." She stared into my eyes. "You think he cares about some old man dying? Or that Frankie might have had a part in it? Jonny is a piece of work. Let me tell you. Frankie—he got him a wise mouth and he thinks he's tougher than iron—but he's scared of his brother. Real scared. Jonny don't like something Frankie done, and he sits down for breakfast with a black eye."

The door to the apartment opened. Jonny stepped in, tossed a pack of cigarettes onto a shelf near the door, and nudged Frankie into the room. The boy stood near the sofa, his eyes moving from me to his mother, his expression stony. "Well, I'm back." Flat, bored. "Yeah?"

His mother prompted me. "Get this over, okay?" She kept her eyes on Jonny.

"Frankie, we had that talk at the diner, but since then—anything? Did you and Simon talk afterwards?"

"Naw."

"You two took off with two Vietnamese guys."

Jonny broke in, surprised, glaring at his younger brother. "Kenny and Joey?"

"Yeah, they gave us a ride."

Jonny fumed and pointed a finger at his brother. "Christ, Frankie. I warned you about them two fuckers." He turned away. "You heard me, you little shit-head."

Frankie faced me. "I got nothing to say. I told you everything."

"Nothing, huh?" I waited.

He tightened his face. "No. Nothing. I told that asshole Ardolino the same thing."

"Christ, Frankie." His mother took a drag on her cigarette.

"This is all bullshit." Jonny had taken off his leather jacket and slung it over the back of a chair. He slipped into the chair, pulled his legs up onto an end table, and lit his own cigarette. "Frankie says he ain't done it."

"JD told me…"

"Yeah, JD told you. The alibi, right?"

"Were you there?" I asked him.

He sucked on his cigarette, blew rings into the air. "I was gonna pick up the boys but the damn street was blocked. The Portuguese church down the block had some parade. The priest holding a statue, a brass band…"

Frankie jumped in. "Yeah, like a funeral. People…like in ribbons. With crosses. We saw that."

I smiled. "Thank you. That's something."

"How?" asked Doris.

"I don't know." I waited a bit, then looked at Jonny. "I saw you on Farmington Avenue yesterday. On a motorcycle. With two friends. Maybe Asian. You had a fight with a driver."

He seethed. "Christ, what are you—spying on me?"

"So it was you?"

"So what? There's a motorcycle shop at the end of the block. Next to Moe's. I get breakfast and a part for my bike."

"Are you on Farmington Avenue a lot?"

Now he waited a bit. "None of your goddamn business, man."

"Did you ever see Ralph on the Avenue?"

"Why would I? I don't know who the fuck he is."

"I'll tell you. He lived in a group home. He drank a bit. He liked to walk up and down the street."

"I seen a lot of people. And lots of old drunks on that street." A harsh laugh. "I bet there's already a filthy drunk taking his place, annoying the shit outta folks."

"He liked to pick fights with people."

Another throaty laugh as Jonny shot a look at Frankie. "Well, so do I. The only difference is that I always win."

"Always?"

He stood up and grabbed his jacket. "Fuck you."

He stormed out of the apartment, his fist banging the door, and Frankie, glaring at me, squeaked out a "Goddamn" and followed after his brother. Their footsteps banged down the stairwell. Loud fiery curses.

Jonny's voice echoed in the hallway. "The guy's a fucking asshole, Frankie. He ain't gonna save anybody's ass."

Whatever Frankie answered was lost in the slamming of the front door.

Doris Croix stood up, a sickly grin on her face. "Well, that went better than I expected." She walked to the front window and gazed down into the street. "He's gonna get killed on that bike someday. And Frankie on the back, hanging on like a rag doll." She sighed and looked for her cigarettes. "You have to go now," she said abruptly.

"Tell me something, Mrs. Croix."

"Yeah?"

"Do you think Frankie was involved in Ralph's death?"

She gave it some thought. "I don't know. Maybe not, as he says. It's just that he does everything else *wrong*. Like what you just watched happen here. He can be a bullshit artist, let me tell you. That's the least of his mistakes. But—look, I don't got time to care about it."

"But he may be charged in Ralph's death. This time tried as an adult. Serious prison time. A man was killed. Maybe by his hand."

"Look, mister," as she pointed to the door with her cigarette, "if it ain't this killing, well, there'll be another down the road. Sooner or later one of my boys will get the chair."

Chapter Seventeen

Jimmy and Gracie were now an old married couple, long settled into companionable silence. As I walked in late in the afternoon, the two of them were drowsing on the sofa. Jimmy's foot was still in a cast and elevated on the coffee table, his chest covered with the sports page of the *Courant*, a raspy snore escaping his throat. A bottle of Budweiser on the end table. No glass, I noticed. Empty.

Next to him Gracie snuggled into the end of the sofa, her arms folded across her chest. She wore a pristine blue duster covered with hibiscus blooms, on her feet the most outrageous pink slippers, an uncharted life form with their abundant furry fabric and gigantic pompoms. She snored in a wispy, hiccoughing hum. A syncopated rhythm as befit a former Rockette from the golden age. Just out of her reach on the end table was another bottle of beer, also Budweiser. Also empty.

I cleared my throat. Jimmy popped open one eye. "We're busy watching TV."

"Then maybe you should turn it on."

He glanced at the set across the room. "These new ones go off when you turn your head for a second."

"Right."

"What do you want?"

I stopped in every day, and every day he asked the same question.

"Work to do." The same answer every day.

For a half-hour or so, until I noticed him starting to fade, we would discuss business, reviewing his cases I was finishing up. "I miss the view from the window," he told me now.

"What? Pizza Palace?"

He grinned widely. "At night they have a huge neon-lit pizza in the window, with twinkling lights."

"Yeah, seductive."

"Don't play holier-than-thou with me, Rick." A sidelong glance toward Gracie, rousing herself and listening to everything. "I've seen you swallow a meatball grinder from Subway in three real unattractive chomps." He watched Gracie move into the kitchen.

"I had to. You were eyeing it with a rapacious look in your eye."

He frowned. "I ain't never had a rapacious look in my eye. Ever."

From the kitchen Gracie's amused soprano. "You can say that again."

Jimmy leaned in, a conspiratorial whisper. "She's trying to kill me with good food."

"Call the cops."

Plied with a cup of coffee from Gracie, I ran through Jimmy's cases, bringing up his files on my laptop. But he lacked interest, his gaze drifting toward the window. The caged bird, I thought. Gracie buzzed around him, quietly placing another bottle of beer at his elbow, but largely silent. At one point I caught her eye, a cloudy, faraway expression that I found hard to read. Yes, I understood that she enjoyed Jimmy under her constant and loving care, but her charge was no easy task. Jimmy belched and grunted and heaved his way through her rooms. Perhaps their bizarre flirtation was best played out across a table at Zeke's Olde Tavern, neutral ground where the give-and-take of geriatric titillation had a natural end when last call was trumpeted. Proximity, alas, did bring—well, not contempt, but heavy sighing.

Jimmy watched Gracie's retreating back. "I'm hobbling on crutches to Zeke's tomorrow. The doctor said it's okay."

"And?"

"And you gotta be there in case I fall."

A short time later Liz waltzed in. "Does everyone leave doors wide open in this high crime neighborhood?" She gave Jimmy a quick peck on the cheek. Of course, he squirmed, delighted. She gave Gracie a quick hug, and I heard Gracie whisper to her, "We women have trials to bear, right, dear Liz?"

Liz nodded, mumbled something that included my name and a throwaway reference to our life in Manhattan. Liz poured herself coffee, and Jimmy and Gracie, next to each other on the sofa, began watching the local news, volume turned up because each contended the other was deaf but wouldn't acknowledge it.

Liz motioned me into the kitchen, where she closed the door behind her. "I need to talk."

I pulled up a chair and poured myself another cup of coffee. When I went to put a second teaspoon of sugar into the cup, Liz reached out and touched the back of my hand. "You should cut that out."

"Just one."

She said nothing but watched me closely. When we were married, she fed me Brussels sprouts, kale, and seaweed. Protein smoothies the color of marsh grass. Sometimes I liked them.

"Talk about what?" I asked now.

Tapping her fingers on the enamel tabletop, she began, "The Tran family saga, Hazel Tran episode, continued."

"Christ," I swore. "Not Judd Snow?"

"Of course. The complication or rising action in this off-Broadway tragedy."

"Tell me what happened."

She sipped her coffee. "It wasn't pretty, Rick. But then I think most stories that involve Judd and Hazel these days are piddling tragedies." She breathed out. "I had to go to a meeting at Town Hall but stopped at that little coffee shop down from the Farmington Country Club, next to the famous bakery I've never been in."

"A digression, Liz?"

"I'm at the counter ordering a cup of java and I hear familiar, raised voices from a booth across from me. Of course, being nosy, I stepped toward the sound and came face to face with Hazel and Judd." She made a face. "God hates me, Rick."

"He hates everyone sooner or later. We tend to disappoint Him."

"Hardly a Buddhist sentiment."

"Don't tell Grandma I said that."

"You know I will, but she won't believe me." Her voice got low, confidential. "Anyway, they were obviously in the middle of a spat, Hazel fairly hissing her words and Judd, the lummox, grunting his disapproval. It all stopped, like a slap to the face, when Judd spotted me. His angry red face suddenly showed the peppy grin of a boy on a Sunkist TV commercial."

"Throwing a beach ball toward the sun?"

"Yeah, that one." She fiddled with the handle of her coffee cup. "He jumped up, obsequious to a fault, with that slimy grin he seems to have invented. For a handsome young man, he sure can look—ugly."

I wasn't happy. "You should have walked away."

"I should have walked away," she echoed. "Indeed. Hindsight and all that. What I did do was the exact wrong thing. He asked me to join them and nudged Hazel, who'd been crying. She looked so—so hurt. I worried about her. I don't trust him. So I'm filled with a wash of conflicting emotions as I stared down into her face. I slid into the seat next to her. Big mistake."

"Did you learn anything?"

"I learned more than I expected."

I sat up, leaned forward. "Anything I should know?"

She drew her lips into a thin line. "Well, yes." The last word stressed. "Otherwise, why am I talking to you now? Our days of end-of-the-day bedroom gossip are long over."

"I sometimes wonder about that."

She smiled, amused. "Sometimes you're actually right." Another deep sigh. "Anyway, it was as though poor Hazel the doormat wasn't even there. Judd the Obscure starts to flirt outrageously with me. I mean, blatant. Fawning, humming, leaning across the table, resting his hand too close to mine, batting those eyelids as though he had cinders in his eyes. He tells me how beautiful I am—and I cringe. Something so wrong—a boy like that. To *me*. Hazel starts to sob again, and I pat her hand. Judd reaches over and grabs her hand, in the process grasping mine, squeezing it. I swear, I jumped as though I'd touched a live wire."

"Christ, he has no boundaries."

"This is an eighteen-year-old man who is one step ahead of the rest of us. He scares me. I swear I see him—or that red Audi—too often these days. Or, at least I think it's him cruising by. I'm backing out of the parking lot and down the street is a flash of red car. Judd, I believe."

I rushed my words. "Then what happened?"

"Well, he dominates the conversation. But in the middle—I swear at one point he winks, and I shivered—he brings up an encounter with Simon and Frankie at the mall. He's trying to get to Hazel—to *hurt* her. 'Your asshole brother,' he says to her. 'A killer, they tell me. Your sad family.' Hazel cries louder now."

"Why mention Simon?"

"Well, earlier that day they bumped into Frankie and Simon at West Farms Mall. Again. A bunch of kids, shooed out of the stores by security. Judd bullied Simon, calling him a wimp. 'Like everybody in the Tran family.' His words, not mine. Simon starts getting tough, in his face, but Frankie barges in, actually shoves Judd. And for a second the two tussle until friends pull Frankie off."

"Why would Frankie do that again?"

"Have you met the boy? He's a brawler, Rick. Fistfight, part two. But it seems he was angry because Judd had emptied his backpack during the first Punic War and had pilfered a video game. 'It's a goddamn rental,' Frankie yelled at him. 'They gonna charge me an arm and a leg.' 'Fuck you.' Judd's words, not

mine. Threats to kill each other." Liz sat back. "Anyway, that's
the Homeric tale Judd now tells me, spun with embellishment
to impress. He puffed out his chest and waited for me to faint
in the aisle."

I chuckled. "I'm assuming you didn't?"

A shrug. "Not this time. The last time I fainted was when
you proposed marriage." A pause. "No, I'm wrong. It was when
they refused to double bag my groceries at Fairway."

"Was that what Hazel and Judd were fighting about?"

"I guess. 'Simon the murderer.' Again Judd's chant, calculated to send Hazel off into a spasm of grief." Liz deliberated.
"And something else I just remembered. Another remark about
the sad Tran family, even though he's sleeping with one of the
members, I'm sure. He said he was sick of Wilson, the namby-
pamby brother."

"Yes, that's how he met Hazel. A chess competition at
Kingswood-Oxford."

"So I learned. Both are on the chess team. Judd taught Wilson
how to play, and Wilson took off, beating him. Judd, infuriated,
said, 'I'm sick of that little creep.'"

"What does that mean?"

"The faculty advisor likes Wilson more than Judd. In some
community outreach program he has upperclassmen visit local
boys' and girls' clubs to teach chess. Judd considers it a rung of
Dante's hell. The advisor put them together, and all hell broke
out."

"Wilson is studious."

Liz laughed out loud. "And, I gather, arrogant. What roiled
poor Judd on the way to a missed anger-management class is that
Wilson repeatedly tells him—and I quote Judd's high-pitched
imitation of Wilson—'I just realized I'm smarter than you, Judd.
Quicker. I just realized it.'"

I burst out laughing. "I would've loved to have heard that.
That little pipsqueak taking on the bully."

"So Judd starts yelling at Hazel about the egomaniacs in her
family, and Hazel sits there trembling."

"And then you left?"

"No, I stayed to listen to Hazel's surprising revenge." Liz's eyes sparkled. "Of course, I stayed."

"Tell me."

Her eyes flashed. "One of the reasons I'm telling you this, Rick, is that Judd kept hissing one word at her. 'Simon.' Then 'Guess who's going back to the slammer?' At first Hazel begged him to stop, but he yelled, 'No, you stop.' That made no sense, of course, and she looked at me, as if I could translate her boyfriend's verbal hieroglyphics. I wanted to get away, but I felt protective of her."

"How did she get back at him?"

"It was as though something finally clicked inside her, some flash that told her she could get Judd. That she had ammo to defeat him."

"Tell me."

Liz's fingertips played with the coffee cup, but finally pushed it away. "She must have seen something in his face because in her next breath she leveled a salvo into his bloated ego."

"Like?"

"'I'm not coming to your house anymore, Judd.' That stunned him. She told him. 'Your father came on to me again.' It was an explosive line, said evenly, deliberately."

"Again? He's done it before?" Foster Snow. The playboy in a college boy's clothing scooting around town in the sports car.

The kitchen door opened and Gracie walked in, the two empty beer bottles in her hands. She walked by us, set the bottles on the counter, but turned toward us, listening.

Liz glanced up at her, smiled, but stopped talking.

"How did Judd react to that?" I went on.

"Steamed. He slammed his palm down on the table. 'Are you sure?' he asked her. 'Yes,' she told him, 'your father is a creep, Judd. He tries to be...you know...near me. When you're not looking, he...'" Liz stopped, glanced at Gracie, and explained to her. "Hazel Tran and her troglodyte boyfriend, Judd Snow."

Gracie was nodding. "I know all about it. I have ears, Liz."

"I feel sorry for Hazel."

Gracie made a face. "I don't."

That startled me. "Gracie, what?"

She pulled out a chair and sat down, folding her arms on the table. "One thing I learned when I was a young girl starting out, when I traveled with Bob Hope to Korea. I was barely sixteen. Then in Manhattan, at Radio City. What I learned is that a girl gotta be ready for anything. Hazel runs into a schmuck like Judd. Sometimes young girls are like wind chimes waiting for a breeze. Talk to her, Liz. Tell her to run."

Liz was smiling. "Exactly, Gracie. But she can't see beyond Judd's controlling hand."

"Then she's a fool."

Jimmy called from the living room. Gracie threw back her head and roared. "Obviously I haven't learned the lesson myself." She sailed by us, back out into the living room.

"Finish the story, Liz."

She leaned in. "I'm sitting there, witness to the scene, but Judd doesn't care. He lost it. Of course, he already knew about his father's peccadillos. And, I guess, Daddy's attraction to pretty Hazel. It wasn't the first time, I'm guessing. He stood up, slammed some cash onto the table, threw a warning look at her. But as he moved, his arm slid against my shoulder, a deliberate move, and he whispered into my neck, 'If you give me a minute, you'll beg for an hour.' And he was out the door."

"Jesus Christ, Liz."

"A slimebag."

"So you sat with Hazel. Did you try to talk some sense into her?"

"I started to. Rick, she's *scared* of him. I could tell—real fear. I softened my voice, put on my psychologist cap, and began a careful…well, intervention of sorts."

"Did she listen to you?"

"There was no time. She sat there, furious, tight-lipped. She whispered—'Liz, he hits me.' But then her phone rang, and she switched it on. I could hear Judd's demanding voice. He was outside in the car. At the sound of his voice, she wilted, apologized to me, and ran out of the restaurant."

"My God."

"Yes. My God, indeed. I sat there, my coffee cold in front of me, and I told myself: This is a story that's going to have an unhappy ending."

Chapter Eighteen

Hank and I spent the afternoon on Park Street, wandering through the shops and cafés of Little Saigon, covering the same ground we'd surveyed earlier. "One more time," I told him. "Maybe we'll find new people."

Carrying the photos of Frankie and Simon—those deadpan black-and-white photos—we asked the same questions, hoping for different responses. Back to the afternoon of April 10, around four or so, the beginning of rush hour as the streets were clogged with commuters escaping Hartford. Did you happen to spot these boys? In the arcade? In the convenience store on the corner? Anywhere around here? Together, both of them, not one, but both Simon and Frankie, an unlikely twosome, buddies wandering the streets, in-your-face tough guys. Surely you noticed them, no? Anybody? Wise guys, maybe. People notice wise guys.

"Maybe there are just too many wise guys around these days," Hank concluded.

"Yeah, sure," said one man who ran a convenience store that local kids robbed over and over. "All I got in here is wise guys. One buys a soda while the other pockets candy and gum and hot-rod magazines."

No one remembered the boys. I was not surprised, though I hoped for some spark of recognition. Days later, weeks later, there might be someone who'd recall the boys, someone skipped by the police. Out sick, out of town, indifferent. "Oh yeah, sure thing. I remember the Asian kid. He bought a *ban mi* from me. Complained the pork tasted like crap. I thought—shit, the kid's a black boy. But those eyes."

No such luck this time.

Hank and I had lunch at Bo Kien Restaurant. At midday on Sunday the small restaurant, a narrow corner space with an unpainted plywood counter and mismatched tables and chairs, was filled with Vietnamese. Old shriveled women with worn canvas bags of groceries from Saigon Market, young families speaking in Vietnamese and English, sliding from one language to the other, the small children glib and fluent. Hank and I sat at the smallest table for two, wedged into the narrow space that led to the bathroom.

Hank looked around the room at the chattering families. "Little Simon," he whispered, "what's your story?"

"The boys who won't be helped."

"Are we going down Russell Street? VietBoyz?"

"We have no choice."

"They're not gonna be happy to see us."

"I don't expect they will be."

"We're not gonna learn anything there." He glanced toward the street.

"No, Hank, I don't believe that—otherwise I wouldn't go. Maybe JD'll say something different today."

"Because of the morning's *Courant*? The arrest?"

"Bingo. That's why I want to stop in. That gangland world may have shifted overnight."

That morning's *Courant* reported that Hartford police, working with a state police task force, had arrested Mickey Tinh late yesterday afternoon. He'd been identified as the sole shooter of a Chinese banker during a home invasion on Prospect Avenue. The BTK New York gang had been known for such home invasions, often the homes of Asian businessmen who famously kept wads of cash hidden in plain sight. Three or four thugs had stormed the Prospect Avenue mansion. But only Mickey had been caught.

"The scary one from our last visit," Hank commented.

"They were all scary. But that Born To Kill tattoo on Mickey was a little…disconcerting."

Hank mocked me, a gleam in his eye. "Yeah, Rick, that's the word that comes to mind…disconcerting."

Mickey, son of one of the most notorious BTK gunmen from Chinatown. The father, Voung Ky Tinh—Vick— had been killed in a shootout with FBI agents, a chase that moved through Canal Street and also resulted in the death of a woman visiting from Iowa who happened to be in the line of Vick's firepower. The *Courant* noted that authorities had been monitoring the move of Vick's son, Ming, a.k.a. Mickey Tinh, since his arrival at the VietBoyz storefront. In fact, the *Courant* used the arrest of Tinh as a focal point for an article about the "alleged" gang activity on Russell Street, a fact that must have jarred the placid citizenry of the town. "One more gang," Detective Ardolino was quoted as telling the reporter. "You got you the Nelson Court, the Solidos, the new generation Latin Kings, the Asylum Hill Marauders." He'd ended with a sarcastic remark to the reporter. "I can keep going, lady. There's a gang on every corner. When do you want me to stop?"

Over my morning coffee I'd read that passage, and grinned— good old Ardolino, making friends with the Fourth Estate.

Ardolino was also quoted talking about the Russell Street storefront. He hinted at drug trafficking, money laundering, extortion, threats to local businesses, mysterious explosions in noncompliant Chinese restaurants, and the familiar home invasions of Asian success stories.

A security camera had caught Mickey's unmasked face as he fled, unlike the others whose faces remained hidden. He was picked up after using a stolen credit card. A Korean dry cleaner on South Whitney had argued with him about the card, and Mickey, never the most serene of customers, had gone berserk, shoving the shopkeeper, pushing over a rack of clothing, unaware that the Korean owner's trembling wife, hidden in back, phoned 911. The state police already had an APB out on him and arrived at the dry cleaner's just as Mickey was storming out. Cornered, he reached for his .45, tucked into the waistband of his jogging suit. A state cop shot him in the shoulder.

"One down," Hank commented now.

When we walked into the storefront, JD looked up. He'd been sitting by the doorway, a wad of cash gripped in his hand as he counted out bills into neat piles. He jumped, the money sliding to the floor. His face flushed with anger, he ducked down, scooped up the scattered bills and jammed them into a drawer. Standing, he faced us. Behind him, a group of young men sat playing cards at a table. Others were gathered around a tablet. The sound of gunfire, screeching tires, yelling. A Hong Kong kung-fu flick. I heard dubbed-in Vietnamese. A classic—*Love and Death in Little Saigon*. Probably an initiation film for the young street soldiers, mind-boggling violence shown in slow motion.

"You got a fucking invitation?"

"Open house." Hank's head swung left and right, taking in the room.

JD let out a false laugh. "Yeah, more like open season."

"You lost one of your boys," I said.

Unblinking, cold. "A visiting lecturer from New York."

That surprised me. "Very nice. A lecturer?"

"We're a social club."

"Can we sign up?" Hank asked.

"Yeah, a state cop. Gonna make you Secretary of Hate."

"A pun?" I asked.

He turned away and checked out the room. "Can I help you? Again?"

The card players had stopped to watch us, but the young guys watching the video could care less. Mainly young Asian boys, perhaps late teens, early twenties. They all looked similar with their close-cropped shaved heads or their slicked-back hair gleaming with mousse, gold stud earrings, bulky sports jerseys, shit-kicking boots, and tight, unhappy mouths. A shooting on the screen, and their bodies shifted to the side, heads rolled back, delighted. Shoot-'em-up music, a drumbeat.

One of the card players nodded at another. A young guy with a nose ring quietly moved his jacket, covering up what I realized was a .357 resting on an seat. Someone shifted an carton of Chinese food while his elbow bumped an empty beer can. It hit the floor and rolled.

"You know why we're here," I told JD. "Thought we'd check in."

JD debated what to say, looking back at the rows of upturned young faces, expectant, hostile.

"Maybe it ain't your job to do that." JD spoke quietly.

"I got nothing else to do." I watched his face.

Some kid behind him tittered, then thought better of it when the guy next to him shot him a questioning look.

"No one in Little Saigon saw them that afternoon—except you."

JD's voice got louder. "I told you that." His hand waved around the room. An unfunny smile covered his face. "I guess I ain't a good witness for the cops."

"Maybe it's the folks you hang out with."

"I'm the leader of the pack. *Dai lao*." Big brother. But he leaned closer, his voice confidential. "Maybe they're doomed, them boys. Saigon and Frankie. They're just—wannabe gangsters, the two of them." His words were spaced out, menacing. "Maybe they hangin' these days with new friends who ain't the kind you can bring home to Mommy."

"Tell me something, JD. Frankie's brother Jonny"—I saw his eyes widen, wary—"says he couldn't get here that afternoon. The Portuguese church a had a procession down Park."

He spoke over my words, "Yeah, so what?"

"Well, Frankie mentioned it. Sort of tells me he *was* here."

"Shit. I already told you that."

"I'm checking it out."

"Good for you. But there ain't no answers here." Again he waved his hand around the room.

"They're hard boys to save."

"Maybe they don't believe they can be saved." He pointed behind him. "None of us can be saved."

"A rung of hell, this place?"

He sneered. "You got that right. Hell is the only place open at night."

I shifted gears. "So the cops swarmed all over you yesterday?" I waited a bit. Then, slowly, "After they picked up Mickey Tinh across town."

"Yeah, local pigs and the fucking F's." The FBI. "That Ardolino is a bulldog. An asshole. I keep telling him we're a social club. No drugs here. No crime spree. No nothing."

I laughed. "I bet he doesn't believe you."

"Well, neither do you."

"There must be a reason for that, no?"

"Yeah, pigs gotta act a certain way."

"I'm not a cop."

He pointed at Hank. "He is. A general in Uncle Ho's Cong army."

Hank bristled, looked ready to say something, but kept quiet.

"My only concern is Simon Tran."

"And Frankie Croix, no? Don't forget the white boy."

"I wasn't planning on it."

He looked bored now, enough game-playing. "Well." He glanced behind him at the upturned young faces. "Time for you to go."

The young girl I remembered as Lana sidled up to him, blended into his side, and he wrapped his arm around her waist, pulled her closer. I noticed a tattoo on her forearm. Green-and-red lettering. *Doi la so khong.* Life is worthless. Another above it: *Tien.* Money. For a second he buried his face in her neck, whispered something that made her giggle, and then he pushed her away. She pouted.

I nudged Hank, who turned toward the door. Reaching into my breast pocket. I took out one of my business cards. It seemed a foolish act, but I handed it to JD, who debated taking it. Finally, reluctantly, he did, but he stared down at it, eyes narrowed. For a moment I wondered if he knew how to read. So many of these lost boys, street wanderers, were illiterate— I knew that from dealing with such kids back in Manhattan many years back. They survived with an "X" in the appropriate box, but unfortunately that box often led them into deep and troubled waters. But JD, fingering the card, read the words out loud: "Rick Van Lam, Private Investigator, Gaddy Associates." He read the address, but in a slow, jerky voice, as if unsure of pronunciation. I took the card back. On the back I wrote my Farmington address and my phone number.

"Call me if you hear anything." I pointed. "My home."

"I never leave the city," JD announced.

"Why not?"

"I go to a place like Farmington and all I see is white people."

"I'm there."

"Yeah," he laughed, "but you got most of your foot solid in some country club. Your Viet Cong blood is like a bad cold that you can't shake."

With that he stepped back, bowed toward the doorway. Flicking my index finger toward him in what I hoped was a friendly valedictory, I left, one step behind Hank.

"Follow me," I told Hank.

We returned to Bo Kien Restaurant where we ordered jasmine tea and bean pudding. The waitress, startled by our return, smiled at Hank. She was a pretty girl, maybe twenty, in painted-on jeans, a loose peasant blouse, and rap-video gold loop earrings that made too much noise. She smelled of gardenia perfume. She gave Hank a lot of attention. "*Toi ten la Emily.*" My name is Emily.

"We're going to watch that doorway," I told Hank.

Sitting by the front window, we could see, at a crooked angle, the dead-end street and the doorway of the storefront.

"What for?"

"You know, Hank, we did learn something from JD."

"What?" He tilted his head. "Sounded liked the same bullshit to me."

"Well, he confirmed that the Portuguese church blocked the street that afternoon. Score one for Frankie telling the truth. And, more importantly, he talked of Simon and Frankie as wannabes, suggesting he sees them as hangers-on, not really part of the gang but there, hungry to be included. But JD is bothered by something else. He was telling us something is going on."

"But we're still back to square one."

"Maybe. Maybe not." I nodded toward the street. "I want to see what happens there."

We waited. A long, drifting afternoon, the two of us lingering over tea. The young waitress Emily flirted with Hank, which flattered him, insisting he knew her family. But she also gave us a certain grace because no one asked us to leave. At one point Hank began fidgeting, twisting in his seat, and I suggested he go for a walk. I'd sit there alone. After all, I was the investigator—and one used to the long, dreadful empty hours of surveillance.

He rejected that idea. "The only problem is that I may end up married by the time we leave."

At one point Lana left the storefront, but returned with a paper bag, a two-liter bottle of Coke tucked under her arm. Two or three anonymous boys left, sullen youngsters who plowed their gangland way through clusters of old women with shopping carts filled with lemongrass and soymilk. A kid walked in, almost a jaunty skip to his walk. But largely the storefront was quiet.

Late in the afternoon a car turned the corner and parked close to the entrance, its front wheels up on the cracked sidewalk. I poked Hank. "Look."

The massive white guy I recalled as T-Boy stepped out, scratched his belly exposed under the T-shirt, lit a cigarette. He looked back toward the street, his eyes searching for something—or someone. His passenger door opened and Frankie Croix's brother, Jonny, slinked out, looking over the roof of the car toward T-Boy. He gestured angrily, and T-Boy, unhappy, gave him the finger and flicked his cigarette over the top of the car. Jonny roared and headed into the storefront, T-Boy close behind him, yelling after him.

"Probably prison buddies," Hank commented.

"Yeah. But maybe that's how young Frankie came to meet Simon. Here—at the storefront. Hanging out with his older brother. One day little lost Simon comes in for succor."

Hank grinned. "Succor? More likely a joint. Or maybe Frankie and Simon hung out there first."

"Unlikely. I don't think a creep like Jonny follows anyone. Frankie hero-worships that piece of goods."

"Maybe they're having a board meeting this afternoon," Hank went on. "Executive chambers."

I flicked my head toward the street. "Look."

We hadn't noticed a low-slung Toyota with dark tinted windows pulling up at the corner, five or six car-lengths down from the storefront, idling in a fire hydrant zone. Even from inside the restaurant I could hear the *thump thump thump* of a heavy bass line.

"They just get here?" Hank asked.

I nodded. While we watched, both doors opened. Two Asian men walked out, both peering anxiously at the front right tire. Conferring, evaluating, one kicking the rubber as if to test its air power. One guy said something to the other, who didn't look happy.

"Christ, the guys who picked up Simon and Frankie from the Coffee Pot," Hank said.

The same two men, one carefully buttoning his black linen sports jacket, adjusting his metallic wraparound sunglasses. The other one was shorter, sporting the same metallic sunglasses. But he wore a white cotton shirt under his black jacket, on his feet, black kung-fu slippers. No socks. Vietnamese, yes, and even from where I watched I could discern a splash of green tattoo across the neck of the taller one. Both stared at the storefront, but didn't move.

Hank and I looked at each other. "Gang members?" he asked.

"Probably, but they're not going inside—no official homage to JD, it seems. A violation?"

"What does it mean?"

"Thugs moving in on JD's territory? Outsiders? Making themselves known? Maybe up from Bridgeport."

"JD's gonna declare war, Rick."

They stood next to their car, the music blaring, too loud, making a point. A presence on Russell Street, but something was wrong. Who were they? A New York gang? D.O.A. from Canal Street? The Viet Crips, a bloodthirsty gang, muscling in? A gang known for robbing banks, hitting massage parlors and pool halls. Was JD's world threatened?

I started to say something but abruptly stopped. Scooting around the corner, looking out of breath, Simon and Frankie flew across the street, dodged a Budget rental truck lumbering by, and stopped short next to the Toyota. Frankie called out, "Joey. Diep." The taller Vietnamese took off his sunglasses, pointed at Frankie, and Frankie threw up his hands in the air. An it-ain't-my-fault gesture. The smaller man pointed to the backseat, and Simon and Frankie tumbled in. The other man hopped into the front seat and the car backed out of the space and squealed off, swerving, in a burst of speed that left a strip of rubber behind. The bass line of some rap song grew louder as the car streamed past the window where I stood. The dark tinted windows hid the occupants.

I looked at Hank. "*Van hoa toc do.*" A life devoted to speed and sensation. The wild life. A candle burning at both its ends. "They believe they can tackle any ghosts they meet."

"What are you talking about?" From Hank. "I can't believe it—Simon and Frankie with those thugs?"

"That's what JD hinted at, Hank. Another camp, moving in. The young soldiers have no allegiance to him."

"But they look like hit men."

"None of this is good," I said. I looked down the street—the car had disappeared. "None of it."

Chapter Nineteen

Mike Tran asked me to stop in at his shop the next day. He called from the garage where he worked, machines clanging and hissing behind him. Another mechanic yelling out, the *whop whop whop* of an air gun loosening tire bolts.

"I gotta work overtime, but I wanna touch base with you. You ain't called me." He must have regretted his sharp tone because his words were followed by a tinny laugh. "I mean, I don't know how you guys work."

Yes, I told him. I'd stop in the next day at lunchtime.

"Fine." A wail of noise erupted behind him. The shriek of metal against metal. "I gotta go." The line went dead.

Mike worked as a grease monkey at Lesso's Auto Body and Repair on Route 6, a three-bay garage connected to a Dunkin' Donuts and an Indian grocery. When I arrived just before noon, he was waiting for me in the small reception room, a paper cup of vending-machine coffee in his hand. He'd rolled up the sleeves of his blue work shirt, a sewn-on name tag identifying him as "Mike."

"I can't leave," he said. "But we can get a bite in the back office. Just us."

I trailed him through the busy garage, cars up on lifts, another with a fender being primed for painting. A chubby man in dungarees and a baseball cap yelled out, "Hey, Mike, you got you a half hour, okay?"

Mike nodded back at him.

We sat on hard-backed chairs in a small room that also held a corner desk covered with work orders. Dixie cups, crumpled-up McDonald's wrappers. A small refrigerator covered with magnets. A wall calendar that featured a rustic covered bridge for the month of April. A pot with coffee so thick it could be classified as tree resin. I shook my head: no thanks. No coffee.

"Wise choice," he laughed.

He took out two bottles of spring water from the fridge, snapped off the caps. He reached into the back and took out a brown paper bag. "I took the liberty, Rick. I got you the wife's *ban mi*. Okay?"

I nodded.

He handed me the Vietnamese sandwich: a crispy baguette filled with sliced pork, pickled carrots, daikon, and cucumber. "The wife's special," he commented. "Nothing like it."

He was right: marinated pork with a rich paté. He watched my face carefully, noting my approval.

"You wanted to talk to me?"

He put down his sandwich, his face folding in.

"Things happening," he said slowly. "I mean, I read in the *Courant* about that arrest in Little Saigon, that gang thug Mickey Tinh. The cops…they got an eye on that place now. This JD character. The *Courant* said he charms the reporters…"

"You're afraid for Simon?"

He nodded vigorously, his eyes suddenly moist.

"This ain't good, Rick." A deep intake of breath as he fumbled with the pack of cigarettes in his breast pocket. "Can't smoke in here. Christ. The world we created." Angry, he looked into my face. "I want you to understand something about my kids."

"All right." I waited.

Another intake of breath, a nervous twist of his head. "I think I came off as a bastard when you came to my house that time. With Hank. I think you got the wrong impression of me."

I held up my hand. "Mike, the impression I got was of a man devoted to his kids."

A broad smile. "You got that right." The smile disappeared. "But my wife says I come off too…harsh…like I'm always demanding…judging."

"Mike, I don't judge you."

He clicked his tongue. "Sometimes I think everybody else does. Especially my kids. I can't do nothing right by them. All I ever wanted was that they have a life that…ain't like mine." He made a fist and rapped the table. "This life of grease and oil."

"You've made a decent life, Mike."

"Yeah, I got a house, a good wife, good schools."

"Then what?"

A helpless look covered his face. An explosive bang from the shop—he jumped, stammered, "Shit." Then, slowly, "It's like I don't understand the world I created. Take Simon. Like he's in trouble. Probably gonna get in more trouble. It's like I don't know who he is anymore. Sixteen now, a dropout. I can't control that…and since coming home from Long Lane he's different. And now this old guy attacked and dying like that and the cops blaming Simon and Frankie. Well, Rick, Simon's *worse* now. He tells me he never wants to go to prison, but he's in the streets, he goes to that VietBoyz place."

"I know."

He leaned forward, anxious to say something. "Now the boys are hanging with two older Vietnamese guys. Twice I seen them riding in their car. It's—it's like, I don't know, the boys got brainwashed by these punks. I trailed that car 'cause I seen Simon hop in. They drive around, slow down, here and there, and I start to sweat. Are they gonna rob somebody? With my boy in the backseat? Shit, I almost rammed their car with my truck. I don't say nothing to Simon. He'll flip out. I, well"—he stared into my face—"that's why I talk to you."

"What do you think of Frankie?"

"You know, when he first brought this kid Frankie to the house, I was happy. Simon never had no friends at school. A scholarship to Kingswood-Oxford but he's lonely there. He got kicked out. Michael and Wilson—they love it there. Well, I think they do. Secrets—they keep secrets from me. So Simon goes to public high school. No friends. Always in his room. Him and Wilson share a room but they're like strangers. Except when they play those goddamned video games and crap like that."

"Yeah, I know." For a second he turned away, his lips trembling. "It's okay, Mike."

He smiled back at me. "This Frankie, yes, a little rough at the edges, a coarse mouth, everything 'fuck this, fuck that.' Even in front of me and my wife. But I think—okay, a friend. Then I learn Simon met him at the VietBoyz headquarters—Simon says Frankie's older brother hangs there—so I start to worry. But he's always okay with me, quiet-like. It's just the...eyes. They stare at you, like mean and hard. I had a neighbor who had a dog with those eyes. You always kept your distance."

"And then they got sent to Long Lane."

His fist hit the edge of the table. A piece of waxed paper slipped to the floor. When I bent to pick it up, he told me, "Leave it, for Christ's sake. I'll never understand that shit. Knocking folks over for the fun of it. Maybe 'cause they smoke weed. Who knows what else? I don't know. It's like I tell Lucy—who are these kids today? You know, Simon was my favorite. I know I shouldn't say that, but he was. The baby who looked like me. A curse, it turned out. Black *bui doi*. Double whammy, no? You and me, right, Rick? But you got you some white blood. You're... halfway home to America."

"Still and all."

He watched my face. "All right, all right. It don't matter now. I know I pushed Simon hard—I pushed all the kids hard. Maybe I forgot to smile at them. I *demanded*. You know, that was a mistake, I realize now. Christ, I drove them so that each one found a way to get back at me. With Simon he closed down. Just shut down, like he found the 'on' switch and clicked it to 'off.' The more I yelled, the more I pushed his face into books, the more he became...a stone. My fault. I know that now. I only wanted..."

"The best," I finished. "Nothing wrong with that."

Fury in his voice. "Yes, there is, as it turns out. That's when he found the streets. Out there"—he pointed through the cement wall toward the outside—"there were assholes that told him to do whatever the fuck he wanted to do."

"Except listen to you."

"You got that right. But what I'm telling you, Rick, is that I made a big mistake. I wanted perfection from my kids, and now I know nobody gets perfection in this world. You don't even come close. I punished…imperfection. Everything backfired."

"Not everything, Mike."

His voice bitter, "Yes, everything. I made mistakes not knowing they was mistakes. I spanked my boys, Rick, and a teacher spotted it—called DCF on me." He fumed. "The fucking Department of Children and Families. They warned me, so I stopped. But that's not the way it is—the way I grew up." A strange smile. "You know what they tell us—If you don't love your kids, give them candy. If you do love then, take the stick to them. Rick, I *love* my kids."

"I know that, Mike."

He mumbled to himself, "*Giau con hon giau cua.*"

Kids are a poor man's wealth.

"But the others stayed with the books, no? Scholarships."

A sarcastic grunt. "Yeah, if that's what you wanna call success." He took a quick bite out of his sandwich. Then he drained half of the bottle of water, smacked his lips. "Yeah, right."

"Tell me."

"Hazel's grades are slipping at Miss Porter's, and she's on scholarship. All A's, all her life. You know why, don't you?"

"Judd Snow."

His eyes got wide. "You guessed that?"

I smiled thinly. "Nor much investigating there, Mike. I've seen them together. He's very controlling."

His hand slammed the table. "He's gonna ruin her life. Lucy tells me Hazel is scared of him at times—she cries in her room."

"She doesn't know how to get away from him. She thinks she loves him."

"Wow," he said. "You called that one on the money."

"Again, not much investigating."

"He's more than that. She fell for him the first time they met. I blame Wilson—he wanted to learn how to play chess. Well, I don't really blame him—not really. An accident. But she got drunk with him, and he liked it. He got drunk with her. Such a pretty girl—and bright. Miss Porter's. He tells her to jump, and she does. And he tells her to jump not because she needs to but because he knows he can make her. You follow what I'm saying?"

"Yes, I do. Not a boy easy to like."

An unhappy laugh. "To put it mildly. And Michael won't talk to me—told me I want *his* life. I can't even follow what the hell he's talking about. 'Look what you done to me.' Like what? He—well, I have to give up on him."

"And then there's Wilson."

For the first time a genuine laugh. "Christ, the bookworm. If I got to hear him talk about... *Moby Dick* or something, I think I'll go nuts. Yeah, he's become a cocky little shit. You know what he said to me? One day at the supper table? We're sitting there and he says my fingernails are dirty. He's disgusted. 'I'll never have dirty fingernails,' he tells me. I almost smacked him on the side of the head. I'm the garage mechanic that pays the fuckin' bills." A sad hound-dog look swept over his features. "Christ, Rick, my own kids look at me like I'm a disease." His voice trembled.

"I'm sorry, Mike."

"I ain't telling you this to make you feel sorry for me, Rick."

"I know that."

"I don't know why I'm telling all this to you now."

"We're having a talk, Mike."

"You know, Wilson is this chess prodigy. He beats Judd, even his teacher. One time, picking up Wilson at the campus, I saw Judd and some bullies shove Wilson into a wall. When I yelled, Wilson said it was no big deal. 'He's a simple ape.' That's what he said. Calm, like it was nothing. 'Shut up about it.' That's what he yells at me. I think he was embarrassed that I saw. Maybe scared. Rick, Wilson is afraid of Judd. And that bothers me.

One time when Judd was at the house he said something—I don't know what—but Wilson started to shake. Another time Judd said to him, 'My shining knight takes your measly pawn.' Wilson looked hurt. I still don't know what that meant."

A head poked into the room, startling us. "Mike, what the hell?"

Mike rustled the papers on the table. "I'm over. I'll work overtime. But I wanted to—one of the reasons I asked you here today is—the fee? What do I owe you for your work? We ain't talked about it."

"No, Mike, no charge."

He got flustered. "I ain't a charity case."

"It's not charity. It's something I want to do."

He sat back, considered my words, and said "No."

"How about this, Mike? If I solve anything, you write a check to the Boys' Club of Hartford."

He nodded. "You sure?"

"Positive."

"It's a Vietnamese thing, right?" A sloppy grin.

"You could put it that way."

He stood up, swept the sandwich wrappings into a trash bin. "Follow me out back."

I sat in the passenger seat of his dented Ford pickup, the cloth upholstery ripped and stained, the radio missing a knob. Food wrappings on the floor. A smashed-in Budweiser can. A carton from a Chinese restaurant, dried soy sauce on the flap. An ashtray pulled out and overflowing with Camel butts. The acrid smell of old cigarette smoke and fast food. Watching me, he rolled down his window. "Nobody sits in this truck but me."

"And me?"

"An experience you probably won't repeat." He laughed at his own joke.

"What do you want to show me, Mike?"

He reached over and opened the glove compartment and pulled out a large manila envelope, wrinkled, grease-stained. It was thick with newspaper clippings. Quietly, a bunch at a time, he handed me clippings from the *Courant*, from the *New Britain Herald*, from the *West Hartford News*, carefully scissored clippings. Some yellowed and torn, dirt stains, coffee stains. Awards for his children, Dean's List, Honor Society, Woodsman of the World medallions, scholarships from a women's club. A library commendation for Wilson. Dozens of them. Michael, Hazel, Wilson, even Simon. A middle-school commendation, Simon accepting the award in front of the school sign. He looked joyous. I'd never seen Simon look—joyous.

"Impressive."

Mike grabbed them back from me, stuffed them back into the envelope, and dropped the envelope into his lap. His hands rested on the folder, his fingers interlaced.

When he faced me, his face was broken and tired. "Sometimes I think that if I threw this envelope away, I could start all over."

"Why?"

His voice shook. "Then maybe I could do it right this time."

Chapter Twenty

The message from Michael Tran on my home phone sounded urgent. When I reached him late at night, the urgency had passed. Instead, in a yawning, lazy voice he said something had come up that bothered him.

"Urgent? That's what you said."

"Well, yes. I don't misuse the English language, you know."

"What is it?"

A long pause. "You woke me up."

"Urgent, you said." Now I was impatient. "I also understand the English language."

I could hear him laugh. "Touché. It's just that…well, a couple of things are bothering me…worrying me. Actually, yes." He deliberated. "I've tried to stay out of my family's petty nonsense, but that seems impossible."

"Tell me."

"A call from Hazel, who never calls me. She's worried about Simon, which I don't think she ever is. And a visit from Simon who slept on my couch again but who is…different. Also, well, worried, if I can judge by the look on his face and his muttered conversation about the state of things in his part of the world."

"I still don't understand why you're calling me."

An edge to his voice. "Well, you are the investigator in all this, as I recall from your visit to my apartment. If anyone can give me a perspective on what's happening, it has to be you."

"And you want a perspective?"

A sardonic laugh. "Amazing, isn't it, Mr. Lam? I surprised myself by making that phone call to you. Maybe there's hope for me after all." He laughed outright, but immediately stopped. "I have no proof of anything, but suspicions, worries. Could we meet tomorrow for a drink? Right now I'm sleeping. You did wake me up. Otherwise you'd have heard more worry—maybe wonder—in my voice."

I agreed, hung up the phone, and sat back in my chair, mulling over a conversation that bothered me—because I realized how much I disliked the smug young man.

Late the next afternoon I met him at a tavern on Park called Gully's, a watering hole a block or so from Little Saigon. He'd nixed my suggestion to meet at a small bar and grill called Xuong's, a dark hole-in-the-wall largely populated by Vietnamese workers straggling back after numbing shifts in the nearby Colt factory on New Park. "No, Gully's," he said. "I don't go into Little Saigon without a court order." Then that arch laugh. "Sometimes I meet friends at Gully's."

A local college bar with wet T-shirt contests and sloppy pitchers of sticky green beer on St. Patrick's Day. University of Hartford frat house celebrations that spilled into the pizza joint next door. Ecstasy with a chaser of spicy pepperoni.

At mid-afternoon the place was nearly empty, a booth of shaggy men in splotchy painter's pants and white caps lingering over a pitcher of beer. Now and then a heated exchange. Thick Slavic accents. Refugees from Little Bosnia by Barry Square in the south end of Hartford. They faced each other across a table with looks that suggested they'd never met one another before and were resentful that strangers had plopped down uninvited opposite them.

I sat across the room, ordered a bottle of Tsingtao, stared out the window, and watched Michael parking his old Lexus in front. He hadn't won his National Merit Fellowship to Trinity based on his parallel parking skills. I was sure of that.

He shook my hand and smiled as he slipped into a seat opposite me. Dressed in a brilliant purple polo shirt and creased khakis over brown loafers, a light tan spring jacket hugging his shoulders, he looked relaxed. A recent haircut, neat and conservative, a hint of scissored hair across his ear lobes. "Good to get out of the apartment for a bit. Too much studying makes me a dull boy."

For all his mission of urgency he now acted breezy, nonchalant, with all the time in the world. Even his voice had lost the tempered, stilted inflection I'd noticed in his apartment and even last night on the phone. A performance? I wondered. Perhaps the lazy-eyed girlfriend who'd watched us from across the room in his apartment—probably occupying a pillow last night as I roused him from sleep—compelled him to affectation and attitude.

He glanced around the place. "At night, sitting here with friends from Trinity, the place is hard-core rock 'n' roll. And pseudo-intellectual pyrotechnics from the pretenders."

I pointed to the inebriated house painters. "Now it's round one."

He squinted at them. "They look angry."

"And drunk."

"That, too." He ordered a beer—Heineken—and admonished the barmaid, "Make sure it's ice cold."

She smiled at him. "I'll fly it in from Alaska."

He winked at her, which bothered me. But she seemed to expect it from him.

"You come here a lot?"

He ignored the question, instead leaning in, arms folded on the table. "You know, Hazel never calls me. We're not that close. She thinks I've left the family."

"You have."

His kneejerk smirk annoyed me. "Well, there *is* that. But for her to call me, well, I guess I had to sit up and take notice."

"What did she say?"

But Michael wanted to tell his story with his own syncopated rhythm. He waited a bit, watching me closely, and then said, "We were never close."

"You already told me that."

Now he grinned. "At first I didn't even recognize her voice. It sounded—strained, echoey, like she was calling from a tunnel. Then she said, 'It's me. Hazel.' Then she yelled, 'Your sister.' That was unnecessary. So I waited and she started to ramble on and on until I broke in. 'Hazel, what the hell? What's the matter?' Then she started to sob."

He paused as the barmaid set down the beer and stood there, waiting for his comment. But he didn't even look up at her. She walked away, her shoulders tight.

Women probably found Michael attractive: a long narrow face, rich mocha skin, lazy eyes, that shock of neatly barbered hair, even modest dimples when he smiled. But more so, I realized, was the aura of aloofness he projected, a suggestion of erotic distance that probably drew women in, challenged them, made them hungry to earn a hesitant grin from him. He'd written his script, and knew its nuances and triggers.

Back when I was a National Merit Fellow who still believed I had no right to be anywhere in the world—and that at any minute someone would snatch everything away from me—I wore a medieval hair shirt to class. Michael obviously suffered no such squeamishness. For a second I was jealous of that self-possession. Me, forty years old, staring at a boy who could be my Vietnamese son. Like me, mixed blood. Unlike me, ignoring it.

He was talking in a slow drawl, hypnotic. "First off, there's this Judd character. The blond white boy from Avon that I've never met but heard lots about from Simon. The über-male, Nietzsche's Will to Power Nazi. Hazel, at least according to Simon, can't stay away from him—yet *wants* to. I love you but please leave me alone. Simon hates him. I guess there have been run-ins, especially with Simon's dim-watt buddy, Frankie." He stopped, flicked his head to the side. "Anyway, that's a different story. Sort of. Hazel told me she wants to get away from Judd— break it off. But she can't. I guess she's been building her—her what?—liberation? She told me he hit her. *Hit her!*" He yelled out the words. "That fucking cave man. That was the last straw. She mentioned your ex-wife, Liz. Helping her."

"Well, she has to leave Judd." I locked eyes with him. "Hazel has no choice."

"But she can't break it off. Whenever she talks of taking time off—that lovely euphemism for desertion and abandonment—he goes ape-shit." Michael looked into my face and repeated, fury in his voice, "He *hit* her."

I cringed. "Liz'll know what to do. She occupies an office in a police station."

"No," Michael thundered. "No."

"What? Why?"

"Hazel told me she'd handle it. She wants to keep Liz away. I guess this Neanderthal has a thing for Liz." Michael threw his hands into the air. "I don't know. It's so messy, and I have tried to keep my life away from all that." He fluttered his fingers as though shooing away pesky gnats.

"If she's afraid of Judd…"

He drained the last of his beer. "No cops, she said." A sly grin. "Aren't there enough cops slithering around the Tran household?"

"Still and all…"

He signaled the barmaid for another beer. "But that's not the only reason she called me. And the reason I finally called *you*. She mentioned being worried about Simon. And that surprised me."

"So she never expressed worries before?"

"Not to me, at least. When he was hauled off to Long Lane and exile in that penal colony, she was indifferent, shrugging her shoulders. Simon as dumb kid. That was her attitude, at least as I heard it from my mother. I never talked to Hazel about it."

"But something has changed?"

The barmaid put two beers on the table. She leaned into Michael. "Cold as your heart."

He looked into her face. "Sally, you need a new line."

She tapped him affectionately on the shoulder. His eyes followed her back to the kitchen. "Anyway," Michael continued, "Hazel says that Simon talked to her when she came home for the weekend—hinted that he had a secret that he couldn't tell her. Something he found out—suspected maybe. Lord, a secret.

What? Hazel said he sounded real scared. And that affected her—made her stop checking her lipstick in the mirror or ordering another Hermès scarf online."

"You're cruel."

"Thank you."

"But what secret?" I wondered out loud. "I mean, Simon slinks around the streets, a boy who likes to play tough with the VietBoyz"—Michael raised his eyebrows, dismissive—"so I can't imagine what would finally get to him."

"Hazel didn't know, but it bothered her enough to reach out to—me. Me! I've become the family confessor. Father Michael of Our Lady of Perpetual Misery Day Camp."

I laughed. "I grew up in a Catholic orphanage in Vietnam."

"It shows."

That rankled me. "Really?"

"Yeah, you look at the world as a big cesspool, your eyes filled with wonder. That's why you chose your profession."

"A reading from the Missal of St. Michael the Arch-Villain, Reader's Digest Condensed Version."

He grinned widely now. "I get around."

"Do you think it has anything to do with the death of Ralph Gervase?"

"Who?"

That annoyed me. "The old man knocked over and killed, the man who…"

He broke in. "Oh, him. Sorry, I can't remember the name of every old drunk toppling over on Hartford streets. But, to answer your question, I have no idea."

"Maybe Judd Snow?"

"I can't imagine what Simon has to do with that. Although Hazel did say Judd likes to refer to Simon as 'the family murderer,' much to her chagrin. She told him to stop, but telling Judd to stop is to open the floodgates of verbal assault." He started to peel off the paper label the bottle of beer, his fingernails scratching the wet paper, balling it up, flicking the round missiles away from the table.

"Maybe Simon knows something about Frankie. The Viet-Boyz. His older brother, Jonny."

"Christ, what are you talking about? Simon is turning informant for the Feds? They'll put him in a witness protection program and change his name to...Jackie Chan." He pointed a finger at me. "I do remember something Hazel said. When she told Judd boy she wanted her 'space'"—Michael mimed two quotation marks in the air—"he said that her brother Wilson could have a convenient accident."

"What?"

"I guess Wilson's on his shit list since he's become the chess master royal of the prep school. The new darling of the chess club advisor, sent into North Hartford to instruct minority kids in the rudiments of a game they can't afford to play. Judd was the star of that outreach camp. But Wilson refused to ride with Judd. He takes the bus—two buses to the boys' club. Can you blame him?"

"Maybe Simon confided in Wilson—his secret."

He was shaking his head vigorously. "No, I asked her that. She said that if it isn't about a chess move or...or *Huck Finn* or some god-awful term paper that's due tomorrow, rush, rush—well, he's not listening." He tapped the bottle with his finger. "The boys like each other—don't like each other."

"So what do you want me to do? You asked for this meeting."

He sat back and smirked. "You're an investigator, no? Credentialed and certified and solidified and verified? Find out what's tearing apart my family."

"And your role?"

His eyes widened. "Well, I just did my part. I off-loaded the misery onto you." He reached into his pocket and took out a wallet, signaled to the barmaid. "I have to leave." He started to slide out of the booth.

"One minute, Michael. Sit down."

He did, though reluctantly.

"I want you to call Hazel and tell her to call Liz. I'm going to talk to Liz later. You need to encourage Hazel to get help. She can't do this alone. If Hazel wants to end this thing with Judd, she'll need support."

He didn't answer, but I could tell he was thinking of what to say. Finally, scratching the side of his face, he mumbled, "Will do."

"Thanks."

He leaned forward across the table, his voice low. "Another thing, now that I think of it. Simon slept on the sofa the other night. This was before Hazel's call. No secrets revealed to me, by the way. Anyway, the next day I decided to drive him back home. But when we turned off New Britain Avenue, headed to our home, he tensed up. There was some beat-up Toyota parked at the end of our street. He ducked down in the seat."

"Tinted windows?"

"Yeah."

"Two Vietnamese guys."

"You know them?"

"I've seen them, Simon and Frankie in the backseat of that car."

"Well, Simon wasn't happy. I asked him what the hell was going on. He mumbled two names. Diep and Khoa. And then sneered, Joey and Kenny. Brothers. Diep the older. The only thing he said was that he knew them and they were looking for him and Frankie."

"Why?"

He shrugged. "He knows them from Little Saigon, I guess. And I guess Frankie—he says it was Frankie—snagged some weed from the guys. A big no-no in gangster land." He breathed out. "Christ, that boy's nothing but trouble."

"What happened?"

"Nothing. By the time I pulled into our driveway and Simon scooted out, hunched over like a corrupt Hartford mayor avoiding the photographers, the Toyota was gone."

"Christ," I mumbled.

Michael stood up, slapped some cash on the table, and nodded at me. "Out of here. Things to do."

I called after him. "Sounds to me like you're becoming part of the family again?"

He stopped walking. "Don't count on it."

"It wouldn't hurt."

"Of course, it always hurts—family."

He started to walk away but turned back. "Well, think about it, Rick. I don't want my brothers and sister—hurt."

I threw out a line in Vietnamese. "*Mot giot mau dao hon ao nuoc la.*" It gave him pause. I could see him translating. I helped him along. "Blood is thicker than water."

"Did you make that up? So clever, the modern PI running with chopsticks at the ready." He sighed. "But I suppose it's true."

"Blood being thicker than water?"

"Blood being preferable to slaughter."

Chapter Twenty-one

Hank bustled into my apartment. "News, news, glorious news." He bowed. "The venerable town crier has arrived." He placed his laptop on my coffee table, and switched it on. "News, news."

"Did you call Big Nose?"

"Of course."

"Big Nose is the real town crier, Hank. Did he come through?"

With the appearance of the Vietnamese gangsters in the low-slung Toyota, I needed information. Kenny and Joey. Khoa and Diep. The slick punks in the black linen suits.

"Yeah," Hank began, "lots to say, running his mouth."

I smiled. "An understatement, Hank."

"Big Nose got the dope from Frankie. The duo moved up from Bridgeport, two slimy brothers. They beat up a massage parlor owner there. They'd been part of the Saigon Crips gang out of Canal Street. They got into trouble there, so they had to get out of town. Loose cannons, nuts. They gravitated to Viet-Boyz because that's what you do if you're a thug, but JD isn't happy with them."

"A power play?"

"Maybe. Probably they want in on the action."

"Which is?"

"Drug activity, mainly. But also extortion, protection. Hookers—pimps." Hank grinned. "Big Nose recited a laundry list."

"So they're not welcome at Russell Street?"

"Big Nose thinks JD is playing them—to keep an eye on them. He's waiting to make a move on them. But they're ruthless—or at least that's the reputation they like. JD is cunning, plays the friendly gangster—we've seen bits of that, no?—but at heart he's dangerous. Some of the young soldiers think the brothers are cool. Those Miami Vice black-linen duds, the guns."

"And Simon and Frankie?"

"JD isn't happy that they're grooming the boys as runners. Flattery—then control."

"Why them?"

"I guess Frankie screwed up bad—ripped them off. Now they got their hooks into the boys. Threats, mainly. Big Nose is scared shitless of them."

"Maybe Simon and Frankie, too."

"They use them as drug runners." A bewildered smile. "Sort of like what JD himself does. Kenny and Joey splashed cash on them, a little weed for their troubles, maybe some liquor, probably not girls but who knows, and the boys got drunk with it."

"Not anymore."

"Right. Diep, the older one, likes to shoot off his gun. Target practice. A real mean streak. Big Nose says he held a gun to Frankie's head—a sort of joke, but Frankie wasn't laughing. Khoa is a little simple-minded, laughs a lot at things that aren't funny. They like to go to bars and pick fights. Flash their guns. Or knives. They brag about ripping off convenience stores. Shoving clerks, hauling off cartons of Marlboros. Mind you, this is Big Nose talking. The boys are afraid to disobey them now. They're in a bind."

"Michael said the guys lay in wait for Simon on his street."

"Yeah, Big Nose said that after Frankie ripped off some weed, a dumb act, things got scary. This is after the gun-to-the-head act. A stupid boy."

"Christ."

"Big Nose says the boys are nervous as hell now."

"What's next?"

"He doesn't know. He no longer stops at Russell Street. Too messed up, he said. 'I seen the blood in their eyes.' That's his line. 'I don't think they're fun anymore.' An epiphany in a sixteen-year-old." Hank waved his hand in the air. "Sort of gives you hope, right, Rick?"

"Yeah, civilization has arrived." I walked to the window, gazed down into the street. "So what'll happen to Simon and Frankie?"

Hank gave it some thought. "Big Nose says he's washed his hands of them. He's staying away. He told me he has a girlfriend now." He laughed. "Big Nose seemed surprised that a girl would *like* him."

I was thinking of Frankie and Simon. "None of this sounds good."

Hank pointed to his laptop on my coffee table, the screensaver an image of a state trooper leaning into the driver's window of a stopped speeding car. "And it's going to get worse."

"What?"

Hank's eyes brightened. "I know folks of your advanced age view social media as one more communicable disease. You refuse to believe that real life is being tweeted and Facebooked and texted nanosecond by nanosecond. Now Big Nose, who travels with a cell phone, a tablet, an MP3 player, and a knapsack filled with violent video games, probably a pair of Google eyeglasses and an Apple watch, and only seems to lack an active account at LinkedIn, asked me innocently what I thought of Simon and Frankie's video, uploaded onto YouTube. Well, that took me by surprise."

I counted a beat. "Well, at *your* advanced age…"

While he was talking, he tapped on the keyboard, brought up the site, typed in a few words, and suddenly there was a line of bold capital letters: SAIGONSEZ—NO GOOD TO CRY.

Hank translated for me. "Do you get it? Simon Says. Saigon…"

"I get it."

The first image was startling. Shot probably in Simon's living room with a backdrop of his mother's knickknacks on a shelf and a curtain slipping off a rod, I marveled at Simon and Frankie's…

well, presence. Both boys gloriously filled the screen. A still shot,
black and white, both assuming slovenly gangsta poses as the
video began: arms folded over their bony chests, heads tilted back
and to the side, eyes narrowed, lips drawn into a belligerent line.
That rhythmic nodding that punctuated a hip-hop performance.
They were dressed in familiar outlaw-boy attire: oversized jerseys
promoting the New England Patriots, tremendously baggy blue
jeans that cascaded over brown work shoes, Alaskan Klondike
gold-nugget necklaces around their necks. Assorted plastic bands
around their wrists. Oddly both boys had braided their shortish
hair into sloppy Bob Marley dreadlocks so that both looked like
country-bumpkin cartoon characters from the old funny papers.

"My God," I said to Hank. "What the hell?"

"Wait," Hank cautioned. "You gotta hear this."

The still shot of the boys dissolved as the video began with
jerky movement, Simon stepping closer to Frankie, then stepping away. Both boys stared into the camera with tough-guy
demeanor. The next shot was a close-up, waist-high. Simon
stared into the camera and announced in an amazingly sure
but high-pitched voice: "We are Saigon"—he pointed to his
own chest—"and Frankie"—a nod toward his partner. "And
we are"—both boys together—"SaigonSez." An uncomfortable
moment as the boys looked at each other.

Frankie then picked up the narration, his voice rough at
the edges, clipped in some tough-guy inflection that reminded
me of James Cagney but was probably stolen from LLCoolJ or
Eminem. *Mama said knock you out… Trailer park girls go round…*

"This here is our first rap. 'No Good to Cry.' Because it ain't
no good to cry. Look around you." Frankie punched the air
with his fist. "You ain't gonna change nothing in the world. Shit
happens. No good to cry."

Simon a.k.a Saigon spoke over his words with a sheepish
grin that belied the words he spoke: "In the name of the devil."

Frankie added, "The situation in Afghanistan."

Saigon echoed, "Afghanistan blood bath, you know." A slight
giggle. "ISIS. Ice baby, ice."

I glanced at Hank. "Current events? Really?"

Frankie repeated in a singsong voice: "Seat-u-a-tion. Seat-u-a-SHUN." Stressed.

Then Frankie reached out of camera range and obviously pressed an "on" button because a driving, iterated bass line began, too loud, a rhythmic duh duh DUH duh duh DUH Boom. And over again. Repeated a couple times, and then Frankie began rapping in a deep heartfelt voice:

In the name of the devil
awright you go to hell
In the name of the devil
awright I'll go to hell.

He paused as Saigon jumped in, spat out the words:

Boys with black and hooded heads
Cool and classy in the street
Talking trash and keeping time
Tattooed savage digs the beat.

Punctuating Simon's lines Frankie sang out in counterpoint:

hide a secret
hide a secret

A pause, then Frankie repeated the refrain:

In the name of the devil
awright you go to hell
In the name of the devil
awright I'll go to hell

Saigon, more confident now, stared into the camera with fierce, penetrating eyes:

See a coffin passing by
It ain't Satan—never never
You and me—no good to cry
Only Satan lives forever.

Frankie's new backing:

practical joke
practical joke
In the name of the devil
awright you go to hell
In the name of the devil
awright I'll go to hell

Saigon thrust his arms out toward the camera, a boxer's aggressive fists:

No tomorrow for a fool
Laugh today, it's all a fake
Forbidden streets ain't got no map
Nowhere to run when you awake

Frankie's parting shot:

hats off to you
hats off to you

Both boys ended with:

In the name of the devil
awright you go to hell
In the name of the devil
awright I'll go to hell

Hank stopped the video. We stared at each other, eyes glazed.
"You look stunned," he said.
"I am stunned. I can't believe this."
"You know what this sounds like, don't you?"
I closed my eyes for a second. Chaotic zigzags of brilliant light in the dark. "Yes, a confession."
"Bingo." Hank pointed at the computer screen. "What in the world are they thinking of?"
"They're thinking of rap music fame, of MTV appearances, streaming video, girls hanging off their beltless pants,

of becoming Justin Bieber, Dr. Dre hustling them off to the Bahamas for lunch with Jay-Z and Beyoncé."

Hank laughed. "You've been watching the E! Network."

"No matter." I pressed a key and the screen woke up. "When was it posted?" I scrolled down.

"That's the kicker. "The day before Jimmy and Ralph were attacked."

"Christ." I saw something else. "There are 8,756 LIKES, Hank. They're finding an audience."

"Well, it's not exactly going viral, Rick. That's a blip on the radar screen of social media."

"Well, all it takes is Detective Ardolino to print out the words and hand them to the D.A. It's…well, a celebration of street thuggery. In the name of the devil no less."

Hank chimed in with a run of quotations. "I've seen it a dozen times, Rick. Boys with black hoodies. Trash talk. Laugh today because it's all a fake. Forbidden streets. A secret. A practical joke. Satan lives forever. Man, you can picture them strutting down the sidewalk, hoodies up, menacing, having the time of their lives because…you're gonna die someday. Only Satan lives forever. So you might as well do your joke, knock your way through life. Hats off to you, boys. Life is short—no good to cry."

I held up my hand. "Enough. I get it." I slumped in the seat. "What are they telling us here, Hank?"

"They're telling us that they work for the devil."

"Not good."

A world-weary smile. "Not good at all. In fact, no good to cry."

Chapter Twenty-two

Late in the afternoon I wrapped up a fraud investigation for Cigna Insurance, pressed SEND, and stood up, stretching out my limbs. I needed to grade papers for my one-night-a-week Criminology class, but I put it off. Time for a nap. The sameness of my investigations sometimes got to me—white-collar crime exhibited a pathetic redundancy. So much of my work involved picayune plodding, and surprisingly the conclusions were often transparent—folks always thought their way to embezzled riches was pioneering. In truth, it was as if the crook simply pressed "replay" on an LP on a turntable that went round and round.

My cell phone jangled. I grabbed it.

I was expecting a return call from Detective Ardolino. Earlier that day, I'd phoned the Hartford policeman but neglected to reach him. I'd left a detailed message on his office machine—"Detective Ardolino's office, I'm not here. This better be important"—letting him know about the incendiary YouTube video from SaigonSez. Though it cast Simon and his cohort in a bad light, I always agreed with Jimmy who stressed transparency. Sooner or later Ardolino would return the favor. A gruff officer of the law, he possessed an abiding if quirky sense of right and wrong.

I hung on his line a little too long, hoping he'd pick up, and ended feebly. "I just thought you should know."

When I told Hank about it, he'd roared, "I'd love to be there when Ardolino brings up YouTube and stares into the quasi-gangsta faces of those boys. All that teenaged testosterone and in-your-face attitude."

I'd thought about that. "I have a feeling Ardolino slams up against that street attitude every day of his working life."

In my phone message I summarized the video, even read a few choice passages from our transcript. Hank had transcribed its curious helter-skelter language. Hank insisted the urban vocabulary and syntax of rap videos demanded *all right* be written *alright*. Or, worse, *awright*. That *you* become *ya*. I cringed at that. That the apostrophe become invisible. And that first person singular, as in *doesn't*, become *don't*—

"Stop," I'd pleaded. "I get it."

So I was expecting a call back from Ardolino, perhaps one laced with sarcasm, a shot of bile, and perhaps a reluctant modicum of thanks.

"Rick." Liz, her voice frantic.

"Oh no."

"Exactly. I'm at work, and we just got a buzz out of Hartford. Seconds ago. Another knockdown attack. This time on Whitney off Farmington. Another man attacked. Violent, cruel. An old man slugged in the side of his head."

"Dead."

"Yes."

My heart raced. "My God."

She hesitated but went on, "APB for two young men last seen running south on Whitney, one report saying they headed toward Sisson. Black hoodies."

A refrain from SaigonSez echoed in my head:
Boys with black and hooded heads.
Cool and classy in the street.

"Christ, Liz."

Liz's voice was scratchy. "There's no proof it's Simon and Frankie."

I grit my teeth. "Yeah. Tell that to Ardolino."

"I'll keep you posted. I'm reading the wires as they come in. It wasn't on the media when I got it, though the TV stations are probably there now."

"I'm headed there. Call me on my cell."

Her voice had an edge. "Rick, maybe you shouldn't go there."

But I was already hanging up and grabbing my jacket. I considered calling Hank, but I knew he was at the Academy, spending the day with some other new recruits he'd become friendly with, the group of four or five young men and women catching a movie and a few beers at a cop bar in Meriden.

I parked at a small strip mall on Farmington Avenue, a line of struggling businesses with lackluster 1950s façades, faded pastel signs with blinking neon. A failed beauty academy, boarded up. A take-out Chinese restaurant notorious for being blown up by Chinatown extortionists—and, I wondered, possibly a recent visit from the VietBoyz. A Spanish bodega with the plate-glass window plastered with LOTTO and MEGA MILLIONS signs. "We had a $1000 Winner!" "You Can't Win If You Don't Play!" "We accept W.I.C. Food Stamps."

A fat man in a greasy T-shirt stood in front, rocking on his heels, a cigarette between his lips, and he frowned as I stepped out of the car. He pointed his cigarette down toward the intersection of Whitney and Farmington. I turned to look—a kaleidoscope of flashing police lights, fire engines, spotlights, and TV satellite trucks. A growing rumble of noise. Screeching tires, a two-way radio blast, a police cruiser taking the corner, siren blaring.

"There," the man said quietly to me. "It ain't safe to leave the house nowadays. *Que lastima!*" I nodded back at him. He rocked on his heels. "Somebody is gonna get you sooner or later. If it ain't those bastard ISIS killers…" He shrugged as I walked away.

No good to cry about it.

As I suspected, the corner of Whitney and Evergreen was cordoned off, a line of yellow tape stretched from a stop sign across the street, wrapped around a light pole, and circled back through a row of cars. A patrolman stood on the perimeter, arms folded, bored.

A crowd of stragglers bunched at the tape, peering, demanding, gossiping. I joined them, pushing to the front, though an old woman clutching a shopping bag filled with empty deposit cans and bottles elbowed me. "My spot." Her fierce voice in my ear made me jump. I ignored her and she elbowed me again. "I was here first."

I waited. I spotted Ardolino conferring with another man by the State Police evidence van, Ardolino dressed in a light tan raincoat that flapped open. Hunched over, speaking into the neck of the other man, he kept pointing his finger toward the body, which lay under a blanket on the pavement. Every so often, though engrossed in the conversation, his eyes swept the crowd, quick penetrating glances that missed nothing. Inevitably his eyes caught me, pressed against the yellow tape. He started, straightened up, and whistled to a patrolman.

He pointed. "Him. The Oriental."

But the cop was confused. Alongside me were two cooks from the Chinese take-out, both in grimy white aprons. Both were chattering in an excited Fujian dialect, and I was surprised that I caught a few words—"bad luck" and "dead." The rest a mishmash. A buddy in college spoke that parochial dialect.

The patrolman was gazing at the two men, who suddenly looked scared, backing off and trying to maneuver themselves away from the crowd. Headed toward them, the cop looked ready to pursue, his hand on his revolver, but Ardolino, frustrated, yelled out, "You damned fool. Are you blind? The one that looks like he got a golf club stuck up his suburban ass."

I bowed.

The cop wasn't happy but let me slip under the tape.

"Your boss is a charmer," I whispered.

"Yeah," he grinned back at me, "a charm-school dropout."

"How did I know you'd be prowling these streets?" Ardolino began.

"Of course I had to come here. I heard it on…"

He held up his hand. "I ain't got time to chat with the likes of you." He started to walk away but swung back, stepped close to me. "But don't go away. Somehow I'm gonna end up talking to you about this shit, and I might as well get it over tonight. Stay right there." He actually pointed to a spot on the pavement, back behind the yellow tape. I took my position, and waited.

As I stood there, a woman rushed up the sidewalk, a policewoman cradling her elbow, and she tried to break free, headed toward the body. Another cop grabbed her arm, but she shrugged him off, wailing, arms flailing, until she stumbled. It was an awful moment, the crowd around me becoming silent as her body rolled back and forth. I breathed in, caught by the raw display, and the moment took me back to New York, to my flatfoot beat in Chelsea. How many times had such a scene played out on a bloody sidewalk? The awful grief that hit a loved one like a senseless tsunami, the dark engulfing sorrow. I'd witnessed it too many times, yet it never failed to stun me. Now, again, this anonymous woman shrieking about the old man dead on the sidewalk.

Ardolino, watching, his pad in hand, didn't budge. But when he looked around again, I noticed that his face was pale as dust.

An hour later, the body removed after the medical examiner made his official pronouncement of death and the evidence squad photographed and bagged and labeled, the crowd drifted away. I waited by the tape with a few stragglers.

At one point, looking back toward Farmington Avenue, I spotted a low-slung Toyota with dark tinted windows idling at the light. Khoa and Diep? Kenny and Joey? They were too far away to tell. The light turned green, but the car didn't move. A red light, then green again. A car behind them blew its horn, but still the Toyota refused to move. Finally, one insistent horn blast erupted from behind, the driver maddened and leaning on the horn, and the Toyota whipped forward, backfired, its occupants returning the horn fire. It disappeared. The Vietnamese brothers? With Simon and Frankie in the backseat?

Finally, darkness falling, streetlights popping on, the street shadowy and bleak, I watched Ardolino nod to another man, tuck his pad into a breast pocket, button the raincoat, and walk away. A dozen yards away he opened the door of George's Pizzeria, but deliberated. He yelled back to the patrolman, "Hey, Sanchez. Yeah, you. Do you see any other cops named Sanchez earning a buck for just hanging around? Yeah, him. Get that guy."

That guy: me. I slipped under the tape and walked by Sanchez.

"As I said," he whispered to me as I passed, a knowing grin on his face, "the dunce sitting in the corner of charm school." I saluted him, and he smiled. "Good luck, amigo."

Inside Ardolino was already sitting at a booth, still in his buttoned-up tan raincoat, hunched over the table. I slid into a seat across from him as he signaled to the waitress. "Honey, a Bud Lite. I'm off-duty." The last was addressed to me. "Don't call the fucking commissioner, Lam boy."

"I probably still have him on speed dial."

"Funny man." He bit his tongue. "Christ, murder makes me thirsty." A sickly smile. "So maybe your bad little boys are back at work. The first one was practice, sort of whetting the appetite. This one was a direct hit." He mimed a fist connecting to the side of my temple. Instinctively I jerked back, which made him laugh.

"What happened, Detective?"

A disingenuous smile. "Maybe Saigon sez…may I take a giant step toward prison?"

"Tell me what happened."

The waitress placed a bottle of beer on the table, waited, looking at me, but I shrugged her off. Ardolino took the paper menu that was wedged between an old-fashioned jukebox player and a crusty sugar container and skimmed the offerings. His finger drummed the laminated paper. "I can't decide if I'm hungry or not."

"Detective, come on."

He dropped the menu and locked eyes with mine. "It's the same goddamned M.O., Rick. You know what I'm saying? Listen to me. This old man, Christ, he had a cane no less, half-blind fucker, and he's hobbling in broad daylight down the sidewalk. He just left his daughter's house. She works as a school aide—you saw her fall to pieces. Every afternoon a walk—for his health. Doctor's orders. So he'll live to a hundred-and-ten. Like anyone wants to in this town. Anyway, he's making his way slow and sure, baby steps, and he's down here on Whitney. Just down from the shops. Here on a stretch where the welfare apartment houses are. No one around. Well, maybe one person. Maybe. Suddenly—and this is from that one person—two figures in black come running breakneck speed, weaving in and around parked cars, yelling and laughing, and the old man, startled, I guess, he stops to wait for the dumb kids to run past him. Instead one of them sucker-punches the old fart in the side of the head. Like he planned it. Heavy-duty punch, mind you. And they run off."

"The witness saw this?"

He nodded and took a long sip of his beer, wiped the beer foam off his lips. "Think I'll have the pastrami grinder." He signaled the waitress and gave the order. "Make it to go, darling. The missus misses me when I'm late at work. Women die from loneliness, Rick." A huckleberry smile that broke at the edges. "Write that down. Seen that looker who dumped you in New York. I should write a manual and give it to you."

"Yeah, twenty-four words or less." Impatient, I leaned forward. "Detective, the witness?"

"A woman who just entered the foyer of her slum housing, for some reason looks back out, sees two young guys, both dressed in black hoodies, running. She sees one of them slam the old guy so she dials 911. Babbling in Spanish, of course. Sees them running, turning that corner toward Sisson, she thinks. End of story."

"She never saw their faces?"

"What do you think?"

"Then why do you assume it's Simon and Frankie?"

He finished the beer, smacked his lips. "Ain't you been listening to me? Doesn't this sound like a certain story you and I been through before?"

"C'mon, Detective. You and I both know there's no evidence the attack on Ralph was done by Simon and Frankie."

"Then why are you here?" he asked. "Why did you break every speed law getting to the scene of this crime? A simple public citizen posing as a voyeur?"

"You know why I'm here."

'That's what I said—Simon and Frankie."

I was getting frustrated. "We're talking in circles." I watched his face. Something was going on—a mischievous grin, a twinkling eye, his tongue rolling over his lips.

"What?" I said. "You're not telling me something."

"What if I told you that I got proof firsthand?"

My heart sank. "What?"

He took his time, fiddling with the empty beer bottle, pulling at the lapel of the raincoat, gazing around the room.

"I love moments like this." A devious smile. "It almost makes all the bullshit worthwhile."

"Proof? Like what?"

He was taking his time. "This is like...*CSI: Hartford. Asshole Division.* You see, the evidence squad is picking up all the debris around the victim, bagging everything. Not just the shit he had on him, like the cane. And his wallet, by the way. It fell outta his pocket. But all the litter—paper cups, Coke cans, French fries wrappers, even a brittle condom—hey, it's a dark stretch of Whitney and some dudes are in a hurry—even a rusted penny that ain't gonna bring nobody any luck."

My voice was hollow. "And they found?"

He did a fake drum roll. "Ta dah! I wish I had it here to show you. To see your face. Something musta fell out of the perp's pockets as he bumped off the old geezer. Maybe he slipped. Who knows? But there's this crumpled postcard from a store in Bloomfield called GameStop. It's telling the recipient that the video game he ordered and put down a five-dollar deposit on... well, guess what? It's arrived! Come pick it up."

"And the card..."

"Is addressed to someone named Frankie Croix, a nasty piece of work that lives in Frog Hollow."

Ardolino stopped, the teacher's pet in class finishing his drill and expecting cheers and huzzahs.

"Say something," he told me.

I had nothing to say.

Ardolino slipped out of the booth, grabbed the pastrami grinder the waitress had left on the edge, dropped a ten-dollar bill on the table, and looked down at me. "Oh, by the way. I got your call about that...that YouTube video from...SaigonSez. Clever boys, no? Thanks for the tip. It's like they're providing a scenario for some low-budget movie they're gonna film on the sorry streets of Hartford. Today was the second rehearsal, wouldn't you say?"

I still said nothing. That postcard. Frankie Croix. What in the world?

Finally, standing myself, I looked into his face. "Is that why you asked me to stay? To have this little conversation?"

He let out a belly laugh that broke into a raspy, smoker's cough. "Hey, I need a little drama in my life, too."

"You couldn't wait to tell me, could you?"

He started to walk away, but turned back, a broad smile covering his features. "Yeah, well"—a long pause as he formed the line I'd used to end my phone message earlier that day—"I just wanted to let you know."

Chapter Twenty-three

At midday on Saturday Liz picked me up at my apartment, the two of us headed to Mike Tran's home.

After much coaxing and tender direction, Liz had helped Hazel orchestrate her separation from Judd. Now she was taking Hazel out to lunch, picking her up at her home. Yesterday, at Liz's insistence, Hazel had made the perilous call to Judd. "We rehearsed the call over and over," Liz told me. "I wrote down the words. I made her recite them to me repeatedly."

"I'm surprised she went through with it," I told her.

Liz looked weary. "A lot of smooth talk—and an appeal to her own self-worth. She still possessed a stupid, lingering belief that I"—Liz raised her voice—"me! me!—was interested in that overgrown lummox. Once I disavowed her of that silly notion, she confessed being scared of him—wanting to be away from him. She cried. Lord, Rick, she told me that he hit her—and more than once."

I shivered. "I know. Good for you, Liz. But what now?"

"Now is a follow-up lunch to reinforce. To talk about strategies. Restraining orders, if necessary. He has to be convinced to stay away from her. Police intervention. I called the Avon cops, filled them in, and a cop was going to pay a casual but forceful visit to the lad at his daddy's bachelor lair. Yesterday I called Miss Porter's and got a sympathetic counselor. Hazel will not be alone as she walks to class."

Liz gripped the steering wheel tightly.

"Judd's gonna be a problem." I stared at her profile. Her jaw was rigid, determined.

"I figured that." She glanced back at me. "You know, Rick, he was vicious on the phone. Told her she didn't know what she was doing. After all, they've been together a long time. Rick, I'm afraid she might become a problem—a backslider. But at least she hung up on him."

Earlier when she'd called me, I'd mentioned that I'd received a frantic call from Mike Tran—a plea that I stop over. He also mentioned Liz's visit.

"I'll pick you up," Liz had told me. "Afterward, you and I can talk about Hazel."

"And Simon," I added.

"And Simon," she echoed.

Mike Tran's early morning call resulted from reading the front page of the *Courant*. The splashy headline: "Man Murdered in West End." A subheading: "Second knockout attack." The dead man was identified as Horace Timball, eighty-one, a retired accountant who'd worked for the Democratic Party machine for decades. A well-known politico. He'd served as financial advisor to old-time Governor Bill O'Neill. Governor Dannel Malloy issued a statement celebrating his long service to Connecticut. My first thought: high-profile. Trouble. Friends in high places.

I'd read the same article and found myself recalling that low-slung Toyota idling too long at the intersection last night. It was the same car driven by Diep and Khoa—I was sure of it. That murky dark blue paint, the one fender primed for painting, the tinted windows. Idling, watching, refusing to move.

I wanted to talk to them. But how? A visit to JD and the VietBoyz?

Then Mike called, rattled. "Can you come over? My wife… me…We're going nuts."

"Is Simon there?" I'd asked.

"In his room. Hiding. He won't come out. Playing video games non-stop. I *asked* him about it. Again. He won't answer me. Christ, Rick, I ain't going in to work today, and I don't give a damn. Can you...?"

I'd stopped him, mid-sentence. "I'll ride over, Mike. Don't worry."

But I did worry as Liz and drove to the house. The *Courant* hinted that a piece of incriminating evidence had been discovered at the scene, a scrap of paper that linked this killing to that of Ralph Gervase. But "suspects previously interviewed at that time are now persons of interest again." The words sounded like Ardolino stumbling through a press release.

Lucy opened the front door and stepped back, a barely audible greeting escaping her throat. Liz hugged her. Silently, Lucy nodded toward the living room where Mike sat on the sofa next to Hazel, who looked none too happy. No makeup, her hair uncombed, bags under her eyes. He tried to smile as Liz and I neared, but finally he sank back into the cushions, a hound-dog look on his face. He looked old, beaten up. A copy of the *Hartford Courant* rested between him and Hazel, folded neatly but with the front page ominously evident. That awful headline. The granite tombstone of his dreams. As Liz and I sat down, Mike picked up the paper and waved it at us. "How did the world get to be so mean, fall apart?"

"Pop..." Hazel began.

But Lucy interrupted. "Coffee. I have coffee ready." Her words were so high-pitched and frenetic she could have been screaming for help.

Liz spoke up. "Maybe later. Hazel, are you ready?"

The girl nodded, though she glanced at her father. He smiled at her, and then at Liz. A murmured "Thank you." He swallowed. "Thank you for my daughter." Liz nodded back. Then, more forcefully, "I never liked that boy." He gripped her hand.

Hazel trembled, and I wondered what she thought of her father's condemnation. Yes, Hazel might fear Judd now, dread his furious slap, but I knew that abuse victims often harbored lingering affection, a hope of reform. Redemption. A spotless phoenix rising from the ashes of his dirty game. A persistent girlish crush on her first boyfriend?

"It's gonna be all right," Liz said, her expression taking in Mike and Lucy but resting on Hazel. "The police..."

Hazel blurted out, "I don't want the police."

Liz spoke in a clipped voice. "Hazel, you have to trust me."

Silence in the room. Mike watched his wife, nodded at her.

"Judd called here this morning." Lucy made a clicking sound, annoyed. "I mean, I didn't talk to him, but I could hear his voice."

Liz fumed. "He was told *not* to call."

"Go now." Lucy pointed at Liz, and Hazel jumped up, grabbed a jacket lying on the sofa, and followed Liz out the door. Liz caught my eye—take care of this, Rick.

"It's gonna be all right," I assured Mike and Lucy when we were alone.

Mike's mouth tightened. "It ain't never gonna be all right."

"Minh," his wife consoled. "Please. Minh."

But he shrugged her off. "And that...that Judd ain't the real problem." He looked toward the staircase—and doubtless Simon's bedroom. I could hear ping and zap noises from a video game—followed by the boys whooping it up.

Mike grumbled. "Listen to that. Simon and Wilson—like nothing in the goddamn world happened yesterday."

Lucy caught my eye. "Simon talked to me this morning. He told me he was with Frankie at West Farms Mall. You know, like hanging out. For hours. The same time that..." Her voice trailed off.

"Okay," I said. "Perhaps there's surveillance tape. I'll check into that. The mall is good about that."

She sounded apologetic. "He says he was in the parking lot, not inside. Sitting in a car, driving around."

"Great," Mike thundered. "One goddamn excuse after the other. A boy who wants the world to put a noose around his neck."

Lucy squealed. "Minh, no."

"He won't talk to me, Rick. He talks to—her." He pointed at his wife, his finger trembling. Breathing in, Lucy looked away.

"Will he talk to me now?" I asked.

"Fat chance," Mike answered, biting his lower lip.

Lucy leaned into me, confidential. "That detective called here this morning. He wanted to know about Simon—was he here? I said yes, and he says—keep him home." A bewildered look in her eyes. "Why, Rick? What's gonna happen?"

Her husband seethed. "What's gonna happen? Christ, Lucy, smell the goddamned coffee. They're gonna take the boy away. Didn't you read the paper? They got—proof."

"Hold on," I cautioned. "No one is taking Simon anywhere yet."

Lucy's voice was stronger now. "He told me Frankie's taking the bus here. I guess they want to talk things over."

Mike snarled, "What? Plan a defense?"

A sudden spurt of anger in Lucy. "You *yell* at him, Minh. You don't talk to him."

"He's up there...stony...stubborn." Mike walked to the foot of the stairs and yelled, "Simon. Wilson. You boys come down here. Mr. Lam is here to talk." Silence. "Your mother made lunch."

The last line struck me as bizarre. "Lunch," she mumbled. "Yes."

Mike looked at me. "Rick, go upstairs. Talk—without us. Maybe he'll...talk..."

Quietly I walked up the stairs, though a little hesitant. From the open doorway of their bedroom, unseen, I stared at their backs as they leaned into their PlayStation consoles. Not a gamer myself, I'd watched Hank and his younger brother going hell-bent to leather on some fast-and-furious adventure projected on their big-screen TV.

Now, watching the two brothers, I was intrigued by the difference. Wilson was on the edge of his seat, his neck stiff, his chin jutted forward, eyes locked on the screen, a boy determined to win. But Simon sat back, a lazy posture, his fingers moving slowly but deftly on the console, almost indifferent. On the screen a nerdy kid with cowlick and buckteeth ambled home from school. Suddenly the boy hurls away his books, the buttons on his white dress shirt pop open, his eyeglasses morph into some sort of laser goggles, and muscles bulge. A superhero. *Pop pop pop*—street corner bullies dropped, one after another, exploding into bits. Simon and Wilson were yelling out—"I got this one." "No—me." Sashaying hookers with mile-high hair had something to say about the loss, but they were also summarily dismissed. A puff of smoke. Gone. "Yes, yes, yes," roared Wilson, excited. Simon gave up, sitting back.

Simon waved the jewel box in the air, dismissing it. "Junk," he mouthed.

I caught a glimpse of the title on the slick jewel box: KILL POWER 3: THE REVENGE OF EINSTEIN.

"It ain't like real life, Wilson," Simon said to his beaming brother.

Wilson snapped back, "Yeah, like you know street life."

Suddenly Wilson shut off the PlayStation and the TV screen went black.

Simon was seething, and I sensed that he resented losing to Wilson. "You live your dumb life through a book." He assumed a tough-guy posture, pulling his lips together. His head swiveled, and I realized he knew I was standing in the doorway. "I got friends who can fuck up your life."

The line bothered Wilson, who squinted at his brother. "What?" Then, quietly, he muttered, "Yeah, but they're already starting with your life."

At that moment Wilson spotted me.

He turned to face me but looked sideways at his brother. The two started some teenaged boy guffaw that was half-pretense, half-boyish glee.

"Shit." Simon was looking into my face.

Wilson poked him in the shoulder. "Sherlock Holmes is here."

Simon moved quickly, slamming the door in my face.

Back downstairs, defeated, I shrugged my shoulders as Mike watched me. The three of us ate a quiet lunch, then sat in the living room making small talk. Silence from upstairs. Every so often Mike's eyes checked the staircase.

◇◇◇

When the front door opened and Liz and Hazel walked in, Liz sought my eye. I must have looked panicky because inadvertently she grinned. I read her mind—as she could always read mine. Hers now said, blatantly—Sometimes there is no escape clause for the harried investigator.

But what thrilled was Hazel's lively face. Her eyes danced around the room. Doubtless buoyed by Liz's rousing cheer, Hazel was smiling. No, smiling is too anemic a word—Hazel bubbled.

"Everything okay?" Lucy asked, anxious.

Liz nodded as Hazel looked warmly at Liz. "Yeah, okay. Liz helped me to see that even though I've been with him so long… but Liz…anyway, Judd…something is…She stopped. "I'm gonna allow myself to be happy."

Liz wagged a finger at her. "Those are my words, Hazel. Remember that. You still have to make them your own words."

Mike looked confused, but pleased.

He started to say something, but suddenly we heard high-pitched yelling from outside. It echoed off the walls. Growled curses, fury, sputtered grunts. A rat-a-tat volley of *fuck yous*. We rushed to the front window, standing shoulder-to-shoulder, peering out.

Hazel sucked in her breath, trembled, and reached for Liz, who draped her arm across her shoulder, whispering something in her ear.

Judd Snow had pulled his car up into the driveway. The driver's side door of the red Audi was wide open, and he leaned against a fender, as if gaining his balance. The car was mud-splattered, as if he'd driven it through spring puddles, careless, crazy. Streaks of dirt smeared the windshield, but he'd switched on the wipers, which left an arc of clean glass.

He stumbled away from the car and pivoted toward the house. A bellowing voice. "You called the fucking cops on me, Hazel. You think I want those yokels from Avon knocking on my door? My dad…he's pissed." A torrent of nonsense syllables, slurred, nasty.

"A goddamn drunk. Christ." Mike's hand touched Hazel's arm, and she started.

"Come out, Hazel. Right now. You get in this car and…" His voice broke, a sloppy sob. "You and me…you know. Come on. Now. Fuck them all." He slumped backwards against the car. His voice grew shrill. "Right now. You hear me. Right now. I'm not gonna wait here forever." A heavy sigh. "I'm not gonna let you walk away from me. I'm sick of people walking away from me. You hear me?"

He swung his fist in the air, as if battling an enemy.

Gasping, Hazel pulled back away from the window, swallowed by her father's arms, hugging her, drawing her into the room. I looked at Liz and mouthed one word: Police. She nodded, reaching into her purse for her cell phone, headed into the hallway.

While we watched, Judd suddenly stopped his drunken gyrations, backed away, and I thought he was getting back into his car. Instead, he was looking to his left, down the street, and he let out a loud hiss. "Goddamn."

Frankie Croix was ambling up the sidewalk from the bus stop, earbuds on, oblivious, nodding his head to music only he could hear, his gait a casual hip-hop swagger. Craning my neck, I could see him pause, suddenly conscious of Judd Snow in the driveway. Watching him.

His face got flushed as he pulled off the earbuds. He stormed at Judd, pointing a finger in his face. "Asshole."

I could hear Liz on the phone talking to the cops. Her voice was clipped, sure. "Now."

I threw open the front door, but by the time I hit the top stair, Judd and Frankie were hurling punches at each other, both guys slugging wildly, Frankie landing a blow to Judd's belly so that he doubled over. Frankie repeatedly kicked Judd, who howled, grabbed his shin, tottered.

Staggering, tipsy, Judd managed to pummel Frankie's face, causing Frankie to dip his head and dive into Judd's chest. They banged against Judd's car, slipped to the ground, rolled over, and Frankie crawled away, his face bloodied.

It was a spitfire skirmish that ended almost as quickly as it began. Frankie swore as he rubbed his bruised face, hunched over on the sidewalk, but looking back at Judd who careened into his car door, hobbled, bent over, started to throw up. Frankie pulled himself up and slowly moved toward the house, a triumphant look on his face—a victor's puffy smugness. He arched his back. He had a bloody nose, and he rubbed it, smearing the back of his hand. Judd, teetering, limped toward his car, dragging his injured foot, a string of "fuck you, assholes" punctuating the quiet lawn. He toppled into his seat.

He looked toward the house.

Mike and Lucy stood behind me, watching. Mike surprised me—he was holding Lucy's hand. Her head was bent into his shoulder. Hazel was somewhere inside, though through the open door I could hear Hazel's hiccoughing sob.

Judd scrunched his eyes at us. "Hazel." A plaintive keening. "Hazel, Come on."

Frankie was standing at the foot of the steps, but turned and gave him the finger. He raised his fist, blood stained, scraped. "Teach you, fucker, to knock me around."

Furious, Judd returned the finger but was surprised to see blood dripping down his arm. "Fuck."

I was suddenly aware of movement behind me. Simon appeared, slipping onto the top stair, maneuvering himself around his parents, tucking his body behind me, staring around me toward Judd. I could feel his hot breath on my arm.

"Get back in the house," I told him. His arm jerked against my side, and I grabbed it.

He ignored me, refused to move. Instead, twisting in front of me, he yelled, "Frankie, did you kill the bastard?"

Mike grabbed his shoulders, pulled him back. "Get the hell back in the house. You hear me?"

Simon didn't move.

A car careened around the corner, blew a stop sign, and screeched to a stop behind Judd's car. Foster Judd leapt out, spun around like a wobbly top, ran toward his son while leaving his own car running. He reached for his son but was suddenly aware of the audience on the steps. His face tightened, but he turned his back to us.

His voice sailed over the street. "For Christ's sake, Judd. I knew I'd find you here. The cops said stay away, and what do you do—you come here. Did you think I didn't know where the fuck you were going? You want to be dragged to jail again?"

He circled the car, thrust out a hand and slapped Judd in the face. Already bloodied, Judd let out a wounded moan. But at that moment Foster became aware of the blood, the dirt stains on his clothing, the scraped knuckles, the torn shirt, the shattered face.

"What the hell happened? What's going on here?" Confused, he spun around, for the first time taking in the frieze on the front porch: Mike, Lucy, Simon, and me. And huddled against an evergreen near the bottom step a bloodied Frankie. "What?" He squinted. "What the hell is going on at this house?"

He looked at Frankie, a shock of recognition. "You're that punk kid…that murderer." He laughed wildly. "Did you read the *Courant*, you loser? You're on the front page again. You and…" He glanced at Simon.

Mike bristled, took a step forward, but I held onto his shoulder. "No, Mike."

"Asshole," he muttered.

Lucy squeezed his arm. "Minh."

The sudden wail of a police siren. Foster's mouth dropped as he spoke through clenched teeth to his son. "Start the fuckin' car and drive away. You don't want to be here. I'll take care of this."

But Judd wasn't moving. "You can't have Hazel."

His father seethed. "Damn you, this isn't the time."

Judd was sobbing. "Every girl I ever dated you…you…move in."

His father shot forward and slapped him again. "Bullshit."

Judd flinched, his sobbing louder.

Mike bristled. "Mr. Snow, I don't think…"

He didn't get far. Foster swiveled around, shoulders tense, eyes slatted. "Don't you talk shit to me, Tran. You got a son that spends time in juvie and…*kills* people…and…and your daughter…" His voice began ragged, broken. "Your daughter ruined my boy's life. Look at him. She made him into a boy I don't even know anymore. He could have been…been…"

His jaw went slack as a squad car pulled to a stop.

Slowly I walked down the path toward the cop, but looked back at the awful tableau on the landing. Lucy had disappeared, though Mike stood with his arms draped loosely around Simon's shoulders. Simon looked frozen. Frankie had joined them, his face still tight with anger. A large purplish bruise covered his cheek, a swollen eye.

For some reason my eyes swept up to the second floor window, the boys' bedroom, where Wilson pressed his face against the window, watching. His arms were folded over his chest and seemed to be cradling a book. But it was the look on his face that jarred me. Mouth agape, eyes unblinking, he had the look of someone who'd read about the evil in the world and was now, on this quiet suburban lawn, seeing it for the first time.

Chapter Twenty-four

Simon disappeared.

Mike Tran called me the next night, panic in his voice. "Like he goes off all the time, running the streets. I know that. I can't stop that." He sucked in his breath. "But, you know, we sort of always knew where he was."

"At Michael's."

I could hear him lighting a cigarette, dragging in the smoke, exhaling. "Yeah, like we couldn't tell him, though. Lucy—she… well, a mother, you know. She calls Michael. She even calls Frankie's mom, who isn't happy but would say, yeah, the boys ain't there—or they're together."

"But not this time? Different?"

A long pause. "Yeah."

"How?"

"A note." His voice broke. "He left a note."

"What does it say?"

He swallowed. "That's what got to us. Two words. 'Don't worry.' He didn't even sign it."

"But maybe after that scene at your house yesterday—I mean, the police and Judd and his father and Frankie, all that insanity—maybe, he thought he'd better say something."

"But no one knows where he is."

"No one?"

He waited a heartbeat. "Could you do me a favor, Rick? I mean, a big favor."

"If I can."

"Could you check—maybe Frankie? Maybe. I don't know. Go to Russell Street? That…those VietBoyz. That JD guy. The only time we can't find him—well, we know he's *there*. I can't go there. I can't. I'm afraid of what I'll do."

"I'll take care of it, Mike."

After I hung up the phone, I sat on my sofa, staring at my comfortable life—the wall of old leather-bound books, the stunning lithograph by Robert De Niro Sr. of Greta Garbo in *Anna Christie* that I bought at a charity auction at the Farmington Country Club. The oil painting by French-Vietnamese artist Le Pho that I paid too much money for at Zillow's Gallery on West Fifty-seventh Street last year. A sunset in old Saigon that I tried to remember. The weathered oriental carpet under my feet. The old oak desk that once sat in a country store. Here was my careful life fashioned after I'd fled Manhattan madness and street violence. Serene, mostly, my life here, and comfortable. Chiseled out of a helter-skelter past. A faraway Manhattan. Farmington as refuge. Sitting there, surveying my room, I trembled—brutal images of Mike Tran's chaotic and troubled family assailed me. The struggling Vietnamese man who wanted the same life I had now—quiet mornings, placid suppers, loving people at his side, restful sleeps.

I phoned Hank and told him about Simon disappearing— and Mike's anguish.

"I think the boy may be running," I told him. "Running scared."

Hank promised he'd be at my apartment within the hour. While I waited, I jotted down possibilities. First off was Michael. A woman's voice, laughing into the phone, in the background a man's playful tease. "For God's sake, give me the phone."

"Oh, it's you." His abrupt beginning when he came on the line. "Did they find Simon?" Laughter behind him, a voice disappearing into another room. A door slammed.

I waited for the laughter to end. "No."

Distracted, he spoke into the receiver. "Sorry, Rick." A familiarity that annoyed me, frankly. Frat brothers discussing the loss of a keg of beer at the toga party on Saturday night. "I mean, my mother called and I told her I haven't seen him. But he did call me."

"When?"

"Well…" he paused, deliberating, "early yesterday. No, during the afternoon. From the house, I guess. I wasn't here and my cell was off. He left a message, something about the craziness at the house. Frankie trashes Judd—something he celebrated, a tick in his voice—and the police blocking the street. A short message, but excited." A deep sigh. "Like I need to know all this."

"Did you call him back?"

"No. I just assumed he was playing reporter and a lot of what he said was, well, embellished. He's always trying to get my attention—to notice him."

My mouth was dry. "And he always seems to fail."

He clicked his tongue. "That's not fair, Rick. It isn't. I told you I let him sack out on my sofa when he's running from home."

"So you don't know where he went?"

Irritated, his voice clipped: "I told you." Then, softening, "I suggested Frankie, but…"

I broke in sharply. "No."

"Look, I have to run. There are people here." Then he regretted his words. "I *am* concerned. I read the *Courant* about the… the attack on Whitney. I'm not heartless, Rick."

"If he calls you…" I began, my voice cold.

"I'll have him call you. I promise."

The line went dead.

When Hank arrived, bounding up the stairs two at a time and ignoring Jimmy's insistent demands from inside Gracie's apartment where the door was wide open—"Where the hell you rushing to? A fire?"—he confided that Jimmy was sitting in a chair near the doorway, injured foot up on an ottoman, but facing the hallway.

Hank chuckled. "Planning his escape." Then, sheepish, "I didn't stop to talk."

"You better say hello."

Hank smiled. "I figured we'd be interrogated, you and me, on the way out."

I walked to the front window, gazed down at the street. A quiet afternoon, one lone girl walking by with her schoolbooks. I turned back to Hank. "I'm hoping he's all right, Hank. That he hasn't done anything stupid. Probably not—he's not with Frankie. Supposedly. It's just that…well, yesterday had to be traumatic for any kid."

Hank watched me grab my jacket. "Where to, then?"

I shrugged, helpless. "Where would a teenage boy go when he's running from his family?"

"To a girl's house."

I shook my head. "No. You've seen him. A baby."

"He's sixteen. Don't underestimate the hormones of a teenage boy."

"A baby." I debated my move. "Mike wants us to check out Russell Street. We will. But first let's check out Frankie's place. Just in case someone is lying to Mike."

Hank persisted. "At sixteen I would run to a girl's house. One I was sweet on."

I punched him in the shoulder, grinning. "Yeah, but unlike you, Simon doesn't like to set himself up for quick rejection."

Hank's eyes glistened. "Ouch, Rick." He preened, stretched his head toward the small mirror I had hanging over a sideboard. He exaggerated his grin. He tapped his flexed bicep.

"Come on. Let's go."

With a passing hello to Jimmy—"No one tells me anything and Hank here runs by me like I'm a pest"—we left the house. Jimmy's voice followed us out the door, though I also heard Gracie's demand that he lower it. "What neighbors?" he bellowed. "Rick? You call him a neighbor?"

"Why would Simon leave a note this time?" Hank wondered.

"Let's find out."

"This may be a wild goose chase," Hank said as he drove into Frog Hollow and pulled up in front of Frankie's apartment house. The front door was cracked open, a brick wedged in place, the buzzer in the lobby disconnected. We trudged up the two flights of stairs, stepping past graffiti-smeared walls, a burnt-out light bulb on the second floor landing, and rapped on the door. No answer. I knocked again. From inside the garbled cough of a smoker, a spat-out "goddamn," and the sound of feet dragged across a hardwood floor. The door squeaked open, and Doris Croix, her head wreathed in cigarette smoke and a narcotic haze, peered out.

"Christ, what is it? Can't I get a little sleep?"

I leaned in, and she jumped back, startled. "Mrs. Croix."

"Oh, it's you."

"We're looking for Frankie and Simon."

The hallway light made her face waxy, grayish. Looking up into the light, she blinked her eyes rapidly, and then squinted. "Somebody already called. Earlier." A harsh, unhappy laugh. "Woke me up then, too. Frankie left with his brother some time ago. And no, they said nothing about Saigon. Is something happening?" For a moment her eyes widened. "Is Frankie gonna be taken in again?"

I didn't answer. "Where did your boys go?" I asked.

But she was already closing the door. Through the closed door, she muttered, "Jesus Christ. I had more peace when he was at Long Lane juvie."

In the car, fuming, Hank said, "Well, she may get her wish again—for all she gives a damn." His knuckles drummed the dashboard nervously. "Well, I don't think Simon is with his buddy."

"Not if Frankie is with Jonny."

Hank grinned. "Okay, Sherlock, where to next?'

"Russell Street, Hank. Where I knew we'd end up. Two birds with one stone, I hope. JD may know something—God, I hope Simon is there, for once—and I want to get in contact with Diep and Khoa."

"Why?"

"Their story is connected with Frankie and Simon. And I swear they were near the attack on Whitney Street, idling in that Toyota. Maybe Simon is with them."

"That's not good news."

"I don't think anything to do with that pair can be good news."

"I don't trust a guy with a tattoo that wraps around his neck."

"Even if it's a good-luck dragon?"

"I don't care if it's a four-leaf clover inside a horseshoe."

But the Russell Street storefront was closed, though I noticed a dim light somewhere at the back of the room. Peering into the plate-glass window that hadn't been scrubbed in ages, I detected ghostlike movement. I waited. I knocked. Suddenly bright light flashed throughout the room as an overhead light was switched on. A shadowy figure paused at the back, then disappeared, then reappeared near the front door, standing to the side, looking out, suspicious. The door opened. JD stood there, his face stony and his clothing rumpled. A shirt hastily donned, some military-style olive green fatigue, but left open so his chest showed. A landscape of tattoos. Curlicues, arabesques, Chinese symbols, daggers, the patchwork quilt of a drunken sailor. An irregular heart with one word: *Toi*. Green lettering. Crime. Another word below that. *Tien*. Money. Across his navel, jagged letters. *DOA*.

"Yeah?"

"We're looking for Simon."

"He ain't here." A thin smile. "Every time you come here you ask the same question."

I moved closer. "Well, one day maybe you'll give me the right answer."

He yawned. "He ain't here."

"Was he here today? His family's worried."

He scratched his stomach absently. "They have a lot to worry about."

"What does that mean?"

"It means nothing." He started to turn away.

"Have you seen Frankie?"

He was already closing the door but stopped, deliberated. A quick glance toward the back room. "Yeah, as a matter of fact, yes. Him and his brother, Jonny. Looking for T-Boy."

"Where's T-boy?"

"You got a lot of questions."

"And still no answers."

He grinned at me, though when Hank grumbled, the grin disappeared. "You got the cop with you."

"He's my protection."

"Low rent," JD said, but there was a curious humor in his tone. I watched Hank, who spotted it. He actually smiled.

"Is Simon with them?"

"God, no. Saigon don't like Jonny, and Jonny don't like Saigon. Jonny don't like most dudes."

"So you can't help me?" I looked into his face.

"No."

"One more question. I'd like to talk to the brothers. Diep and Khoa. Joey and Kenny."

His body stiffened. "Them?" He took a step backwards. "I ain't too keen on them boys."

"Why's that?"

A quizzical smile. "Shit. Another question. Man, you got a truckload of them."

I laughed. "And still no answers. Look, JD, I'm looking for Simon. He's in trouble. Two men dead now. Help me out, okay?"

He watched me closely for a minute. "Diep and Khoa are trouble. They moved up from Bridgeport, gun-happy, talking smack, acting like wild cards, telling me what's what, and they impress the boys with shit. We don't want them around here. I told them to stay away." A wide, happy grin. "Our revolution wants brains, not trigger-happy punks."

"Brains?" From Hank.

JD considered him for a while, a burning stare, his head nodding up and down. "You heard me." But then he looked at me. "They buy off the kids with cash and...ugly promises. They *scare* them. That ain't my style." He waved his hand behind him. "The VietBoyz got a code. It ain't your code, but it's a code."

"I believe you."

"Well, that's nice for me then." Sarcastic, his tongue running over his lower lip. "So I ain't seen them around here lately because they bring the cops here. Now and then"—he paused, looking over my shoulder into the street—"they bump their piece-of-shit car up to the door, *boom boom boom*, but they ain't scaring nobody. And I don't know where they hanging out, and I don't give a damn. Don't push it."

"I want to find Simon."

"Then you better look somewhere else."

With that he closed the door quietly. In a second the overhead light switched off, plunging the room into darkness. A shadow drifted across the room, disappearing into the backroom. I heard a girl's high soprano, a laugh that only stopped when JD barked, "Shut the fuck up."

She did.

In the car I turned to Hank. "I don't know if he's telling us the truth. But it's clear he's not a friend of Diep and Khoa."

"Who knows where Simon is?"

"C'mon, Hank. Any ideas?"

He was smiling. "Yeah. The mall."

I pointed a finger at him. "The mall."

A teenage boy's miraculous mecca. Nirvana for the wandering kids with bus tickets or their father's cars. Fast food courts and video arcades and girls walking by. Lots of girls.

◇◇◇

Simon was sitting by himself on a wooden bench outside a busy Arby's. He was staring into space, ignoring the bustle of strolling shoppers. Slouched on the bench, the collar of his spring jacket turned up around his neck, his legs stretched out, his arms folded over his chest, he looked dazed. He also looked a bit menacing, as in—Don't come near me. As we approached, I noticed the laces of his oversized, clunky sneakers were undone, though the brilliant red stripes seemed freshly painted on. He was wearing baggy jeans, the cuffs rolled up, and under his jacket a black T-shirt. I read the message: EVERYTHING IS A

LIE. In huge black block letters. But tiny cursive letters below it said: *Especially This.*

"Simon." I stood ten feet away and tried not to sound threatening.

He looked up.

"It's okay," Hank reassured him, sliding into the seat next to him.

"No, it ain't."

"I was worried about you," I began. "You left that note."

He looked up into my face, his cheeks becoming pink. "I didn't know what to do."

"Why leave home?"

He closed his eyes for a minute. When he opened them, they were fiery. "There was so much yelling yesterday. Everybody so crazy. And Wilson said it was my fault—I brought it on. Me and Frankie. He said it was all right, but...I don't know." A boyish shrug of his shoulders. "So I took the bus here."

"Not with Frankie?" Hank asked.

"He's with his brother. They didn't ask me. I don't got Frankie. I got...no one."

For a second his eyes shot around the open space, finally resting on a beefy security guard who'd been eyeing him.

"You could have stayed in your room. With Wilson. Video games."

He scoffed. "Yeah, Wilson beats me at everything. He's smarter. And when he wins he gloats. Like a victory lap or something. Lords it over me. It's..."

"Hard to take," Hank finished.

Simon snickered. "It's worse when he feels sorry for me and lets me win. Then his—like triumph—is so disgusting because it's not, you know, said. Just the looks."

He pointed around the mall. "I just didn't know where to go. This is a place we come to...me and Frankie. Other guys. They only throw us out when we stay too long or get loud or take things."

"You take things?"

A crooked grin. "Not here."

Hank's words were soft, comfortable, as he leaned in, his hand brushing the boy's shoulder. "You have to come home with us."

Simon look confused, his head bobbing. A round head, I realized, too large for his scrawny short body. Those long ears— Buddha's ears. A constellation of acne gracing his forehead, his nose. A small, sensitive mouth and a tiny chin. He looked like those Chinese kids on the Asian Relief charity ads you see on late-night TV. Faces to warm your heart.

He nodded and stood up. "Yeah. Home."

I dialed Mike Tran from the car, reassured him that Simon was fine, that he was in our care, and that we'd be home shortly. "Thank God," he said, and Simon, listening. When we got to the house, darkness had fallen, the street dark. Yet the Tran household was ablaze with light—upstairs, downstairs, front yard light, even a sweep of spotlight that stretched in the backyard to a neighbor's fence.

We sat for a minute in the car, Simon hesitant to get out. "Saigon," I said slowly, "can I ask you about Khoa and Diep?"

He sucked in his breath. "No, they're nothing."

"You told Hazel you had a secret—you were scared."

He resented the questions, fidgeting, pulling at his jacket. He opened the door and slipped his feet out. Still he didn't move.

Lucy and Mike stood on the front steps, illuminated by bright light behind then, silhouettes unmoving, waiting.

"Go," I prodded Simon.

Then he started to run toward the house, but stopped, looked back and began to say a thank you—it emerged as a grunted "thank"—which was, I suppose, enough at the moment. Then he scooted toward his parents. When he reached them, they looked ready to grab him, squeeze, but Simon plowed between them and disappeared into the house. Lucy immediately disappeared. Mike stood in the doorway, facing out, watching the street and us, and finally, looking defeated, offered a hesitant wave. We waved back, and he waved again. It was like he didn't know how to say goodbye.

Chapter Twenty-five

Napping on my sofa, I dreamed of the market in old Saigon. Nguyen Tat Thanh in District Four. The aroma of potent coffee. Monks beat hollow wooden drums and chant, *"Kinh mu sieu."* A prayer for peace. A woman sits over a basket of dragon fruit, her teeth stained from chewing betel nuts. Horse flies buzz around her head. She whispers to me that ginger will let me see in the dark. Avoid ghosts. It is December. *Chap ma.* Time to look after my dead ancestors. The woman laughs—You, boy, have none.

It's a dream I often have. Usually it forces me awake and into the kitchen where, groggy and unhappy, I brew my own anemic American coffee. But the raw power of Vietnamese coffee lingers in my head, and makes me smile.

But sudden thumping on the floorboards roused me. Since Jimmy was housed below in Gracie's apartment, I'd been through this routine a couple times. Not exactly smoke signals, but the pounding of the war drums. Jimmy stretching up to the high ceiling and banging with a broom handle.

"I have two telephones," I told him the first time after I scooted down the stairs in my boxer shorts and U.S. Open T-shirt.

"Which you ignore," he grumbled. He pointed to the broom handle. "It worked, no?"

Now, again, I stood before him, scratching my side and realizing I had a magnificent hole in my *Born in the USSR* T-shirt. "Can I help you, Jimmy?"

"You don't tell me nothing, Rick."

"There's nothing to tell."

Jimmy was eating take-out from Wah's Garden. He dripped soy sauce onto his sweatshirt, and ignored it. He reached for the General Tso's chicken and slobbered it onto his lap. A chunk of crispy chicken toppled onto the carpet, and Gracie scurried after it. He examined a floret of broccoli as though it were an insult to epicures everywhere. When he was finished, he tore the cellophane from the fortune cookie and read out loud: "15 19 55 67 34. My lucky numbers. Rick, remember to pick me up a Mega Millions ticket at the gas station, okay?" I nodded. "And," he went on, "my fortune: 'Wisdom is what you offer the world.'" He waved the slip at me. "Now you know."

I smiled. "Hey, Jimmy, I've known that for years."

He pushed his plate away. The plastic fork he'd used flipped onto the carpet, and his unused chopsticks disappeared into the sofa cushions. "All right, let's get busy. Rick, fill me in."

So I did, beginning with the unpleasant incident in Mike Tran's front yard, the ugly incident with Judd Snow and Frankie. "He's trouble," I said. "Slumped in his car, getting out when the police ordered him to and staggering on a bum leg, Judd still looked at the cops like he was going to spit at them. The cops gave him a warning, maybe because his father was there, promising that his son would comply, not show up again."

"A mistake," Jimmy said. "Hazel isn't out of danger yet."

"Liz sent me a text and said Judd's daddy is raising the roof, his turn to call the cops, blaming everybody, accusing Mike Tran, throwing out phrases like 'alienation of affection' and other insults, talking of hiring lawyers."

"The man's a fool," Jimmy noted.

"He is that. A playboy daddy who envies his son's life—maybe."

Jimmy eyed me closely. "For all your running around, Rick"—he smirked—"and Hank, who is not a part of my firm but serves as mascot, what have you found to *prove* Simon *didn't* attack me and Ralph?"

"Nothing."

"Nothing?" he echoed.

"There are two dangerous players, Diep and Khoa, who are grooming them for more serious crime."

Jimmy listened closely. "Well, what are you gonna do about it?"

"I'm gonna track them down."

He waited a second. "Bring your gun."

"It's in my glove compartment, Jimmy. Locked."

"It should be in your lap."

Gracie chuckled. "The Wild West, Jimmy?"

"Second amendment. You heard of it?"

"I've also heard of the first amendment, Jimmy, but you seem to forget that sometimes." Gracie smiled innocently.

"Okay, here's how I see things." Jimmy's eyes were bright pinpoints, focused. "That family is like an old pinball game, metals balls pinging off each other. So much so that nobody can see straight."

"But how does this help me clear Simon?" I wondered.

"Maybe it don't, Rick. But you gotta keep in mind that maybe Ralph's death got nothing to do with this family. But—and this is a big 'but'—if they are involved, it's because one of those pinball pellets banged into them."

"Chance?"

"Choices," he stressed. "So everybody's got it into their heads that the boys got a bad reputation. A locked-in image of the bad boys roaming the streets. Probably the whole Vietnamese community." He thought for a second. "Even Detective Ardolino zeroed in right away. He assumed Ralph's attack was by the boys because, well, they'd cemented that image into his head. Farmington Avenue, late afternoon. Bingo, now they're back home. The assaults begin right away, this time deadly. Who else?"

"So," I nodded my head, "someone might be taking advantage of their bad-boy reputation."

"Maybe," said Jimmy. "Maybe not. Keep in mind there's been another attack."

"Which," I went on, "could be a distraction. Or, maybe, the culprits found out they liked hurting people."

"That's ugly," Gracie said.

"But it happens," Jimmy told her. "Jackasses get intoxicated with what they can get away with."

I summed up, "So maybe somebody *wants* us to believe it was Simon and Frankie."

"Meanwhile," Gracie said, "there's Hazel to watch out for."

"I talked to Liz. She's moving through channels. She'll orchestrate whatever needs to be done. She said that Judd tried to reach her through Facebook, but she'd unfriended him."

Gracie frowned. "Whatever that means. How do you unfriend someone? In my day you waited until they walked by you, and then you cut them dead. Very Victorian, and very effective."

"But then he sent a tweet—'Goodbye, Hazel.' Just those words. And those words scared Hazel more than anything."

"Choices," Jimmy broke in. "The Tran family. Choices."

"But," I said, "maybe someone is making the choices for them."

Jimmy yawned. "Well, Rick, it's up to you to do your job. Your name is in gold lettering on the office door, no? Under mine. Not as big, of course, but there. Investigate."

◇◇◇

Thinking of Jimmy's words, I sat in the Hartford office, lazily staring down into the street. My cell phone rang. Detective Ardolino.

In the morning's *Courant* there was a short page-six piece about the delays in the arrests for the two deaths in the West End, as well as a snide, accusatory commentary on the editorial page. Citizens, the editors noted, were squawking, fearful of strolling the popular streets. Business was impacted. Folks from the suburbs heading for Japanese food at Ginza or Portuguese food at Porto's changed their minds. Somehow I suspected the reporter's piece and the editorial board's testy, slap on the wrist rankled Ardolino, and he'd be itchy for an arrest.

"I was expecting your call," I told him.

"Yeah, like we got this psychic bond, you and I."

"Maybe we do. We're destined…"

He cut me off. "Quiet, Lam. By August I'm gonna be lying in the shade of a palm tree in Porto Gordo while the missus merrily wades too far out in shark-infested waters."

I laughed. "Then you'll have to rescue her."

"It's bad enough I gotta constantly save your ass."

That surprised me. "I thought we were a team."

"I work alone."

"Which explains why you're calling me now?"

"Don't be a wise guy. I'm calling because…well, just listen to me. There was another incident yesterday afternoon. Can you believe it? My fucking luck. Same time. Four o'clock. The hour when everybody in the world is hiding office supplies in their trousers and getting ready to leave good old Hartford."

"Except the school kids," I said. "Prime time for wandering the streets, no?"

"And the dropouts like your boys."

"They're not my boys."

"Look, Lam. This nuttiness got to stop."

"Tell me what happened. There wasn't anything in the papers this morning except…"

He rushed his words. "Yeah, I read that shit. The editors of the *Courant* are noted for gazing off into the sky while some pervert diddles their privates. If you know what I mean."

"That's not a good image."

"Are you saying I ain't a poet?" He chuckled to himself. "There was nothing in the paper because nothing happened. Sort of. I mean, this happened right in Little Saigon, go figure. This old Asian fart tells a cop two boys dressed in black hoodies run past him, and the big one is breathing down his neck. He sees a fist go up, he ducks 'cause he got this survival instinct, I guess, but down the street two cars slam into each other, a loud bang that has everyone running out of their skin, and the boys run on. Nothing happened. But he calls the cops. All the old folks buying their dog meat at some Vietnamese market think they're next. Christ, they expect to see it on *CBS Evening News* or on

Anderson Cooper—that ass gets all excited over a homeless guy sneezing on the subway—and that's that."

"Almost a knockdown," I said, almost to myself.

He echoed my words. "Almost. Yeah, an almost-killing."

"Same culprits?"

"Bingo."

"No exact identification?"

"What do you think?"

"I would've thought Simon and Frankie would be taken in by now."

A rasp in his throat, angry. "Yeah, you'd think so. So would any decent person on this earth. But the D.A. is dragging his heels, biding time. No visuals, no witness identification, just that lousy postcard that could mean nothing—he says. It's a bus stop, he says. Lots of kids step off the bus there. The bus to Frog Hollow. Where Frankie lives. He says a defense lawyer can eat up that bit of evidence in court. But it seems to me…" His voice trailed off. "Never mind."

"What do you want from me, Detective?"

"Here's the deal. Go to Little Saigon, Rick. Talk around. Those VietBoyz losers. This is your territory, man. You speak the language. I walk those streets and I'm in never-never land. Every store looks like a kung-fu palace or something. Christ, in the Minh Loc Pool Hall even the cue balls look foreign to me. Nobody talks English." A pause. "Maybe they'll tell you things."

"Maybe not. I've gone there a few times. Talked to folks." I was ready to hang up. "You know, Detective, maybe you should get some Vietnamese cops on the force."

"There's a rumor that we got one or two, but maybe they're Chinese." His voice was laced with laughter. "And, besides, I hear there's gonna be a Vietnamese state trooper coming up. Excuse me—Vietnamese-*American* trooper. It's a new America."

"Thank God."

"From sea to shining sea."

"Goodbye, Detective."

"As I say, I like to look at the larger picture." The line went dead.

◇◇◇

Near dusk someone rapped on the downstairs door, and I looked out the window. I'd been home for an hour, reviewing my files, getting nowhere. The "almost" attack on Park Street. Little Saigon. The "almost" knockdown. A different area of Hartford. Different attackers? But two boys in black hoodies? Copycats?

The rapping got louder.

A Harley motorcycle was parked in front of the house, nosed into the curb. I'd heard the loud rumble of the bike, but paid it no mind. The tenant on the top floor, a fortyish manager of a local Pizza Hut, rode bikes, had friends who disturbed our quiet evenings. Gracie repeatedly asked me whether she should ask him to leave, but Gracie was too kind-hearted to evict anyone. "I told him I want a quiet building. He said he worked for Pizza Hut." At the time I thought—there's no connection between these two sentences, but I let it go. "Talk to him, Rick."

Again the loud knocking, insistent. Regular visitors knew to open the front door, always unlatched, and check the three mailboxes. Gracie's apartment door faced the mailboxes. Now, listening, Gracie's voice rang out. "Door's open, whoever you are."

I smiled and opened my door and peered down the stairwell.

JD walked into the vestibule, stood there looking lost, and Gracie, stepping into her doorway, said, "From the looks of you, I guess you want Rick. Second floor."

JD said nothing but glanced up the staircase where I stood on the landing, waving him up. Slowly he climbed the stairs.

He didn't look happy. We watched each other, feet apart, me in the doorway now, arms folded across my chest, and JD stopped in place at the top of the stairs. Dressed in an old brown leather bomber jacket with a ratty fur collar, unzipped over a camouflage T-shirt, tapping a biker's boot on the floor, he was waiting for my move.

I smiled. "I thought you said you never went to the suburbs."

A quirky smile. "You believe everything I say?"

"Why not?"

"Then you're a fool."

"I've heard that before."

I motioned him into my apartment, but he hesitated, unsure. I stepped back, leaving the door wide open, and he walked in, though he lingered just feet inside. Nodding his head up and down, his tongue rolled into the corner of his mouth, he surveyed the room.

"You want to sit down?" I asked him.

"No."

"You want to stand there?"

"That's what I'm already doing." His eyes swept around the walls, stopping on the wall of leather-bound books. Ignoring me, he walked up to the floor-to-ceiling hardwood bookcases and ran his fingers across some flaky bindings. "You read all these?"

"No."

"I didn't think so."

He walked past me to the front of the apartment and gazed out the window into the street below. The skittishness was gone now, replaced with his gangland swagger, as if he'd decided to own the space. A crooked smile. "Is my bike safe around here?"

"Probably not."

He swung back quickly. "Then I gotta get going."

"Well…"

He thrust out his arm. "This is for you." In his hand was a CD in a plastic jewel case, unlabeled. I reached for it. For a second he kept his hand suspended, his fingertips gripping the plastic. Broken nails, I noticed, dried blood at the nub of his fingernails, a smear of splotchy bike grease. He made me yank it from him. He dropped his hand to his side and backed up.

"I don't understand."

"You hear about the thing in Little Saigon?" He waited. "I mean, the old guy almost attacked. Nothing happened but the police swarm the streets like it's Pearl Harbor Day in a Japanese restaurant."

"That's funny." I said. "That line."

"It ain't original with me."

"I still don't understand."

"As I say, nothing happened, but the old guy is the grandfather of a friend of mine. So the whole thing got real personal real fast." He pointed to the CD in my hand. "Le Hanh Fashions a block away got this security camera. This here is the video. It's shitty 'cause all it shows is blurry figures and a lot of bright sunlight shining off the cars. The guys ran into the sun. But it's the only video."

I fingered the plastic case. "Why don't you give it to Ardolino?"

A phony laugh. "Yeah, are you serious? Can you imagine that scene? I ain't got street cred walking up your damn stairs right now. And I don't wanna find myself in a goddamn police lineup. You hear me?" He moved toward the doorway.

"What can I see on it?"

"Nothing. I seen nothing." But he grinned. "But maybe you're a magician."

He turned to go.

"Wait," I said. "I want to ask you…"

He waved me off. "No, I don't think so."

"Why are you doing this?"

His words came out fierce, hostile. "Because no one fucks people over in Little Saigon on my turf and gets away with it."

"Understood."

"No one."

He stepped into the hallway, but then he deliberated, looked back at me. He fiddled with a gold stud in his ear. Then, zipping up his bomber jacket, he reached into the pocket and took out a slip of paper. "Here."

I read the scribbled pencil. "87 Buckingham. Room 3."

"What's this?"

"You figure it out."

Chapter Twenty-six

The video was useless. Or that's how it struck me when I first played it. That night Hank and I watched it over and over. Slow motion, zooming in, zooming out. All the pyrotechnics whiz-kid Hank could muster on a computer screen. Nothing: splashes of intense sunlight, vague ghostlike figures running. A shaft of piercing sunlight on a car fender, blinding. Nothing.

The perps on the screen for—ten seconds. Tops.

"What we can see," I summarized, frustrated, "is a tottering, slow-moving figure brushed by two wisps speeding past. Paranormal activity."

Hank watched the screen closely. "But there's a reason JD gave it to you."

"What he wants is no trouble on his block. Bad for business."

Hank made a face. "There is that."

I shrugged, watching as he pressed "Replay." "Maybe he just wanted to prove to me that he wants justice for Simon and Frankie."

Hank stood up, yawned. "Thanks for the movie. Next time make some buttered popcorn. I gotta get some sleep."

I waved the slip of paper at him. "You're forgetting he gave me an address."

Hank sat back down. "Yeah, what did you find out?"

"A rooming house a few blocks down from Farmington. A dead-end street. On the edge of Little Saigon. A little seedy, a drug den maybe. I know there's drug activity there. But also, I suspect, where I can find Diep and Khoa."

"But he didn't tell you that."

"In his own way he did."

◇◇◇

Another night of dreaming. The orphanage. The boy named Le Xinh Phong. The black kid that allowed me a little breathing room—for a second. The gang of boys chasing him. Waking, the image of that face metamorphosed into that of Simon, running, running. Police dogs tracking him, crying on the banks of the South China Sea during the monsoon season. I woke, gasped out loud. Did he live? Some hardscrabble, piddling life, the boy in the corner. Did he make it to America? Like Mike, was he slipped into the family tree of greedy folks, shuttled to America, and then abandoned? Did he come to understand that none of this was his fault, that he was an accident of war and disaster, that his American father might still remember his mother, the… maybe nothing at all. His GI Joe father. Back in America, a life lived with new children, a wife, a Chevrolet, breakfast special at Denny's. A summer vacation at Disney World.

No. I shook myself awake. Stop it. No. Because thoughts of that boy—and Simon—came cascading back into my own life. And I didn't want to think about it.

But I had to. Early, perhaps seven, the sound of the garbage truck clamoring on the street, the phone rang. It was Mike Tran.

"What happened?" I got out.

The black boy. The orphanage. The Most Blessed Mother Orphanage. Don't hurt me, Viet.

Please.

Mike took some time to answer, and I thought the line had gone dead. But I could hear tinny radio music behind him, drifting in from another room. An oldies station. Johnny Cash, I thought. Or Glen Campbell. A country guitar, twang and strumming.

Finally, clearing his throat, he said, "Maybe it ain't nothing, but last night I heard Simon on the phone. He was calling this other guy. Kenny, I think. Sounded like he said Kenny. But he was whispering, secret-like, but I heard him say something about, well—'I don't wanna do that.' But then, he said 'All right, all right. Tomorrow. Frankie said yes.' When I walked into the room and snatched the phone from him, he beat it out of there, hiding in his room. I couldn't sleep all night, worrying. Should I be worried?" An exaggerated laugh. "I mean, any more worried than the kid makes me already? Who is Kenny? I woke up and thought—something bad is gonna happen to my boy today." A deep sigh. "So I called you."

"I'm glad you did, Mike."

"I didn't know."

"Is he there?"

"Locked in his room, but that don't mean nothing. He runs when he wants to. You know that. I can't lock him in no more."

"I'll look into it," I promised him.

"You will?"

"I will."

◇◇◇

A day of surveillance then. Now that I knew where they lived, I'd been planning on checking out Khoa and Diep—Kenny and Joey. Maybe trail them—learn their habits. They loomed too large in Simon and Frankie's world. JD's dislike—and his sending me in their direction—suggested what? Time for me to move?

If Simon and Frankie hooked up with the brothers today, I'd know about it because I'd be their persistent shadow.

By nine in the morning I sat in my car across the street from 81 Buckingham, idling in the parking lot of a Shell station that had gone out of business, the windows boarded up, a few old cars lined up near the curb, all with For Sale signs on the inside windshields. A number to call. My ancient Beamer fit in nicely with the old rusted relics.

I waited.

I kept an eye on the small parking lot on the side of the old rooming house. The low-slung Toyota with the dark tinted windows sat there, front bumped up against a crashed-in chain-link fence. The guys were sleeping in—or they'd gone somewhere on foot. But I suspected they were late-sleepers. Night clubbers, party boys in their high-life duds, smoking reefer in the parking lot of the Boom Boom Room, a hot-as-hell Asian New Wave night spot, dancing till dawn. A seedy venue, often raided. Gunfire. Fistfights. Kewpie-doll Vietnamese hookers. Kenny and Joey's world, I believed. At nine in the morning, they'd be yawning and stretching like alley cats facing sunlight.

I sat with a bag of buttery croissants from Amy's Bakery on Buckingham and Farmington, a huge mug of coffee, and three Hershey chocolate bars if I got peckish later in the morning. If they were at home, I'd tag them.

The rooming house was an ancient ramshackle Dutch Colonial with green asphalt shingles and white peeling shutters. To the left and right were cheap brick five-story apartment buildings, and across the street were mom-and-pop businesses, an Asian grocery, a beauty parlor called Hair for Now, the deserted Shell station next to a thriving Mobil station, and an auto body repair shop, already doing a brisk morning business. A neighborhood of shops and poor people. The sign that advertised the rooming house announced, honestly: ROOMS. CHEAP. DAY RATES. Then, an afterthought: Mrs. Homer's Rooms.

I sipped coffee slowly, leaned my head back against the headrest, nibbled on the corner of a croissant, and waited. Just waited. At ten o'clock I sat up sharply when the front door opened and the two brothers walked out. They were laughing at something. The taller one, in front, swiveled around and playfully headbutted his shorter brother, who jumped back, then clipped the other with the back of his hand. Even from across the street, crouched low in my seat, I could hear their boisterous humor, overlapping voices in Vietnamese.

"Toi doi." One was hungry.

His brother teased him. *"An khoe nhu voi."* An appetite like an elephant.

At the edge of the sidewalk both paused, debated the direction, and the taller one nodded down the street. A small art deco diner on the corner, a gigantic roof sign that announced: AETNA DINER 24 Hours. But the "E" and the "I" had darkened, and the "R" flickered. ATNA DINE. Brilliant even with the morning sunlight hitting it. "Diep," the shorter brother called out and pointed.

Both brothers were dressed in black clothing, hooded sweatshirts under black vinyl windbreakers, black jeans, military boots. The hoods were up, pulled over their foreheads, but there was no mistaking who they were. A different look from before—gone were the sleek linen suits, the silk black shirts.

I watched as they disappeared into the diner.

I waited.

With my window rolled down, I could smell bacon grease from a block away. Burnt coffee. Garbage overflowing bins. A breeze carried a whiff of motor oil from the auto body shop. A smoky backfire from a lumbering city bus that chugged by. My stomach turned.

A half-hour later they walked out, looked up and down the street as if waiting for someone, lit cigarettes as they strolled back to Mrs. Homer's. They stood on the front porch, silent now, inhaling, then flipping the butts into the bushes. Again they looked up and down the street, leaning into each other. They looked angry as they went into the rooming house.

I waited.

My mind wandered as I daydreamed about a new fraud case that involved an office manager at the Cigna in Bloomfield. Complicated, sensitive investigation. Higher-ups. I was nodding to myself, eyes half-shut, when I realized that the brothers were leaving Mrs. Homer's, both toting over-the-shoulder satchels. Khoa carried a pair of work boots, the laces tied together and draped over his shoulder. They popped the trunk of the Toyota and slipped in the bags. In seconds the car pulled out onto Buckingham, headed toward Little Saigon, three or four blocks away.

I slid out into traffic, two car lengths behind them. Khoa was driving, and jerkily, shifting lanes, tailgating, at one point irritated, leaning on his horn. They stopped at a red light, and even before it turned green, the Toyota jumped ahead, almost sideswiping another car. Gunning it, slowing down, shifting lanes erratically. A heavy-footed driver.

The car pulled into a parking lot of Enterprise Rental, just across from a Subway, and idled. Pulled over on the street, a half-block back, I could see the driver's door open and Khoa step out, looking down the street, shielding his eyes from the sun. Arms waving, he said something to Diep, but then got back into the car.

The car jerked out into traffic so quickly that a passing car slammed on its brakes, the driver raising a fist. Khoa, glancing in the mirror, gave the woman the finger.

I followed, watched them circle back to Buckingham, idle by the Enterprise lot, and then speed away.

The car stopped at a Mini-Mart, and Khoa left the car running, rushing in for a pack of cigarettes, ripping off the cellophane as he pushed open the door. He lit a cigarette and looked up and down the sidewalk. I could tell he was irritated—body stiff, jaw set, head jerking left and right. The car didn't move, idling at the curb, waiting. Then it darted out onto the street.

A stupid game, this rushing up and down the street, but finally the Toyota cruised slowly toward Park Street, maneuvered its way to Little Saigon. Then, suddenly, it pulled up a half-block away from a Second Niagara Bank on the corner of Maynard and Park, then inched its way forward. Again, the waiting. Then, finally, it slowly moved around the corner, stopping alongside a fire hydrant. Diep stepped out of the passenger's side, leaned back in for a second. I'd pulled across the street, parallel but unseen behind a panel truck.

Casually he strolled into the bank.

I waited.

I didn't feel good about the move, but I told myself that even thugs do legitimate banking.

A short wait.

The sudden wail of an alarm, piercing, intense.

A shot fired.

Yet Diep strolled back out in a sleepwalker's gait, his hood pulled over his forehead, his head dipped into his chest. He had a leisurely amble, but his arms cradled a canvas bag. He turned the corner, and Khoa plunged the Toyota forward, and Diep, now trotting alongside, leaped in. The door still wide open, the car pushed ahead, and Diep's arm reached out to shut the door.

My heart pounding, my throat dry, I trailed the car. A block away it slowed, as though going about its normal business, easing its way across a lane, slipping in front of a Connecticut transit bus.

I tapped out 911 and told the dispatcher what I'd seen.

"We have officers heading to the scene." The dispatcher sounded harried. "The bank called in."

"I'm following the car," I told her.

A slight pause. "You're what?"

Stepping on the gas, I got close to the Toyota. I provided the license plate number and a description of the car. "Headed east on Park, almost at the intersection of Ledger. It's slowing…"

She interrupted. "Stay on the line, sir."

"I plan to."

I heard the wail of distant police sirens.

The Toyota hesitated.

Then, just as they neared the turn off Park, I spotted Simon and Frankie walking up the sidewalk. They'd stopped, probably caught by the wail of police sirens coming from different directions, but they seemed to spot the Toyota the same moment I spotted them.

No, God, I thought. No.

The Toyota pulled over behind a stopped transit bus, its front tires scraping the curb. The passenger window rolled down. Diep yelled at the boys, who hesitated, backing off, jittery. Simon turned, as though ready to run, but Frankie looked paralyzed. The bus pulled away, and the Toyota jerked forward, then stopped. An arm reached out. Simon moved, but Frankie ducked down. The glint of a gun, waved wildly at them.

Simon pulled at Frankie, who stumbled.

The gun on them.

Bumping into each other, fumbling with the door, the boys toppled into the backseat, and the car sped off.

I caught my breath.

Maneuvering in front of another car, shifting lanes, I struggled to stay with the Toyota as it careened down the street. No longer the slow pace now, but a wild ride. In the distance a police car's flashing lights. The Toyota scraped the fender of a parked car, a high-pitched whinnying squeal of metal against metal. The car blew through a red light and two other cars, reacting, crashed into each other. One car spun onto the sidewalk and plowed into a plate-glass window. The other rested against a trash bin, its radiator smoking.

I was behind the Toyota, maybe ten feet, maybe less.

It was impossible to see through the dark tinted windows, but I detected movement—the boys in the backseat squirming, twisting around.

The Toyota did not slow down now, whipping past other cars, weaving in and out of lanes, tailgating, swerving, a bumper-car frenzy. The squeal of brakes. Khoa was heading toward the entrance to I-84.

In my rearview mirror I spotted the flashing lights of two squad cars. Cars behind me were pulling off to the side, stopping. Double-parked cars blocked lanes. The cop cars careened left, then right.

I kept going.

Then, approaching a red light, the Toyota suddenly swung to the right, but a Coca Cola delivery truck occupied the right lane, idling. In the left lane a transit bus. Both were waiting for the light to change. The Toyota considered squeezing through—I could see the car edge close to the back bumper of the truck—but couldn't. The light changed, but the truck and bus hesitated.

Police sirens shrieked from behind. No one moved. The Toyota tried to swerve around them into the opposing lane, but a sudden rush of opposing traffic blocked that escape. The Toyota swerved back to the right, smashed into the curb, and seemed to be trying to ride the sidewalk. But the right front fender snared a trash barrel, and the car limped along but finally squealed to a stop.

The Toyota shifted back and forth, managing to shake off the bin, but the car hesitated. Suddenly, as I watched, the right back door swung open, and Simon and Frankie toppled out, hitting the sidewalk, managing to crouch behind a parked car. The Toyota plunged forward and swerved back into traffic, nearly rear-ended by the Coca Cola truck.

I breathed in, closed my eyes.

The boys were nowhere in sight.

A squad car hit the intersection, another blocked the street from the front, and the Toyota tried to jump the sidewalk again but managed only to careen into a streetlight. The hiss of a blown tire. The crunch of fender against metal. The front hood flew up, steam bellowing out. Cop cars everywhere, sirens wailing, a bull horn, yelled orders.

Unable to move forward, I'd pulled over and jumped out of my car. Crouched behind a parked car, perhaps thirty yards away, I watched cops circling the faltering Toyota, rushing out, assuming position, guns drawn.

The grinding of gears as the Toyota belched and shimmied.

Suddenly Khoa opened his door and jumped out. He fired a single shot at the cop facing him. An insane move as the shot ricocheted off a street sign. A ping and an echo. He hunched over, a madman, extending his arm as though at a firing range, his face contorted.

"*Do mami*," he screamed. Fuck you. The words sailed back over the paralyzed street corner. "*Do mami.*" Again. "You fuckin' assholes."

Wildly, he twisted around, losing balance, and fired another shot, willy-nilly, at a cop car. The windshield shattered. Then, his eye obviously on the cop he faced, he pointed the gun.

A shot from the cop hit him in the head. His face bloodied, a hole in his skull, his head lolled to the side like a rag doll's.

Another shot caught him in the chest. A third penetrated his side. His body folded, jerked back, bent.

Then it was over.

His body slipped onto the pavement, the gun still gripped in his right hand. On his back, his other hand twitched and slapped the cement.

It was over. Within minutes Diep was sitting on the sidewalk, legs stretched out in front of him, his hands cuffed behind his back. A sullen look on his face. Muttering, cursing, a volley of Vietnamese filth directed at any cop who neared him. He tried to shift his shoulders, but a cop yelled, "Don't fuckin' move." Diep stared up into his face, turned his head toward the cop, and spat.

The area was cordoned off, cops everywhere, reporters, gawkers, the world come to see. I lingered at the edge of the yellow tape, watching, lost in the crowd. I looked for Ardolino, but there was no one I recognized. It didn't matter. It was over.

But I stood there a long time.

No one touched Khoa's body. He lay in a pool of blood now, his face contorted in an awful grimace. A trickle of blood seeped down the sidewalk, pooled in a crack.

Suddenly I felt pressure on my lower back, a hand digging into my spine. Simon and Frankie had come out of hiding. Little Simon was so close to me that his shoulders brushed against my jacket, his knees trembled against the backs of my legs. I could hear him breathing hard. One of his hands was moving, brushing my side. Startled, I turned and stared down into his face. Bloody, a face and hands scrapped from hitting the pavement, a purple welt on his lip, a swollen eye. He'd been crying, I could tell, wet puffy eyes, streaks of tears down his bruised cheeks. His face had broken out in red blotches, and he was blinking his eyes wildly. Next to him Frankie looked paralyzed, white as parchment, the gaunt look of a cadaver. A smear of dark blood on his temple, clumps of dirt in his hair, a closed eye.

"Simon," I began, but stopped. These boys were scarcely aware of my presence.

Instead their eyes focused on the awful scene feet away.

The death car was still idling, the engine groaning, up against a streetlight. A wispy plume of smoke drifted from the radiator. The kaleidoscopic flash of police lights, a dance-floor light-show cast macabre illumination on the street. Diep, handcuffed, rocking back and forth, quiet now, his face frozen in hate. That gigantic red-and-green dragon tattoo across his neck. But what held the boys' rapt attention was the twisted body of Khoa: blood-splattered, stiff, an arm unnaturally bent, that horrible death grimace gazing up from the pavement, his mouth agape, his tongue hanging to the side. The gun catching the brilliant sunlight. The outstretched hand that no longer twitched.

Chapter Twenty-seven

"Diep and Khoa wanted them to be scouts. Lookouts."

I was sitting with Hank the next morning at Lucille's Breakfast Bar across from the Farmington Courthouse, a room filled with lawyers and clerks and vacant-eyed defendants and accusers—a wholly curious mix of people. Hank had arrived late, but immediately pummeled me with questions about yesterday's shoot-'em-up events. That bloody street scene was splashed across the front page of the *Courant*, not only the wrecked car against the streetlight, but two old mug shots of the brothers Pham—Diep before the dragon tattoo, and Khoa, his eyes half-shut and his mouth twisted. Neither looked happy. Bridgeport police had a warrant out for the two on suspicion of the murder of a Vietnamese restaurateur who famously kept cash in a home vault.

Hank had the newspaper tucked under his arm.

"Simon and Frankie," he said matter-of-factly. "They were moments away from ruining their lives."

"Tell me about it." I sighed, sipping coffee. "When it was all over, the two boys crowding me on that street corner, I drove them to Gracie's apartment—I'd called her first—where she bandaged them up. I mean, she was a delightful Florence Nightingale, mothering, feeding them. She calmed them down. They fell in love with her. Jimmy glowered through it all."

"But you didn't tell the cops about them." He glanced at the next booth where two Farmington cops were contemplating the menu.

I shook my head. "No, I didn't. Jimmy had a problem with that, but only for a minute."

"But is that right, Rick? They were in that car."

I ran my finger along the edge of the cup. "No, Hank. Think about it. They chose *not* to be on that corner where they were supposed to meet Khoa and Diep. They hesitated. And yet, by chance, they were forced into that car. A gun pointed at them. I saw that. Luckily they bailed out. For once they made the right choice. They were *not* a part of that bank robbery."

"But they could have been." A note of pique in his voice.

I smiled. "Sometimes there are different laws that govern the universe. There's no good that could come of handing them over to the police. What would be gained? I want to move them *away* from crime, not reinforce it."

He smiled back. "And so you saved them?" He reached over and broke off a corner of the wheat toast on my plate, swallowed it. My frown meant little to him.

"I don't know about saving them, but I know that they may have been scared straight, to use that awful and familiar phrase my captain bandied about during my Manhattan cop days."

"Scraped and bruised?"

"Yeah, but they're tough kids."

"I can't believe the brothers planned to use them."

"Simon said the brothers had cased that bank, purposely near Little Saigon. I mean, JD had ordered them to leave town because he'd had it with them. But I suppose they were hoping the finger of the law would point back to VietBoyz—at JD. But extortion and petty graft are the bread-and-butter of VietBoyz, small-time crime, drug trafficking in the city. They want to keep it in Little Saigon. Simon told me Khoa knew there was a security guard stationed there some days, different hours, nothing constant. They wanted Frankie or Simon to walk in, stroll around, ask a question maybe, play stupid, then walk out, communicate with the brothers. The other boy would wait by the entrance, watch for any problems outside the bank. No one would pay attention to two young boys."

"Devilish." Hank was shaking his head.

"Yeah, fiendish. They'd already groomed them with weed, money, and gifts like bootleg watches and electronics. Most of all they gave praise, taking two boys with poor self-esteem and building them up. Big brothers, looking out for them. Simon figured they'd use them as shields—or foils."

"But what would have happened to them if the robbery had gone off without a hitch?"

I drummed my fingers on the table. "The brothers were headed out of town. They'd left another car off I-91 in a Newington commuter lot. Ditch the Toyota. Let the cops find it—what did it matter? They'd be gone. They didn't count on me IDing the car to 911 so fast. They'd leave the boys behind. As it was, they were furious the boys didn't show up, so when they saw them walking by, they forced them into that car. Maybe they were thinking, I don't know—hostages, insurance. It never happened."

He laughed. "I can't believe they rolled out of the backseat."

"Simon's idea, he told me. Frankie whispered that the police would kill them, shoot at them through the rear window, and Simon whispered back, 'Now. Get out.' The car hesitated and they toppled out."

"It saved their lives."

"And it may have been the moment that they needed to—well, wake up. Life suddenly got a little too heavy-duty. Hey, the big boys carry guns. And they use them. Christ, Diep fired a shot in the bank, grazed a teller."

"So they're back home now."

"Frankie delivered to his mother's home, where no one was home. Simon into the arms of his mother, who wept when she saw the bandages. And we're back where we started. Ardolino still on their case. Nothing has changed."

Hank bit his lip. "Except maybe *they* have."

"Ardolino's a stubborn guy. He insists they were the ones in the 'almost' mugging in Little Saigon. He followed up on that, talking to the old man who had nothing to offer. But Mike Tran told me Hazel insists she was with her brother on Franklin

Avenue the same time as that incident. She's vouched for him. And she told Ardolino that Frankie showed up. The three of them were slurping shakes at Pinkberry a couple streets over from their house."

"What did Ardolino say about that?"

"Not happy. I told him Hazel wouldn't lie, but he didn't buy that."

"Well, I hope Simon has come to his senses. His days as a juvenile delinquent need to be over."

I puffed out my cheeks. "Lord, I hope so. As Buddha said, You need to prune the growing plant when its leaves are still tender."

Hank's eyebrows shot up, a quirky smile on his face. "Grandma always says to me, *Ai lam nay chiu.*"

You blow an evil wind and soon you'll have a raging storm. I was surprised. "You're finally starting to listen to her."

He smirked. "When did I ever have a choice?"

While Hank wandered across the room to say hello to a state police lieutenant he knew, buzzing as though surprised by a celebrity popping up in a donut shop, I typed some notes into my laptop while idly sipping my third cup of good coffee. Sleepy, I stretched my back and told myself I needed to get back to running, maybe take in a swim at the college pool, write a final exam for my night class. My phone rang.

"Liz." I snapped shut the laptop, sat up. "Hello."

"Where are you?"

I told her. "I'm with Hank."

"I'll drive over. I was just leaving the office." Then, a rousing laugh. "Tell Hank to save me one of Lucille's chocolate croissants."

"You're thinking of Jimmy, Liz," I said, laughing. "Hank only eats protein bars that resemble wood planks, omelets fashioned from the whites of free-range eggs, and kale smoothies that look like a baby's digestive surprise."

"Okay, thanks. There went my appetite."

By the time Hank returned to the booth, Liz was walking into the eatery. She waved from across the room.

She slipped into a seat and poured herself a cup of coffee from the carafe. "Lord, I know everyone in this place," she whispered. "Even some of the criminals twirling around on the stools at the counter."

I checked the time on my phone. "You have news, Liz?"

"You bet." She took a sip of coffee, sighed. "The best, always. Anyway, news on the Judd Snow front. Good in its own bizarre way, but also bad. Maybe 'sad' is the word I want."

"He's leaving Hazel alone, I hope." Hank sounded angry.

"Well, he has no choice these days. But there's more to the story."

"There always is." I leaned forward in the booth.

"Here's the deal. I've been working with a colleague to get a restraining order for Hazel, who now talks to me every day, I am happy to say. Warm, friendly talks. She's starting to feel good about herself—not in the cocky teenage pretty-girl way but, well, genuinely. Talking to her dad. More attention to schoolbooks. I gather Judd had been making her life miserable for a long time, and she never told anyone. Ashamed—blamed herself. He helped that idea take root. She kept it hidden last year. I never knew."

"What about you?" I asked.

She smiled. "Yes, that too." She laughed. "Yes, a fortyish woman has to petition for a restraining order against an eighteen-year-old boy."

"Man." I stressed the word. "A man."

"Yes, of course." She glanced around the crowded room. "A troubled man, that one." She shuddered. "Hazel now confides horrible stories to me. The slaps, the raw, verbal assault."

"So what happened?" Hank was anxious, leaning in.

"Liz," I said, "you're leading up to something."

She smiled at me. "So impatient. At this moment he's cooling his heels in a Hartford jail."

"What?" I blurted out.

Liz sat back, narrowed her eyes, savoring the tale. "Well, we've talked about the toxic relationship he has with his father. Hazel insists there's some truth to Judd whining that Daddy hits on young girls. Namely, Hazel. Makes your skin crawl, no? Daddy slinks around town in Mick Jagger's rock 'n' roll discards. Now that Hazel has told Judd to get lost, Judd's hormones compelled a new girl into his lair. One of them sneaking away from Kingswood, much to the delight of Daddy who came home from the office to discover the pair. Oddly, learning of it, Hazel got jealous, angry. A typical reaction, if an unappealing one."

"Fireworks?"

"You got it. Judd and Daddy Leerest got into it yesterday, and Judd, the poster boy for failed anger-management classes, beats up his father. Okay, Judd is already a wounded animal from the kerfuffle with Frankie, but, though he's hobbling around, he tackles his father, bloodies him, until the neighbors call for help. Judd is carted away, and because this isn't his first foray at the rodeo, he's actually booked, fingerprinted, the whole nine yards. A night in the slammer, where, as I say, he now sits, though not for long."

"Let me guess," I volunteered, "Daddy's posting bail."

"Exactly. A father's love and devotion for an errant child. Sort of sounds like he should be a member of the Tran clan."

"That's not fair," I said sharply. "Simon would never punch out his father."

Hank jumped in. "Because Mike Tran would run the game on that skinny little body."

I shook my head slowly. "This is horrible. But at least Hazel is free of him."

"Well." Liz stretched out the word.

"Christ, no. What?" I raised my voice.

"There's always a second act to a domestic tragedy, no? Well, it seems Daddy called Hazel last night, imploring her to forgive Judd. To take him back. He's hurting. He's in love. His behavior was unseemly. The courts will look upon Judd with more forgiving eyes if she withdraws her plans for a restraining order. No need to testify before a judge. Why would she want to hurt him? He's been hurt so much. On and on—drivel."

"You're kidding." Hank slammed his fist down on the table. "He *called* her?"

"Sweet-talking her. Pleading. 'My only son. There's just the two of us. Mommy ran off with the candlestick maker. The bitch abandoned him—walked away and never looked back. He still has nightmares—cries out in his sleep.' Hazel hung up the phone and called me."

"The man is a creep." Hank lowered his voice. "A damned creep."

"Which one?" Liz arched her voice. "The father or the son."

"They're both cut from the same cloth," I noted.

"Daddy is bandaged up." A pause. "Well, then, so is Junior." Liz took a final sip of her coffee. "Gotta run, gentlemen. The world of criminal psychology is demanding. Every detective on the Farmington force is a manic-depressive. I mean—bipolar. But I knew you'd want to hear the latest from the *Avon Mountain Gazette and Coupon Clipper*. Liz Sanburn, editor-in-chief. One subscriber."

"Call me later," I said as she walked away.

"Are you taking me out to dinner?"

I glanced at Hank, who was grinning. "Well, of course. You pick the restaurant. How did you know?"

She laughed. "One thing about being married to you in the golden age of Ronald Reagan, Rick—I could always read your mind."

She walked away.

"I love her," Hank said. "I think you two will end up remarried. God's plan. Buddha's magic."

I said nothing.

"Say something," Hank insisted.

"I have nothing to say."

◇◇◇

Hank had orchestrated a plan for later that afternoon. We'd watched the brief video given me by JD—what amounted to ten seconds of impossible images: cloudy, a flash of quick moment and blinding reflection of sunlight. Worthless. I'd emailed a file to Detective Ardolino, and he'd left a message on my machine:

"Are you nuts? My alcoholic nephew shoots better footage when he's heaving in a corner. This is supposed to help the case—how?"

Ten seconds of video, but definitely an intended assault in Little Saigon, one that was thwarted by the car crash that sent the culprits scurrying away. Worthless. I agreed with Ardolino.

Not so, Hank. "A video is a video," he said, a line I frowned upon because it told me nothing.

"And a rose is a rose," I told him.

"That makes no sense, Rick."

"Gertrude Stein."

"An old girlfriend?"

"Yeah. How'd you know?"

He was adamant. "What I'm saying is that there is something there. Yes, hard to read. Maybe impossible. But I have an idea."

What Hank had done was to edit the snippet of footage, slowing it down, breaking it into ten distinct seconds, each the equivalent of a still photograph. I'd watched it with him, but still saw nothing. But Hank wasn't through.

"We're going to reenact the ten seconds, frame by frame. With space between. With real people, not frenzied flashes of movement and light. We'll try to approximate the real action of those ten seconds. Same time of day, same direction—into the sun."

"How?"

A mischievous grin. "You ever want to star in a video?"

He had it all worked out. At four that afternoon, the approximate time of the footage, Gracie, Jimmy, Hank, and I stood on the sidewalk in front of Gracie's house, positioning ourselves according to Hank's direction so that we were at the camera's angle, facing the bright sunlight. Gracie was commandeered to use Hank's phone camera, a task that stymied her. "Oh, I can't." But of course she was game.

Jimmy was now walking without crutches, though his foot was still bandaged. "I'm up for this."

Our director Hank named Jimmy the victim, the old Vietnamese man. Hank and I would be the miscreants, aborted in our knockout endeavor. Hank positioned his laptop on a chair dragged from Gracie's apartment, and the second-by-second slow-motion video was to be our script. Our abbreviated scenario.

We rehearsed. The culprits were on camera for ten seconds. A blink of an eye. The old man walked slowly. Someone runs up, flying up the street, suddenly in the frame, near the old man. A movement—perhaps a thrust of arm in the air, raised. A blur. Meanwhile the second culprit, smaller, is not seen until the final seconds, off camera until the sound of the car crash, at which time he steps into the frame but turns suddenly, rushes away, disappears. We see him for two or three seconds.

"But they're all ghosts," I complained to Hank. "You can't even tell if the moving figures are—male. Or young. Old. It's a scene shot through a plywood lens."

"It's something." He shot me a look. "C'mon, Rick. Game up for this."

So Jimmy stood still, stopped by the movement behind him. I was the assaulting figure, rushing in, raising my fist. Hank was the shorter figure, stepping into the frame, twisting around toward the camera angle, and disappearing.

We rehearsed. Gracie recorded the ten seconds. We did it over and over.

Dressed in an oversized I Luv NY sweatshirt and misshapen stretched-out sweat pants—the logo of the New England Patriots had almost disappeared—Jimmy had also donned a World War Two vintage feathered fedora. "A chill in the air," he explained.

"Where in the world did you get that?" I asked.

Gracie spoke through clenched teeth. "My dead husband's wardrobe, which I keep in a back closet. Off limits. Jimmy rifled through it."

"Hey, I'm an investigator."

A gaggle of girls from Miss Porter's, strolling by, stopped to gape, and looked ready to applaud wildly. Perhaps because of the fedora, but more likely enthralled by Gracie, dressed as she was in some 1940s Betty Grable cocktail dress with bunches of red silk roses at the bodice, her notorious black cape dramatically draped over her shoulders. She managed the camera with the care and attention of Cecil B. De Mille staging *Birth of a Nation* with megaphone and safari hat. Apropos of nothing, she sang out to the girls, "I was a Rockette at Radio City Music Hall."

They bustled away.

"They know nothing about art," she grumbled.

Jimmy, standing in position but wobbly on his bum foot, smirked, "Yeah, I'd like to thank the Academy…"

Back in Gracie's apartment we watched ourselves. Hank fed the cell video through the TV, and put it on a loop. Juxtaposed with the original video. Back to back. Over and over, ten grim seconds. We were a fleshed-out version of the original's opaque images.

'What do we see?" I asked.

"Well, the original video is jerky," Hank said. "Look. The Rick/evil person is moving in on the old man. In the original sequence the image is broken by starts-and-stops."

"But," I said, "that isn't the case with the other perp. The Hank/evil person flows in and out smoothly, though in a flash."

"Yeah," Jimmy said. "But look at Hank/evil person's head? When you look at the original, there's…a sudden glare. Like a light in your eye? A spotlight? What in the world?"

"Have we learned anything?" I asked again.

"Yeah," Jimmy said. "I'm the only one with talent. Someone's lifting an arm to slug me and I stand there. In character."

"Method acting." Gracie smiled at him sweetly. "Yeah, you and Brando."

Chapter Twenty-eight

Grandma's kitchen smelled of diced ginger. She stood at the counter, an oversized cleaver in her small, frail hand, and she wailed at the brown fibrous tubers. At one point she stopped, picked up a few flecks of the savory herb and handed them to me. "Chew these." I placed them in my mouth: potent, tangy, my nose twitching. She smiled. "A cure for everything that can be cured."

"Well, I don't know about that," I laughed. "I've heard you can see in the dark."

"It's seeing in broad daylight that's the real problem for so many folks."

On the late April afternoon, a chilly day, the kitchen was warm and toasty. Not only the heavenly scent of chopped ginger, but a small bowl of grated garlic, a colander of freshly rinsed broccoli, the florets gleaming as if waxed. Long strands of lemongrass lay like marsh reeds across a cutting board. The rice cooker hummed, whiffs of steam seeping out. On a cutting board a plump bitter melon.

A drifting afternoon in the kitchen, as I sat at the oilcloth-covered table, quietly sipping jasmine tea and munching on ginger candy so tart my eyes teared and my mouth puckered.

"This is nice." Grandma walked by and patted my wrist. "You stay away too long." She was wearing one of her daughter's old housedresses, too big on her small frame, bunched at the waist.

I smiled up at her. "Busy, Grandma."

She swung her head back and forth and looked like a small doll that might shatter. "Foolish boy. You have to always come home."

"I'm here."

She squinted at me, her foggy eyes trying to focus. "You look tired. This...this Tran boy...this case." We were chatting in Vietnamese, hers a slow drawl and mine a hesitant attempt, but now she lapsed into English, always a strain for her. "I watch TV, Rick. Americans like to talk of dying." Then, back to Vietnamese. "They think if they talk about it, it will not come for them. They don't understand that we have no choice but to suffer." She tapped my wrist. *"Lua thu vang, gian nan thu suc."*

A man's misfortune is the touchstone of his life.

I laughed as I dropped another candy into my mouth. "Everyone wants to live forever."

"Then they are foolish," she answered.

She bent over the cutting board, intent on what she was doing. I heard her chuckle, and mutter, "The act of living is the act of dying. One and the same." But she seemed to be saying it to herself.

Grandma's kitchen. Of course, Hank's Grandma, but mine by love and possession. And I cherished the time sitting alone with the old woman, a woman so tiny she came up to the world's hip but oddly dominated any room she walked into. That wrinkled prune face, wreathed by a halo of brilliant white hair. Slightly hunchbacked, she shuffled along, at your side, leaning in, whispering, smiling, holding your hand. She was medicine for any day of blues.

Hank was at the Academy, so he couldn't make supper. His mother and father were somewhere in town, dragging along Vu and Linh, Hank's younger brother and sister. Grandpa, never a fan of mine, was somewhere in the house, doubtless listening to Grandma's encouragement of me—and shuddering. No matter: I loved this late afternoon with Grandma.

Grandma finally sat down opposite me, her hands circling a small cup of tea. "Yesterday I spent the day with Lucy."

Grandma had undergone a painful reckoning. She wanted to undo the transgression she believed she'd committed years back when she let the friendship die after Lucy's marriage to an untouchable. They'd talked a few times on the phone, both overjoyed with their rediscovery. Now another milestone: Lucy had invited Grandma for lunch. The two women, after all these years, a lunch.

She whispered, "Decades of my shame leave me now."

I said nothing.

She sat still. Finally, "*Doi cha an man, doi con khat nuoc.*"

She saw the question in my eyes, and translated in slow, fractured words. "When parents eat salt"—she struggled.

But I knew the rest: "The children die for water."

She smiled. "The horrible things we do to our children." A heavy sigh. "The years are nothing now. I was a foolish woman who let others tell me how to live my life. As Buddha would say"—now she pointedly looked at me—"*Di hoa vi quy.*" The need for cherished peace.

So she'd spent a lovely day at the Tran household, Mike Tran working at the garage all day. Lucy alone in her kitchen.

"I'm glad you two are friends again."

She shrugged away that comment. "We were always friends, but I listened to the wrong voice inside me." A wistful smile. "Now I listen."

"I'm happy."

"She tells me you brought Simon home. A boy covered with bandages. Black and blue."

I nodded. "I took him first to Gracie's. He's all right."

"He told her that you saved him."

"No, he saved himself."

"She's hoping you saved him."

"But I…"

She held up her hand. "The boy is home safe. Thank God. But she's worried what will happen." She looked into my eyes. "Talk to me about him."

So I told her about the shooting, Khoa's death. Diep's capture.
But also little Simon behind me, frightened, weeping.

She nodded. "So he learns, that boy."

"I hope so."

"Oh yes, he learns. Now he witnessed that life is not a game.
Chim bi ban nut gap canh cay cong cung so."

I didn't understand. "A child who…" I stopped.

She finished in English. "A child who is burned will always
run from fire."

"I hope so, Grandma."

"But she's worried. That goes without saying. She wakes up
in the morning and she thinks of Simon. She has trouble talking
to her husband because he is a little…"

"Pig-headed," I finished.

She laughed. "A good man but fighting his own demons. The
dark that stays inside him." A sigh. "Because of Simon, he feels
he's failed as a father. It pulls him apart, making him *more* severe.
He won't ever say anything—you know Vietnamese men, silent,
running away from emotions—but he's ready to…shatter. And
maybe…it's up to you…maybe you can talk to him." Her face
reddened, her eyes flickering. "You understand what he went
through. The horrors there. The horrors here. The old country."
Her voice got so low I had trouble hearing her. "This is a man
who still cries out at night from his nightmares, his boyhood in
the streets." She stopped, out of breath.

"He is hoping I can clear Simon's name. I don't know."

Her voice hardened. "Do you hear yourself, Rick? That's not
you talking. Of course, you can help."

"I don't know."

"You probably already know the answer."

"You think so?"

She wagged a finger at me. "Lucy tells me you take no money
for this. Like a good son of Vietnam. So that tells me you are
looking with your heart as well as your head." She tapped my
temple. Her fingertip was warm to the touch.

"I remember a saying from the little book my mother left with me in the orphanage. *Ngay dai nhat cung phai qua di.*"

Even a long, long day will come to an end.

"Your mother was a wise woman."

I felt a tugging at my heart. My mother—a vague image of a woman holding me, crying, letting go of me, sending me away. My mother, lost. Another country. Lost.

A new land. America. This warm kitchen.

I stared around the cluttered kitchen. On each wall a calendar, perhaps five in total, something I'd never understood in Asian kitchens. Chinese markets, Vietnamese restaurants, Korean gift shops, Laotian health stores. New Year's gifts in the marketplace. This household of Catholic and Buddhism. A mother and a father, happy together. And Grandma in the center of it all, the moral heartbeat.

"My mother," I whispered.

Grandma stared into my eyes. "I have something to say. Something that comes to me as I hear your story."

I waited. "I was hoping you would."

"Simon. The lost boy. You are convinced he has nothing to do with the street violence?"

I nodded. "Yes. Without proof."

"Instinct?"

"Maybe."

She sat back in her seat, watched me closely. "It seems to me, Rick, that you believe that young boy is innocent, but all your focus is on *him*. All your energy is on his story. You keep asking him to help you. You look to…him."

Feebly, I protested, "I have to. What else is there?"

"But you already *believe* him innocent. Then he has nothing to do with the crime, yes? Maybe it is time to look at a world where he is *not* the center of your attention."

"What does that mean?"

"It means this—is there anyone who *wants* him to be guilty? You tell me the two street crimes—maybe three—resemble the foolishness he did that got him sent away."

"Grandma, who would want to frame a young boy? It makes no sense."

She held up a finger. "Wait. Maybe not *wants* him to be guilty but—well, *allows* him to be guilty." She glanced toward the counter where the vegetables sat, waiting for her touch. "The boy that everyone expects to be bad."

"I just don't see it." I sighed and remembered Jimmy's remarks. "Jimmy told me something similar—others using the boy."

She stood up, smiled. "A great mind, that man. Think about it."

"Thank you."

She motioned with her hand. "Come with me."

I followed her into the hallway, toward the back of the house. She opened the door to Hank's bedroom and switched on the light. She walked in, motioning me to follow.

"I don't know if Hank would like…"

She stopped me. "Of course he wouldn't mind. You're his brother."

She pointed to a Connecticut state trooper's formal uniform hanging on a post. Pristine, sharp, the gray shirt with the royal blue epaulets with gold piping. A run of gold brass buttons down the front. The dark navy blue trousers with a crease so sharp it could be knifepoint. On the dresser the gray Stetson-style hat. A gold pin on the front that said "State Police."

Grandma pointed at it. "His pride," she said, beaming.

"It looks…chiseled."

"He irons and steams and fiddles with it. For him, it is a piece of art."

I laughed. "The ceremony is coming up."

"His pride," she repeated, running her fingers over the fabric.

"His mother worries."

She looked into my face. "*I* worry. Of course, I worry." But she added, "But I understand that it's the life he demands of himself. Duty, honor, service. Heroism is never ego. My grandson. My Hank. Number one son. I worry, too. But I understand that there is no other road for him to follow."

"Why are you showing me this, Grandma?"

We stepped out of the bedroom and she clicked off the light. "Because you are a part of what makes him a man. He honors you because you honor him."

"But I worry, too."

Manhattan. Hell's Kitchen. A gun to my head. My trigger finger. The bloody body. My rage, out of control.

She wasn't listening. Instead she mentioned Liz's name, which surprised me. "He tells me she is helping young Hazel find her way."

"Yes. Another troubled Tran child."

She tossed her head back and forth. "Those children. A blessing and a curse. A family loses happiness when a child is lost."

"Liz is helping."

Grandma looked into my face. "A good wife to you."

"Grandma, you know that we're divorced, Liz and I."

She waved her hand in my face. "That means nothing. A piece of paper...no matter."

I gave her a quick hug. "You know, Grandma, little Simon actually said the same thing to me—that Liz and I will always be married."

A quiet laugh. "Maybe that little boy is not as lost as people say. Buddha speaks to his heart."

"He's a Catholic, I think."

"Everybody walks with Buddha, Rick."

I followed her back into the kitchen and was surprised to see Grandpa sitting at the table, sipping tea. He looked up and frowned. My heart sank. The last frontier in this Nguyen household, the last and most harrowing barrier. Grandpa, the man refused to speak to me.

"Hello," I said respectfully. *"Ban co khoe khong?"* How are you?

He hesitated. For a moment he blew across the hot tea, then put the cup down. As I watched, he extended his hand. Surprised, I stared at it, the gnarly arthritic fingers, twisted. In a barely croaked-out voice, he cleared his throat.

"Hello," he said slowly. *"Chao mung bau."*

Awkwardly, we shook hands.

Behind him, already at the counter, her fingers running over reeds of lemongrass, Grandma was smiling.

◇◇◇

Back in my apartment, I reflected on Grandma's words, although I also obsessed about Grandpa's magnanimous gesture. I smiled to myself. Perhaps the axis of earth could shift. Perhaps snow could fall in August. Perhaps fate does surprise you with a happy ending. Ever since last year when I helped solve the murder of two of Grandma's relatives, Hank had hinted that his grandfather admitted a begrudged respect for me. But in all my visits to the household, he'd never extended his hand. Until today.

I liked that.

Grandma's chilling words: who knowingly would *allow* Simon and Frankie to take the blame? Allow—permit—maybe welcome. To abet—to encourage. Who?

I made myself a cup of coffee, munched on a stale butter roll I'd left out on the counter that morning, and decided to play the video. *Let's go to the tape.* That horrid line used on scandal TV. Cop shows. *Let's look at the tape. CSI: Everywhere.* The muck-raking reporters trailing after errant politicians. *Let's take a look at the video. The tape shows...*

The tapes. More than one.

I played the ten-second video of the Little Saigon incident and then played it against the one produced by my own amateur acting troop, Gracie Patroni, director. Something was starting to click. The anomaly of movement. Something there. Yes.

The tape from the first crime—the death of Ralph. Jimmy stumbling into traffic.

Nothing.

Then I logged onto my computer, brought up YouTube, and found that rap video from SaigonSez. I'd watched it over and over, the gangsta stances, the in-your-face menace. Simon as thug. Frankie as thug. Worse, the bleak outlook on life. The dead-end philosophy. In the name of the devil. But oddly it always struck me now as the product of two half-baked wanna-nabes dressing up for an amateur hour in a suburban school hall. Yet…there was a message there, perhaps not the one they might glibly proclaim.

I watched it again.

A teenaged fatalistic vision. The raw power of boys exalting evil. Celebrating the vainglorious ego of Satan. No good to cry. This is the way the world is, and it isn't pretty. Only evil lasts forever. Shakespeare: the evil that men do lives after them. The good is buried with the dead. Don't cry. No good to cry.

Simon and Frankie as Elizabethan troubadours on a dark landscape.

> *In the name of the devil*
> > *(awright you go to hell)*
> *In the name of the devil*
> > *(awright I'll go to hell)*
> Did they describe themselves?
> *Boys with black and hooded heads*
> > *Cool and classy in the street*
> *You and me—no good to cry*
> > *Only Satan lives forever.*

I found myself thinking back to my literature classes. John Milton: Satan thundering after exile from heaven—better to rule in hell rather than serve in heaven.

What fresh hell is this?

> *Forbidden streets ain't got no map*
> *Nowhere to run when you awake*

A civics lesson, no less—bloodbath in Afghanistan.

Little Simon watching CNN and taking notes? What would Wolf Blitzer say?

I scrolled down the page. The number of "likes" had increased in a few days to 11,732. Who were these online viewers? Young kids? Disgruntled grownups? How did young folks navigate social media and discover SaigonSez? Lost Vietnamese immigrants pining in the Diaspora for a city that no longer existed? Sai Gon. Saigon.

Sez.

But there were fifty-seven "dislikes."

I skimmed through the comments:

You boyz is all there is…You nail it.

This is a masterpiece. Somebody got real talent rap lyric telling.

I put this on my MP3 player and it plays thru my schoolday.

You got anymore raps? Upload.

SaigonSez a lot to me.

Yet some were negative, even strident:

What the hell you talkin about.

White boyz cant rap or jump and Asians too.

Find Jesus and cut the crap.

You sound like boys that kill for the hell of it. Awright then you can go to hell for all I care.

…Boys that kill for the hell of it…

Go to hell…

Awright…

The lines stopped me cold. I found myself playing and replaying the video. I reread the comments. Then I saw something. I scrolled up and down. I sat up, startled. Why hadn't I seen it before? How had I missed it?

I returned to my laptop and played the ten-second video from Little Saigon.

Over and over.

Sunlight on a city sidewalk, late in the afternoon.

Suddenly I had an idea of what had happened.

Chapter Twenty-nine

I called Hank to tell him my idea, and his long silence convinced me that I'd hit on a real possibility.

"But there's no proof," he protested. "And it's a little preposterous."

"But possible?"

As we spoke, I was pacing my rooms, antsy, manic. I straightened a picture on the wall, decided it had to be moved. Then I changed my mind. I looked out the front window at the street. A cloudy day, windswept. It started to rain, a driving spring shower, and a girl from Miss Porter's ran for shelter. I peered through the rain-splattered window, and my mind riveted to that cloudy ten-second video. So much revealed in so short a tape. Yes. An awful epiphany. There, hidden under all that brilliant sunlight.

"Yes." Hank sucked in his breath.

I waited for that one word: yes.

As I was hanging up my phone, my land line rang. My mind elsewhere, I picked up the phone absently.

"Ardolino here." The grumpy voice waited. "You there?"

I focused. "Yes."

"It's polite to say hello, you know. Were you raised in a barn?"

"What is it, Detective?"

He made a gulping sound, then swore. "These goddamn lids don't stay on a cup, you know. Like that old lady, I should sue McDonald's for millions. Then I wouldn't have to be calling you with news."

"You don't sound happy. Let me guess—good news for me?"

"Dream on." Another slurping sound. "Well, I guess it is. We got hold of this surveillance video from this Pinkberry place where Hazel Tran said she was with your boys. Time of day, etcetera, etcetera. As it turns out, there they are, Hazel and criminal-at-large Simon, merrily chugalugging milk shakes without a care in the world."

"They're kids," I told him. "They *should* have a world without cares."

"I believe in giving kids a dose of reality right off the bat."

"Scare them straight?"

A forced laugh. "That way life ain't gonna take them off guard later on in life."

"Is that how you raised your kids, Detective?"

The sound of gulping. "Whatever happened to my kids was the result of my wife hiding them from the truth."

"Why'd you call?" I asked. "An apology?"

"Well, Simon and weasel Frankie—yes, even Frankie makes a guest appearance at Pinkberry. Christ, in my day no boy would never walk into a place called Pinkberry."

"They also didn't have frozen yogurt in your day."

A snarky laugh. "Yeah, like I'm one day older than water, Lam boy."

I broke in, content. "So the boys couldn't have been the culprits in Little Saigon."

"No, they couldn't. Not *that* episode. I mean, they ain't off scot-free from the other two—the ones that resulted in someone buying final lunch. But most likely not."

"Good news, then."

"Yeah, yeah." I could hear him getting ready to hang up, his voice moving away from the receiver.

"Hold on, Detective," I yelled into the phone.

He barked into the phone. "Yeah? More pleasant conversation? I guess you don't get to talk to cheerful souls like me on a regular basis."

"Listen, Detective. I have a theory of what happened." I could hear him bring the phone closer to his mouth. "Hear me out. Okay?"

"This better be good."

I hesitated. "It's a conversation I really don't want to have. It's...sad..."

He cut in. "For Christ's sake, just tell me."

I sat down on the sofa. "I have a favor to ask of you."

Slowly, point by point, without any interruption from Ardolino—except now and a muttered "yeah, yeah, shit"—I outlined my theory, why I'd come to have it, what I needed from him.

"I don't think I can—"

A sinking feeling in the pit of my stomach. "C'mon, Detective."

"But...all right." He stopped. "I'll call you back in a few hours. I'll make a couple calls. This better not be a wild goose chase, Lam."

"I'm on to something."

"Maybe. Give me three hours. Tops." The line went dead.

◇◇◇

Ardolino was a man of his word. Three hours later, almost to the second, my phone jangled, and his smoker's cough took up the first few seconds. I waited. A monstrous, phlegmatic bark. He muttered, "Jesus H. Christ." Then, abruptly, "Lam?"

"What did you find out?" I held my breath.

"You were right on the money, Lam."

I slapped my hand on the table. "I knew it."

"Don't get too cocky. It ain't a nice character trait. But, yeah, the house of cards collapsed. All the pieces fitting in. Little Simon and his Neanderthal buddy Frankie get to bother a few more of my days."

Then, wound up, he filled me in on what had transpired during that three-hour block of time: back-and-forth telephone calls, checking in with forensics, interrogation, and finally capitulation. Ardolino related the information piecemeal, with stammered gaps as he checked his notes. Consultations with superiors, faxes ignored, at one point a nasty call from a lawyer.

But he persisted in the probe. A bulldog, driven, once he was convinced that I was right.

"A confession, no less. Signed and sealed. I can sleep a little better tonight." A pause. "Just that one loose end to take care of. The D.A. is preparing a warrant as I speak to you."

I rushed my words. "Let me do something first."

"Like what?"

I told him.

"Is that a good idea?" Then, his voice dropping, "What the hell. All the pieces coming together. You have an hour. Hear me? Have a good time."

That bothered me. "I'm not enjoying this."

He made a clicking sound. "Well, yeah, I can understand that. You got a soft spot inside you."

"And you don't?"

"It's my secret, Lam." Someone behind him yelled to him. For a second he covered the receiver. "Gotta run."

"You're welcome, Detective."

"Like I said, arrogance ain't attractive, Lam. Didn't they teach you that in immigration school?"

"Goodbye, Detective."

◇◇◇

I pulled into Mike Tran's driveway, hoping Simon was at home to receive the good news. I wanted to watch his face—gauge how he'd changed, if at all. He'd no longer have Ardolino hounding him, threatening, accusing, a noisome shadow that never disappeared. I wondered if the boy would care—all along he copped that tough-boy attitude, indifferent to his fate. A simple protestation of innocence. Believe me or not, it's up to you. Then he went about his boyhood business, sinking deeper into quicksand.

Now it was over.

I rang the doorbell, and Michael Tran opened the door. I suppose I looked surprised because he laughed out loud. "I'm not an apparition, Rick."

"But a rare visitor to the homestead, no?"

He was wearing a navy blue polo shirt that said Trinity Crew in gold stitching. "Time for a visit." He stared over my shoulder. "And I had to deliver Simon back once again. That boy likes to run."

"You're talking to your father?"

"My, my. Standing in the doorway and already the personal questions." But he looked over his shoulder again. "As a matter of fact, yes. I like to surprise people."

"So do I."

He watched me closely, his eyes cold. "That's what I'm afraid of. Why are you here?"

"Can I come in?"

He stepped back. "Of course."

Rushing from the hallway, Mike grabbed my hand and shook it too long. He put his arm over my shoulder and steered me into the living room. Lucy sat on the sofa, her body pressed against Hazel's. The girl looked weary, ready to cry. I nodded at her, but she looked away. Lucy nodded to a side chair, and I sat. Simon was not in the room, but I heard the *ping ping ping* of a video game played in the family room. For a second the noise stopped as a head peeked around the corner, checking out the living room—Simon's face, expressionless, staring. It disappeared.

Looking anxious to leave, Michael stood by the front door with his jacket in his hand.

"You're here for a reason," he said.

"Call Simon," I said.

His father panicked. He rushed toward the family room, but he stopped abruptly, faced me, beads of sweat on his forehead.

"It's all right, Mike," I told him. "It's okay."

"Simon," he called out. A voice hollow, breathy. "I let them play video games today."

Simon and Wilson stopped their game playing, though one of the boys let out a disgusted groan. Probably Simon. Both joined us, dragging their feet. Simon stood behind Wilson, eyes slatted, uncertain, unhappy.

"I didn't do nothing." A scratchy voice.

"I know that," I said to him. "We all know that now." I caught Mike's eye. "I just spoke with Detective Ardolino. He's made an arrest. Simon and Frankie are in the clear."

I expected some reaction from Simon. But there was none, simply the calculated indifference of a teenaged boy, shoulders hunched, eyes blank. Next to him his brother Wilson turned to look at him as though he expected Simon to say something. A quizzical smile on his face. He scratched absently at a pimple on his chin. Acne on his forehead, picked at until the spots bled.

Something happened in the room. Lucy stood up and stared out the front window, her hand clutching a curtain. She swiveled around, faced the TV, but seemed unable to settle down. We all watched her. She wore a haunted look as though expecting disaster. Her husband eyed her from his seat, his eyes hooded, and he said in a raspy, angry voice, "*Dung lo*, Lucy." Don't worry. Then, softly, in English, "Sit down. It's all over." Immediately she sat back down next to Hazel, who stared straight ahead. Silence, awful.

Michael was the first to speak. "Then, I suppose, we can get back to our boring lives."

Mike, relief on his face, asked, "Then who? Why?"

I waited a heartbeat. "Judd Snow."

Hazel screamed as her mother gripped her shoulder.

Mike looked puzzled. "But that makes no sense, Rick."

Simon stepped back toward the family room, his face pale.

"Judd Snow," I repeated. "An hour ago he confessed. He was already in jail for beating up his father but, questioned by Avon cops, he broke down, confessed."

"But why?" From Lucy.

Michael's voice was tinny. "None of this is coming together for me. Really, Rick. I'm curious. How did they catch him?"

Suddenly Hazel was sobbing out of control. Every eye found her. She was wearing some eye makeup, and now it streaked her face, ran down her cheeks. When I repeated Judd's name, she squirmed, twisted out of her mother's tight hold. A low moan escaped from her throat.

We waited.

"No." Only that one word. "No." She repeated it. Then, slowly, "He…?"

She dipped her head into her lap. Lucy rocked with her. A choked sound, whispered. "No."

I went on. "Judd Snow is an angry boy—man. You all know that. Striking out, battles in public." I softened my words. "The way he treated Hazel for so long a time. The need to dominate— to *hit* her." Her head jerked up for a second, then dropped back down. "And a toxic relationship with his father. A screwed-up childhood, filled with rage. A home life that…" I stopped. "Enough. Anyway, he told the cops he thought of doing those knockdowns because it was thrilling, forbidden. Bored, he could get his heart racing."

"That seems extreme," Michael protested.

"It is, and only one part of the story. The truth of the matter, as he acknowledged to the cops, was that he'd had that brawl with Frankie"—I shot a look at Simon who looked nervous—"a fistfight that ended with both taken to a police station. He was humiliated. You remember that he said he'd kill Frankie if they crossed paths again. Well, he harbored growing resentment— fury—at Frankie. Another scuffle at the mall. Then another fight on the lawn outside. He stalked Frankie the way he stalked Hazel, the way he stalked Liz. But then he decided a better way."

"What?" Michael's voice was too loud.

"He was sitting in Burger King and was irritated by Ralph Gervase. They may have exchanged words, obscene gestures. He wanted to hurt him. So the opportunity presented itself— unplanned, most likely. He said he'd been talking of Frankie and Simon and their months in juvie. Knocking folks around. At that moment he thought—why not get back at Frankie that way? He says it was spur of the moment. But ratchet it up a bit. Copy Frankie and Simon all over again. Get Frankie sent to prison. Revenge. Stupid, yeah, but it's the thinking of a guy filled with hate he couldn't understand."

"Diabolical," said Michael. "But that would mean Simon would be implicated, sent away. The brother of his girlfriend? Why?"

"What did he care?"

Michael's eyes widened. "You mean, he confessed to all this?"

I nodded. "But only after he was shown proof. The second killing on Whitney was different. I imagine he was looking for blood—thrills, excitement. The cops found a postcard from GameStop, addressed to Frankie Croix. It could have meant nothing, but this morning I asked Detective Ardolino if they'd dusted it for fingerprints. Of course, they had. Ardolino's a stickler for detail. Mostly smudges, unreadable, Frankie's own print, but one partial print of a thumb at the edge of the card. Unidentifiable. No way to use it. But I remembered that Judd was booked and fingerprinted for the assault on his father, and I wondered about it. Anyway, Ardolino had the two compared. It has Judd's thumb on that card."

"But how?" Michael asked. "How would his print be there?"

Simon spoke up, "That fight in the mall. He dumped out Frankie's backpack for spite, kicked it around. He took a video game. He stepped on his stuff."

I nodded. "Yes, and he obviously pocketed a postcard that fell out. Or maybe it was attached to the game. In any event he pocketed it, saved it."

"But to kill guys? To *hurt* them?" From Lucy, her voice trembling.

"He may not have intended to kill. Or maybe he did. The idea of inflicting real pain…well, perhaps he wanted the feel of fist against bone. It happens."

Lucy shivered. "How sad."

"But there's something I don't get." Michael looked puzzled. "He had a buddy with him, no? And didn't I read that one witness thought that he was Chinese or something?"

The room felt hot, close, no windows opened to let in the brisk spring air. A cluttered room, too much furniture packed into the small space. I found myself staring at the wall of awards and commendations. A family's proud display of academic achievement. Plaques from the American Legion and the D.A.R. Too many of them.

I looked at no one but said in a loud voice, *"Ego non baptize te in nomine patris, sed in nomine diabolic."*

I waited, watching the stunned faces.

All but one, that is. One face offered a wistful smile.

Mike frowned. "What the hell you talking about?"

Michael, brow furrowed, translated. "I baptize you not in the name of the father but in the name of the devil. Latin 101. Thank you, Kingswood-Oxford."

I hesitated a moment, nodding at him, but continued. "Hank told me about a video on YouTube uploaded by Simon and Frankie. SaigonSez." Simon, I noticed, blinked wildly. "I watched it over and over, fascinated. Clever, really. Intriguing."

Simon spoke up. "Yeah, it's cool. All my friends…"

"What's this?" Mike thundered.

I went on. "A celebration of Satan. A dark view of the world. Life is tough. It's no good to cry about it. Give the devil his due. We mortals end up in hell, but Satan lives forever." I waved my hands in the air. "Sort of a quick summary of it."

Simon was not happy with my glib summary, and looked ready to argue the point.

"I don't understand," Lucy added.

"At first I thought the YouTube video was a confession from the boys, given that it talked of street life, souls in black hoods, practical jokes, an unforgiving world. I watched it over and over. All the time I never noticed one thing about it." I paused, deliberated, uncertain.

"Well?" From Michael, impatient.

I lowered my voice. "Tell us about it, Wilson."

Every eye shot to the young boy, standing by his brother but shuffling from one foot to the other. "Come on, Wilson. I saw the credits. Those rap lyrics were written by you. W. Tran."

"So what?" From Simon, feisty. "He writes stuff."

"No, Simon. Suddenly some things made sense. Wilson, the would-be writer, lost in his room and his books, punished by his father for not studying. Hazel had told Michael that she was afraid of something. Simon told her he had a secret, but kept it to himself."

"A secret?" asked Mike.

"I suspect Simon suddenly realized something one day."

Simon quaked. "No, I…"

"He put two and two together. Smart boy. I remember watching him play a video game with Wilson. A familiar storyline—the bookish nerd who overtakes the powerful evil force, becomes the hero, triumphs. Exalts. A violent game. The hero leveling foes."

"So what?" From Michael.

"But I also remembered his love of *Moby Dick*. I checked out my copy. Captain Ahab, filled with overweening pride. 'I'd strike the sun if it insulted me.' A baptism in the name of the devil. The lyrics on YouTube came from Melville. 'Who ever heard that the devil was dead?' 'I was a black and hooded head.' Ishmael, plagued with boredom and ennui, going to sea to prevent him 'from deliberately stepping into the street and methodically knocking peoples' hats off.' Other lines." I struggled to recall and slipped a note card from my breast pocket. "'I love to sail forbidden seas, and land on barbarous coasts.' 'It is the easiest thing in the world for a man to look as if he had a great secret in him.' A great secret. So many lines taken from *Moby Dick*. Even that line about a bloody battle in Afghanistan. Melville, over and over. And the last bit from Mark Twain, Huck Finn when he decides to give up his soul for a black man. 'I'll go to hell.' A refrain—'Awright I'll go to hell.'" I stopped. "Enough."

"Still…" said Michael, faltering. "I mean…"

"Stop," I demanded. "The first clue for me was a ten-second tape from Little Saigon, an aborted attack. Reconstructed by Hank, played in slow motion, rehearsed by friends, I was bothered by two things. One was that the attacker moved jerkily, while the other didn't, even though the video was unclear. Then I realized the attacker was limping. Judd Snow with the bum leg after the fistfight with Frankie in front of this house."

"And the second?" Michael again, his voice sharp.

"The second culprit, smaller, standing apart, appearing for a second but turning into the sun. A sharp piercing light on his head."

"Which was?"

"It took me a while but I realized that person was wearing thick eyeglasses, and the glint from the sun was what the camera picked up."

"I don't understand this." Mike Tran was looking at Wilson.

"Tell us, Wilson," I said softly. "Tell us."

The boy fidgeted, looked over his shoulder toward the hallway. He wrapped his skinny arms around his chest, and for a second I thought his look was cocksure, his eyes steely. Captain Ahab. *I'd strike the sun if it insulted me.*

"Tell us," Michael coaxed, surprisingly gentle.

I prodded him. "Judd Snow has already told us your name, Wilson."

That startled him. In a surprisingly strong voice, he said, "He promised."

"But why?" From his father. "You hated him. He pushed you around. He..."

"He told me I had to be quiet about it. He threatened—scared me."

"Is that true?" I asked, suspicious.

He nodded furiously. "We went to the boys' club to teach chess. The advisor sent us, you know. I took the bus but sometimes he said—ride with him. He told me...he said, 'You wanna get a thrill? You wanna make some excitement in your boring life?' He drove around the city like a maniac, top speed, daredevil. He told me I was a wimp. He...you gotta slap the world in the face. He didn't *like* me. I didn't *like* him. But I felt...you know...important in that car, his attention, laughing, making fun of people...walking down the street. But I didn't know he was going to hit that man from Burger King. Yeah, he was pissed off and we followed them. I mean, he just ran at the guy."

I broke in. "But after the first time you did, Wilson. You knew what to expect. Come on."

He looked wild-eyed. "It always surprised me. It did. He said—'I can get away with murder.'"

"You didn't have to go."

He looked up into my face, his glasses slipping down his nose. "I *had* to. He told me I had to." His eyes sought his father. "I had to, Pop. He said you only live once. He used to whisper: 'YOLO.' You only live once. Grab it. Seize the day. *Carpe diem.* You gotta feel…like the world is yours. For a minute I felt like I was on top of the world. 'Come with me,' he said. 'Get in the car now. I don't wanna have to hurt you.' 'I will *hurt* you.' I mean, he *told* me."

He kept talking until he ran out of words. He rocked back and forth on his heels.

A long silence settled in that stifling room. Lucy's eyes were stark, frightened. No one moved. The clock on the wall tick-tocked monotonously. The shape of Vietnam. Tick tock. The same clock that Grandma had in her house. One that I'd seen in so many Vietnamese restaurants. Cheap kitsch, yes, but an odd reminder that once upon a time we all lived in a tropical country, where water buffalo grazed next to the Saigon River under the shade of banyan trees…rattled by *cyclos* zipping through the narrow streets…the helicopters and the napalm and the B-52s and the VC hiding in the elephant grass…where there was a different sense of time and place…the long tropical nights filled with green bottle flies. A land of exile and longing. The geography of memory. In America everybody looks at those clocks. Every day. They took you back to New Year's. Tet. Everyone listening for the first sound after the clock struck twelve. A rooster's cluck signaled a bad harvest. A dog's yip meant good fortune.

My mind replayed some words from my childhood. The good nun telling me it was all right to hit the little black *bui doi*. The black monkey. *Khi den.* A mongrel race, she insisted. The mother a whore, the father American scum. Like you, Lam Van Viet, touching my forehead. But worse than you, if possible. Hit him. Hit him. Knock the devil out of him. Satan has branded his black soul.

No good to cry.

A bout of dizziness, my eyes blurred.

Then, an awful keening began. Mike Tran slumped against a wall and moaned like a wounded animal. The cries grew louder and louder until the only sound in that room was his unbearable sobbing.

Epilogue

Jimmy returned back to his tiny apartment in Hartford's West End. Though he hobbled a bit, dragging his foot, he managed to climb the one flight to our office, settling in with a look that suggested I'd let things fall apart. He pointed out an empty Arizona Iced Tea can I'd left on the windowsill. Mayhem and disaster. Now we'd get back to the real work of the firm. When I stopped in to check on him, he'd pulled a chair up to the front window, a stubby cigar gripped in his hand, and he was nodding merrily at the Pizza Palace and Best Wings in Town, fast-food places across the street. He looked unnaturally content.

Gracie had become flustered when Jimmy packed his scant belongings and left, though he did nod his thanks to her. Later, taking her out to lunch, I watched her choke up. Jimmy surprised everyone by sending a bouquet of red roses to her, a gesture that made Gracie cry.

When he was gone one day, she whispered to me, "He was a pain in the ass but now I miss him."

Every day as I scooted past her open front door, I'd see her sitting in an easy chair, sometimes staring into the hallway absently.

"Give him a call," I advised.

She made a face. "In my day a lady never called a gentleman."

"A gentleman?"

She wagged a finger at me. "Watch your mouth, young man."

A cut-glass vase by the door displayed the roses, though they were beginning to wilt. Brown petals clustered on the table. I leaned in to smell the roses. "Nice."

"They're mine to smell, Rick."

I backed away.

The first morning back in the office Jimmy and I reviewed the cases I'd closed—or continued. The monotonous fraud investigations that kept our financial life afloat. But after an hour he'd fallen asleep in the chair, and I assumed his medications were kicking in. Gently I removed the cigar from the hand that rested on the arm of a chair. He stretched out, his sweatshirt rising and falling with his heavy breathing, and I noticed unfortunate hot sauce stains on the shirt. I smiled—back to normal.

Earlier that morning we'd talked of news in the morning's *Courant*. A front-page article chronicled a police raid on the Russell Street storefront, the arrest of JD and other members of the VietBoyz. Some courageous shopkeepers, fed up, had rallied and sought help—they were tired of extortion, handing over envelopes of cash to safeguard their livelihood. A few intrepid shopkeepers told stories of intimidation, threats, scare tactics. So the storefront was boarded up, though Jimmy insisted it would be business as usual within weeks. JD was released on bail—and a reporter noted he was spotted sitting in the doorway of Le Thang Barber Shop.

Maybe he was waiting for a haircut.

The other news that morning was a small item in the police-blotter column: Jonny Croix had been arrested for beating up his mother in their Frog Hollow apartment, so vicious an assault that his mother was hospitalized with a broken arm. Jonny was behind bars. The only salutary end, I told Jimmy, was that the *Courant* reporter noted that Jonny had been wrestled to the ground by his younger brother. Frankie had sustained bruises trying to rescue his mother.

"The better angels of his nature," I told Jimmy.

"What the hell is that supposed to mean?"

"Think about it."

Jimmy puffed on his cigar. "You're not gonna start annoying me again, are you?"

"I wouldn't think of it, Jimmy."

◇◇◇

Liz and I met for dinner one night at a favorite Thai place in the south end of West Hartford. Thai One On, a name that always made me cringe, though I forgave them when I tasted the salted shrimp. She'd come straight from work, but still looked fresh and lovely. A gray tailored suit that would have looked dowdy on a less beautiful woman, a string of cultured pearls, a white silk blouse with a lace collar. "Beautiful," I told her. "You always look beautiful."

"Are you proposing?" she said.

I said nothing.

We talked about Wilson Tran and the shattered Tran family. Since that painful afternoon at their home, I'd not spoken to Mike or anyone else in the family. But I understood from Hank, who relayed stories from his grandmother, that the family had rallied around Wilson, hiring a lawyer, anxious as the case moved through the police and court channels.

"I'll never understand it," I told Liz.

She sighed. "Not an unfamiliar story, Rick. Like the other Tran children, Wilson slipped easily into an obedient role, nodding weakly at authority, a pattern learned under Mike Tran's Draconian discipline. Some part of it has to do with his defiance of his father, a taskmaster, but that doesn't excuse it. The all-A student, bookish, hungry for sensation that would take him momentarily from his monotonous world of study, study, study. His father with a whip. He…well, succumbed to Judd's authority."

"Judd." I thundered the name. "How many lives can one person ruin?"

She shook her head back and forth. "No one addressed his anger over the years. Anger at his mother for deserting them. His father for…well, being the ass he is. Hazel for leaving. This grievance, that one. Like Wilson, a stellar student, if a lout, but one who craved thrills, sensation, law-breaking. Mostly domination—if necessary by force. Fueled by stories in the press about knockout punches. Knocking his way through the world."

"But devious. The bit with the postcard."

Liz sipped her gin-and-tonic. "Judd planned revenge. It was sweet to him. Frankie had come to represent everything he despised—a white trash boy who challenged him. Who beat him up. Well, he'd send him back to jail."

"Wilson hated him."

"Maybe, but Wilson was very afraid of him," Liz said. "Afraid to defy him. Judd knocked the boy around, we learned. He terrorized him."

"But Wilson played along. And a part of him reveled in it—that swelling up of his chest. Pride. Captain Ahab cursing the sun. Power. Intoxicating. The exhilaration of literature translated into the stuff of everyday boyish dreams." I thought of something he'd said to me one time. "'Call me Will.'"

Call me Ishmael.

"What will happen to that boy?" Liz asked.

"Well, to Judd's credit, he did confess to coercing Wilson. He also said he never warned Wilson about the attacks. The one outside the Burger King with Ralph—he said Ralph angered him in the restaurant. Only when they were walking down the sidewalk and spotted Jimmy and Ralph ahead did he rush into action. He just wanted to knock him over. Not kill him."

"But the second one? The others? Maybe some we don't know about?" Liz watched me closely.

"Yes, planned, once he hit on that scheme to get Frankie and Simon arrested again. After the first, he realized he could set the maniacal plan into motion."

"Cruel."

I sat back. "But he says Wilson was just there. And the videos sort of show that. And Wilson came tumbling after. Wilson turning from behind, always a few steps away. Wilson never hitting anyone."

"But he was an accomplice," Liz insisted. "By law."

"And that's the problem." I sighed heavily. "The courts have no sympathy for accomplices when someone dies. Manslaughter, whatever charge will be leveled finally against Judd."

"But Wilson?"

"Hank tells me the D.A. is not unsympathetic to the boy, given all the circumstances. The video. Judd's confession. Counseling, probation, therapy. All options on the table. I don't know if they'll put him away. I doubt it."

"That'll serve no purpose."

"I agree. It's a hurting family." I drummed my fingers on the table. "Hank said Simon is undergoing counseling. Even Mike and Lucy are involved. Michael has stepped up, a part of the family. Mike and Simon are talking. Mike is trying to understand his family."

"Poor Mike and Lucy." Liz's words had finality to them.

"The awful job of being a parent," I said. "And the awful burden of Mike's childhood—that desire to escape a past."

"And Lucy's, too," Liz added. "Don't forget her, too."

"Orphans in the storm."

Liz smiled wistfully. "'O my America, my new found land.' John Dunne."

I shook my head. "I know, I know." I smiled at her. "But, Liz, I think I've had enough literary quotation lately to last a lifetime."

◇◇◇

On Saturday we celebrated. Early in the afternoon Gracie met me outside her apartment where she'd been waiting, anxious. She'd had her hair done at the beauty parlor down the street, a rare occurrence for her, and I complimented her. Silvery white curls ringed her lively face. A pill-box hat with a fringe veil. A trace of peach lipstick, also unusual. I always insisted that Gracie was a glamorous woman without any makeup. The aristocratic thrust of her chin, the dark flashing eyes, the impish smile, the ballet dancer's stance. Now, dressed in a longish dress the color of spring lilacs, a polished rhinestone brooch pinned to her lapel, she looked ready for the dance.

"You stole that brooch from one of the Andrews Sisters."

She eyed me mischievously. "It was a gift from Arthur Godfrey."

I teased her. "You think I don't know who that is, right?"

"You don't."

"He was vice-president under Coolidge."

"Smart mouth."

She tucked her elbow under my arm, and we strolled out to my car.

We met Jimmy and Liz in the lobby of the State Armory on Capital Avenue. Liz and Gracie hugged, and Liz asked Gracie if she'd let her borrow the brooch at some future time.

"It was a gift from Arthur Godfrey," I told her.

Jimmy frowned, itching to get to his seat. "I never liked that man. Especially after he fired Julius LaRosa from his show. Right on the air."

Gracie's hand grazed Jimmy's sleeve. "Jimmy, you wore a suit."

"I clean up real nice."

She smiled at him.

Hank's family had saved seats a few rows from the stage, and I sat down next to Grandma. She'd been craning her neck back toward the entrance, expectant. She'd motioned me to hurry. Now she grasped my hand and squeezed it. Hank's mother, father, brother, and sisters filled the rest of the aisle, but I noticed the two rows behind us were packed with Vietnamese I'd never met. "Who are they?" I whispered to Grandma.

"Family."

"All Vietnamese are family," I said.

"If you knew that, then why did you ask me?" She tapped my wrist.

We watched as Governor Dannel Malloy solemnly swore in twenty-seven young recruits, a line of radiant men and women who stood, accepted congratulations, and officially became state troopers. When Hank was announced—"Hank Ky Tan Nguyen," a mouthful—we erupted into applause. Grandma cheered. His mother wept. His father beamed. I got all choked up, and Liz, on my left, leaned into me, her hand brushing my sleeve.

"A Vietnamese state trooper," Liz hummed, thrilled.

Hank looked smart and resplendent in his pristine uniform, and I recalled the careful attention he'd paid to it, as pointed out by Grandma. Gold and blue and gray—the line of recruits was a frieze of colorful magic. Handsome, trim, a rise of color in his cheeks, his hair clipped military style, Hank strode across the stage. I swear he hesitated a second when he heard Grandma's loud squeal, a slight twist of his head toward the audience, a hint of a smile.

Afterwards we gathered at the VFW Hall in East Hartford for a long, rousing celebration that would go on till the morning. Long tables of food, streamers suspended from the ceiling, a South Vietnam flag suspended next to an American one, a new-wave orange-haired teenaged Vietnamese DJ happily spinning Vietnamese house music on a turntable, headphones covering his ears, his head bobbing up and down. A stoned look in his eyes.

Hank walked in, and we circled him, yelled, clapped, and slapped his back. We hugged. "I just wrinkled your uniform," I whispered.

"I do own an iron, you know."

He'd driven over with a girl who looked a little familiar. A gorgeous girl, Vietnamese, with straight black hair and wide, midnight eyes. He'd told me he was bringing a girl because he thought he might be in love. Of course, I'd heard that before, as Hank moved like a punch-drunk Lothario through a succession of pretty girls. He was always in love—or falling out of it.

"Emily Phoung," he told us.

She smiled but said nothing.

Then I realized how I knew her. She was the waitress at Bo Kien on Russell and Park. The one where Hank and I had spent the afternoon monitoring the storefront of the VietBoyz. The pretty girl who craved his attention, flirting, teasing. Obviously it worked.

I turned to Grandma. "Hank's new girl is pretty."

Grandma said in a deadpan voice. "He told me she was Miss South Windsor." She shrugged. "Imagine that."

Gracie leaned in. "I was a Rockette a hundred years ago."

"That recent?" From Jimmy.

Gracie winked at him.

I sat back, contented. I gazed at my friends. My family. An orphan like Mike and Lucy, I suddenly thought. Yes, one more orphan in the storm. So many of us, drifting, drifting. But as I watched everyone laughing, happy, I thanked God. My boat had found safe harbor.

Liz was watching me closely, a mysterious smile on her face. "You look so—happy."

"I'm rowing in Eden."

"Hey," Hank's younger brother Vu blurted out, "That's Emily Dickinson. We just read that in school."

Liz laughed. "All of your good lines are stolen, Rick."

"Don't tell. They'll banish me."

To receive a free catalog of Poisoned Pen Press titles, please provide your name, address, and email address in one of the following ways:

Phone: 1-800-421-3976
Facsimile: 1-480-949-1707
Email: info@poisonedpenpress.com
Website: www.poisonedpenpress.com

Poisoned Pen Press
6962 E. First Ave. Ste 103
Scottsdale, AZ 85251

CPSIA information can be obtained at www.ICGtesting.com
Printed in the USA
BVOW08s0950090616

451373BV00003B/40/P